FACE OF DEATH

Slowly Tundree got to his feet, leaving the Sharps where it lay.

"Turn around an' face me," Long John said.

Stoney was out of range and while he couldn't fire, he could see what was coming. "Long John!" he shouted.

Tundree carried a second Colt under his belt, and when he whirled to face Long John, the weapon was roaring and spitting lead. The first slug ripped off Long John's hat, while the second burned a fiery path along his neck beneath his left ear. But Long John didn't flinch, and he fired just once. Dust puffed from Tundree's shirt, and then his knees buckled. . . .

St. Martin's Paperbacks Titles
by Ralph Compton

The Trail Drive Series

THE GOODNIGHT TRAIL
THE WESTERN TRAIL
THE CHISHOLM TRAIL
THE BANDERA TRAIL
THE CALIFORNIA TRAIL
THE SHAWNEE TRAIL
THE VIRGINIA CITY TRAIL
THE DODGE CITY TRAIL
THE OREGON TRAIL
THE SANTA FE TRAIL
THE OLD SPANISH TRAIL
THE GREEN RIVER TRAIL
THE DEADWOOD TRAIL

The Sundown Riders Series

NORTH TO THE BITTERROOT
ACROSS THE RIO COLORADO
THE WINCHESTER RUN

THE SHAWNEE TRAIL

RALPH COMPTON

St. Martin's Paperbacks

The Shawnee Trail is respectfully
dedicated to Sidney Lee Linard, 1936–1994.
Vaya con Dios, amigo.

This is a work of fiction, based on actual trail drives of the Old West. Many of the characters appearing in the Trail Drive Series were very real, and some of the trail drives actually took place. But the reader should be aware that, in the developing of characters and events, some fictional literary license has been employed. While some of the characters and events herein are purely the creation of the author, every effort has been made to portray them with accuracy. However, the inherent dangers of the trail are real, sufficient unto themselves, and seldom has it been necessary to enhance their reality.

THE SHAWNEE TRAIL

Cover illustration by Bob Larkin.
Map illustration on cover by Dennis Lyall.
Cover type by Jim Lebbad.
Map on p. vii by David Lindroth, based upon material supplied by the author.

ISBN: 0-312-95241-4

Printed in the United States of America

St. Martin's Paperbacks edition/June 1994

10 9 8 7

AUTHOR'S FOREWORD

In America, trailing cattle to market was common long before the longhorn era. It was done in Texas under Spanish and Mexican rule, and in the early days of the Republic, Texas longhorns were driven into Louisiana and points east. Trailing north began in the early 1840s, and the Shawnee Trail became the route most commonly used, for until 1861 St. Louis was the nearest railhead. The Shawnee led from Brownsville, in southwest Texas, and reaching the north, it kept to the high prairies. Herds swam the Red River at Rock Bluff Crossing, where a natural rock formation provided easy entry into the river. A sloping north bank offered a convenient exit into Indian Territory.

Just why, or when, it was first called the Shawnee Trail is uncertain. Perhaps the name was taken from a Shawnee Indian village on the Texas side of the Red, below the crossing. Or it could have come from the Shawnee Hills, near which the trail passed before crossing the Canadian River. From Dallas to the Red the trail was first known as the Preston Road, taking its name from Captain William Preston, who was in charge of a company of men at Fort Johnson, a stockade and supply post built near the crossing in 1840.

The Shawnee crossed the Red, veering northeast,

toward Fort Washita. But the herds bypassed the fort a few miles to the east. The Shawnee and the Preston routes came together some fifty miles north of the Red, and the Shawnee crossed the Canadian River just before the joining of the north and south forks. Stretching across Creek country to the Arkansas, the trail crossed just above the mouth of the Neosho River and below the mouth of the Verdigris. The earliest trail crossed into Missouri just south of Baxter Springs, Kansas. In later years, after the railroad reached Sedalia and Kansas City, the Shawnee Trail followed the east bank of the Grand River almost to the Kansas line. Crossing to the east bank, it entered southeastern Kansas and continued north to the Missouri River. The trail then followed the Missouri to Kansas City, Sedalia, or St. Louis.

By 1850, thanks to the Missouri Pacific Railroad at St. Louis, the Shawnee Trail had become the most important cattle route from Texas to the northern markets. But in June 1853 there was an outbreak of Texas fever, and angry cattlemen in western Missouri forced a herd of Texas longhorns to turn back. The Texas cattle carried ticks, and while they had no effect on the longhorns, the ticks were deadly to other cattle. In 1855 Missouri passed a law banning Texans and their tick-infested longhorns. The Kansas legislature soon adopted a similar law, but the courts of Missouri and Kansas did little to enforce these laws. Instead there were confrontations —some of them ugly—between Texas cattlemen and angry farmers and ranchers of Kansas and Missouri.

But the tick fever controversy was only part of the problem. In Kansas and Missouri bands of terrorists—pro-slavery and abolitionist—were fanning the flames of war. And when war came in 1861, the Shawnee Trail was closed. On April 19 President Lincoln ordered a blockade of the coast of all seceding states, and further ordered, on August 16, that all trade with the South cease. During the war, except for a few eastward drives to feed

Confederate soldiers, there was no movement of Texas cattle.

When the North-South conflict finally ended, it was 1866 before war-weary Texans were able to gather their scattered cattle and again trail them north. But nothing had been done to resolve the tick fever problem, and Texas longhorns were as unwelcome as ever in Kansas and Missouri. Texans and their herds were met by armed men and forced to turn back. Some Texans died and many herds were stampeded or shot. The Union Pacific Railroad reached Abilene in 1867, and Joseph McCoy, a young Illinois cattle dealer, persuaded the governor of Kansas to lift the ban on Texas longhorns so that they might be trailed to the railroad at Abilene. Only then did the violence cease, for the Chisholm Trail became a more direct route to end-of-track. The old Shawnee Trail was closed. Forever.

PROLOGUE

March 1858. North of San Antonio, Texas, along the Rio Colorado.

Long John Coons was curious as to the identity of the three riders. After all, this was his spread, the L-J Connected, and the trail was fresh. He forded the river and his horse was clambering up the opposite bank when a shot shattered the stillness. Lead nicked the brim of Long John's Stetson, and he rolled out of the saddle, pulling his Colt and slapping his horse on its flank. The horse went on, trotting through the underbrush and low-hanging willows. Long John circled in the opposite direction, depending on the riderless horse to cover the sound of his own movement. Reaching the edge of the thicket, Long John could see three horses, but only two of the riders. They had roped a mealy-nosed, line backed, black, two-year-old heifer, and had the animal hog-tied. But where was the third man? Until he knew, Long John couldn't make a move. He waited, and his patience was rewarded when the third man emerged from the willows leading Long John's horse. He spoke confidently to his companions.

"He's somewheres in the thicket. I nailed the bastard with one shot. You reckon *that* ain't damn good shootin'?"

"Bandy," said a second man, "I admire modesty in a man. Somebody in your family got it all, 'cause you shore as hell ain't got none."

"Them's my sentiments too," the third man said.

"Only a damn fool counts coup on a kill he ain't sure of. That hombre could have us under his gun this very minute."

"Yer damn right he could," said Long John Coons, "an' he has." The cocked Colt was steady in Long John's fist, and slowly the trio raised their hands.

"Now," said the lanky Long John, "I'm wantin' to know what the three o' ye are doin' on my range, ropin' my cows."

"We been ridin' the grub line," said one of the men, "an' we're damn near starved."

"I ain't begrudgin' a man beef if'n he's hungry," Long John said, "but I don't see the need of brandin' the critter 'fore ye kill an' eat it. You, with the cinch ring. Now, most hombres don't tote cinch rings around, less'n they aims to use 'em, an' they're mighty handy fer alterin' brands. Like my L-J Connected, on that mealy-nosed critter. Hungry, are ye?"

"Damn you," said the man called Bandy, "we ain't needin' your charity."

"That bein' the case," Long John said coldly, "I reckon we'll jist call this what it is. Rustlin'. Ye hanker to be strung up, er gut-shot?"

"Shut up, Bandy," snarled one of his companions. "This gent's holdin' aces and we got a busted flush. You got us cold," he said, turning to Long John. "We're Texans, and we know the code, but what'n hell could we do with just one cow, 'cept cook an' eat the critter?"

"I'm countin' that in yer favor," said Long John, less hostile now. "I reckon they ain't much use fer one cow, 'cept fer grub. Was I sure ye jaybirds was hungry grub-line riders, like ye say, maybe I'd have a place fer ye. I'm needin' riders fer a drive up the Shawnee, to the railroad, in Missouri."

"Hell," Bandy said, "there's a shootin' war goin' on in Kansas and Missouri atwixt them pro-slavers and abolitionists. Besides that, ain't you heard of the laws agin Texas longhorns, 'cause of tick fever?"

"Ye ain't tellin' me nothin' I don't know," said Long John, "an' that war ye hear of in Kansas an' Missouri is comin' fer real. When it comes, it'll likely close the Shawnee fer good, an' I got to git me a herd to market 'fore that happens. Now I'm needin' riders. Men with the bark on. Forty an' found, all yer shells, an' a hunnert dollar bonus fer ever' man that finishes the drive to the railroad."

"Mister," said the most apologetic member of the trio, "I'm Dent Briano. I'll ride with you, and count it a privilege. These other peckerwoods is Bandy Darden and Quando Miller, an' they can do their own talkin'."

"Count me in," said Miller. "It wasn't me or Dent that took a shot at you."

"I done it," Darden said. "You still want me ridin' with you?"

"I allow a man one mistake," said Long John, "but if ye ever throw lead at me again—fer any reason—ye better make it good the first shot. Elsewise, I'll kill ye grave-yard dead. Now ye ridin' with us er not?"

"I'll ride," Bandy Darden said, but his eyes were hard and cold. Long John could read sign, and somewhere on the long trail to Missouri, he could expect a showdown with Darden.

"Cut that cow loose," said Long John, "and let's ride. Ye'll git supper at the cook house, an' they'll be plenty of it."

Long John's ranch consisted of a series of log buildings strung end to end, with a swift running creek passing near the barn. There was a rambling house with a front porch running the length of it. Next to that was the cook shack, and then a bunkhouse large enough to accommodate a dozen riders. Half a mile distant was the big log barn with hayloft, and at one end a corral with a six-rail-high fence. It angled across the creek, providing fresh water for the horses. It was near suppertime when Long John and his newly hired trio reined up before the bunkhouse, and only four of Long John's crew ambled out to greet the new arrivals. There was Llano Dupree, Stoney Winters, Deuce Gitano, and an arrogant two-gun rider not even out of his teens, known only as "the Kid."

"New riders fer the trail drive," bawled Long John. "Sky Pilot, three more fer supper."

"Wal, thank God," growled the old cook, leaning out the cook shack door. "You be the answer to a man's prayers, Long John Coons. I been shovelin' out grub to this no-account bunch nineteen hours ever' day, wonderin' what'n hell I was goin' to do with all my extry time."

Used to the old man's grousing, Long John grinned at him and rode on to the house. After supper, except for their coffee cups, Long John's dark-eyed, black-haired Cajun woman cleared the table. Suzanne had said nothing throughout the meal, and Long John well knew the reason. When she finally spoke, it was with the question Long John had expected.

"Who are the new riders, and where did you get them?"

"Darden, Miller, and Briano," said Long John. "Hungry grub-line riders. Found 'em about to have supper off'n one of our heifers."

"Rustlers, then," Suzanne snapped, her dark eyes flashing in the pale lamplight. "You'd hire these damn down-at-the-heels rustlers for the drive, but I'm not good enough, am I? Well, I ain't stayin' in Texas while you take a herd to Missouri. Maybe I'll just go back to New Orleans, to the Quarter."

"Now, Suzy—" Long John began.

"Stop calling me that!" Suzanne shouted. "You know I *hate* that name. It—It makes me feel like one of Madame Toussard's whores."

"So ye keep tellin' me," Long John growled, "an' I'm a mite fed up with ye spoutin' off about Toussard's whorehouse. I'm startin' to wonder how'n hell ye got so familiar with the place."

Suzanne's coffee cup was full, and she flung the steaming brew in Long John's face. He kicked back his chair, lurched to his feet and whacked his head against the hanging lamp. His lean face white with fury, Long John seized the front of the girl's shirt, dragging her bodily across the table. Equally furious, Suzanne went for Long John's face, fingers splayed out like an eagle's talons, but Long John had expected that. He snatched the front of her flannel shirt, using its long sleeves to imprison her flailing arms. He got a grip at the waist of her Levi's with his big left hand and dragged the kicking, screeching Suzanne across the table belly down, flopping her across his knees. Holding her in place with his left hand, he used the right to lay some well-placed blows on her backside. Only when her furious yowls and swearing dwindled to genuine sobs did he relent. He allowed her to slide to the floor on her back. When her sobbing finally ceased, Long John helped her to her feet, easing her into the chair in which she'd been sitting. She sat sideways, favoring her sore bottom, her dark head bowed, tears still trailing down her cheeks. Long John knelt before her, looking up into her eyes, and spoke in a gentle voice few had ever heard.

"Girl, I care fer ye, an' that's why I ain't wantin' ye on the drive. I look fer the Shawnee to be hell with the lid off. It'll be man's work."

Slowly Suzanne's arms reached for Long John, and he held her close for a while before either of them spoke.

"I can ride, rope, and shoot as good as any man," said the girl. "Am I all that different?"

"Ye are," Long John said, grinning up at her, "an' in ways that matter the most. I never had, an' never hoped to have, a woman the likes o' ye. Any woman takin' a look at my ugly mug was off an' runnin' t'other way. Damn it, I purely can't afford fer nothin' to happen to ye."

"An' I can't afford fer nothin' to happen to ye," she said, laughing, imitating his drawl. "That's why I'm going with you on this trail drive to Missouri. My God, Long John, you have maybe three riders I'd trust not to turn on you in a showdown. Please take me with you, if only to watch your back."

"Go, then," Long John said with a sigh. "What ye jist said matches my gut feelin' that we'll be ridin' into trouble. 'Fore we git to the railroad we're likely to need ever' damn gun in the outfit, an' then some."

"I'm sorry I . . . I threw the coffee, Long John. You have a right to know why I . . . I did that, why I . . . why I hate that name you've been calling me. It—Suzy— was my name when I . . . when I was at Madame Toussard's."

After all these months—with Long John caring for her, believing in her—why had she told him? Her hands trembled, and the frantic thudding of her heart seemed to vibrate her entire body. For a long moment Long John Coons said nothing, and Suzanne looked fearfully into his pale blue eyes. It was as though Long John looked beyond her, into some private hell she had created for him. Finally his eyes softened and he spoke.

"I reckon we all done some things we ain't proud of. Ye got sand, girl, an' all I can see is what an' who ye are now. I never knowed anybody by that other name. Ye'll always be Suzanne to me."

1

Long John Coons stood an inch over six feet, without his hat and Texas boots. His Colt six-shooter was thonged low on his right hip, and his Bowie hung down his back beneath his shirt, Indian fashion, from a rawhide thong around his neck. While Long John's mama was a Louisiana conjuring woman, his daddy had been a hell-for-leather Texan who had died at San Jacinto. Long John had his daddy's pale blue eyes and his swiftness with Colt and Bowie.

In 1850 Gil and Van Austin, owners of land grants from the Bandera Mountains east to the Rio Colorado, had taken a herd of Texas longhorns to hungry miners in the California goldfields. Long John had been part of that historic drive. The Austins had been generous to their riders, paying them in cows because there had been little money in Texas in the years after the war with Mexico. More than a hundred of the cows sold in California had belonged to Long John. Near Fort Yuma, Arizona Territory, a band of Mexican outlaws had murdered Bo, Long John's friend, and the vengeful Cajun had gunned down the gang to the last man. There had been a substantial reward, and that, combined with the sale of his cows, had allowed Long John to return to Texas with more than $12,000.*

Long John had bought several grants along the Colorado, some seed cattle from the Austins, and a few blooded horses from Clay Duval's Winged M. Duval and his friends, Gil and Van Austin, had brought the famed Mendoza horses—along with five thousand Spanish longhorns—from Mexico in 1844.**

Suzanne, Long John's Cajun woman, was twenty-five, half a dozen years younger than Long John. The two had met in California, and Long John had known nothing about the girl, but she seemed interested in him, and wished to return to New Orleans. But when they reached Texas, Suzanne had remained with Long John, and only when they'd had an occasional fight did the girl threaten to return to New Orleans. By the time Long John learned of her unsavory past, she'd become so much a part of his life that he found himself unable to part with her. Suzanne was a foot shorter than Long John, her eyes as black as her hair. Her temper equaled Long John's, and there were times when she swore at him, and he at her. But on this day—the last day of March 1858—they rode in peace, bound for the Austin grants, near Bandera.

"You expect a lot of your friends," Suzanne said, "asking them for riders to look after our place while we take a trail drive to Missouri. We may be gone for months."

"Wal, hell," said Long John, "it was them that made the offer. They come back from Californy with twenty times as much gold as I did, an' they ain't hurtin' fer money. Fact is, they tried to lend me money till all this hell-raisin' in Kansas an' Missouri is done. But I ain't the kind to run from a fight, an' I ain't in the wrong. So

* Trail Drive Series #5, *The California Trail*
** Trail Drive Series #4, *The Bandera Trail*

Gil an' Van says if'n I'm hell-bent on fightin' my way to Missouri, they'll send me four er five riders to look after our spread whilst we're gone. I aim to take 'em up on that, long as they'll let me pay them riders fer the time they're workin' fer us."

"After we've sold the herd and ridden back to Texas," said Suzanne, "and that's assuming we make it back alive, of course."

"Yeah," Long John said, ignoring her sarcasm. "They know we won't have the money till we sells the herd. Clay Duval's offered us extry horses fer the remuda, if'n we need 'em, an' we do."

"If something happens to the herd," said Suzanne, "we'll have to sell the spread to pay what we owe."

"Wal, hell's fire, woman, if'n we don't at least try to git a herd north to market, we'll be losin' the damn place anyhow. By God, I'd ruther go down fightin' than git shot to ribbons doin' nothin'. I ain't worryin', 'cause I reckon ye'll be doin' enough fer the both o' us. Anything else on yer mind?"

"Yes," Suzanne said. "Those Indians, Malo Coyote and Naked Horse. All they have favoring them is that they rode in with Winters and Dupree."

"Hell's bells," said Long John, "they're Cherokees from the nation, an' they ain't after scalps. They're good protection agin them damn Comanches, an' they're the best horse wranglers I ever seen. Why, a horse'll foller them Injuns anywhere."

"Yes," Suzanne said. "Right out of Texas and into Indian Territory. Don't you think these blooded horses Clay Duval's promised will be just a little too much temptation for this shifty-eyed pair of Cherokees?"

"Wal, dammit," growled Long John, "we got to trust *somebody*. With all the hell-raisin' goin' on betwixt here an' Missouri, they ain't that many riders hankerin' to go on this drive. On other drives, they's been riders shot, cows shot, an' herds stampeded to hell an' gone."

"Any you think this bunch of riders we have can break through where others have failed?"

"At least they ain't scairt to try," Long John said. "Gil an' Van reckons they'll be a shootin' war a-goin' on in a year er two, and they ain't no tellin' how long it'll last. We got to trail a herd north an' git some gold whilst we can. Right now, it's jist pro-slave an' abolitionist hell-raisers, an' a few ranchers scairt o' tick fever. Nex' year we may have the whole damn Union army atwixt us an' that railroad in Missouri."

Long John and Suzanne would be away at least three days, and young Stoney Winters had been left in charge. The outfit would begin rounding up the cows needed for the trail drive. Stoney was barely twenty-one, a year older than his saddle pard, Llano Dupree. The two riders, with Long John's outfit less than a month, hunkered under an oak, awaiting supper. Facing them, sitting cross-legged, was Naked Horse and Malo Coyote.

"Jugar," suggested Naked Horse, deftly shuffling a deck of cards.

"Like hell," said Llano. "No way am I gamblin' with you *pelados*. You damn Injuns has got more'n one way of scalpin' a man."

Stoney Winters laughed, and the pair of Cherokees grinned. They were a disreputable duo with whom Llano and Stoney had an uncertain alliance. The Texans had been riding from Omaha back to Texas, and just after crossing the Red, had sighted a Comanche camp. Sneaking close, they discovered that the Comanches, two dozen strong, were torturing Malo Coyote and Naked Horse. The captives were bound to trees, with dry leaves and brush heaped about them. There was little doubt as to their fate, once the Comanches had grown tired of the torture. But darkness was near, and Llano and Stoney had managed to free the unfortunate Cherokees, a deed they soon had regretted. The Texans, along with

Malo Coyote and Naked Horse, had been forced to ride for their lives, pursued by the furious Comanches.

"We be *companeros,*" said Malo Coyote.

"I ain't sure we need or want *companeros* like you and Naked Horse," said Stoney Winters. "You thievin' varmints was caught stealin' Comanche horses. That's enough to get a man hung, and you two was guilty as sin. If we'd of knowed that at the time, we'd have backed off and let them Comanches roast the pair of you alive."

"Damn right," said Llano. "I reckon there's gonna be hell enough on the Shawnee, without you varmints addin' to it. I know Long John's damn hard up for riders, and I just hope when he comes down on the pair of you, he forgets you rode in with us."

Suddenly there was a shot from the bunkhouse, the breaking of glass and the clatter of overturned chairs. Stoney lit out on the run, Llano at his heels. Malo Coyote and Naked Horse remained where they were. Llano held back, allowing Stoney to enter the bunkhouse first. Five chairs and the rickety table had been overturned, and glass from the shattered lamp littered the floor. Against one wall stood the three new riders Long John had hired. With them—seeming to have become a companion—was Deuce Gitano. Against the other wall, his right-hand Colt cocked and ready, stood the surly young man known only as the Kid.

"Long John left me in charge here," Stoney said. "Kid, put away the gun."

"This ain't none of your affair, boy segundo," said the contemptuous kid. "These thievin' bastards teamed up to cheat me. That first shot was to get their attention. I don't miss. Now, you buyin' in or backin' out?"

Stoney Winters seemed to stumble to the left, pulling his Colt as he went down. The Kid's slug tore into the door frame where Stoney had been standing, while Stoney's lead slammed into the cylinder of the Kid's Colt. The remaining three shells in the cylinder chain-fired as the Colt was torn from the Kid's hand. Unbelieving, the young gunman stared first at his mangled Colt on the floor and then at Stoney Winters.

"I'll kill you for that," he snarled at Stoney.

"You have another Colt," said Stoney, holstering his own. "When you're ready, draw."

"My time, my place," said the Kid. "It's a long trail to Missouri."

"It is," Stoney said coldly. "Pull a gun on me again, and you won't be seein' Missouri."

The tension was broken when Sky Pilot banged open the door to the cook shack, announcing supper.

"Come an' git it, you ongrateful coyotes, 'fore I throw it out."

There were two long split-log tables, each with a split-log bench down either side. Long John's three new riders took one of the tables, Deuce Gitano joining them. The Kid sat at the farthest end of the second table. Llano and Stoney took the opposite end of the same table. The Kid was eating awkwardly with his left hand, and Llano grinned at him. Only when the seven riders were seated and eating did Malo Coyote and Naked Horse enter the cook shack. Wordlessly, Sky Pilot heaped their plates, and the Indian duo went outside. Sitting cross-legged, their backs to the log wall of the cook shack, they ate their supper. They shied away from the bunkhouse, preferring to sleep in the brush. It was a habit Long John Coons favored, for the Comanches were still a threat. With Malo Coyote and Naked Horse well away from the ranch buildings, Comanches planning a surprise attack would be in for a surprise of their own.

The Kid finished first, got up and stalked out. He was a good four inches shy of six feet, even with the high crown of his hat uncreased so that he might seem taller. When the four men at the second table were down to their last cup of coffee, Deuce Gitano broke out a deck of cards.

"That table's fer eatin'," growled Sky Pilot. "When yer done, git th' hell outta here."

Silently the four got up and went out. Sky Pilot glowered sullenly at Llano and Stoney, but they ignored him. He began gathering the dirty tin plates, cups, and eating tools the others had left.

The three new riders—Bandy Darden, Dent Briano, and Quando Miller—accompanied by Deuce Gitano, returned to the bunkhouse. The Kid wasn't there, and the four righted the table, the chairs, and lit another lamp. Old habits being hard to break, Deuce Gitano still carried a .31 caliber Colt pocket pistol in an inside pocket beneath his coat. He was well under six feet, and although he wore Levi's and rough-out, runover boots, the rest of his outfit attested to days when his attire might have been that of a saloon dandy. The ring finger was missing from his left hand, a constant, bitter reminder of that night in El Paso when he'd been caught cheating. He'd worn a "cheater," a ring whose mirrored set faced his palm, allowing him to read the cards as he dealt them. He could have been shot dead, but the men he'd cheated devised a fate worse than death. With a Bowie knife, using the poker table as a chop block, they had severed his ring finger, ring and all. Like rustlers who had been permanently marked by having their ears cropped, Deuce Gitano had been forever branded a cheat. It had become a stigma, a dead giveaway where men gathered to gamble for high stakes. Only on the range could he get by with the lame excuse that he'd lost the finger in a roping accident. Someday Gitano would kill the man who'd wielded the knife.

Bandy Darden had hair as black as an Indian, wearing it long. His eyes seemed as black as his hair, and he had a thin face, like a ferret. His Colt was thonged low on his right hip. Darden was under six feet, even with his hat

and boots. He wore Levi's and a flannel shirt, as did
Dent Briano and Quando Miller. But Dent and Quando
were both over six feet, and there was a kindness in their
eyes that was lacking in Bandy Darden's. Briano had
pale blue eyes, while Miller's were hazel. Both men had
sandy hair, wore their Colts on their right hips, and were
five years younger than the thirty-four-year-old Bandy
Darden. While the three of them had "cinch ringed"
enough cows to get a man shot or hanged, only Darden
was a killer. The cantankerous old cook—Sky Pilot—
was so named because when he got drunk enough, he
took to preaching. Like most cowboy cooks, a horse had
rolled on him, ending his days in the saddle forever.

It was well after sundown when Long John and Suzanne
reached Van Austin's spread, near the Bandera Mountains. Van, his wife Dorinda, and little Van, now ten, had
greeted them. When supper was over, they all sat
around the big kitchen table. Long John wasted no time.

"Tomorrer," said the Cajun, "I reckon ye'd oughta
send fer Gil an' Clay. I—me an' Suzanne, that is—will
be takin' a herd up the Shawnee Trail, whilst we still got
a chanct. Ye offered—an' so did Gil—to lend me some
good hombres to look after our buildings, cows, an'
range whilst we're gone. I'm takin' ye up on that, per-
vidin' ye let me pay these gents forty an' found.
'Course, I can't pay till we git the herd to the railroad
an' collect fer 'em. I'll be needin' horses too, an' that's
where ol' Clay Duval comes in. They'll be 'leven, includin' Suzanne an' me, so I'm aimin' t' hit Clay up fer
twenty-two o' them Mendozas. We'll be owin' him too,
till we're able to sell some cows."

"Long John," Van said, "we offered to help you, and
we will. So will Clay. But do you have enough riders for
the drive? Some of those bulls you got from us—the
Corrientes—are fighting bulls, from the arenas of Old

Mexico. They're likely to be hell on the trail, if you aim to add any of them to the drive."*

"I aim to take some of the critters," Long John said. "The increase has been good, an' we got way too many bulls, so I'm trailin' the oldest. Like ye said, them Corrientes bastards is always tryin' to gore somethin', somebody, er one another. I got too damn many, an' it's time some of 'em went to market."

"That's why I'm wondering if you have enough riders," said Van. "With conditions bein' what they are in Kansas and Missouri, and your cows never having been off your range, you'll need a rider for every two hundred head."

"Yer right," Long John said, "an' that's what I'm figgerin' on. There'll be 'leven riders, includin' Suzanne, an' I aim to take two thousant head."

"Good thinking," said Van. "When do you aim to move 'em out?"

"Soon as we can git the brutes gathered. I reckoned, since I'm hirin' yer riders to watch our spread whilst we're gone, that I'd take 'em back with us an' use 'em fer the gather. With extry help, I figger we can be on the trail in a week."

"No problem," said Van, "far as Gil an me's concerned. While both of us are pardners with Clay in the Winged M, we generally let him make most of the decisions regarding the horses. If we can spare twenty-two horses, you got 'em."

Next morning after breakfast, Van sent riders for Gil Austin and Clay Duval. Gil arrived first, and swinging out of the saddle, gripped Long John's hand.

"By God," Gil grinned, "you never stop tryin' to get yourself killed, do you? I've about decided you're inde-

* The Corrientes bulls were stocky, with shorter legs and horns. While the longhorn was ornery when prodded, the Corrientes were naturally mean.

structible, after you gunned down that bunch of outlaws at Fort Yuma."*

"He's never told me about that," said Suzanne.

"You don't want to know," Van said.

Quickly Long John repeated to Gil what he'd already discussed with Van.

"I can spare you a couple of riders," said Gil, "and we'll get with Clay about the horses."

When Clay Duval arrived, he slapped Long John on the back and told the Cajun what he wanted to hear.

"We can spare you the horses," said Clay, "and you can pay when you've sold the herd. For anybody else," he grinned, "they'd be a hundred dollars a head, but for you, two hundred."

Once they'd had a laugh at Long John's expense, Gil turned to Long John.

"I can send you a couple of my Lipan Apache riders. I'd trust 'em with my life."

"I can send you two more," Van said. "You sure that'll be enough?"

"Yeah," said Long John. "All I'm expectin' 'em to do is ride the range, seein' that the rest o' our stock is bein' left alone, an' to be sure the house, the barn, the bunkhouse, an' the cook shack is still standin' when we git back."

"Easy work," Gil said. "If we ain't careful, we'll have them Injuns fightin' amongst themselves, all of 'em wantin' to go."

"Wal," said Long John, "I reckon we'd best pick up them extry riders an' go with Clay to git the horses."

The Lipan Apaches were a peaceful tribe, having settled along the Medina River, south of San Antonio. They hated only the Comanches, and the Austins had found them fearless, faithful, dependable riders. Van chose two from his outfit to accompany Long John, and the pair grinned at the Cajun, knowing him from his years as part of the Austin outfit. Long John and Suzanne rode out, accompanied by the Lipans, Clay Duval, and Gil Austin. They would pick up a second pair of Austin riders at Gil's spread, and from there they would accompany Clay to the Winged M, where his riders would cut out the horses Long John needed.

Before Long John had ridden out, he'd instructed the riders to begin rounding up cattle for the proposed trail drive. With Stoney Winters in charge, the first day's work had been fruitful. But the morning following Stoney's fight with the Kid, there was another confrontation, this time in the cook shack. The Kid remained at the table until all the riders had gone out except Llano and Stoney.

"Boy segundo," said the Kid, "I ain't ropin' cows today. My hand's all swole up, and it's your fault."

"Kid," Stoney said coldly, "when a man pulls a gun, he ain't entitled to cry over the consequences. You notice I'm talkin' about a *man.*"

"You sayin' I ain't a man?"

"Take it any way you damn please," said Stoney. "I'm in charge till Long John returns, and you'll do what I say."

"And if I don't," the kid smirked, "you'll go whining to your daddy."

"Wrong," Stoney said. "I can stomp my own snakes. But you're right about one thing. You won't be worth a damn on the range, and I won't have you out there, slowin' down the gather. But you won't be layin' on your backside while the rest of us work. You'll stick close by and spend the day helpin' Sky Pilot. You can carry wood, wash pots and pans . . ."

It was the ultimate insult. Sky Pilot detested the arrogant Kid, and the old cook chuckled with delight.

"By God," bawled the Kid, "I won't do it. Nobody—you, with this old buzzard throwed in—can make me!"

From beneath his dirty apron Sky Pilot whipped a Colt, cocking the weapon as he drew. He rammed the deadly muzzle under the Kid's nose and then he spoke.

"Boy, this old buzzard can still shoot, an' he ain't reluctant to bore any cocky young bastard what's needful of it. Now you lift that pistol out'n the holster, an' you do it slow. Then lay the gun on the table."

A drop of sweat dripped off the Kid's nose, and he cut his eyes to Stoney in a mute appeal for help. Stoney said nothing, coldly indifferent, while Llano strove to hide a grin. White-lipped, the Kid slowly lifted his remaining Colt from its holster and placed the weapon on the table. Sky Pilot took the Colt, slipped it under his belt, and backed away.

"After supper," said the old cook, "when the place is clean an' cookin' is done fer the day, you git the gun. Now git up an' bring in a couple loads of wood. Move, dammit. There ain't nothin' wrong with yer legs."

The Kid got up, and in blind fury stumbled out the door. Stoney looked at Sky Pilot and the old cook glared at him. He eased down the hammer of his Colt and shoved it back under his waistband, handy for a right-hand draw. He then went about his business, totally ignoring Llano and Stoney. They left the cook shack and headed for the barn, where the rest of the outfit was about to ride out. Most of them—even Malo Coyote and Naked Horse—were grinning, for they could see the Kid making his way toward the cook shack with a load of wood.

"If I'm any judge," said Llano, "it ain't a question of *whether* you'll have to kill that little coyote, but *when.* Long John didn't do you any favor, leavin' you in charge of this outfit."

"All I can do is agree with you, but seein' what he had to choose from, who would *you* have picked?"

"You, I reckon," Llano said, "but if the old devil wasn't so stove up, I'd take a hard look at Sky Pilot."

"He's plenty salty, but his life won't be worth a plugged peso if he turns his back while that Kid has a gun. I'm beginnin' to wonder if hiring on for this trail drive was such a good idea. Most of these hombres—but for Long John and Sky Pilot—look like they've been run off from somewhere else. Maybe two jumps ahead of the law."

"Trouble is," said Llano, "with this tick fever scare in Kansas and Missouri, and with war threatenin' to bust loose, nobody's needin' riders, except Long John. Everybody else is standin' pat, waitin' to see what's goin' to happen, not wantin' to get caught in the middle. What's botherin' me is them Injuns, Malo Coyote and Naked Horse. You reckon that pair can be trusted from here to Missouri, or will we roll out some mornin' and find them gone? Them and the whole damn horse remuda?"

"I warned Long John about them, but thanks to the Comanche problem, he likes the idea of having these Comanche-hating Cherokees in the outfit. Hell of it is, when it comes to horses, an Indian will steal from anybody. Who else but Malo Coyote and Naked Horse would try to grab the horses of more'n twenty Comanches?"

"It wasn't the smartest thing we've ever done," Llano said, "saving their thieving hides almost at the expense of our own. They talk and act friendly toward us, but what would they do if you and me was captured by a bunch of Comanches?"

"I ain't completely sure," Stoney grinned, "but I can guess. While you and me was bein' roasted over a slow fire, Malo Coyote and Naked Horse would use it as a diversion while they stole the Comanche horses."

An hour before sundown Long John and Suzanne returned. With them rode four Lipan Apache riders who would remain at the L-J Connected while Long John

trailed the herd to Missouri. The Lipans drove before
them the twenty-two Winged M horses Clay Duval had
supplied. Naked Horse and Malo Coyote concerned
themselves for only a moment with the new Indian riders. The two Cherokees then turned their eyes to the
magnificent Mendoza blacks. Long John Coons eyed his
outfit, pausing a moment on the Kid's surly face, wondering why the little catamount wore only one Colt in a
two-gun rig. Finally Long John's eyes sought Stoney
Winters, and Stoney's eyes told him nothing. The Cajun
recalled Suzanne's warning, and was silently thankful for
Stoney Winters and his young friend, Llano Dupree. He
believed they were the kind of Texans he needed, men to
ride the river with, although he'd known them but a few
days. At first opportunity Long John would talk to the
grouchy old cook and learn what had really happened in
his absence.

2

The day following Long John's return, the roundup began in earnest. Suzanne had been excluded, because they had ten riders—enough for five teams—without her. There might be almost a month of dirty, dangerous work ahead of them. Tempers could flare, so Long John had paired his riders accordingly.

"Here's the order fer the roundup," he said. "Briano an' Darden, Miller an' Gitano, Dupree an' Winters, Naked Horse an' Malo Coyote, an' Kid, ye ride with me."

Clearly the Kid thought he'd been whipsawed, being paired with Long John, and he scowled at Stoney. Bandy Darden was equally resentful, having to ride with the mild-mannered Dent Briano. But neither man wished to risk the potential wrath of Long John Coons.

A week passed uneventfully, and by riding the brakes of the Colorado from dawn to dusk, they had managed to rope and corral 510 longhorns.

"Ain't bad," Long John said. "All three- an' four-year-olds, but not a one o' them mean Mex bulls in the lot. It's time the oldest o' them critters went up the trail."

"Toro matar," said Malo Coyote. *"Malo medicina."*

"Bad medicine they be," Long John said, "an' that's all the more reason to git the cantankerous bastards to market. But I won't see a man er horse gored. Ye rope one an' he gits loose, shoot the varmint."

Supper was done and the outfit sat around the tables finishing their coffee when Long John came in.

"Sky Pilot," said the Cajun, "ye git the time, that ol' wagon's goin' to need greasin'. Might's well cut new canvas fer it too. Whatever else might happen on this drive, we'll have dry blankets, anyhow."

"My God," said Quando Miller, "you ain't aimin' to take a wagon up the Shawnee?"

"I am," Long John said. "Ye got any objections?"

"No," said Miller hastily. "I just never seen it done before. Pack mules is better. We'll likely have to break trail for the wagon, and it'll slow us down."

"Sky Pilot can't ride," Long John said. "It's either a wagon fer Sky Pilot er we do our own cookin' from here to Missouri."

"Then by God, we'll take the wagon," said Dent Briano. "Anybody don't like that, he can answer to me."

"Well, I don't like it," the Kid said, his mean eyes on the bewhiskered old cook. "Longer we're on the trail, the more likely we are to git shot by abolitionists, proslavers, or ranchers scared of tick fever. It'll take forever to git to Missouri with a fool wagon draggin' along. All because of some stove-up old buzzard that can't ride like a man."

There was an embarrassed silence in which the cocking of Sky Pilot's Colt seemed inordinately loud.

"Sky Pilot," said Long John, "pull in yer horns an' put away the Colt."

Reluctantly the old cook eased down the hammer and slipped the weapon under his belt, but his hard old eyes never left the Kid, forcing the young gunman to look away.

"Now," Long John said, his eyes on the Kid, "the wagon goes with us. By the Eternal, this is my trail drive, an' if they's a man what don't like the way I'm ramrod-din' it, he can damn well saddle up an' ride."

The Kid got up, snatched his hat off the floor and stalked out of the cook shack.

Bandy Darden kept his peace, doing his share of the work, becoming so amicable that he aroused the suspicions of Dent Briano. More than once Darden had caught Briano watching him. Finally Darden exploded.

"Why the hell are you always lookin' at me?"

"Tryin' to get a handle on what you're up to," said Briano. "You ain't the kind to ride for forty and found, with the promise of a bonus at the end of the trail. You've never worked with another man's cows any longer than it took to hot up a cinch ring and change the brand."

"Well, by God," said Darden, and his laugh was ugly, "ain't *you* a fine one to be callin' *me* a thief. I disremember you and Quando ever backin' off when it come time to split the money."

"I ain't sayin' Quando and me is any better'n you. I just aim to be sure you ain't leavin' us out of whatever you got in mind. You can't trail this whole damn herd to Missouri by yourself."

"I don't aim to," Darden said. "I got a better idea, and I ain't sure I need you and Quando."

"It was you that took a shot at Long John, and I reckon it wouldn't take much to convince him you're a thievin' little skunk, low-down enough to steal from a man that's payin' you wages."

Bandy Darden went for his Colt. Snake quick, he still found himself looking into the muzzle of Dent Briano's weapon.

"Just hoorawin' you," said Darden, holstering his Colt. He laughed, but the laughter never reached his eyes. They were flint-hard, with a coldness that did not escape Dent Briano.

"Talk, then," said Briano, easing down the hammer and holstering his own Colt.

"I reckon when we git 'em to St. Louis, these cows oughta bring at least forty dollars a head. We git there with two thousand of 'em, that's $80,000. We could blow the rest of our lives grabbin' a cow here and a cow there, without ever havin' two pesos to rub together. This is our big chance. Maybe our only chance, with a war comin'."

Briano said nothing, waiting for Darden to continue.

"With all this hell raisin' in Kansas and Missouri," said Darden, "Coons ain't about to leave the money in a bank. He'll saddlebag it, likely in gold, and head for Texas."

"All we have to do, then," Briano said, "is kill everybody, includin' Long John's woman."

"That's it," said Darden. "Leave just one witness to a thing like this, and somewhere down the trail there'll be a noose waitin' for us. With all this war talk and shootin' goin' on, who can ever prove these poor Texans wasn't gunned down by them pro-slavers and abolitionists? You want me to talk to Quando, see if he's with us?"

"No. Stay away from Quando, and with others around, don't be talkin' to me. Coons is no fool, and if he finds the three of us palaverin' too much, he's likely to get the idea we're up to somethin'. He don't much like you anyhow, and I purely cain't understand why, you're such a lovable little bastard."

While Malo Coyote and Naked Horse did their share of the hard work, they also found time to talk. Somewhere along the Shawnee Trail they too wished to become wealthy, and the potential source of it had nothing to do with the gold from the sale of the longhorns. Their eyes were on the twenty-two horses, all handsome blacks, from Clay Duval's Winged M Ranch.

"Gaupo caballos," said Malo Coyote. *"Cuando nosotros tomar?"**

"Ser largo sendero," Naked Horse replied. *"Nosotros espera. Blanco hombre's guerra venir, guiza pronto."***

As a cowboy, Deuce Gitano was adequate, but that was all. If he could avoid it, he rarely spoke. But the missing ring finger and the undisguised hatred in the man's eyes said much about him. Each night after supper he lovingly cleaned the .31 caliber Colt he carried beneath his coat. Deuce Gitano had the look of a man who rode a vengeance trail; that when he found the man or men he sought, somebody would die. The eventual loser might be Gitano himself, but would the man really care? Quando Miller wondered.

Llano Dupree and Stoney Winters worked well together. They'd been saddle pards since their early teens, and for half a dozen years had been fiddle-footing it from one range to another. Like most Texans, they had "learned cow" early in life and took the hard work in stride.

"Long John Coons is no fool," Llano said. "He rode up, took one look at the Kid, and knew he'd been at the bottom of some kind of ruckus."

"Yeah," said Stoney. "That's why he's paired himself with the Kid, trying to keep peace during the roundup. The Kid's already figurin' I've talked to Long John."

"He'll have it in for you now. Somebody oughta stick a hay fork in the little catamount and let some of that pride ooze out. I just hope you don't have to shoot him before we get to Missouri. I got a feeling we'll need every rider we got, includin' Suzanne."

"I'm a mite uneasy about her bein' along," Stoney

---

* "Handsome horses. When we take?"
** "Be long trail. We wait. White man's war come, maybe soon."

said. "She can ride, rope, and shoot, but she's still a woman. There are limitations."

"She's tough as whang leather, and while I wouldn't say it around Long John, I reckon she's seen some hard livin'."

"Then maybe she *is* tough enough for the Shawnee Trail," said Stoney. "If there's a problem with her, it'll be Long John's worry. There's somethin' else bothering me. While I understand why we have to take the wagon, I can agree with some of the objections they throwed at Long John. You can drive cows over rocks, logs, and through deep arroyos, but not a wagon. If we have to clear a path for the wagon, it'll take us a year to reach the railroad."

"Nothin' we can do about the land," Llano said, "but you'll have to give old Sky Pilot credit. He's doin' all he can to head off the usual problems. He's carryin' a spare wheel and a replacement axle."

The Kid was still nervous after a week of working with Long John. He fumbled with piggin string, missed easy throws, and instead of roping a cow's hind legs, he often caught only one. Long John didn't know whether to laugh at him or swear at him.

"Kid," said the Cajun, after an especially trying day, "startin' tomorrer, you'll ride with Quando Miller. Deuce, you'll be workin' with me."

The Kid's relief was obvious, but Deuce Gitano only shrugged. Nothing seemed to matter to him.

Nearing the end of the second week of the roundup, they roped some of the ill-tempered bulls whose ancestors had fought in the arenas of Old Mexico. Once roped, the brutes had to have their front and hind legs bound. In that position they thrashed about for hours before exhausting themselves. Only then could they be led to holding pens. All the riders hated the savage bulls except Malo Coyote and Naked Horse. The Cherokees seemed to delight in subduing the Mexican bulls. It was near the end of the day, and the outfit had gathered at one of the holding pens as Malo Coyote and Naked Horse brought in their two most recent captives.

"Look at the heathen bastards," said Bandy Darden. "They think they're better'n we are."

"Maybe they are," Llano Dupree said. "They've roped eight of those Mex bulls, and the rest of us haven't roped even one."

"So you're a damn Injun lover," snorted Darden. "You talk like a squaw man."

Long John waited, saying nothing. Bandy Darden had nursed his mad about as long as he could, and needed a dog to kick. Long John could stop it if he saw the need, but he wanted to see how Llano handled himself.

"I've known some Indians," said Llano, "that I thought more of than some of the so-called white men that's runnin' around loose."

"You sayin' that I'm one of 'em, that I ain't good as a heathen Injun?"

"Darden," Llano said coldly, "far as I'm concerned, you'd have to grow some before you'd be even close to any Indian that ever lived."

Bandy Darden's hand was just inches from the butt of his Colt. It was time for Long John to intervene. He couldn't afford to lose a rider; not even a troublesome varmint like Bandy Darden.

"Darden," said Long John, "git yer hand away from that pistol. We're out here to rope cows, an' they's an hour o' daylight. If ye damn roosters is hell-bent on fightin', do it after supper. But ye'll do it with fists, not guns."

It rankled Darden, but he was in no position for a showdown with Long John. Not yet. Instead he turned on Llano Dupree.

"If you got the sand, boy," he said through clenched

teeth, "I'll meet you behind the bunkhouse, after supper."

"Come on," said Llano. "I'll be there."

"Mount up," Long John said. "They's cows to be roped."

"Damn it," Stoney said when he and Llano had ridden away, "what do you expect to accomplish by that?"

"I ain't doin' it to accomplish anything," Llano said angrily. "I'm doin' it because it's somethin' I want to do. Can't a man do somethin' purely because he wants to? Somebody's got to beat that bastard's ears down to his boot tops. Why not me?"

"He ain't tall," said Stoney, "but he's built like a mountain grizzly, and he outweighs you a good twenty pounds. He just might beat *your* ears down to *your* boot tops."

"If he's man enough," Llano said, "when I'm able, I'll shake his hand. But first, by God, he's got some provin' to do."

Supper finished, the outfit gathered behind the bunkhouse. Suzanne was there, despite Long John's objections. Sky Pilot had left all the supper dishes, hoping to see Darden take a licking. Both men had removed shirts, hats, and pistol belts, and stood facing one another, like wary hounds.

"What's wrong with you, boy?" Darden taunted. "Has your feet sprouted roots?"

"This was your idea," said Llano. "Start the dance when you're of a mind to."

Excitement ran high among the rest of the outfit, but Stoney Winters was calm, for he knew something the rest of them did not. While he and Llano had been in Omaha, Llano had become friends with a fighter, had taken an interest in fighting, and had spent some time in the ring. He was fast on his feet, with a deceptive right that held his opponent's attention until he could land a sledgehammer blow with his left. It was Naked Horse who drove Bandy Darden to make the first move.

"El cobarde," said Naked Horse, loud enough for Darden to hear.*

Darden threw caution to the wind, and Llano countered his charge by stepping aside and tripping him. Darden went facedown in the dirt, and there were whoops of laughter from the rest of the riders.

"You look more natural on your belly than on your feet," Llano said.

Darden got to his feet, cautious now, and Llano waited. He ducked under Darden's right, driving a hard left into Darden's belly, and the wind went out of Darden. He doubled up, and when his chin came down, it met Llano's hard driving right. It straightened Darden out, lifted him off his feet, and he came down on his back in a cloud of dust. But the man was game, and tougher than he looked. He shook his head, got to his feet and came after Llano. The wind was to his back, and when he was near enough, he flung two handfuls of dirt into Llano's face. It provided just enough edge for Darden to seize Llano in a grizzly hug, and the two of them went down in a clench. With Darden astride him, Llano couldn't get enough leverage with his legs to buck the heavier man off. Llano raised his shoulders off the ground, seeking to get some force behind his blows, but Darden seemed to ignore them.

Darden had his hands around Llano's throat, cutting off his wind and slamming his head against the hard ground. Llano could feel the gravel cutting into his scalp, but it was Darden's thumbs dug into his windpipe that were killing him. Dizzy, unable to see, he made one last, desperate move. With a mighty heave, he rolled on his right side, breaking Darden's grip on his throat. Darden tried to roll Llano to his belly, but Darden's

---

* Him Coward

position had shifted and he was off balance. Quickly Llano turned on his back. Before Darden could again imprison his legs, Llano lifted them and brought them forward till he was bent like a horseshoe. He wrapped his long legs around Darden's neck and, with a powerful backward thrust, threw the man off, on his back. Llano rolled and got to his feet, winded, only to have Darden come at him again.

Llano's throat ached. He knew he had to stay on his feet. On the ground or in the clinches, Darden had an edge. Confident now, Darden charged. Llano feinted with his right, connected with a left, and halted Darden in his tracks. Blood poured from Darden's smashed nose and dripped off his chin, and with a roar like a wounded bull, he came after Llano again. Although the April sun was down, Llano backhanded sweat from his eyes, and he could feel it soaking the waist of his Levi's. His knees were weak, and he was thankful for the log wall of the bunkhouse at his back. Again Darden came after him, his left arm up, expecting another blow to his battered nose and mouth. Llano again feinted with his right, and with all his failing strength threw a smashing left to Darden's belly. It took the wind out of Darden, and when Darden humped forward, Llano brought up his right knee. It was a brutal blow that caught Darden just above the eyes and laid him flat on his back. Using his elbows for support, he tried to rise, but he hadn't the strength. He fell back, breathing hard. Still on his feet, Llano slumped against the log wall of the bunkhouse. There were no shouts, no laughter, for neither man seemed to have won. Bandy Darden, after several attempts, managed to get to his feet. He was staggering toward Llano when Long John spoke.

"The fun's over. I want the pair o' ye in the saddle tomorrer, not so stove up ye can't move."

"Llano," said Stoney, "let's take a walk down to the

creek. I know this ain't Saturday night, but you could stand a bath."

In silence, Long John and Suzanne returned to the house. Long John went into the kitchen, dragged out a chair and sat down. Suzanne went to the stove, stirred up the coals under the coffeepot, and added a stick of wood. She sat down, resting her elbows on the table, her chin in her cupped hands, facing Long John. Finally he spoke, and there was an edge to his voice.

"Ye don't think I done the right thing, allowin' the fight, do ye?"

"You didn't ask me what I thought before you allowed it. What does it matter what I think now?"

Long John got up, and leaning his big hands on the table, glared at her. Suzanne got up, assumed a stance similar to his own, and glared right back at him. Slowly the tension went out of Long John, and he sighed.

"The coffee's hot," he said. "Git me a cup—please."

Without a word Suzanne brought two cups, poured them full of steaming black coffee, and slid one across the table to Long John. He downed half the coffee before he spoke.

"What should I of done? Bandy Darden needed somebody to stomp a mudhole in his ornery carcass an' then walk it dry."

"Perhaps," said Suzanne, "but it didn't happen. This young man, Llano Dupree, handled himself well, but he didn't win. Neither did Bandy Darden. You know what that means, don't you?"

"Guns, I reckon," said Long John gloomily.

By mid-April, Long John's outfit had gathered 975 head, secured in holding pens that stretched across the creek, so the animals could drink. Four days had passed since the fight between Llano Dupree and Bandy Darden, and there was no evidence that either man intended to resume the conflict, but Long John had a nagging feeling

that Suzanne had been right. Just before supper, a rider
none of them had ever seen before reined up before the
bunkhouse. He had ridden in from the north, and his
horse was well-spent. Long John had seen him coming
and was there in time to invite him to dismount. He
wore sweat-stained range clothes, a battered hat, and a
Colt hung low on his right hip. On the left side of his
cowhide vest was pinned a silver star in a circle. A Texas
Ranger.

"Git down," said Long John. "Supper in a few minutes, an' yer welcome to stay the night, if ye want."

"I'd be obliged," the stranger said, dismounting. He
nodded his thanks to Llano, who took his tired horse
and led it toward the barn. "I'm Eldon Reeves," he said,
turning back to Long John and offering his hand.

"Long John Coons," said the Cajun, extending his
own hand. "Trouble up north o' here?"

"Comanche trouble," said Reeves. "Hell with the lid
off. Cap'n got word there was maybe twenty-five renegades holed up somewhere north of Fort Worth, along
the Red. Four of us rode up there and picked up their
trail, thinkin' we'd lay an ambush. We got two doses of
bad news pronto. First, that bunch we was trailin' was
just part of a larger party. Second, they knowed we was
comin' and had laid an ambush of their own. Must've
been a good hundred of the bastards. Cost us three good
men. They was cut down in the first volley, and so was
my horse. The other three horses lit out back the way
we'd come, and that's how I got out alive. I caught the
reins of one, and we tore out of there like the devil
himself was on our heels."

"That ain't very encouragin'," Long John said.
"Maybe two weeks from now, we're aimin' to take a
herd up the Shawnee, to Missouri."

"I'd think long and hard on it," said Reeves. "Last
two or three drives lost men. Some to the Injuns, some

to the terrorists in Kansas and Missouri. If you go, take plenty of fighting men, and see that they're well-armed."

The following morning after breakfast, Reeves rode out, heading southwest. Long John and his outfit continued the roundup, nobody talking about the news the Ranger had brought. Llano and Stoney spoke of it only when they were well away from the other riders.

"This oughta be some hell of a trail drive," Llano said. "The Kid's got a mad on for you and Sky Pilot, Bandy Darden would like to gut-shoot me, while Malo Coyote and Naked Horse may try to grab the horse remuda."

"Don't forget the long trail across Indian Territory and into Missouri," said Stoney. "While we're fighting among ourselves, wrassling with a herd of longhorns— the pro-slavers, abolitionists, and ranchers afraid of tick fever will be after *us*. All of us."

"There's just one sensible thing for us to do," Llano said.

"Yeah," said Stoney, "but we've given our word, so we can't do it."

"No, but we got an edge, pard. We're Texans."

Late that night, Suzanne tossed and turned, unable to sleep. Finally Long John kicked back the covers and sat up on the edge of the bed.

"What in tarnation's botherin' ye?" he asked irritably.

"This trail drive," said Suzanne. "Except for Llano, Stoney, and old Sky Pilot, I don't trust a' one of them . . ."

"Me neither," Long John said, "but gal, we ain't in a position to be choosy. These gents is willin', takin' their pay when we sell the herd. Fer all I know, the whole damn bunch is runnin' from the law. They all got some reason fer throwin' in with us. We'll likely have to fight our way into Kansas and Missouri, thanks to this damn tick fever, and fer all we know, we may end up smack in the middle of this war that's brewin' betwixt north and south. I agree with ye, we likely got the biggest bunch of misfits that ever forked a bronc, but things bein' like they are, we purely got no choice."

"I know," Suzanne sighed. "I know."

It was far into the night before either of them slept . . .

3

As the outfit began the last week of the roundup, Long John made a change.

"Startin' today, me an' Deuce is goin' to reshoe all the horses," the Cajun said. "Winters, yer in charge o' the roundup. We're still needin' more'n five hunnert cows to complete the herd."

"For sure," said Quando Miller, "you can't say Long John puts all the dirty work off on his riders. I'll rope cows any day, 'fore I'll shoe horses. And them damn mules that'll be pullin' the wagon is mean enough to have you for breakfast."

Llano Dupree and Bandy Darden had avoided one another since the fight. Darden again approached Briano, a week after the little gunman had revealed his devious plan to rob Long John and murder the outfit.

"You was gonna talk to Quando," Darden said. "Did you?"

"I did," Briano said, "and he's with us. But I ain't sure you're gonna be with the outfit long enough to do nothin'. That was a fool move, pickin' a fight with Dupree. Coons could of tallied your time and told you to ride."

"Not much, he won't," said Darden. "He's needin' riders. I don't like Dupree or Winters. When we take the gold, I want the pleasure of borin' the pair of 'em."

"You can try," Briano said, "but you saw Winters draw after the Kid had the drop on him. I got an idea this Winters and Dupree ain't the kind to back off. I've seen you draw, and if Dupree's anywhere close to Winters in speed, he'll fill your gizzard full of lead before you clear leather."

Stoney Winters had a habit of going to the house after supper and reporting to Long John, allowing the Cajun to add the day's gather to his running tally. It was a time to discuss any problems that had arisen, but at the end of the third day, Stoney had nothing negative to report. When he had departed, Long John sat staring at the kitchen door.

"He's hardly more than a boy," said Suzanne, "but you have much faith in him. Is that why you have chosen to shoe the horses, to test him by leaving him in charge of the roundup?"

"Yer always a-studyin' me," Long John said with a sigh, tempering it with a grin. "But yer right. Winters is young in years, but he's a man to ride the river with. I look fer trouble from the Kid and Bandy Darden, an' I'm figgerin' with Winters as segundo, them two troublesome varmints might work off their mad 'fore we take the trail."

"That," said Suzanne, "and you *are* testing Stoney Winters."

"That's part o' it," Long John admitted. "If'n he can keep this outfit in line without me standin' behind him now, then I reckon he can handle 'em on the trail. Unless somebody backs him down 'fore the end o' this week, Stoney will be the trail boss."

While resting their horses in the shade of a cottonwood, Llano and Stoney discussed Long John's probable reasons for leaving Stoney in charge of the roundup.

"Except for me and the kid," Llano said, "you're the youngest hombre in the outfit. The Kid's down on you, and Darden's got it in for me. It's kind of like Long John's makin' you segundo just to rub their noses in it."

"We'll have trouble enough on the trail without fightin' among ourselves," said Stoney. "I don't know why Darden was so hostile, so anxious to fight, but I think I know why Long John allowed it. I reckon Darden's the kind to let his temper build until he's got to let off steam, and Long John hoped to take the fire out of him before we start the drive. But your fight with him settled nothing. The Kid's been avoiding me, so that means trouble somewhere along the trail. It'd be mighty easy durin' an Indian or renegade attack for Darden or the Kid to gun us down."

"Long John's an old hand with enough wrinkles on his horns to have thought of that," Llano said, "but his plan ain't workin'. Once we take the trail, you and me will have to be as ready for gunplay from behind as from ahead."

By noon Saturday—the end of the fourth week—they had, by Long John's tally, 2030 head, twenty-five of which were the Corrientes bulls.

"All o' ye better take tomorrer an' rest," said Long John, when the outfit came together at one of the holding pens. "Come Monday mornin' at first light, we'll move 'em out. Stoney Winters will be trail boss, and ye'll answer to him er to me. If ye got questions er complaints, let's hear 'em now."

They kept their silence. One by one Long John singled out the riders, his questioning eyes pausing the longest on the Kid and Bandy Darden. But their impassive faces told him nothing, and his misgivings grew.

Sky Pilot spent Sunday loading the wagon, and despite the anticipated difficulties, the riders began to see some advantages to having the cumbersome vehicle on the drive. There was plenty of room for extra shoes for the horses and mules, and all necessary tools. There was a

Dutch oven, a full array of pots and pans, eating tools, tin plates and cups. From San Antonio, Long John had brought a barrel of flour, a sack of brown sugar, coffee beans, dried apples, dried beans, four sides of bacon, three hams, and a two-gallon keg of whiskey.

"I got to admit one thing," Quando Miller said. "We're travelin' in style, and the grub's goin' to be good. Usin' pack mules, we couldn't take even half of this."

"Studebaker wagon," said Long John. "She'll take a hell of a beatin'. Got 'er rigged with new canvas, too. Throw yer bedrolls in there an' keep 'em dry."*

"I still say this is a damn tenderfoot idea," scoffed Bandy Darden. "With pack mules we could git by with half of what we're takin', and end the drive a month sooner."

"Darden," Long John said angrily, "this is my idea an' my drive, an' the onliest damn thing we got to look forward to is decent grub at the end o' God knows what kind o' day. The wagon goes, if'n we have to pick the bastard up an' carry her the last fifty mile. Ye don't approve of the wagon, then leave her be. If'n it'll make ye feel better, yer welcome to eat jerked beef an' live out'n yer saddlebag."

The rest of the riders laughed. Even Malo Coyote and Naked Horse knew enough English to appreciate Long John's fiery response. Darden said nothing, silently reminding himself that his time was coming.

April 28, 1858. On the trail north.

"Move 'em out!" Stoney shouted.

Sky Pilot had already taken the lead, and the wagon was out of sight. The longhorns surged forward in a mass, making it all but impossible to control them. Once they became trailwise and manageable, the best formation was three or four abreast, regardless of how long

* In 1839, the Studebaker brothers began building wagons

the column was strung out. Long John and Suzanne brought up the rear, riding drag. Deuce Gitano and Dent Briano rode with them. Except for Stoney, the rest of the outfit flanked the herd, heading bunch quitters breaking left and right.

"Keep 'em bunched," shouted Long John, popping dusty behinds with his lariat. "Keep 'em off'n the back trail. If'n they're hell-bent on quittin', make 'em break from the flanks."

While most bunch quitters sought a path where there were no restraining riders, one old Corrientes bull was determined to go back the way he had come. He whirled, charging the drag riders. Long John's horse sidestepped the charge, and Long John caught the brute with a horn loop. It then became the duty of a second rider—and Suzanne was nearest—to catch the hind legs with an underhand throw. But the bull seemed to anticipate the throw, and with a wild kick he escaped Suzanne's loop. The hostile animal then turned on Long John, intent on goring the Cajun, his horse, or both. Long John drew his Colt and fired once, twice, three times. He swung out of the saddle and was removing his lariat from the dead bull's horns when Suzanne rode up.

"Sorry," she said, unsure as to how Long John might react.

"Nothin' to be sorry about," Long John said. "This bastard was too savvy fer his own good. He knowed ye was after his hind legs, an' he knowed what'd happen if'n ye caught 'em. Mebbe two more hours, an' we'll have to call it a day. Couple o' us can ride back an' cut out a haunch o' this varmint. He won't be a total loss, an' we'll have fresh beef fer supper."

Knowing the first few days of the drive would be man killers, they would follow the Colorado north as far as they could, so there would be no lack of water. While a trailwise herd could be pushed to the nearest water, the outfit had its hands full, just keeping this unorganized bunch moving in the same general direction, without having to guide them to water as well. Near sundown Long John used his hat to signal the nearest flank riders, and they passed it on. Once the leaders were headed and the herd began to mill, Long John spoke to Suzanne.

"Briano an' me are ridin' back fer that haunch o' beef. Git the word to Stoney, an' tell Sky Pilot they's fresh steak fer supper."

The herd had begun milling. Finally they got the idea the drive was over for the day, and began to graze, some of them making their way down the riverbank to the water.

"My God," said Llano, "I feel like I been throwed and dragged through the dust all day."

Stoney grinned. "You look it."

Nobody else had anything to say. They were exhausted, their enthusiasm at a low ebb. Sky Pilot had the rest of the fixings well under way when Long John and Dent Briano returned with the haunch of beef. Little was said until Sky Pilot had fed them Dutch oven biscuits, beans, fresh steak, and plenty of hot coffee. When Long John spoke, it was to Stoney Winters.

"How far, ye reckon?"

"Eight miles, maybe,". said Stoney.

"This is my first trail drive," Suzanne said. "Is it always like this?"

"No, ma'am," said Dent Briano with a tired grin. "Sometimes it's worse."

"I'm taking the first watch," Stoney said, "along with Darden, Briano, Miller, and the Kid. Since there's eleven of us, I'm savin' the heaviest watch for last. We change at midnight."

"That's savvy," said Long John. "If they's trouble— Injun er white—it mostly comes after midnight."

But the night passed uneventfully. The herd, unruly as it was, seemed as tired as the riders, and there were no bunch quitters during the night. But whatever hope they had that the second day's drive might be better than the first lasted only until they got the herd moving at first light. The brutes were as wild as ever, some seeming more so, following a night of rest. More than a hundred head, led by a pair of Corrientes bulls, tore out to the east, and there was little the flankers could do to stop them. Stoney had to halt the drive, while Long John, Llano, Quando Miller, and Deuce Gitano went after the runaways. No sooner had they been returned to the herd when the same bunch again tried to run. Angry now, Long John managed to get ahead of the leaders, turned his horse and charged headlong into them. He swatted tender muzzles with his doubled lariat, swore at them, and screeched like a cougar. The leaders, frightened by this madman, turned and ran bawling back to the herd. Long John and his horse were dripping with sweat. He reined up, dismounted, and began walking the animal. Suzanne caught up, rode alongside and just glared at him. Finally she spoke.

"I've never seen a man do anything as foolish as what you just did," she snapped. She didn't know how he'd take it, and she didn't care. "Suppose when you rode into those charging bulls, they hadn't turned?"

"Then I reckon me an' my horse would of been buzzard bait," said Long John mildly.

Disgusted, words failing her, Suzanne rode away, catching up to the drag. Long John grinned, touched by her concern. Finally, when he and his horse had rested, he mounted and rode on.

Not until their fourth day on the trail did the herd begin to settle down. There were still a few bunch quitters, most of them the ornery Mexican Corrientes bulls. The sun set behind a bank of dark clouds, its rays pinking the sky until they blended with the purple of night. The wind was from the southwest, brisk, bringing with it the unmistakable smell of rain. As dusk approached, jagged slivers of golden lightning darted from the cloud mass.

"Storm buildin'," said Long John. "If'n we're lucky, we'll have time fer supper 'fore she hits."

"Everybody saddle a fresh horse," Stoney said, "and be ready to ride. This herd has some trail savvy, but not enough to weather a storm with lots of thunder and lightning. I reckon we're about to have both."

It was a prophecy that not a man in the outfit doubted would soon be fulfilled. The herd hadn't bedded down, nor would they graze, and some had already begun a nervous lowing. Summoning Malo Coyote and Naked Horse, Stoney spoke to them in Spanish. Immediately they mounted their horses and rode away.

"I'm leavin' Malo Coyote and Naked Horse with the remuda," said Stoney. "They're goin' to move the horses well away from the herd. Then if the longhorns get spooked and scatter from hell to breakfast, they won't be taking the horse remuda with them."

"Damn good plannin'," Long John said approvingly.

"Now," said Stoney, "the rest of us are goin' to circle this herd and do what we can to convince these brutes there's nothin' to get spooked about."

"That bunch is gonna run like hell wouldn't have it," said Bandy Darden, "and there ain't a damn thing we can do about it."

"Maybe not," Stoney said shortly, "but get out there and ride. If they run, do your best to head 'em. Nobody's askin' more of you than that."

The storm came closer, and while the lightning wasn't striking, it had become more intense. Thunder rumbled, and with it came the first big drops of rain. Gone was the purple of the darkening sky with its blanket of stars. The heavens had become a roiling gray mass, seeming all the more eerie as lightning circled the horizon with an almost continuous halo of fire. The longhorns stood with their backs to the approaching storm, waiting. They were going to run, and the only question was when. Circling the herd in an effort to calm them had become an act of futility. Better they should prepare themselves for a hard ride that might put them ahead of the herd. A stampeding herd nearly always ran away from the storm, the wind and rain at their backs. In the almost continuous flare of lightning, Stoney could see Long John and four other riders on the far side of the herd, riding eastward. It was a good move, and Stoney followed their lead. Behind him rode Bandy Darden and the Kid, with Llano following them. He trusted neither of them. There were tales of more than one unpopular segundo being shot in the back in the darkness and confusion of a stampede.

When the lightning finally struck, it illuminated the world from one horizon to the other, and was accompanied by a clap of thunder that shook the earth. As expected, the herd lit out to the east, and while the riders had anticipated it, their efforts were futile. Some of the unruly Mexican bulls had taken the lead and wouldn't be stopped. Stoney galloped his horse, getting ahead of the stampeding herd, and in flashes of lightning he could see other riders on the farthest side doing the same. But they had to ride for their lives, as did Stoney. They *had* gotten ahead of the herd, but the stampeding brutes thundered on in blind terror. Out of danger, Stoney reined up and was joined by the Kid, Bandy Darden, and Llano.

"Damn it, Winters," said Darden sarcastically, "you was ahead of 'em. Why didn't you turn 'em?"

The Kid laughed, but it died away to a nervous giggle as he saw Stoney's face in the flare of lightning. In the wake of the stampede, Long John and the rest of the outfit joined Stoney and his trio of riders.

"Them bastards wouldn't of stopped fer anything less'n a prairie fire," Long John said. "I'm jist glad none of us was hurt an' none of our horses gored. Wonder if

Malo Coyote an' Naked Horse was able to hold the horses?"

"We might as well go and find out," said Llano. "We can't go after the herd until first light."

To their surprise and relief, they found the horse remuda intact, and Long John was jubilant.

"Wal, by God," he chuckled, "they done it. Now all we got to do is round up them blasted cows."

The day dawned clear, the sky as blue as bluebonnets, with a sun that promised to have them sweating before midday. Breakfast done, the outfit saddled up to begin looking for the scattered herd.

"Long John," Stoney said, "take four riders and back-track down the Colorado. I'll take three and follow the path of the stampede. I reckon we'll find some of the herd out on the plains, but not for long. The sun will suck up last night's rain pronto, and the herd will be forced back to the river for water. Naked Horse, you and Malo Coyote stay with the horse remuda."

"I'm a mite tired of you suckin' up to them damn Injuns," said the Kid. "How come they git to stay here and watch the horses, while we all have to wrassle cows out of the brush?"

Long John fought back an angry response, allowing Stoney to handle the situation.

"Two reasons," Stoney said, as calmly as he could. "First, they're only followin' my orders. Second, they've proven themselves better horse wranglers than anybody else. Now mount up."

Stoney took Llano, Deuce Gitano, and Bandy Darden, following the path of the stampeded herd. The water that had accumulated from last night's rain was rapidly disappearing. Reaching the point where the stampede had lost its momentum, Stoney and his companions soon found many tracks turning westward, toward the Colorado. By the time they reached the river, Long John and his riders were already there, chasing cows out of the brush.

"We'll ride on down the river a ways," Stoney told Long John. "All of 'em won't reach the river at the same point. We'll run the others upriver, throwin' 'em in with what you're gathering."

Stoney and his riders rode downriver an estimated five miles, a distance Stoney believed sufficient to gather the rest of the stampeded herd. Rounding a bend in the river, they came face-to-face with a dozen mounted Comanche warriors. One party was as surprised as the other. Stoney and his riders wheeled their horses and tore out back the way they'd come. Six of the Comanches pursued, while the rest of the party crossed the river. It was an obvious move. Using brush along the river for cover, those on the farthest bank would attempt to get ahead of Stoney and his companions.

"Ride," Stoney shouted. "If they get ahead, they'll have us in a cross fire."

Stoney drew his Colt, and turning in the saddle, fired three deliberate shots. He hit none of their pursuers, nor had he intended to. The shots would warn Long John and the rest of the outfit. But the six Comanches on the farthest bank of the river had achieved their purpose. Half a mile ahead of Stoney and his companions, the six rode across the river, shouting their triumph. But suddenly they found themselves in a cross fire of their own. By the time they were aware of the new threat, Long John and the rest of the outfit were within range and shooting. Two of the Comanches were shot off their horses into the river, and a third was cut down as the survivors scrambled their horses up the farthest bank of the river. Stoney looked back, and finding they were no longer pursued, reined up his tired horse.

"Wal," said Long John, grinning, "ye go downriver fer cows, an' ye come back with Comanches."

"We're just almighty lucky we surprised them before they surprised us," Stoney said.

"We shot three of them," said Suzanne, "but is that enough to keep the rest of them from coming after us?"

"No way o' knowin'," Long John said. "I jist wisht I knowed them remainin' nine was all we got t' worry about. This bunch might of been an advance party fer lots more of 'em. Could be fifty more o' the varmints skulkin' around, an' if they is, them three we shot will likely make the rest of 'em killin' mad."

It was a grim prognosis, and for once neither the Kid nor Bandy Darden had anything to say.

"We'd better round up whatever cows we can," said Stoney, "and move 'em upriver. Comanches are horse Indians, and we're taking a risk, having only two men with our remuda. We could ride back to camp, find our grub and our horses gone, with three dead men waitin' for us."

They worked swiftly, flushing out cattle from the thickets along the river and hazing them north. They fought their way upriver, adding to their gather as they went. By the end of the day, Long John's quick tally accounted for only 1600 head.

"Damn it," said Long John, "that's twenny percent. I purely can't take a beatin' like that, jist four days down the trail. If we swaller a loss like this, time we git to Missouri they won't be a thousant head."

"We've pretty well covered the river," Stoney said. "The rest of 'em could have continued east or turned north at some point, but I can't understand why, with the Colorado being the nearest water."

"Maybe somebody was drivin' 'em," Quando Miller suggested.

"Comanches, I reckon," said Bandy Darden, with his usual sarcasm. "What would Injuns want with a herd of cows?"

"Same thing I want with 'em," Long John said. "It

ain't unusual fer the Injuns to steal a herd, drive it to Injun Territory, an' sell fer what they can git. They's guv'mint forts up there, an' quartermasters that don't ask any questions, if'n the price is right."

"With that possibility in mind," said Stoney, "I have a suggestion. Let's put Malo Coyote and Naked Horse on this. Let's let them find a trail, if they can."

"That'll mean layin' over another day or two," Bandy Darden said, "with them damn Comanches mad at us."

"Wrong, Darden," said Stoney. "The drive goes on. With only sixteen hundred head, we can manage without Naked Horse and Malo Coyote. If they find our cows, then we can ride back and take them. If they don't find them, then the drive hasn't lost any time waiting."

"Good thinkin'," Long John approved. "Git them Injuns on the trail, an' the rest o' us can git on with the drive."

"I'll talk to them in the morning," said Stoney. "Time we get these cows back to camp, it'll be too late for them to start today. The trail will be a day old, but unless every one of them four hundred cows took a different direction, there'll still be plenty of sign."

After breakfast the following morning, Stoney explained the mission to Malo Coyote and Naked Horse, and at first light they set out to find the trail. But the unpredictable pair had more on their minds than just finding Long John's missing cows. Once they had ridden away, Naked Horse spoke.

*"Caza vaca, nosotros hallazgo caballo. Comanch' caballo."** *

*"Matar Comanch'," * said Malo Coyote. *"Tomar caballo. Vaca guiza."*** *

---

* "Hunt cow, we find horse. Comanche horse."
** "Kill Comanche. Take horse. Cow maybe."

4

June 2, 1858. Along the Rio Colorado.

*T*he day following the stampede, the outfit bedded down the herd for the last time before leaving the Colorado. As they finished their coffee, darkness was only a few minutes away.

"Startin' tomorrow," Stoney said, "no more river. Long John, how far is it from your spread to where we are now, and how far south of Dallas are we?"

"We come maybe fifty mile," said Long John, "leavin' us 160 mile south o' Dallas, an' 110 mile 'fore we cross the Brazos."

"My God," Suzanne said, "six days on the trail, and we've come just fifty miles?"

"Startin' tomorrow," said Llano, "we'll have to do better, because we'll be scoutin' ahead for water. Either we reach the next water, or spend the night in dry camp."

"I was hopin' them Injuns would git back to us 'fore we left the Colorado," Long John said. "If'n we're goin' after them missin' cows, we need to do it 'fore we have to start huntin' water. I ain't wantin' water problems ahead, whilst we're fightin' Comanches on our back trail."

"Sendin' them two heathen off on a cow hunt wasn't so smart," said Bandy Darden, his hard eyes on Stoney. "We'll likely never see 'em again, and with another rider scoutin' for water, it'll be all the harder on the rest of us."

"That was my decision," Stoney said, "and good or bad, I'm sticking to it. If I want your advice, I'll ask for it."

Long John had witnessed the angry exchange, but said nothing. In the morning, Stoney Winters would be forced to make yet another difficult decision. Should they press on, or risk losing another day? Once they left the Colorado, the daily search for water would take priority over almost everything else. Those four hundred cows—twenty percent of the herd—would be lost. Yet they might wait another day and still lose the cows. It all depended on the unpredictable Malo Coyote and Naked Horse, and already Stoney's mind wrestled with the hard choice he must soon face.

Malo Coyote and Naked Horse followed the path of the stampede, seeking some point at which the missing cows had broken away. But there was, as Stoney Winters had found, no indication the herd had split. Instead, as the Cherokees discovered, the stampede had lost momentum, scattering the herd. Most of them had turned back toward the river. The others had left no definitive trail, but had wandered aimlessly, probably grazing. Naked Horse reined up and dismounted. Among the cow tracks there were also tracks of unshod horses.

"Comanch'," said Naked Horse.

He mounted, and with Malo Coyote following, rode on to the northeast. After several miles, cow tracks became more numerous, and so did the tracks of the unshod horses. Individual riders had driven three or four cows until all the animals had come together, creating a herd. The trail began to veer to the southwest.

"*Agua,*" said Malo Coyote.

Naked Horse nodded. The herd was being circled back toward the Colorado River, but their eventual destination would take them many miles downstream, far beyond the distance Long John's outfit would search. Naked Horse and Malo Coyote rode slowly, reading sign. Once all the cattle converged into a single herd, the Indian duo found tracks of eighteen horses. The longhorns would be driven so far south that Malo Coyote and Naked Horse could expect no help from Long John's outfit. But did they *want* help? The cowboys would concern themselves only with recovery of the cows, and the Comanche horses would be lost. It was time for a decision, and the Cherokees reined up.

"*Sur?*" Malo Coyote asked.

"*Sur,*" Naked Horse replied.*

They turned their horses and rode due south, disregarding the obvious trail. To continue following the herd would be foolish, for it was the logical direction from which any pursuit would come. Besides, an Indian camp might have a formidable pack of dogs. Instead, Naked Horse and Malo Coyote rode far to the south and doubled back up the river. By the time they reached the Colorado, the wind was out of the southwest, and they rode slowly north, listening.

"*Perra,*" said Malo Coyote.

They reined up, listening, and the dog barked again. They dismounted, picketing their horses in a thicket, continuing on foot. The brush along the river was thick and they could see nothing. Suddenly, only yards away, a cow bawled. Malo Coyote looked at Naked Horse, and the latter shook his head, pointing back the way they had come. Silently the pair retreated to their horses,

* South

mounted and rode downriver. Reaching a secluded area where there was graze for the horses and cover for themselves, they waited for darkness. Little was said, Naked Horse speaking only once.

"Vaca, caballo, Comanch'," he said, holding up three fingers.

Malo Coyote nodded. If that proved to be the case— first the cows, then the horses, and finally the Comanche camp—Malo Coyote and Naked Horse could ask for no more. They need only stampede the longhorns and the horses, sending them thundering through the Comanche camp. To set their plan in motion, they needed only darkness, and they settled down to wait.

Llano and Stoney were riding second watch. Come the dawn, Stoney faced a tough decision, and it was that of which Llano spoke.

"Sorry, pard, but I don't believe that pair of Injuns is comin' back. They could of rode all the way back to Long John's spread by sundown. What in tarnation could they be doin' that'd take this long?"

"I don't know," Stoney said, "and I don't know which is worse—losing two riders or costing Long John four hundred cows."

"The cows ain't your fault, and unless we just gave 'em up as lost, somebody had to trail 'em. Who else in this outfit could you have trusted more than the Injuns? Except me, of course."

"I'd counted on Naked Horse and Malo Coyote dis-liking the Comanches enough to help us get our cows back," said Stoney. "What I failed to consider, and what worries me, is—"

"The possibility," Llano cut in, "that these crazy In-juns may try some fool stunt of their own, and get them-selves killed."

"That," said Stoney, "and the fact that we'll still be short two riders and four hundred cows."

* * *

Once darkness had come, Malo Coyote and Naked Horse made their way afoot to within a few hundred yards of where they'd discovered the longhorns. What wind there was came out of the southwest. With the Comanches camped on the east bank of the Colorado, Malo Coyote and Naked Horse moved eastward, circling wide. They knew not to get too close to the horses or longhorns, for some of the Comanches would be on watch. Being downwind, they eventually heard the horses cropping grass, telling them what they had only suspected was true. The horses and longhorns were south of the Comanche camp. There was time before moonrise for Malo Coyote and Naked Horse to work their way closer to the Comanche camp, and they did so.

A fire pit had been dug beneath a huge oak, and the supper fire was only a pink glow in the night. Blanketed Comanches sat around the fire speaking in guttural undertones. Malo Coyote and Naked Horse had seen enough. They slipped away to wait for the moon to rise and set, and for the Comanche camp to settle down. Neither had eaten since breakfast, and returning to their picketed horses, they ate jerked beef and drank river water.

They waited until an hour before first light, when the stars seemed to dim and the darkness grew more intense. Malo Coyote and Naked Horse led their horses to within a few hundred yards of the longhorns, and continued on foot. There they separated, each man drawing his Bowie knife. Malo Coyote crept along the river, while Naked Horse moved silently eastward until he was well beyond the bedded longhorns. From there he crawled as near the herd as he could, and crept along its outer flank.

Malo Coyote caught the first sentry in a stranglehold, driving the big Bowie deep into the Comanche's belly. On the farthest side of the longhorn herd, Naked Horse had performed a similar feat. There were two more Comanches on watch, one on either side of the horse herd. Malo Coyote disposed of the one on his side, while Naked Horse took the other. From there the Cherokee duo could see the Comanche camp. Silently they returned the way they had come, meeting where they had left their horses. Timing was critical. Malo Coyote and Naked Horse must make their move while it was dark enough to safely run the horses and longhorns through the Comanche camp, but they couldn't sustain a stampede in the dark. Success depended on leaving the Comanches afoot, and that could be accomplished only by stampeding the horses from the camp on a dead run, and keeping them running. In the first light of dawn, it was possible that the longhorns, as well as the horses, could be pushed near enough for Long John's outfit to recover them. But only if the Comanches were left afoot.

Leading their horses, Malo Coyote and Naked Horse crept as near the longhorns as they dared. Mounted, they kicked their horses into a gallop, squalling like cougars. Within seconds the longhorns were up and running, led by half a dozen of the ill-tempered Corriente bulls. They charged headlong into the horses, already spooked, and a mix of horses and longhorns thundered through the Comanche camp. Comanches who tried to catch their horses on the run were gored or trampled. Malo Coyote and Naked Horse drew their Colts, cutting down Comanches who tried to grapple with them. Then they were through the Comanche camp, and in the gray of the dawn, Malo Coyote and Naked Horse again cut loose their cougar screeches. But after a few miles the horses and longhorns began to tire. Naked Horse drew his Colt and fired three times.

The outfit had finished breakfast, and Stoney was about to announce his decision. They would have to forget the lost cows and move on. Then, sounding faint and far away, there were three shots.

"Come on, Llano," said Stoney. "The rest of you stay with the herd." They mounted, heading downriver at a fast gallop.

"Could be Malo Coyote and Naked Horse," said Llano. "Hope they ain't got a hundred Comanches on their tails."

Stoney had considered that possibility, and wished he had more than just his and Llano's guns. But they'd have to do, for if the odds were overwhelming, the entire outfit wouldn't be enough.

"Hey, that's one of our Mex bulls!" Llano shouted.

And it was. The animal trotted ahead of a pair of horses, and the trio was followed by a mix of other horses and longhorns. Llano and Stoney reined up and waited until the tag end of the herd reached them. Following it, their grins triumphant, rode Naked Horse and Malo Coyote.

"Comanch'?" Stoney asked, pointing downriver.

"*Ninguno,*" said Malo Coyote. "*Tomar Comanch' caballos.*"

"Well, by God," Llano said, "they grabbed the herd as well as the Comanche horses. That's a good one!"

"Maybe," said Stoney. "It depends on how far downriver those Comanches are, and how many there are." He raised one hand, all his fingers extended. "Comanch'?" he asked.

Naked Horse raised both hands, all his fingers extended. He brought his hands down and raised them again, extending all the fingers on his left hand and three on his right.

"Eighteen of 'em," Llano said, "all afoot and mad as hell."

"*Ninguno,*" said Naked Horse. He raised both hands, all his fingers spread. He then lowered his left hand, showing two fingers on his right.

"Twelve, then," Llano said.

"Still too many," Stoney said. "Let's gather these cows and move 'em upriver with the rest of the herd."

"Caballos," said Malo Coyote, pointing to himself and then to Naked Horse. *"Comanch' caballos."*

"They're claimin' the Comanche horses," said Llano. "That ain't gonna set well with the rest of the outfit."

"You're right," Stoney said, "but there's more at stake here than what the outfit thinks. Leave these cayuses here, and they'll likely wander back to that Comanche camp. Now if six of their bunch has been shot dead, and others maybe trampled or gored, what do you reckon they'll do if suddenly they have horses again?"

"They'll come lookin' for scalps," said Llano. "Ours."

"That's how I see it," Stoney said, and he turned to the Indian duo. *"Caballos,"* he said, *"vaca."*

The pair nodded and then set off in pursuit of the mixed herd.

"I oughta be glad they brought back the cows and got away with their hair," said Llano, "but I can't help wonderin'. Did they bring back the cows for Long John's sake, or was it easier just to stampede the whole damn bunch and pick out the horses later?"

"Do me a favor," Stoney said, "and don't raise that question before the rest of the outfit. Until we learn otherwise, Malo Coyote and Naked Horse are just a pair of *bueno* hombres who found and returned their outfit's stolen cattle. As far as we're concerned, the horses were taken to keep that bunch of Comanches from comin' after us with killing on their minds."

It was an explanation that suited everybody except Bandy Darden.

"We ain't that far from Dallas," Darden grumbled, "and them broncs would bring twenty dollars apiece. That's low-down, Winters, favorin' a scroungy pair of

Injuns. I'm a white man, and by God, I'm demandin' as good as they're gettin'."

"Darden," said Stoney, "I don't favor one man over another. When you've raided a hostile Comanche camp, you're entitled to every horse you can catch."

5

June 3, 1858, 150 miles south of Dallas.

*T*his will be our first day of havin' to scout ahead for water," Stoney said, "and with the Comanches bein' a threat, I'm making some changes in our formation. Malo Coyote and Naked Horse will lead out, keeping the horse remuda well ahead of the herd. Sky Pilot will follow the horses, and the herd will follow the wagon. Now that we're leaving the Colorado, I expect to spend more time scoutin' ahead for water than ridin' point. I'm leavin' Llano and Long John at the near flank, so either of them can take over at point, should it become necessary."

Once the herd was on the trail, Stoney rode out on his first quest for water. He met the trail drive an hour past midday.

"Twelve miles to water, I figure," Stoney said. "It's just a seep, really, but it builds up to a decent runoff."

"It'll be the most miles we've made in a day," said Llano, "if we can do it."

"We'll have to," Stoney said, "because there'll be days when we'll have to travel even farther. If we can't make twelve miles today, how can we make fifteen?"

"We won't," said Bandy Darden. "On a trail drive, ten miles is as good as it gits. Some days, not even that."

"Usin' that as a standard," Stoney said, "we'll never see anything but dry camps. I aim to find water each day, and regardless of how far it is, somehow we'll get the herd there."

Their first day after leaving the Colorado was more difficult than they'd expected. The cattle, especially the cows, began to lag. The drag riders were kept busy keeping them bunched and moving. At sundown they were still more than three miles from the stream Stoney had found. They ate supper in the dark, half the outfit eating while the others nighthawked.

June 4, 1858, 138 miles south of Dallas.

Stoney rode out at dawn, again seeking water. There had been considerable rain during April and May, and there should be water, even in streams a summer sun would later suck dry. But the never-ending search for water was just one of the responsibilities of a trail boss. He must be forever on the alert for hostile Indians. His only warning might be the sudden flight of a bird or a slight movement of grass or bush. Stoney rode with caution. Suspecting the Comanches who'd grabbed part of their herd were just part of a larger band, he wondered where the rest of them were.

Back with the herd, from his flank position, Long John squinted through the dust raised by the horse remuda and Sky Pilot's wagon and teams. The herd seemed to be gaining on the wagon, and Long John soon understood the reason. The wagon wasn't moving, and Sky Pilot stood behind it, waving his hat. Long John kicked his horse into a gallop. Without a point rider, somebody must get ahead of the herd. On the opposite flank Llano had made the same decision, and the two riders came together a few yards shy of the wagon.

"Busted wheel," Sky Pilot yelled.

It would take some time to remove the broken wheel and replace it with the spare. Long John and Llano wheeled their horses and rode back to head the longhorns. When they had the herd milling, and the rest of the riders had seen the stalled wagon, Long John turned to Llano.

"Catch up to Naked Horse an' Malo Coyote an' have 'em hold the remuda. If'n they be too far ahead fer safety, have 'em ease back this way a mite."

Long John then turned to the disabled wagon, to the broken rear wheel. The wide iron tire hung loose, the oak rim had split, and some of the spokes had snapped at the hub. From the toolbox Sky Pilot took an axe, and Long John reached for it.

"When Llano gits back," said Long John, "the two o ye wrassle that extry wheel outta there. Then start gatherin' some stones we can pile under the axle t'git that wheel off'n the ground. I'll go cut us a pole fer the liftin'."

Except for Suzanne, the rest of the riders had remained with the herd. When Llano returned, he and Sky Pilot removed the spare wheel from the wagon and then began gathering stones as large as they could handle. First they built a pyramid on the ground directly behind the shattered wheel. It would become a fulcrum for the pole that would lift the wagon. Once lifted, other stones would be placed beneath the axle, until the wheel could be removed and replaced. By the time Long John returned with a dozen feet of hefty cottonwood, Llano and Sky Pilot had gathered enough stones.

"Llano," Long John said, "ride back yonder an' git a couple o' them cow nurses to help us lift this wagon. Them cows ain't goin' nowhere till we git this new wheel on."

Llano returned with Deuce Gitano and Quando Miller.

"Now," said Long John, "Quando, Deuce, Llano, an' me is gonna raise that busted wheel off'n the ground. Sky Pilot, git under there an' stack them rocks agin that axle tight as ye can."

Long John had already taken a wrench to the hub, and once the wheel was off the ground, Quando and Llano removed the broken wheel.

"I got the grease," Sky Pilot said, digging a handful from the tin.

Once the new wheel was in place and Long John had tightened the hub nut, they again used the pole to lift the wagon while Sky Pilot removed the stones from beneath the axle.

"Wal," said Long John, looking at the sun, "that wasn't too costly. We lost maybe an hour. Llano, ride ahead an' tell Malo Coyote an' Naked Horse to git the remuda movin'. Might be a long ways to the next water, an' we got some time to make up."

Stoney rode what he estimated to be fifteen miles before finding a spring with a decent runoff. To his dismay, he also found the hoofprints of more than twenty unshod horses. Indians! The tracks came in from the west, and after stopping at the spring, continued eastward. The trail was two days old, and there was one chance in three the Indians had some destination in mind and had kept riding. The other two possibilities came into play if the band was aware of the approaching trail drive. Comanches were fond of leaving an obvious and misleading trail. Then, when they were miles away, they rode well ahead, paralleling their quarry, and laid an ambush. Or they doubled back and came up the back trail in a surprise attack. But Stoney had no time to trail them, to investigate either of these possibilities. After resting and watering his horse, he rode back the way he'd come.

This day's drive would be the longest yet, and the sooner he returned, the better their chances. Long John's herd was mixed, and it would be hell on the riders as they forced the brutes to a faster pace than they were accustomed. When Stoney finally met the horse remuda, he nodded to Malo Coyote and Naked Horse and rode on. He passed the wagon without even a nod from Sky Pilot, and rode back to Long John's flank position.

"It's a good ten more miles to water," Stoney said. "We'll have to double this pace, or there's no way we'll get there before dark."

"The wagon busted a wheel an' we lost some time," Long John said. "Ye best tell ever'body else, an' git 'em started whoppin' some behinds."

Stoney rode to the tag end of the herd and back along the opposite flank to his point position. The leaders had already begun bawling their protests, as they were forced to trot. Anything less and they were prodded by the horns of their companions as they pushed from behind. Stoney looked at the sun. They had maybe five more hours of daylight. The shirts of the riders were dark with sweat, as were the hides of the horses and longhorns. Before they reached water, all the animals would be consumed with thirst, and under such conditions there was a danger that some of the horses might be gored as they tried to get to the water. Stoney had an alternative, but remembering the many tracks of Indian horses near the spring, Long John had a right to know the risk involved. The Cajun listened as Stoney told him of the two-day-old trail.

"I'm telling you this," said Stoney, "because if that bunch of Indians doubled back, what I aim to do could cost us our horse remuda."

"Ye can't let ever'thing rest on what Injuns is liable t'do," Long John said. "They's always risk on ever' trail. Use yer best judgement, an' I'll back ye."

"In that case," said Stoney, "I'm sending Malo Coyote and Naked Horse on ahead. They'll reach water well ahead of the herd. The horses can be watered and taken to graze. This bunch of longhorns is goin' to be almighty thirsty and hard to handle, and when they smell water, I doubt we can hold them. I'd feel better if the horses were watered and out of the way. Cantankerous and unruly as the herd's goin' to be, we can't send any more riders with the horse remuda. So that means risking our horses for the time it takes the rest of us to get the herd to water."

"Hour er two, maybe," Long John said, "but yer right about these critters makin' a run fer the water. Git 'em all mixed up with the horses, an' likely we'd have half the remuda horn-raked an' gored. With the cows laggin' behind, they ain't no way we'll ever git this bunch to water 'fore dark. I reckon ye know that."

"I could," said Stoney, "if these were my cows."

For a while Long John said nothing. When he finally spoke, there was that lopsided grin Stoney had seen only a time or two.

"I took yer measure 'fore we took the trail. When I trust a man, by God, I'll stay with 'im till hell freezes, an' we'll skate on the ice t'gether."

"Thanks," Stoney said. "We'll drive as hard as we can until sundown, and with the horses watered and out of the way, we'll stampede the herd."

6

While Sky Pilot seldom spoke to the riders, he wasn't unpleasant. When Stoney trotted his horse alongside the wagon, the old cook said nothing, waiting for Stoney to say what was on his mind.

"I'm sending the horse remuda ahead," Stoney said, "so they can be watered and taken to graze. Come sundown, we're gonna stampede the herd. It's the only way we can get them to water before dark. Might be a good idea for you to go on with the horse remuda."

Sky Pilot shifted a wad of tobacco to his other jaw, spat a stream of juice to the ground, and urged his teams to a faster gait. Stoney rode on, catching up to the horse remuda. When he had spoken to Naked Horse and Malo Coyote, he rode back to join the herd, finding that Sky Pilot was closing the gap between the wagon and the horse remuda. This, Stoney reflected, might be a good daily procedure, if they could avoid Indians. It would depend on him, on his judgment, as he rode out to search for water. When he reached the herd, he found the flank riders having problems with bunch quitters. The herd—especially the temperamental bulls—didn't like the faster gait, and were objecting to it by breaking away.

"Cows is ornery, ongrateful bastards," Long John

said. "Their tongues can be draggin' from thirst, an' they're wantin' to go anywheres 'cept toward the water."

The day had been humid, with little wind, and that wasn't in their favor. Come sundown the herd would be tired, and the last thing they'd want to do was run. But a light breeze, with just a hint of water, could change their minds. With the wagon and horse remuda gone on ahead, Stoney had to continue riding point. Behind him the bawling of cows, the whapping of lariats against dusty behinds, and the shouts of the riders testified to the difficulty the outfit was having with the unruly herd. The sun was two hours high, and they had to diminish the distance as much as possible before they forced the herd to run. Far to the west a dirty smudge of gray streaked the horizon, and Stoney's hopes rose. Where there was rain, there should be some wind, and it was what they needed. They pushed on, the longhorns bawling their thirst and weariness, the riders and their horses sweat-soaked and exhausted. The sun was only minutes away from slipping behind the cloud bank far to the west, when the first cooling breeze touched their sweaty faces. Quickly the heads of the thirsty longhorns came up, and they seemed to pause, like gigantic hounds keening the wind. Then they lit out, a bawling, frenzied, longhorned avalanche. The riders had only to get out of the way.

"Let's ride!" Stoney shouted.

They couldn't nighthawk a herd scattered along a stream. They had to get the brutes together and out to graze before it was too dark to see. Along the way they found three animals that had to be shot, one with a broken leg, and two gored beyond recovery. Well beyond the stream, Naked Horse and Malo Coyote had moved the horses to graze, and Sky Pilot already had his supper fire going.

The longhorns were scattered the length of the stream, from the spring until the runoff played out. One stubborn longhorn bull stood in the stream, defying any effort to remove him. Llano and Quando Miller roped the brute and dragged him out. Slowly but surely they gathered the herd and drove them out to graze. Full darkness was only minutes away, and the cooling wind from the northwest had picked up.

"Long John, Suzanne, Llano, Deuce, and Quando, go ahead and eat," Stoney said. "Rest of us will watch the herd till you finish. Way that wind's risin', we could be in for a storm later tonight."

But there was no storm. There was faraway lightning and thunder, and a continuing wind, but nothing serious enough to trigger a stampede. The night passed without incident, and Stoney had the herd on the trail by first light. Before riding ahead to scout the trail, he spoke to Long John.

"I'll try to be back here by noon," Stoney said. "If it's another long drive to water, we need to know as early in the day as possible."

The faraway storm of the night before had done nothing to lessen the heat of the coming day. Before the sun was an hour high, horses and men were all sweat-soaked and plastered with trail dust. Stoney had riders changing their positions daily, so that nobody had to eat dust at drag more than a day at a time. Llano found himself riding drag with Deuce Gitano, Bandy Darden, and Suzanne. Llano had spoken to the girl only a time or two, and he was a bit surprised to find her riding alongside him.

"I like the mornings best," she said, "before the cows get tired and want to run away."

"Yeah," Llano said, "they do get a mite troublesome on up in the day."

Bandy Darden was far enough away that he couldn't hear their words, but Llano could see Darden giving them the eye. It would be just like the mean-spirited little rider to try and make something of it, so Llano did nothing to encourage Suzanne to further conversation. But Suzanne wanted to talk.

"I'm glad you're with us on this drive," she said. "You and Stoney. I wish . . . oh, how can I say it? I wish Long John wasn't so . . . so tolerant of his men. He says a man's got to have a little bit of rattlesnake in him —a little poison—or he's not man enough to survive on the frontier."

"He's mostly right, ma'am," Llano said. He was becoming uncomfortable, uncertain as to what she was leading up to.

"But can't you—shouldn't you—draw the line somewhere? These last three riders Long John hired, did you know he caught them stealing one of our cows?"

"No, ma'am," said Llano, "I didn't know. But these ain't good times. Maybe they was just grub-line riders who was hungry."

"That's the story they told Long John, but he admitted one of them had a cinch ring. Wouldn't you be suspicious of men who were about to alter the brand of a cow they claimed they were going to kill for food?"

"I reckon I would," Llano said, "but his only other choice would of been to kill the three of them. It takes a big man—a man with courage—to give a thief another chance."

For a while she said nothing, and when she finally spoke, there was bitterness in her voice.

"There's truth in what you say, but however big and courageous a man is, he still bleeds and dies when he's shot in the back."

"And you think Long John might be riskin' that?"

"Oh, I don't know *what* I feel," she said. "This drive . . . I haven't felt right about it from the first. Long John wanted me to stay with our friends, the Austins, at Bandera."

"Perhaps you should have," said Llano. "Why didn't you?"

"I thought—hoped—I might be of some help to him, to . . . to watch his back. But I can't always be that close to him. When there's a stampede, the cows running in the darkness, anything might happen. I feel so . . . helpless."

"Ma'am," Llano said, "me and Stoney ain't perfect, but we never shot a man in the back who was payin' us wages. I can promise you, we'll do all in our power to see that nobody else does, if that'll make you feel better."

"It will," she said, "and I hope you'll ride with care. Whatever else he is, this Bandy Darden's a killer."

"I expect you're right," said Llano. "He's been watching ever since you started talkin' to me. He's buildin' up to something."

"If he provokes you," she said venomously, "kill him. Long John won't fault you for it."

"I can take care of myself," Llano said, "and I ain't askin' anybody's approval for doin' what I have to."

Llano rode away, discouraging further conversation. While he understood her concern for Long John, and her words had given him much to think about, he hadn't liked the turn the conversation had taken. Had he gone too far, when he'd committed Stoney and himself to watching Long John's back? Thinking about it, he wondered if he and Stoney weren't in more danger than Long John. The Kid had a mad on for Stoney, and Llano believed it was only a matter of time until he was forced into a shoot-or-be-shot situation with Bandy Darden. He needed to talk to Stoney, and the sooner the better.

Again Stoney rode almost fifteen miles before finding a creek. He rode several miles beyond it, riding a circle back to where he'd started, looking for sign. Finding no tracks, nothing to arouse his suspicions, he rode back to meet the herd. Again they'd have to drive the herd, pushing them beyond their comfortable gait, or risk a dry camp. There was little wind, and not a cloud in the sky. When Stoney first sighted the horse remuda, the sun was noon high. Starting with the left flank, he rode all the way to the tag end of the drive and back up the right flank. Immediately the riders began pushing the herd, seeking to double the pace, racing with the evening sun.

The longhorns didn't like the faster gait the riders demanded, and showed their resentment by breaking ranks at every opportunity. Others—the smarter ones—didn't quit the herd and run. They just broke rank, stepping aside and forming slower moving columns left and right. Eventually the drag riders found themselves not with four columns of cows, but with a dozen or more. The glut increased as more of the animals broke and dropped back.

"Where'n hell is them flank riders?" Bandy Darden bawled.

Nobody answered him. There wasn't time. One old bull saw his chance and tore off down the back trail. Bandy Darden did exactly the wrong thing, catching the brute with a horn loop. To save Darden or his horse from being gored, Llano went for the hind legs, but his underhand throw missed. Leaving no doubt as to his intentions, the bull charged Darden. Deuce Gitano caught the beast with a second horn loop, saving Darden, and while the bull was unable to charge either rider, neither could they free themselves of him. Two of the flank riders—Dent Briano and Quando Miller—had dropped back and were doing their best to help Suzanne keep the herd together and moving. It was a foolish situation, Gitano and Darden roped to a bull that neither rider could turn loose. Somehow they had to throw the brute and tie his front and hind legs.

"Keep the ropes tight," Llano shouted. "I'll try and wrassle him down!"

Kicking free of the stirrups, Llano rode as near the bull as he dared, and leaning to the far side, caught the brute by his massive horns. Leaving the saddle, he threw all his weight to the bull's left side. Darden wisely stepped his horse closer, leaving some slack in the rope, while Gitano backstepped his horse. Llano already had the bull off balance, and with the help of Gitano's horse, the bull was thrown to the ground. Llano sat on the bull's head. Seconds counted. Darden had back-stepped his horse again, taking up slack in the rope. Darden came out of the saddle, piggin string in his teeth, and caught the bull's flailing front legs. Deuce Gitano had captured and tied the hind legs, and Llano got away from the lethal horns as quickly as he could. By then the herd had ceased moving altogether, and Long John rode up.

"Can one o' ye tell me what'n hell's goin' on back here?"

"Long John—" Suzanne began.

"Back off, woman," said Long John. "I'm talkin' to these hombres that's been roped to one damn bull whilst the rest of the herd scatters to hell an' gone."

"The bull broke away," Darden said angrily, "and I caught him with a horn loop. Dupree's throw missed the hind legs, and the bull was comin' after me and my horse. Gitano stopped him with another horn loop. Dupree, damn him—"

"I seen Dupree wrassle him down," said Long John. "Onct ye got in that damn fool mess, ye done what had to be did, gittin' out. Now I got jus' one thing t'say. When half the damn herd's tryin' to run, we purely ain't got the time to rope an' hog-tie them cows one at a time. Is they any one o' ye that can't git a handle on that?"

"You're layin' it all on me," Darden said, "because I roped the bull."

"I am," said Long John. "Ye got yerself in neck-deep, and the others had to let ever'thing else go an' haul ye out. Ye could of cost us half the herd whilst ye wrassled with one bull. All I ask o' ye is to head the varmints an' *drive* 'em back to the herd. Git in front o' the critters, double yer rope, an' swat hell out'n 'em."

"Tally my time," Darden said, "and I'll ride."

"I'll fergive a man a mistake," said Long John, "but not fer breakin' his word. Ye signed on fer this drive, an' by God, yer goin' to finish it. Now mount up. We're puttin' this herd back t'gether, an' it's stayin' t'gether."

Bandy Darden said no more. Llano mounted his horse, and for a fleeting moment Suzanne's eyes met his. The girl was afraid, and from the undisguised hate in Darden's face, Llano now believed she had cause.

"Move 'em out!" Stoney shouted.

They'd lost an hour or more, gathering the bunch quitters and changing the order of the drive. Stoney rode alongside Long John for some needed talk.

"I reckon I'll have to take some of the blame for the herd comin' apart," said Stoney. "Because the cows have shorter strides, I've tried makin' it a mite easier on them, by keeping 'em mostly toward the end of the herd. But no more. Some of them are gonna get horn-raked across their rumps, but it's the surest way of keeping the herd bunched."

"Like I tol' ye," said Long John, "use yer best judgment. Ye been right more'n ye been wrong, an' I'm satisfied with that."

Stoney rode on, saying no more, yet feeling uneasy. Long John now rode drag, having moved Bandy Darden to flank. Like it or not, the herd had more than doubled their previous gait, but it wasn't going to be enough. The sun dropped steadily toward its evening rendezvous with the western horizon, and an hour before sundown, Long John rode ahead for a talk with Stoney.

"What ye reckon?" Long John asked.

"We could try runnin' 'em again," said Stoney, "but they're tired, and we're still too far from water. I don't think we could keep 'em running that far. Without the smell of water somewhere ahead, they could just scatter all over hell and half of Texas. Our only other choice is dry camp, but while they're dry, they won't bed down or graze."

"Two trails we kin ride, one hard as the other."

"That's it," Stoney said, "and I'd choose a dry camp over an uncontrolled stampede. Unless they're close enough to water to smell it, there's nothin' to keep 'em from scattering in every direction. I'll ride on ahead and find some good graze. There'll be dewfall tonight, and that'll wet the grass."

"If'n they got sense enough to graze."

"We'll hit the trail at first light," said Stoney, "but it'll still cost us a day. After we reach water tomorrow, it'll depend on how far it is to the next water. By my thinking, it's better to lose a day tomorrow than spend two nights in dry camp."

"I ain't arguin' with that," Long John said. "Ride on, find the graze, an' I'll git word to the rest o' the riders."

Stoney overtook the wagon and caught up to the horse remuda. Malo Coyote and Naked Horse received word of the dry camp in silence. Stoney rode a mile farther, found the graze he sought, and waited for Malo Coyote and Naked Horse to arrive with the horse remuda. He then rode back and met the wagon, thankful for the water keg Long John had insisted on bringing. It held enough water for the outfit for two days.

"Dry camp," Stoney yelled as he passed the wagon. When he reached the herd, he found Long John riding point, prepared to help head the herd when they reached the graze Stoney had chosen. The herd again trailed at their own gait. They would easily reach camp by sundown, but there would be no water.

Reaching the graze, Stoney noted with approval that Naked Horse and Malo Coyote had taken the horse remuda well beyond the area where the longhorns would be bedded down. If the worst happened and the longhorns stampeded, they still might control the horse remuda. It became immediately obvious that the cattle had no intention of grazing or bedding down until they'd been watered. They stood there lowing mournfully, looking in vain for the water that was always there at the end of the day's drive.

"It'll take the lot o' us to keep that bunch from gettin' spooked," said Long John. "Don't nobody plan on sleepin' t'night."

"Won't make no difference," Dent Briano said. "With all that bellerin' goin' on, there'll be folks awake in Dallas."

"Dent," said Stoney, "take the Kid and Quando, and the three of you start circlin' that herd. Llano, you come with me. We'll watch the horses while Malo Coyote and Naked Horse ride in for supper."

It was Llano's first opportunity to discuss with Stoney that strange conversation with Suzanne and her fears for Long John.

"Maybe she's got reason to worry," said Stoney. "Especially after that set-to with Bandy Darden today. It's interesting that Long John caught them three hombres about to cinch-ring a cow. Briano and Miller seem straight enough, but if they are, why were they ridin' with that weasel, Bandy Darden?"

"I've been watchin' the three of 'em," Llano said, "and I don't see Briano and Miller talkin' to Darden. Maybe they ain't all that fond of the little varmint."

"Or maybe they want the rest of us to think that," said Stoney. "I reckon we ought to take Suzanne serious. When you get down to it, we don't know any of these hombres all that well."

"We know Naked Horse and Malo Coyote," Llano said, "and I still say they're just waitin' for the time they can grab the whole damn horse remuda and vamoose."

"I got the same feeling," said Stoney, "but Long John

don't see 'em in that light. Startin' tonight, I aim for every rider to have a fresh horse handy. Before the first bunch of nighthawks turn in at midnight, when they leave their horses with the remuda, I want every rider to take a fresh horse."

"So if them horse-crazy Injuns make off with the remuda, we won't be left afoot."

"That's part of it," Stoney said, "but from here to the crossing of the Red, we're likely to have the Comanches stalking us. From there on, we may be up against owlhoots and renegades."

Long John had been right. Nobody slept. There was a continual mournful lowing from the herd, and tired as they were, they refused to bed down or graze.

"I've never been so glad to see daylight in my life," said Suzanne, as the first rays of the rising sun lighted the eastern horizon.

"I reckon we'd better take these brutes on to water," Stoney said, "and then we'll have our breakfast."

"I'm for that," said Quando Miller. "I just hanker to rest a little while, without ever' blasted cow in the herd bawlin' at once."

Stoney again sent the horse remuda ahead, so that the horses could be watered and out of the way of the thirsty longhorns. In the early morning stillness there was no wind, and the herd was within a few hundred yards of the water before they were aware of it. Holding them was impossible, and the riders didn't try. Twenty-eight hours without water, they'd go no farther than the stream.

"I expect we'll be spending the night here," Stoney told them after breakfast. "By the time I find the next water, it'll be too late in the day for us to reach it. Since nobody slept last night, we'll make up for some of it today, a few of us at a time. Long John, Suzanne, Darden, and the Kid will sleep three hours. Then, while they watch the herd and the camp, the rest of you will catch three hours. I aim to ride ahead and find the next water, so we can be that much ahead on tomorrow's drive."

Stoney rode what he figured was ten miles before finding a sandy-bottomed creek. He was tempted to return to the herd and try to bring them to this water before sundown, but a look at the sun told him they'd never make it. When his horse had rested, he led the animal to water. He then dropped the reins, allowing the black to pick at the grass along the creek bank. Stoney bellied down to satisfy his own thirst. Coming up for air, he could see the reflection of his horse in the water, and suddenly the animal's head came up. It was the only warning Stoney had. He rolled to his left, drawing his Colt as he turned. An arrow thudded into the creek bank where he'd been seconds before. The Comanche had nocked a second arrow when Stoney, belly down, shot him. Colt still in his hand, Stoney leaped into the saddle and kicked his horse into a fast gallop. He rode north, away from the direction of the attack. He thought it unlikely that there'd be just one Comanche, and wondered where the others were. Could they have backtrailed him, and at this moment be attacking the camp? With half the outfit asleep, it was a sobering thought. He turned west for a mile, then south, and finally east. Eventually he cut his own trail as he'd ridden north, and to his relief, found no tracks following his back trail. As he rode he was all the more troubled by the presence of a single Indian. Even if the Comanche had been alone, he would have friends, and they'd come looking for him. Comanches could read sign like a printed page, and they could be on his trail in a matter of minutes. Stoney rode into camp and found Long John and Suzanne there. The Kid and Bandy Darden were with the herd. Quickly Stoney told Long John of the incident at the creek.

"Yer right," Long John said. "Ain't no doubt they's more of 'em. Looks like another sleepless night fer us."

"Only if we set on our hunkers and wait for 'em to come after us," said Stoney. "Couple of us can watch the horse remuda while Malo Coyote and Naked Horse do some scoutin' for us. We have to know where the rest of that bunch is and how many there are."

"Then we'll git 'em 'fore they git us," Long John said.

"If we don't," said Stoney, "they'll stalk us and strike when we're least expecting it. Once you know you've got to fight, attack."

"Ye got it," Long John said approvingly. "Git that pair of Injuns on the trail."

Stoney spoke in Spanish and by sign to Malo Coyote and Naked Horse. At first they seemed indifferent, but their eyes lighted at the mention of the hated Comanches. They rode out astride two of the Comanche horses they had captured.

"Since we have to take the trail drive through there," Llano said, "I hope that weird pair don't just run off the horses, leavin' them Comanches afoot and ready to take our scalps."

"I don't much think they will," said Stoney. "They're part of this drive too, and after taking their horses, I doubt they'd want to meet that bunch of Comanches on up the trail. I can't believe they'd swap their lives for a few Comanche broomtails."

"I reckon you're right," Llano said. "I'm doin' my best to believe in that pair, but it ain't easy."

7

Naked Horse and Malo Coyote rode north, dismounting and leaving their horses a mile south of the creek. They did not follow Stoney's trail, but crept through the brush to the east a good distance before again turning north toward the creek. They were considerably east of the place where Stoney had shot the Comanche, and it was there that they found a single moccasin print. The Indian duo continued along the creek bank until they reached the scene of the shooting. The body was gone, of course, and there was only a spot of dried blood on a fallen cottonwood leaf.

The trail Malo Coyote and Naked Horse expected to find led west along the creek bank. Eventually they found where three horses had been picketed. Horse droppings told them one horse had been there much longer than the others. From that they knew the Comanche Stoney had shot had been alone, and when his companions came looking for him, they had left their horses with his. Naked Horse and Malo Coyote returned to their own horses and took up the trail. The two Comanches had ridden side by side, one of them leading the third horse. The sun was an hour high, partially obscured by clouds, and there was a rising wind out of the southwest. Being downwind, Malo Coyote and Naked

Horse were aware of the Comanche camp long before reaching it. The first sound they heard was an eerie chanting. A death song was being sung for the Comanche Stoney Winters had shot. Malo Coyote and Naked Horse left their horses and continued on foot. Their first objective was to learn how many Comanches they faced. They waited until it was good and dark and the first stars were out before approaching the camp. There was the continual barking of a dog, until it ended with a yelp of pain. Somebody had grown tired of the noise. There was the smell of wood smoke, and it grew stronger. Finally there was the low murmur of voices.

The supper fire had burned down to a bed of coals, and there wasn't much light, but Naked Horse and Malo Coyote could see enough to guess there might be trouble ahead. They counted fifteen Comanche warriors, and there would be others watching the horses. Even in the poor light from the fire, some of the Comanches were daubing their ponies with war paint. Some tribes wouldn't attack at night, believing that if they died in battle, their spirits would wander forever in darkness. But it was a superstition the Comanches didn't share. While their favorite time to attack was just before dawn, they'd ride at midnight when circumstances demanded it. This was a band strong enough to wipe out Long John's outfit to the last man, to take every horse. It was threat enough to draw Malo Coyote and Naked Horse away, sending them hastily to recover their horses and ride to alert the outfit.

"About what I expected," Stoney said when Malo Coyote and Naked Horse had brought him the news. "All that'll save us is a surprise attack, and it may be too late for that, unless they're holdin' back to hit us at dawn."

"We'd need every gun in the outfit to go after that many Comanches," said Dent Briano. "Who's stayin' with the herd and the horse remuda?"

"Sky Pilot can't ride," said Stoney, "so he'll be here. Suzanne will be staying with him."

"Winters," Bandy Darden said, "that don't make sense. If that bunch of Comanches hit this camp 'fore we git to them, the woman and the old man will be dead dogies."

"Darden," said Stoney, "unless we hit them first, and hit hard, we'll all be dead as last year's cottonwood leaves. Malo Coyote and Naked Horse know where the Comanche camp is. We'll split our forces and try to ambush them in a cross fire. Now saddle up and let's ride."

Stoney turned to Naked Horse and Malo Coyote, for they had to understand what he planned to do. Suzanne sought out Long John, and he had a pretty good idea what was coming.

"I don't want to stay here," she said. "I can shoot, and I'm not afraid." She half expected his temper to flare up like a prairie fire, but he surprised her with an uncharacteristically mild response.

"Suzanne, I ain't doubtin' yer courage, an' I know ye can shoot. But ye got no Injun fightin' behind ye. Was ye out there, I'd be so afraid fer ye, I'd not be worth a damn to the outfit. This'll be a dirty, dangerous, killin' job, and it'll pleasure me if ye ain't part of it."

"I'll stay," she said, pleased at his concern. "Just please, please be careful."

They rode out, ten strong, Malo Coyote and Naked Horse taking the lead. There was no moon, and through ragged holes in the low-hanging clouds only an occasional star twinkled. The wind had risen, and there was still a promise of rain out of the southwest, perhaps before morning. Stoney eyed the ominous gray clouds with misgiving. So far there was no sign of lightning or rumble of thunder, but in Texas that could change within the hour. They were in a race with time. Could they finish this grisly task that lay ahead, and return to the herd before the storm struck? Reaching the creek, Malo

Coyote and Naked Horse reined up, the rest of the outfit gathering around them.

"This is where we divide the outfit," said Stoney softly. "Long John, you'll go with Malo Coyote. Take Deuce, Dent, and Quando with you. I'm goin' with Naked Horse, taking Llano, the Kid, and Bandy Darden. Once we're all in position, Naked Horse and Malo Coyote will open fire, and that'll be the time for the rest of us to join in. Make every shot count. They'll scatter with the first volley, and any that escape may come after us later."

They left the horses and proceeded on foot. Malo Coyote and his four men turned north. Once they were a few hundred yards north of the Comanche camp, they would circle west and then south, allowing them to approach the camp from the west. Naked Horse held them back for what Stoney believed was half an hour. When the Indian finally gave the sign, the four of them followed silently. Somewhere in the night a coyote howled, and a chorus of others responded. Dark masses of clouds rolled across the sky, and the wind seemed cold. Somewhere ahead a dog yipped once, and Naked Horse halted them with an upraised hand. Malo Coyote and his men would have the wind at their backs, and if the dog continued barking, it could mean the five men approaching from the west had been discovered. Stoney held his breath, but there was only silence, and Naked Horse led them on.

To the west of the Comanche camp, Malo Coyote had halted all movement when the dog barked, and then they resumed their stealthy approach. Now they were in position, within pistol range. The wind whipped through the ashes of the Comanche cook fire, spiraling a few sparks toward the murky sky. In the clearing ahead, Long John could see the dark blobs of blanket-wrapped sleeping men. Where were the horses, and why hadn't there been Comanches on watch? Then suddenly, to the south, a horse nickered, and the troublesome dog barked again. Some of the blanketed Comanches stirred, and Malo Coyote drew his Colt. The time had come.

On the east side of the camp, Stoney had his hand on the butt of his Colt when the horse nickered and the dog barked. Stoney's eyes were on Naked Horse, and he saw the Indian draw his Colt. Then they were all firing, as were their comrades to the west of the camp. It was a deadly cross fire of lead, and when the firing ceased, none of the blanketed forms moved. To the south there was a patter of hoofbeats. Two fast-running horses.

"That's where their lookouts were," Stoney said. "With the horses. Two of them got away."

"Yeah," said Llano, "but we got the rest. How much damage can two of 'em do?"

"It depends on how far away the next Comanche camp is," Stoney said. "If we're goin' to beat that storm, we'd better be gettin' back to our horses."

"Ninguno," said Naked Horse. He slipped cautiously into the clearing, and Malo Coyote came in from the opposite side. Drawing their Colts, they went from one blanketed form to the other, ripping away blankets. All too often, an enemy presumed dead had suddenly come to life with knife or gun in hand. Satisfied that the slaughter had been total, Malo Coyote and Naked Horse holstered their Colts and drew their Bowie knives.

"The rest of you come on," Stoney said, "and let's get back to the horses. Our part in this is finished, and you don't want to see the rest."

Stoney headed for the horses and the others followed, nobody speaking until they were well away from the blood-drenched Comanche camp.

"You left them cold-blooded bastards back there to take scalps," Bandy Darden said accusingly.

"Sorry I left you out, Darden," said Stoney. "You're welcome to go back and join them."

Nobody laughed at the macabre humor. They rode in silence, and by the time they reined up in camp, the promise of rain had become reality. There was no fire. Suzanne and Sky Pilot stood near the wagon.

"Everybody catch a fresh horse," Stoney said. "Llano and me will stay with the horse remuda until Malo Coyote and Naked Horse return. The rest of you begin circling the herd. While there's no thunder or lightning yet, we can't rule it out. Soon as it's light enough to see, I want this herd on the trail."

As the riders circled the herd, Suzanne wasted no time in getting to Long John with her questions.

"Tell me about it," she said.

"Not much to tell," Long John replied. "We split up, five o' us to a bunch. Caught them Comanches in a cross fire, them sleepin'. They didn't git off a shot. The two of 'em that was watchin' the horses skeedaddled, but I reckon we kilt the rest."

"What a terrible thing," she said. "So much killing."

"No more turrible than what they'd of done to us," Long John said.

"Llano and Stoney are with the horse remuda. What happened to our horse wranglers, Malo Coyote and Naked Horse?"

"They had some finishin' up to do at the Comanche camp," said Long John.

"What kind of—" And then it hit her. "You left those . . . savages there to mutilate the dead?"

"Woman," Long John said, his patience wearing thin, "them savages saved our hair by scoutin' that camp an' leadin' that attack. Fer as I'm concerned, they're welcome to whatever pieces o' them Comanches they want."

That ended the conversation, and there was only the

patter of rain and the splash of horses's hoofs as the riders circled the drowsing herd.

June 6, 1858, 123 miles south of Dallas.

The day dawned dark and dismal, with low-hanging gray clouds, and the rain continued.

"We ain't gotta worry about reachin' water tonight," said Quando Miller. "The water's comin' to us."

Nobody appreciated his humor. Sky Pilot carried dry firewood in a cowhide slung under the wagon, so at least they would have breakfast and hot coffee. Thinking ahead, Sky Pilot had used a big square of canvas to create a shelter behind the wagon, room enough for a fire and for cooking. One side of the canvas had been rawhided to the top of the last wagon bow, while the other two corners were attached to cottonwood poles driven into the soggy ground. Sometime during the night, Malo Coyote and Naked Horse had returned. Each had an ugly, hairy bundle thonged about his middle, and Suzanne crept away from the wagon when the Indian duo came for their breakfast. Sky Pilot eyed the pair distastefully, and Long John laughed.

"Move 'em out," Stoney shouted. Malo Coyote and Naked Horse led out with the horse remuda, followed by Sky Pilot's wagon. The herd fell in behind, slogging through the mud, and the drive again took the long trail north.

June 7, 1858, 113 miles south of Dallas.

Despite the rain, it was the easiest day they'd had. There was no heat, no dust, no bunch quitters. The rain ceased before sundown, and the sun set in a glorious burst of red. Reaching the creek where Stoney had shot the Comanche, they bedded down the herd. A curtain of darkness transformed the clear blue of the sky to deep purple, and stars winked on like distant fire flies.

"The usual watch tonight," said Stoney, "but no dozin' in the saddle. We lost a pair of Comanches in that ambush, and they could still be around, with ideas of getting even."

But the night was quiet. Not a cow bawled, and even the coyotes were silent. At dawn, once the herd was on the trail, Stoney rode north. After the Indian trouble they'd had, he was especially watchful. With a day and a night of rain, even an Indian couldn't avoid leaving some sign. On the other hand, the rain had wiped out all previous sign, and any Comanches ahead of them might come as an unpleasant surprise. It was still too early for the sun to have swallowed up the effects of the rain, and there was plenty of water in the wet weather seeps and arroyos.

Watered, grazed, and rested, the herd was trailing well. There was no dust, and a cooling westwind brought blessed relief from the heat. For the first time since Suzanne had confided in Llano, he was again riding drag with her. The Kid and Bandy Darden were also at drag, and for that reason Llano hoped Suzanne would keep her thoughts and problems to herself. Sooner or later the Kid or Darden would try to make something of his conversations with the girl. They'd been watching him, and they'd been watching Suzanne, and she was well aware of it. Llano wasn't in the least surprised to find her riding alongside him.

"You purely believe in stokin' the fire, don't you?" he said.

"I don't trust them," she said, "and I wish we were rid of them. I can't stand them always looking at me that way."

"Is that why you're wrangling things around so me or Long John will have to shoot one or both of 'em?"

"I don't know what—"

"Oh yes you do," Llano said angrily. "That's why you're talking to me now. I give you the benefit of the doubt the first time, believin' you was afraid for Long John. The Kid and Darden are a pair of troublemakers, and you know that. How long will it be until they start askin' nasty questions? Such as why are you and me spendin' so much time together?"

"Why that . . . that's foolish," she said. "I spend my nights with Long John, just as I've done for eight years. I've only talked to you while we are riding drag, where anybody can see."

"Long John didn't see," said Llano. "Did you tell him you'd talked to me, and why?"

"Of course I didn't," she snapped. "There are times when Long John's pride gets in the way of his common sense. He'd resent me asking for anybody's help, believing that I think he's not man enough to take care of himself."

"Any man with sand in his craw would rather be shot dead than have his woman think he's a yellow coyote," said Llano. "So I couldn't fault Long John for feelin' that way, with you comin' to me behind his back."

"So you fault *me,*" she said bitterly, "for asking for help without him knowing, because I'm fearful he'll be shot in the back."

"No," said Llano, "I don't fault you for that. That's natural. I just don't believe you can protect Long John by gunning down every hombre who looks like trouble. It ain't the western way. When a man pulls a gun on Long John, then the code says Long John can protect himself. It don't say you can shoot every suspicious-lookin' varmint before he shoots you."

"Then you don't intend to help. . . ."

"I don't aim to be prodded into a gunfight over what these hombres *might* do. Damn it, I told you Stoney and me would stand by Long John if there's trouble. We ride for the brand. Now don't be askin' more than that."

With that, Llano rode away from her. She was beginning to irritate him. Long John was fully capable of taking care of himself, and he'd purely raise hell if he knew Suzanne was begging for help to keep him alive. Having been with Long John eight years, she hadn't made much progress toward becoming a western woman.

Stoney rode a dozen miles before finding water. It was a shallow and probably wet weather stream that would eventually dry up, but for now it suited their needs. Stoney rode a mile north, and then to the west, making a half-moon swing back to the point from which he'd started. He then rode eastward and turned south, circling back to the west. Having found no sign, he was reasonably confident there had been no Indian movement since the rain. There was always the possibility the Comanches might move into the area before the trail drive reached the stream, but that was a risk they'd have to take. Riding at a fast gallop, Stoney turned south to meet the oncoming herd.

Long John came up with an idea so strong, he was disgusted with himself for not having thought of it sooner. Why wait until Stoney returned, to begin pushing the herd? Then if it was a long drive to the next water, the time it took Stoney to find the water and ride back wouldn't be lost. First, Long John rode ahead, telling the Indian wranglers of the change. He then rode back and passed the word to the rest of the outfit.

"Damn it," Bandy Darden growled, "the mornin' hours wasn't so bad. Now we'll be chasin' them bunch quitters from sunup to sundown."

"I thought," said Long John, controlling his temper, "that's what riders was s'posed to do on a trail drive."

Long John rode on, getting no complaints from the rest of the outfit.

"It's a good plan," Llano said. "When we wait for Stoney to tell us how far it is to water, we end up having to run the herd during the hottest part of the day. Why not just take it for granted we're in for a long drive, and start pushing early? For sure, it'll be harder on us, but not as hard as dry camp."

"That's how I see it," said Long John, pleased. "If'n we kin make two er three extry hours before Stoney rides in, we're that much ahead."

Bandy Darden's prediction proved true, however. Despite the fact it was still early and the sun hadn't yet unleashed its fury, the herd resented being pushed. The brutes showed their displeasure in the usual manner, breaking away at every opportunity. The front ranks consisted mostly of cows, and they were forced to move ahead, for behind them were mean-tempered bulls with sharp horns. The drag riders were keeping the herd bunched, so there was little opportunity for bunch quitting except from right or left flank. Bandy Darden was one of four flank riders, and since his was a forward position, most of his charges were the unruly cows. Time after time they broke away, and before Darden could head one, there would be another. Seeing the problem, Llano Dupree rode forward and began heading troublesome cows. A new pair broke away, and Llano galloped after them, Darden right behind him. Llano got ahead of the ornery cows, swinging his doubled lariat. Knowing what was coming, the cows turned and bolted back toward the herd. Bandy Darden, still behind Llano, had doubled his lariat and deliberately lashed the rump of Llano's horse. The startled animal nickered and began to buck, and Llano was pitched off.

Darden rode on as though nothing unusual had happened, swinging his lariat, driving the pair of wayward cows back into the herd. Furious, Llano got to his feet, swatted his dusty hat against his thigh, and went after his horse. By the time he caught it, the tag end of the herd was near enough for the drag riders to see him. The Kid,

Quando Miller, and Dent Briano kept their positions at drag. Only Suzanne rode forward.

"What happened?" she asked.

"Somethin' spooked my horse and he piled me," Llano said as calmly as he could.

She looked skeptical, but he said no more, so she rode back to join the rest of the drag riders. Llano mounted and rode on, catching up to his flank position. Darden looked back, a smug grin on his face, and Llano ignored him. This wasn't the time or the place, but the time and place would come, and Llano Dupree wouldn't forget.

Stoney met the drive much sooner than he had expected, nodding approvingly when Long John explained the strategy.

"Good move," Stoney said. "Right now we're maybe eight miles from water, and if nothin' goes wrong, we'll get there before sundown."

"Beddin' 'em down early won't hurt none," said Long John. "Fact is, I'll feel a mite better if'n we git supper done an' the fire out before dark."

"I'm going to send the wagon and the horse remuda on ahead," Stoney said. "Long as the wind's out of the southwest, we can control the herd. But let it shift, comin' from the north, and they'll run toward the water. I'll feel a bit easier if the horses are watered and out of the way."

But the wind didn't change, and when the herd reached the stream, Malo Coyote and Naked Horse had watered the horses and taken them to graze. Sky Pilot already had supper well under way. Sunset was a spectacular splash of red in the western sky as it was transformed from blue to deep purple to coax out the first timid stars. Long John, Suzanne, Deuce Gitano, and the Kid took the first watch. Llano, Stoney, Bandy Darden, Dent Briano, and Quando Miller would begin the second watch at midnight. Nothing broke the silence except the chirping of crickets and the occasional distant wail of a coyote. Suddenly the stillness was shattered by the most unharmonious caterwauling imaginable.

"Brangin' in the sheep, brangin' in the sheep . . ."

"God Almighty," said Dent Briano, "what'n hell is *that?*"

"Rest of you stay with the herd," Stoney said. "Llano and me are gonna find out."

The unholy discord was coming from Sky Pilot's wagon, and by the time Llano and Stoney reached it, Long John was already there. Sky Pilot stood on the wagon seat, his arms lifted heavenward. His terrible singing had died away to a melancholy growl, and he began to shout.

"Repent, you bastards, repent!"

"Quiet, ye damn old fool," Long John hissed. "Ye'll have ever' Comanche in East Texas after us."

But Sky Pilot launched into another song as horrendous and unharmonious as the first, and Long John clambered up to the wagon box. Seizing the front of Sky Pilot's shirt with his left hand, Long John fisted his right and slugged the old man just hard enough to silence him. His hands under Sky Pilot's arms, Long John lowered him to the ground on his feet.

"Stoney," said Long John, "ye an' Llano take this old fool to the creek an' sober him up. Drown him if ye want. I don't much give a damn."

Llano caught Sky Pilot under the arms, Stoney took his feet, and they started for the creek.

"His breath's powerful enough to stun a grizzly," Llano said. "Light a match under his nose, and he'd breathe pure fire."

"When this old jaybird sobers up," said Stoney, "it's Long John that'll be breathin' fire."

Reaching the shallow stream, they threw Sky Pilot in, boots and all. The water was cold, and he came up coughing and wheezing.

"You sneakin' bastards," he shouted, "I'll—"

"You'll get out of there and shut up," Stoney said. "Then you're goin' back and listen to whatever Long John has to say."

On hands and knees Sky Pilot crawled out of the creek. With supreme effort he got to his feet and stood there tottering like a tall tree about to fall before a strong wind. Finally, with Stoney on one side of him and Llano on the other, the trio made their way back to the wagon. The moon had risen and they could see Long John rummaging through the toolbox mounted on the side of the wagon. He came out with the axe, and his intention was plain. On the ground was the two-gallon keg that contained the whiskey.

"No," squawked Sky Pilot, "no!"

Long John responded by raising the axe and splitting the keg, spilling the whiskey that remained. Without a word he replaced the axe in the toolbox and closed the lid. The wind had turned cool, and, soaking wet, Sky Pilot's teeth had begun to chatter. But Long John wasn't finished with him.

"Ye old buzzard," Long John said, "ye promised to leave that stuff alone. If'n breakfast ain't done on time, ye better be dead, er by the Eternal, I'll make ye wish ye was! Stoney, you an' Llano pile him in the wagon."

Llano and Stoney hoisted Sky Pilot over the tailgate. At least the canvas would protect him from the wind until he got into dry clothes, but the worst was yet to come. With the dawn would come a towering hangover, and there wouldn't be a drop of whiskey to soothe it.

"The rest of the outfit ain't gonna like this," said Long John, "him havin' all that whiskey and them havin' none. I ought to of knowed better than to bring that stuff along, but it's handy fer wounds an' snakebite."

"Since we're on the second watch," Stoney said, "Llano and me can rustle him out in time to get breakfast. Left on his own, he'd sleep all day tomorrow."

"I'll do the wakin'," said Long John. "I might have to

chew his tail feathers down to a nub. Ye can help me most by playin' this down, so's the other riders don't try to make somethin' big out of it."

"I can think of only one who might," Stoney said, "but don't let it bother you. If he gets on the prod, I'll explain it to him in a way even he can understand."

When Llano and Stoney returned to the herd, nobody said anything, but Stoney knew curiosity was killing them, so he gave it to them straight.

"Sky Pilot got into the whiskey Long John brought along for wounds and snakebite," Stoney said, "but it won't happen again. Long John smashed the keg, and there's no more whiskey."

"Real smart," said Bandy Darden. "Now what's to be done if one of us gits shot or snakebit?"

"If you get shot," Stoney said, "I reckon you'll just have to take your chances. If a rattler bites you, Darden, it'll be the snake that'll die."

8

Breakfast was on time, but Sky Pilot was mean enough and sick enough to have gut-shot anybody who spoke to him, so nobody did. By first light the drive was under way and Stoney had ridden in search of water. Not knowing how long the day's drive might be, Long John had the riders pushing the herd by the time they took the trail. The longhorns had become trailwise to the extent that it was possible to keep them in a long column of fours. As the herd became more strung out, it was more than four flank riders could handle. Long John saw the need for some changes.

"You and me is gonna handle the drag, Suzanne. I'm sendin' Llano to right flank with Quando Miller an' the Kid. Deuce Gitano will ride left flank with Bandy Darden an' Dent Briano."

There was immediate improvement as the added flank riders took up the slack. With Long John and Suzanne riding close on the heels of the drag cows, a potential bunch quitter was limited to right or left flank breakaways. Long John seemed pleased with the progress they were making, and Suzanne made up her mind this was the time to ask him a ticklish question.

"Long John, since we have to stop at Dallas for a new

wagon wheel, can't we stay over one night and spend some time in town?"

"Gittin' homesick fer the city, are ye?"

"No," she said hastily.

Long John put up with a lot from her, but one thing he absolutely refused to tolerate was untruth. From Suzanne or anybody else. He looked at her now, his hat tilted low over his pale blue eyes, and said nothing.

"All right," said Suzanne, irritated, "I *would* like to see somebody other than an occasional Indian and a few down-at-the-heels cowboys with nothing to say. Am I wrong to feel that way?"

Long John continued looking at her for a moment in that noncommittal manner of his that she still hadn't gotten used to. He could go either way, flaring up like a prairie fire in a high wind or with a disarmingly mild response. It surprised her when he chose the latter course, speaking without anger.

"Ye been to San Antone twice."

"Twice in eight years," she said. "I'm not asking you to go out of your way, and I don't expect you to spend any money on me. I'd just . . . like to look in the stores and . . . see what women's clothes are like. I've worn Levi's pants and shirts for so long, I . . . I'd just like to see what women—other women—are wearing. . . ."

Her voice trailed off on a wistful note that wasn't lost on Long John. She wasn't quite twenty-five, and Long John was twice her age. He turned on that half smile that eased the hard lines of his face and melted the frost from his eyes.

"I reckon we kin kill a day in Dallas," he said, "and on the way back, maybe we'll stop fer a while. I reckon it's time ye had some finery of yer own. Yer right. A woman oughtn't to spend her whole life in britches an' shirts."

By Stoney's estimate he'd ridden almost twenty miles before finding a creek. It would be their longest drive, almost twice that of an average day. Long John's idea of hard traveling from sunup to sundown might well be their salvation. Even if they failed to reach water, they might be close enough to stampede the herd the rest of the way. It was a last resort. Some of the animals were becoming gaunt. They needed a week on good graze to bring a good price in Missouri. That was yet another problem he must discuss with Long John. With the tick fever problem, and the dogs of war already loose in Kansas and Missouri, should they linger to fatten the herd, or just take what they could get and ride for Texas? It was a decision Stoney couldn't make, and he doubted that even Long John could. Not until they were in the midst of the conflict could they chart their course.

When Stoney rode back and met the drive, he found they had made much more progress than he'd expected. The herd was trailing well, seeming to have resigned themselves to the faster gait.

"When we git this day behind us," Long John said, "it won't git no worse. Even in unfamiliar country, I can't see us drivin' more'n twenty miles without findin' *some* kind of water."

"That's why it's important that we put this day behind us," said Stoney. "Compared to this, twelve or fifteen miles will seem easy."

Stoney spoke to the rest of the riders, finding no opposition from any of them except the Kid and Bandy Darden.

"I ain't likin' the way you're bossin' this drive," said the Kid. "You're actin' like you own this bunch of cows. You're runnin' us all to death for forty and found."

"It's my job to find water for the herd," Stoney said, "and once I've found it, to get the herd there before dark. I think you have a grudge against me that's got nothing to do with what I do or don't do as trail boss. Now if that's what's eatin' you, before this drive is done, I'll see that you get a shot at whatever satisfaction you got in mind. Until then, be man enough to ride for the brand."

The Kid said nothing and Stoney rode on, receiving about the kind of response he had expected from Bandy Darden:

"I don't like you, Winters, and I especially don't like you as trail boss. You're always suckin' up to Coons, nuzzlin' him, while Dupree's makin' up to his woman."

"Darden," Stoney said, "before this drive is done, somebody's goin' to kill you. I won't be surprised if it becomes such a popular idea, we'll all be drawing lots for the privilege."

Stoney rode on, chills creeping up his spine as he turned his back on Bandy Darden. The man was a killer, waiting for something. What?

When Long John rode back to talk to Stoney, sundown was an hour away. "If'n we ain't gonna make it," said Long John, "it's time we got this herd started runnin'."

"I think we can still make it," Stoney said, "but I'm going to send Malo Coyote and Naked Horse on ahead with the horse remuda. Sky Pilot can go with them. Once the longhorns get a whiff of water, there'll be no stopping them."

Stoney rode ahead, and when he caught up to the wagon, shouted his message to Sky Pilot.

"Keep up to the horse remuda. I'm sendin' 'em on to water."

Sky Pilot said nothing, and Stoney rode on. Malo Coyote and Naked Horse had been expecting an order to take the horse remuda on to water. As Stoney rode back to the herd, he met Sky Pilot catching up to the remuda. The longhorns continued at a mile-eating gait, and Stoney kept his eye on the sun. The wind was light, out of the south, and wouldn't betray the water ahead. Stoney met Llano at the forward flank.

"This is one time we need the wind to change," Llano

said. "The herd's tired, and nothin' but the smell ot water will make 'em run."

It was true. Stoney rode on toward the drag. When longhorns were tired and thirsty, they became more or- nery than ever. Some of the bulls were tossing their heads, hooking at one another, and Stoney had to sepa- rate a pair of them that were disrupting the drive. Reaching the drag, Stoney found Long John and Su- zanne swinging their doubled lariats against the dusty rumps of the many stragglers. The longhorns ignored the punishment, bawling their misery and frustration all the louder.

"The wind purely ain't goin' to change," said Long John. "It'd take a prairie fire to git these varmints a-runnin'."

"Whatever it takes gettin' 'em to water won't be as bad as dry camp," Stoney said. "There's no bad drop- offs or arroyos from here on. We'll keep 'em moving and we'll get 'em there, even if it's in the dark."

But the longhorns had gone as far as they intended to without rest, water, and graze. Tired as they were, they kept breaking ranks, trying to mill. But just when it seemed the cause was lost, the leaders smelled the wa- ter. Or thought they did. They forgot how tired they were and lit out through brush and thicket, and that's all it took to send the rest of the herd thundering in pursuit. The crimson of the setting sun had faded to the gray ot night, and the first stars twinkled against a velvet sky.

"Let's ride," said Stoney, "and get those brutes out ot the creek and onto some graze."

By the time they reached the creek, Sky Pilot had supper ready. "Come and git it, you no account sheep herders, 'fore I throw it out."

"Shut up, ye old coot, an' keep it hot," Long John shouted. "We ain't doin' nothin' till we git these critters out to graze."

As expected, some of the longhorns were still in the creek and had to be dragged out.

"Four of us will stay with the herd while the rest of you eat," said Stoney. "I'll be the first."

"Them cows is on t'other side of the creek," Long John said, "an' we kin see 'em from here. They're so fagged out, they ain't goin' nowhere. Ever' body go ahead an' eat."

Nobody argued with that. Their shirts were still damp with sweat, and every rider was coated with dust from head to toe. They had inhaled so much of it, their food and coffee was gritty, but they were too tired to care. Long John, Suzanne, the Kid, and Deuce Gitano took the first watch. By moonrise the camp was quiet, as riders got what sleep they could before the second watch began at midnight. Suddenly Dent Briano sat up, throwing off blankets and reaching for his Colt.

"Damn it," Darden hissed from the darkness, "it's me."

"Good way to get yourself blowed into the middle of next week," said Dent Briano. "Where you goin'?"

"To the bushes," Darden said, "if it's any of your business."

"When I wake up to somebody rustlin' around in the dark," said Briano, "I make it my business."

The herd was quiet and the riders were not circling. Long John and Suzanne sat their saddles near the creek.

"Long John," Suzanne said, "I'd like to get in the creek long enough to wash off this dust."

"No use. Tomorrer night ye'll have it all over ye again."

"Then I'll wash it off again. I want to feel clean again, if only for tonight."

"Go on, then," said Long John. "The Kid and Deuce is on t'other side of the herd, an' ever'body else is sleepin'."

Suzanne quickly shed her boots and the dusty clothes.

She waded into the creek, and the water was so cold it all but took her breath away. The moon was yellow-gold, and in its light Long John watched Suzanne in silent admiration. Suddenly his horse stopped cropping grass and lifted its head. Long John was out of the saddle in an instant, his Colt cocked and in his hand. The slight sound that had startled his horse had come from the other side of the creek.

"Suzanne," Long John said in scarcely more than a whisper, "git out'n there an' git yer clothes on."

Suzanne did so as quickly as she could.

"Now," said Long John, "ride over there where the Kid and Deuce is, till I git back."

Pausing only long enough to assure himself that Suzanne had done as bidden, Long John headed for camp in a lope, his Colt still cocked and ready.

Llano and Stoney had spread their blankets a distance away from Briano, Miller, and Darden. Nonetheless, they'd heard Darden's exchange with Briano. They were also aware of Darden's hasty return, but thought nothing of it. Such nocturnal trips were necessary and certainly not uncommon.

Long John did not approach the camp, for the moon was bright and there was a clearing he'd have to cross. He paused in the shadow of some cottonwoods but could see no movement in camp. His horse might have been startled by some prowling animal, maybe a skunk. But Long John, though he had no proof, couldn't dismiss the possibility that the intruder had been one of the men from his own outfit. While he couldn't question the men based on suspicion, he was unwilling to let the incident pass. Everybody was accounted for except the five men who would go on watch at midnight. Of the five, Long John ruled out Llano Dupree and Stoney Winters. That left only the three newcomers. Long John eased down the hammer on his Colt and holstered it. Tomorrow he would talk to Stoney, and it would be a natural enough question. Long John had heard something—or somebody—in the night. Could it have been one of his own riders, one of the five men awaiting the second watch?

The second watch took over at midnight, and it was several hours before Dent Briano and Quando Miller found themselves alone with Bandy Darden. It was Quando Miller who had a question.

"Darden, I've seen men have to get up and run for the bushes, but you're the first I ever seen come runnin' back. What you been up to?"

"Who can say I was up to anything more'n a trip to the bushes?"

"We can't prove nothin'," said Dent Briano, "but you come tearin' back like your shirttail was afire, and rolled in your blankets with your boots on. You think Winters and Dupree didn't notice?"

"So what?" Darden said. "They can't prove nothin'."

"Maybe not," said Miller, "but you just proved somethin'. You was up to no good, and somebody was on your tail. Now if you done somethin' to get me and Briano in Dutch, then I ain't holdin' still for that. Talk, damn you."

"He's right," Briano said. "You done some low-down things since we throwed in with you, and I ain't seen any signs that says you've reformed."

"I swear," said Darden with a mocking laugh, "you two got all the sand of a pair of old maid Sunday school teachers. I heard talkin', so I snuck down to the creek. Coons was sittin' his saddle while that woman of his was in the creek, standin' there jaybird naked. Git her outta that shirt and them britches, and by God, she's all woman."

"Darden," said Miller, "you done some things that'd shame a yellow coyote, but this is about the worst."

"Sure as hell is," Briano agreed. "You oughta be strung up."

"I didn't hurt nobody," said Darden defensively. "I reckon I can count on one or both you *asnos* to spill your guts to Coons."

"I ain't volunteerin' nothin'," Miller said, "but if I'm asked straight out, I ain't lyin' for you."

"Me neither," said Briano. "I reckon me and Quando's done some things we ain't proud of, but we ain't slid down as low as you."

"Keep talkin' down to me like you're better'n I am," snarled Darden, "and when we come to the end of this trail, maybe I'll decide I don't need either of you."

"Thanks for the warnin'," Briano said. "We'll keep that in mind."

June 8, 1858. Ninety-three miles south of Dallas.

"Move 'em out!" Stoney shouted. The horse remuda had gone ahead, followed by Sky Pilot and the wagon. Once the herd was strung out and trailing well, Long John rode ahead. Before Stoney rode out on his daily search for water, Long John wanted to talk to him. The Cajun didn't beat around the bush.

"Last night," said Long John, "somethin' er somebody was prowlin' around acrost the creek from wher' the herd was bedded down. Was any of the hombres waitin' fer the second watch up an' about?"

"Maybe a couple of hours before we went on watch, Darden got up and said he was goin' to the bushes. He came back in more of a hurry than he left. Was there trouble?"

"No," said Long John, "nothin' ye need be concerned with. Ride on ahead, find us some water, an' I'll be pushin' the herd as hard as I kin."

When Stoney had ridden away, Long John rode back to Llano's position at right flank. Llano looked questioningly at him.

"Fall back t'drag an' ride with Suzanne," said the Cajun. "I'll take yer place at flank t'day."

With misgivings, Llano did as he was told. That left Long John not too far behind Bandy Darden. While Llano didn't know of Long John's questioning Stoney, he had his suspicions. He reckoned after a day of riding drag with Suzanne, he'd know plenty.

As Stoney rode north he pondered Long John's strange behavior. A trail herd was usually bedded down far enough from camp so that riders might get up as the need arose without disturbing the nighthawks or the herd. It wasn't wise for a cowboy to wander around at night where he wasn't supposed to be. According to Long John's calculations, they were a little more than forty miles south of the Brazos River. After the eventual success of the colony founded by Stephen Austin, some families who missed out on grants along the Colorado had settled on available land on the Brazos. While Stoney dared not relax his vigilance, he believed those settlers along the Brazos might lessen the possibility of Comanche attacks. If that were the case, the trail drive might enjoy a respite from Indian attacks as far as Dallas, almost a hundred miles.

To Llano's surprise, Suzanne apparently had nothing to say. She had left him between a rock and a hard place often enough, so Llano shocked her with a question of his own.

"Long John took my place at the flank and sent me back here. Why?"

"I . . . I don't know."

"I think you do," Llano said. "Was it something that happened last night?"

"Yes . . . No. I . . . I can't tell you."

It was still early and the herd was fresh, trailing well. Llano kept his eyes on her, but she turned away, refusing to look at him. When she did finally face him, her dark eyes sparkled with anger.

"Oh, all right," she snapped. "While we were on watch last night down by the creek, Long John heard something—or somebody—in the brush. He was going to talk to Stoney this morning."

"Now I reckon I know why Long John took my place at flank," said Llano. "Stoney must have told him Bandy Darden got up last night, sayin' he was going to the bushes."

Her face crimsoned and she turned away, but Llano continued.

"So Darden was skulkin' around near the creek, but so what? He might have been shot for a coyote or a Comanche, but the risk was all his. Now that ain't enough to put a burr under Long John's tail. So why is Long John on the prod?"

"Oh, damn you," she cried, "you have to know, don't you?"

"No, ma'am," Llano said, "I don't *have* to, but I think I have a right to. It was you that dragged Stoney and me into this, with your fears for Long John. Now, damn it, you tell me what's put a crimp in his tail."

"I—I . . . It was my fault," she said in a small voice, again refusing to look at him.

Llano said nothing, offering her no encouragement. Slowly she forced her eyes to meet his, and she was blushing furiously.

"I was so dirty," she said, "and I begged Long John to let me get in the creek for a few minutes."

"The moon was full," said Llano, "and I reckon you was jaybird naked."

"Of course I was," she snapped, her anger overcoming her embarrassment. "I've been eight years on that godforsaken Colorado River, but I haven't forgotten how to bathe."

Llano laughed, and it infuriated her all the more. He said nothing until she calmed down.

"So Darden saw you, and now you figure Long John

aims to call him on it. You've been wantin' to get rid of
Darden, and this may be your chance. Long John ain't
no slouch with a Colt."

"I . . . oh, I don't know *what* I want," she cried, "but
I know what I *don't* want. I don't want Long John risking
his life over a—a foolish thing like this."

"Men have died for less," said Llano. "A western man
won't tolerate some hombre jackin' around with his
horse or his woman."

"But Long John doesn't *know* that was Bandy
Darden. It might have been an animal. You told me we
can't shoot men just because we're suspicious of them."

"That's true," Llano said, "and I expect how this turns
out between Darden and Long John will depend on
Darden. If that *was* him, he'd better tell the most con-
vincin' lie he's ever told, else he'll end up with his gizzard full of lead."

While the herd was fresh and trailing well, Long John
rode forward to confront Bandy Darden. While the evidence seemed concrete enough, Long John still had
only his suspicions, so he didn't wish to confront Darden
before the rest of the outfit. Darden saw Long John
coming and waited until the Cajun caught up.

"Last night," said Long John, "about the time ye got
up an' went to the bushes, they was somebody at the
creek, near wher' the herd was bedded down."

"I wasn't near the herd or the creek," Darden said
sullenly. "Hell of an outfit, when a man can't go to the
bushes without bein' raked over."

"I ain't rakin' ye over fer that," said Long John, "an'
ye know it. They's a reason, Darden, fer beddin' down
the herd away from camp, an' no reason fer anybody
else bein' there 'cept the nighthawks. Show up in the
middle of the night when ye ain't s'posed t'be there, an'
ye can die from lead poisonin'. This is Injun country, an'
I won't fault any nighthawk fer cuttin' down on some

hombre skulkin' near the herd. I'm givin' ye the benefit of the doubt this time, but I won't do it again."

With that, Long John turned his horse and rode back to his position. The range over which the herd traveled was flat, virtually treeless, so Llano and Suzanne were able to see Long John as he rode back.

"No shooting," Llano said. "Long John leads his temper on a short rope, but he's fair. He won't kill a man without cause."

But Bandy Darden's pride was more fierce than Long John's, and the little gunman seethed with anger. Darden had killed men on a whim, asking no quarter and giving none. He had just lied his way out of a perilous situation, and as a result, he felt worse than if he'd been shot. He had been spared by a man who had every right to kill him, and for that reason he hated Long John Coons all the more. In his own mind there was the inescapable fact that Long John was a bigger and better man. Besides that, there was a deep down nagging suspicion that if he'd drawn against Long John, the Cajun would have shot him dead. Darden tried to shrug off the doubt, drawing on his hate, but the uneasy feeling plagued him like a persistent devil.

Stoney rode what he estimated to be sixteen miles before finding water for the night's camp. If Long John had again pushed the herd hard all day, they could just about make it by sundown. Stoney scouted the stream for several miles in all directions, finding no Indian sign. He allowed his horse to rest, watered it, and then rode south to meet the herd. The sun was noon high when he met the horse remuda. They were already a little more than halfway to the water, he noted with satisfaction. Stoney rode on, taking the news to Long John, surprised to find the Cajun riding the flank. That likely meant Llano was riding drag with Suzanne. He wouldn't have a chance to talk to Llano until the second watch. Then he reckoned Llano would have something to tell him.

Clouds swept in from the west, hiding the sun, and a gentle west wind made the day bearable. The absence of the Texas sun, which normally sucked all the moisture from man and beast, made the rest of the day's drive almost pleasant. Just in case the wind should shift, bringing the smell of water and stampeding the herd, Stoney again sent the horse remuda on ahead, followed by Sky Pilot and the wagon.

"From the looks of them clouds," said Long John, "we might not need that creek. I'm thinkin' she's gonna blow up one hell of a storm, an' pronto."

The wind shifted, coming from the northwest, bringing the pungent, unmistakable smell of rain. It was all the herd needed. The longhorns in the farthest ranks couldn't wait for those ahead to get out of the way, and the tag end of the herd swung north, like the open end of an enormous horseshoe. As the thunder of the running herd receded and died, there came a new rumbling. Thunder.

"This could be a blessing," Stoney said. "With any luck they'll run themselves out before the storm strikes. Let's ride, and get 'em rounded up and out to graze."

9

In their eagerness to reach water, the longhorns had fanned out in a wide swath that left them scattered along the creek for a mile. A rising wind swept murky gray clouds before it, and by the time the riders reached the creek, the sky was a sea of darkness. Distant lightning flung jagged golden arms into the swirling cloud mass.

"Long John," said Stoney, "it's a lost cause. We can't gather cows in the dark."

"Leave the cows fer daylight," Long John shouted, "an' ride fer camp."

Sky Pilot had positioned the wagon so that a stand of young cottonwoods might provide some protection from the coming storm. The big canvas that sheltered the cooking area had two corners lashed to the arch of a wagon bow and the other two corners rawhided to a pair of cottonwoods. The cook fire roared and crackled in a frenzy of excitement as the rising wind whipped sparks and smoke away into the night. Long John reined up at the wagon, the other riders right behind him.

"Hold supper as best ye can," Long John said to the old biscuit shooter. "We'll be with the horse remuda till the thunder an' lightnin's done."

Sky Pilot said nothing as Long John and the riders

vanished into the night. The first gust of wind-driven rain lashed the wagon canvas, and a golden chain of lightning crackled from one horizon to the other. Even as Long John and the riders drew near, there were nervous nickers from the horse remuda. The riders began circling the frightened horses, seeking to calm them. Every rider's hat was secured with piggin string against the fiendish prying fingers of the wind. The almost continuous glare of lightning revealed Malo Coyote and Naked Horse afoot among the horses. The Indian duo moved from one animal to another, calming them.

Suddenly, even above the roar of the wind and the rumble of thunder, came the frenzied bawling of cattle. In the flare of lightning Llano saw them coming and shouted a warning. It was unnecessary, for the other riders had seen and heard them too. On they came, two hundred horned devils of retribution with the fuse lit. It would take more than hard riding to head them, and they were coming straight toward the horse remuda. Long John led the charge, and once he was far enough from the horse remuda, he began firing his Colt. The rest of the riders, following his lead, began firing. The storm was at the backs of the stampeding longhorns, while the roar and flash of the Colts was right before their eyes. Slowly the leaders turned away and the hard-riding cowboys forced the longhorns into a circle. The lightning had become less frequent, the thunder rumbled off into the distance, and the rain became a steady downpour.

"By the Eternal," Long John said, "we got that many of the varmints we won't have to round up in the mornin'. The Kid, Suzanne, Deuce Gitano, an' me will watch these critters while the rest of ye go eat."

Later, during the second watch, Llano had a chance to tell Stoney what he had learned from Suzanne.

"Darden's a skunk," said Stoney, "but Long John did

the right thing. I can't see killing a man over something that might have been accidental."

"Darden bein' up at that time might have been accidental," Llano said, "but his bein' so far from camp wasn't. He knows the Comanches are a threat, and that if Long John had pulled his Colt and emptied it into the brush, he'd have been within his rights."

"That's likely what Long John told him," said Stoney. "I think you'd best keep your curiosity on a tight rope where Suzanne's concerned. She's pretty as a three-day-old colt, but somewhere down the trail there's gonna be some trouble, and I look for her to be the cause of it, whether she intends to be or not. I think the less involved we are with her, the better off we'll be."

June 9, 1858. Seventy-seven miles south of Dallas.

The first gray light of dawn gave way to a golden aura in the east, heralding another day of brutal Texas sun.

"Wal," said Long John as the outfit began gathering the herd, "it ain't as bad as I expected. I reckon that bunch we headed last night was the only ones spooked enough to run."

"Rest of 'em was give out from that run to the creek," Quando Miller said. "If we'd been all tied up with the cows, we'd of lost the horse remuda. I don't believe that pair of Injuns could of held 'em."

"Like I been sayin' all along," said Bandy Darden, "any outfit that puts too much store in heathen Injuns is askin' for trouble."

"That was a mean storm last night," Stoney said, "and I'm not faultin' Malo Coyote and Naked Horse because the horses were spooked. I doubt any two of us could have done any better. Now let's gather the rest of the herd and move 'em out."

The outfit lost two hours gathering the herd. Most of

them were strung out along the creek, and they didn't want to leave it. Only when the herd was finally on the trail did Stoney ride out on his daily quest for water. To Llano's surprise, Long John again took the flank position behind Bandy Darden, and Llano again found himself riding drag with Suzanne. Recalling Stoney's advice, he decided to ignore her. That lasted for less than a mile, and it was Suzanne who broke the uncomfortable silence.

"You're angry with me, aren't you?"

"No," said Llano, "why should I be angry with you? I'm not your daddy."

They rode on in silence as she digested his words, and she seemed surprised when he spoke to her again.

"You're actin' like you've done something bad, and you're disappointed because nobody's spanked you."

She blushed and turned away, unable to look at him. Finally she did, and when she spoke, it was without the anger he had expected.

"I—That . . . that's kind of how I feel. I know it bothered Long John, but he was kind to me. He told me to put it behind me, to forget it."

"Then why don't you?"

"I—It's . . . him. Bandy Darden and . . . the others. They know, and when they look at me, then I know . . . what they're thinking."

"You're a handsome woman, ma'am, and a man would have to be nigh dead to overlook you. It's no more'n you can expect, and I reckon you and Long John will have to accept that."

"How do you feel . . . about me?"

"I got no right to feel anything," Llano said. "You're the boss's woman, and I'm just a fiddle-foot cowboy, hired on for the drive to market."

"You misunderstood," she said, blushing again. "I mean how do you feel about me being here on the trail?"

"What I feel don't matter," said Llano. "That's between you and Long John. But without referrin' to you in particular, ma'am, a trail drive is no place for a lady. The swearing in particular and the talk in general among these cowboys ain't fit for your ears."

"It's kind of you to say that, but I've heard as bad, and worse. When I was sixteen, I . . . I worked in a saloon in New Orleans. In the Quarter. I've no right to think of myself as a lady. I'm not uncomfortable among swearing, hell-raising cowboys, so perhaps this *is* my place."

"Well, *I* ain't comfortable with you tellin' me all this," Llano said. "It ain't proper. If you feel the need to unload on somebody, it oughta be Long John."

"Long John already knows most of it. But we'd been together eight years before I . . . before I could tell him, and then it was right in the middle of a fight."

"Eight years! That's a mighty long time to live with a man and him knowin' nothing about you."

"We met in California after Long John, as part of the Austin outfit, had driven a herd of Texas longhorns to the goldfields, near San Francisco.* Long John took me for what I was. Or what he thought I was. I'd left New Orleans with barely enough money for passage to California, and when Long John found me, I was desperate."

"So you dabbed a loop on Long John, tellin' him nothing."

"You make it sound so . . . crude," she said. "He asked me only if I wanted to go back to New Orleans. That was the last thing I wanted, but I didn't know what else to do. When we reached Texas, Long John asked me to stay."

"So you did," said Llano, "and eight years later, old Long John learns he's bought a pig in a poke. What's all this leadin' up to?"

* Trail Drive Series #5, *The California Trail*

"My reason for asking you and Stoney to watch Long John's back. Since I told him about . . . me, he's changed, but not in the way you think. He's become more protective, and he was so against me coming on this trail drive, I had to threaten to leave him to go back to New Orleans."

"So it didn't bother *you* all that much, Bandy Darden catching you in the creek, but it pretty much tore up Long John."

"Of course it did," Suzanne said. "He can forgive a man for trying to kill him, but not for sneaking around and seeing me . . . like that. I wish he hadn't spoken to Stoney or Darden, but he wouldn't let it go. He tells me to forget it, to put it behind me, but he won't do that. Now that he knows about my . . . my past, he's become obsessed with the need to protect me from so much as a memory of it. I don't want him fighting because of me."

"At the start, then," said Llano, "Long John was just your ticket out of California. Now, if I'm understandin' what you're trying to say, you're findin' you got some honest feelings for old Long John as a man."

"I have," she said. "He has a temper, too much pride, he's crude, and sometimes we fight, but there are good times. How do you think I've stood it for eight years on that godforsaken Colorado River ranch?"

"It helps, knowin' you ain't about to deal Long John a busted flush," Llano said, "but I still don't think he'd appreciate you unloadin' all this on me."

"He trusts you and Stoney, and so do I. Bandy Darden frightens me. I feel like he's just waiting for the right time and place. Has Long John told you we'll be stopping in Dallas for at least a day and a night?"

"No," said Llano. "Does Long John aim to let the riders go into town?"

"I don't know," Suzanne said, "but if he does, I'd like for you or Stoney to be with Long John."

"I reckon we can manage that," said Llano. "I'll talk to Stoney."

While Bandy Darden would remain a threat, death on the frontier wore many hats. Violence would explode in Dallas, and despite Suzanne's good intentions, it would be she who would light the fuse. . . .

By the time Stoney rode out, the sun was well on its way to drying up all evidence of last night's rain. One of the hazards of traveling in the aftermath of rain was the total absence of any Indian sign. Comanche movement following the storm would be obvious enough, but there was no sign, and Stoney expected none. They'd been fortunate, he reflected, having had an adequate rainfall. Having ridden a little more than twelve miles, he found a spring bubbling from a rock cleft. It formed a pool at the rock base with a substantial runoff. Stoney rode in a widening circle, returning eventually to the point from which he'd first approached the water. For two days there had been no Indian sign, and the total absence of it left him uneasy. If all went as planned, they were two days from the crossing of the Brazos and maybe six days from Dallas. Stoney turned back, and it was almost noon when he met the drive.

"We ain't doin' bad," Long John said, "gittin' started two hours late."

"Keep 'em trailin' like this," Stoney said, "and we'll reach water without a stampede."

Despite the late start, it proved to be one of their better days. Stoney again sent the horse remuda ahead, but for a change the longhorns approached the water in an unusually orderly manner. By sundown the herd had watered and begun to graze. But for the sleepy chirp of a night bird in a nearby cottonwood, the night was quiet as Llano and Stoney rolled out to begin the second watch.

"Well," said Stoney, "after another day at drag, I reckon you got an earful."

"Not much I didn't already know," Llano said. He found himself reluctant to reveal some of what Suzanne had told him. "I did learn that Long John aims to lay-over a night near Dallas."

"We need another wagon wheel," said Stoney, "but it's not an overnight job. Whose idea is this?"

"I don't know," Llano said. "I reckon you'll find out when Long John gets around to tellin' you about it."

June 10, 1858. Sixty-five miles south of Dallas.

"We're goin' to push on to the Brazos today," Stoney said as the outfit gathered for breakfast. "I'll ride ahead lookin' for Indian sign, but not for water. By Long John's reckoning, we're fifteen miles from the Brazos. Might be a little more or a little less."

"Since we're gettin' a new wagon wheel in Dallas," said Bandy Darden, "who goes to town?"

"The wagon goes to town," Stoney said, "and Sky Pilot will take it. If anybody else goes, that'll be up to Long John."

"I'll think on it some betwixt now an' then," said Long John. "Fer now, let's git this herd on the trail."

Stoney rode ahead, to scout for Indian sign. Too, he needed to know how accurate Long John's estimate was. If he'd overestimated and they had less than fifteen miles to the river, all the better. But suppose it was twenty miles, or twenty-five? Besides, Stoney wanted a look at the Brazos, an opportunity to find a suitable ford, lessening the risk of their crossing. There had been considerable rain, and by the time they reached the Brazos it might have become a raging torrent.

Stoney reached the river sooner than he expected, and figured the distance at a little more than twelve miles. But that bit of good news was offset by the fact that the Brazos was running bank full, the muddy brown water sweeping tree limbs and other debris before it. However, there was evidence of past flooding that had been much more severe, backwater extending far beyond the river's banks. Stoney rode several miles along the river, up and downstream, and at only one point—downstream—did it seem possible to cross the wagon. Even there it might be difficult unless the water receded. But it was the luck of the draw. A trail drive had no choice but to push on, nothing certain but the uncertainty. On the western frontier the grassed-over graves on lonely riverbanks were mute testimony to those who had gambled and lost. Stoney rested and watered his horse, and then rode back to meet the drive. He found Llano at right flank and Long John at drag, with Suzanne.

"We'll make the Brazos 'fore sundown, then," said Long John, after Stoney had reported to him. " 'Course, the high water ain't good news, but maybe she'll run down some 'fore morning."

Stoney passed word of the nearness of the river to the other riders without mentioning the high water. As Long John had pointed out, the high water might diminish before morning. On the other hand, it might become worse. With that possibility in mind, Stoney again rode back to talk to Long John.

"Long John," Stoney said, "there's a fifty-fifty chance we'll be wrong, however we do this, but I've seen a few almighty bad river crossings with a tired herd. Once they hit that river, they'll drink. Followin' that, they'll be ready to graze and rest. With that in mind, I favor holdin' off until morning."

"I reckon the risk is about even," said Long John. "On one hand we got an ornery herd, an' on t'other, a cantankerous river. We'll wait fer mornin' an' gamble on the river. How's it look fer crossin' the wagon?"

"Just one promising place," Stoney said, "and we'll lose that if the river continues to rise. How tight is the wagon box?"

"Tight enough to sail the Pacific," said Long John. "She'd damn well better be. Sky Pilot spent two weeks pitchin' the cracks. Used all the tar we could beg, borry, er steal. Sky's a grouchy old coot, but he's crossed his share of water. He can't ride, so that wagon's gotta float, er it's his carcass."

Despite their nearness to the Brazos, Stoney took no chances. He sent the horse remuda ahead, to be watered and taken to graze. The longhorns might not be so thirst-crazed they'd stampede, but there was no assurance of that. A lethal horn could gut a horse. The herd moved on, the riders unconcerned with the westering sun. For once they had time, and it was a welcome change. While the longhorns approached the river in a lope, there was no all out stampede. The water was high enough and swift enough that the animals used some caution in their approach, content to drink from the shallows.

"Look at 'em," said the Kid. "Skeered of it as they are now, we'll play hell gittin' 'em across if it gits any worse."

"It ain't gonna be no Sunday school picnic, whenever we do it," said Briano, "but I can see the sense of waitin' a few more hours. There's always a chance she'll calm down."

"And just as much chance there'll be rain, makin' it all the worse," Bandy Darden said.

The conversation ended when Stoney and Long John returned from downriver, where Stoney had selected a possible crossing. Sky Pilot had supper well under way, as bull bats swept silently out of a darkening sky, seeking their own evening meal.

"Lightning yonder to the west," said Llano.

"Don't necessarily mean rain," Long John said. "It

gits hot enough, ye kin git lightning aplenty without rain."

"True," Stoney said, "but without a drop of rain to-night, enough may have already fallen to strand us for a week. There's trouble and danger enough on the frontier, without worryin' over what *might* happen."

"Yeah," Llano said, "come daybreak, we might all be shot full of Comanche arrows. Then crossin' the river won't be a problem."

"By God," said Quando Miller, "you sure know how to comfort a man."

Seeming dim and faraway, stars twinkled from a velvet sky, and a pale quarter moon seemed suspended from its upper horn. There was no wind. Far into the night, riders circling the herd watched golden tongues of lightning flick across the western horizon.

June 11, 1858. At the Brazos.

At first light, before breakfast, Stoney and Long John walked to the river.

"Wal," said Long John, "waitin' ain't cost us nothin'. She ain't much better an' she ain't no worse."

"You're right," Stoney agreed. "All we have in our favor is a herd that's been rested, watered, and grazed."

"That'll make a difference," said Long John, "and I reckon we'll soon be knowin' how much. Let's git breakfast, and then git this water behind us."

"If there's trouble," Stoney said, "it'll likely be with the wagon. I'd like to take it across before the horse remuda. Besides, if we take the horses across just ahead of the herd, it'll give those longhorns somethin' to follow."

"Can't hurt none," said Long John. "You got any ideas fer crossin' the wagon?"

"Only one way I know of in deep water," Stoney said,

"and that's to unhitch the teams, lash a dead cotton-wood log along each side of the wagon and float it across. But that current's mighty swift. We'll need three riders upstream, their ropes tied tight to that wagon, or the force of the water will tip it over."

"See to gittin' the logs, then," said Long John, "and I'll git a pair o' hombres to ride with me, steadyin' the wagon. You gonna hitch onto the tongue and pull her across?"

"Yeah," Stoney said. When Long John had ridden away, he found himself facing Suzanne. She looked worried. All her conversations had been with Llano, and she'd scarcely spoken to Stoney, but she did now.

"That river worries me. Crossing it, I mean. But we've no choice, do we?"

"Not unless we wait for a drought to dry it up," said Stoney. "Stay at drag. If there's trouble at the crossing, I don't want you sucked into it."

"Damn you," she shouted as he turned away, "you're ordering me around like a . . . a greenhorn."

"You're worse than that," Stoney said, turning to face her. "You're the boss's woman, and I can't treat you like just another cowboy, and you know it. I want you at drag during the river crossing. *Comprender?*"

She turned away without a word, and Stoney didn't know if she had meekly accepted his order or intended to disobey. He took the axe from the wagon and found Llano.

"Come on," Stoney said. "You have the honor of helping me find and cut a pair of dead cottonwoods big enough to float the wagon across."

"Only if you tell me what Suzanne had to say."

"She wants one of us to take Long John piggyback and swim him across the Brazos," said Stoney, "and I told her you'd do it. Now come on."

Once Llano and Stoney found suitable cottonwoods, they were felled, trimmed, and the logs were snaked back to the wagon. While other riders hoisted one of the logs into position, Llano and Stoney lashed it to front and rear axles of the wagon, just shy of the right front and right rear wheels. The second log was secured in the same manner to front and rear axles, beneath the wagon box, just inside the left front and left rear wheels. Sky Pilot had thrown the mule harnesses into the wagon. Malo Coyote and Naked Horse had already crossed the two teams of mules without difficulty. Sky Pilot had climbed to the wagon box and sat there placidly chewing his plug. Long John had chosen Dent Briano and Quando Miller to accompany him in steadying the wagon during the crossing. From the wagon, Stoney had taken a substantial coil of rope brought along for this very purpose, and was securing one end of it to the wagon tongue. That done, he slipknotted the other end to his saddle horn.

"Come on, gents," Long John said. "Let's rope this critter an' move her acrost the water."

Sky Pilot, foreseeing the need, had installed iron rings on both sides, along the bottom of the wagon box. Long John tied his rope to a ring near the front of the wagon, while Quando Miller tied to a ring nearest the back. Dent Briano took his place in the middle, and they were ready. Stoney swam his horse across, and as they clambered up the opposite bank, the slack went out of the rope, and the wagon lurched toward the rushing brown water of the Brazos. The trio of riders kept pace, and when the wagon left solid ground, the current took hold. When the wagon hit the ends of the steadying lines, Long John's horse staggered. Little by little they gained on the river, and Stoney sighed with relief as his horse drew the wagon to safety. Long John, Stoney, Dent, and Quando quickly freed the wagon from the cottonwood logs, as Sky Pilot began harnessing the teams. Seeing the wagon had safely crossed, Malo Coyote and Naked Horse had driven the horse remuda into position. Long

John, Dent, and Quando rode downstream to assist in crossing the horses. Curiously, the Indians didn't drive the horses into the river, but rode in ahead, leading them. The remuda followed willingly, as the rest of the riders already were moving the longhorns toward the river. Llano was at drag, and Stoney noted with satisfaction that Suzanne was with him. Once the horses were safely across, Long John, Dent, and Quando rode out to meet the oncoming herd. The Kid, Stoney, and Bandy Darden were at right flank, on the downriver side. Long John, Dent, and Quando had ridden to left flank, while Deuce Gitano had joined Llano and Suzanne at drag.

"Let's hit 'em hard!" Llano shouted.

Deuce and Suzanne followed his lead, swinging doubled lariats against dusty flanks and screeching like Comanches. The lead steers plunged into the swirling water without hesitation, and it looked good. But it all changed in an instant, and Stoney saw the trouble coming. A broken cottonwood branch had been submerged, but when the butt end hit some obstruction, the leafy end of the branch reared up out of the water directly in front of the lead steers. It literally sprang out of the river like some green apparition, and while it hung there but a few seconds, it was enough to spook the leaders. With the rush of the current to their left and the rest of the herd behind, the lead steers turned downstream, seeking to circle back to the riverbank they'd just left. In doing so, they were about to engulf the three flank riders in the resulting turmoil.

"Ride," Stoney shouted. "Get out of their way!"

Bandy Darden broke free and rode downstream ahead of the longhorns, but the Kid wasn't so lucky. His horse screamed, trying to buck as a flailing horn raked its flank. Even then the Kid might have made it, but another horn ripped into his left side. The force of it drove him out of the saddle, and he disappeared beneath the swirling brown water of the Brazos.

10

Dodging flailing horns, Stoney fought his way to the Kid's frightened horse, to the offside where the young rider had left the saddle. The Kid, had he been trampled beneath the hooves of the milling herd, was finished. There was one chance in a thousand he was hurt but alive. A slashing horn tore a burning gash across Stoney's right thigh as he leaned out of the saddle, seeking the offside stirrup of the Kid's horse. While Stoney could hear someone shouting, he couldn't distinguish the words. Suddenly his frantic fingers touched the toe of a boot. The Kid's foot was caught in the stirrup! Taking a firm grip on the horn with his right hand, Stoney leaned far out of the saddle, his left hand grasping the Kid's pistol belt. The Kid was a dead weight, almost more than Stoney could handle. When Stoney came up, the first person he saw was Llano Dupree, about to rope his horse. With Llano's help, the horse fought its way free of the longhorns. Stoney shook his head, trying to clear his eyes and ears of the muddy water. He had been lucky, but he wasn't so sure about the young rider. The Kid looked dead, or close to it.

The water being deep and swift, the longhorns couldn't remain in the river. As they began milling, they seemed to lose all sense of direction. The path of least resistance being with the current, they drifted downstream and, at the first opportunity, clambered out on the bank toward which they'd been headed. The rest of the herd followed the leaders and the crossing was completed.

"May be . . . too late," Stoney panted, as Long John and Dent Briano eased the Kid to the ground.

"I reckon he's swallered enough o' that river to drown him," said Long John, "an' that horn in the gut won't help him none. Let's peel him outta them clothes an' see what we kin do fer him."

"Our bedrolls is in the wagon," Quando Miller said, "and the wagon's across the river. We ain't got even a blanket."

"Yer right," said Long John. "Ain't nothin' we kin do fer him here. We'll have t'git him acrost the river, if'n he's still alive. Is he?"

"Yes," Stoney said, "but his pulse is weak. Once I'm in the saddle, a couple of you hoist him up to me, and I'll take him across. He'll need warm blankets and that wound tended to."

The rest of the outfit was solemn as they followed Stoney across the river. The Kid hadn't been that well liked, but he was one of the outfit, and what had happened to him might have happened to any one of the rest of them. There were other dangerous rivers to cross, most notably the Red.

"My God," said Dent Briano, when they removed the Kid's muddied, bloody clothes, "that's an awful gash. I don't see how a man can get gored like that without ruinin' his vitals."

"Only piece of luck he's had," Deuce Gitano said. "That wound needs some whiskey poured over it, and then sewed together."

"Yeah," said Bandy Darden with a nasty laugh, "but we ain't got no whiskey, have we, biscuit shooter?"

It was a deliberate attempt to provoke Sky Pilot, but before the cook could explode, Long John spoke up.

"We got medicine that'll disinfect his wound, an' we got needles an' thread fer the sewin'."

"That's ticklish work," Dent Briano said. "Who's gonna do the sewin'?"

"I am," said Sky Pilot, glaring at Bandy Darden through slitted eyes, "and I don't patch up skunks. Think on that some, 'fore you get shot or cut."

"I'll help you," Suzanne said.

For a moment Sky Pilot seemed about to refuse. Finally he nodded, his eyes on Long John, for the Kid had been stripped bare as a skinned coyote. But Long John said nothing, and Sky Pilot went to the wagon for his medicine.

"Come on," said Long John. "Rest of us is gonna git them cows bunched an' ready fer the trail."

When the lead steers found a low bank downstream and left the river, the rest of the herd followed. The riders found them grazing along the bank, and it wasn't difficult to bunch them and drive them to the point where they should have crossed originally. Before they reached the wagon, Suzanne rode out to meet them.

"We did the best we could," she told Long John. "Sky Pilot says we need some whiskey, and we might find some at Waco. It's somewhere to the east of here."

"The Kid goes in the wagon," Long John said. "We'll wrap him in blankets an' go on to Dallas. If'n the Kid ain't no better when we git there, we'll find him a doc."

Suzanne seemed about to question Long John's decision, but thought better of it. She rode away, and when Long John and the rest of the outfit arrived with the herd, Sky Pilot was on the wagon seat, the reins in his hands.

"We've lost some time," Stoney said. "I'll get the horse remuda started and then ride ahead to scout the trail and look for water."

The longhorns took the trail at their usual leisurely gait, but that wouldn't do.

"Keep 'em bunched an' keep 'em moving," Long John shouted. He and Bandy Darden rode the right flank, while Dent Briano and Quando Miller covered the left. Llano, Deuce, and Suzanne rode drag, the herd was fresh, trailing well, and Llano soon found Suzanne riding beside him.

"Your friend Stoney's a strange man," she said.

"Strange to you, maybe," Llano replied, "but not to me. We've sided one another since he was thirteen years old and I was twelve."

"I'm not questioning his loyalty to you," she said, "and you know it. He just saved the life of a man who tried to kill him. Why?"

"Why did you help Sky Pilot tend to that same man, after Stoney hauled him out of the river?"

"I—I don't know," she said, not looking at him.

"Then I'll tell you," Llano said. "On the frontier, an outfit looks after its own. Sure, we'll fight among ourselves, but when a man's in trouble, we'll help him, side him till hell freezes."

"Even knowing that when he's well, he may still try to kill you?"

"Even then," said Llano.

"You don't think very much of me, do you?"

"I think there may be hope for you, after what you done a while ago. You set your prejudice aside and helped a man who was hurt. Who he was and what he was didn't matter. His hurt did."

She said no more, and when she finally looked at him, there was a softness in her eyes that he'd never seen before. She rode away, leaving him to wonder.

Stoney rode almost fifteen miles before finding a creek for the night's camp. From there he rode a two-mile circle, looking for Indian sign, but finding none. Their nearness to Dallas might account for that, if Long

John had his distances right. Stoney rested his horse, allowed it to drink, and then rode back to meet the herd. He passed the horse remuda, waved to the Indian riders, and rode on until he met the wagon. Sky Pilot ignored him.

"The Kid doin' all right?" Stoney asked.

"See for yourself," said Sky Pilot.

Stoney fell back to the rear of the wagon. He stepped out of the saddle, climbed over the wagon's tailgate, and tied the reins of his horse to a rear wagon bow. Sky Pilot had done some drastic rearranging to make room for the Kid. He was surrounded by barrels and crates, with bags of various goods piled all the way to the wagon's canvas top. His eyes still not accustomed to the gloom, Stoney was trying to hunker down when the Kid spoke.

"Why'd you do it, Winters?"

"You were in trouble," Stoney said. "Given a choice, would you have preferred that I let you drown or be trampled by the longhorns?"

"God, no, but I ain't deservin' of what you done for me. I tried to kill you, and I . . . I swore I would, 'fore this drive is done."

"Do you still aim to?"

"No," said the Kid, "but I made a damn fool of myself, and I feel lower than an egg-suckin' dog. How can I ever make up for that?"

"By gettin' back on your feet," Stoney said, "and doing a man-size job on this trail drive. What do I call you besides 'the Kid'?"

It wasn't a fair question for the time and place. Many a man had lost himself on the frontier, hoping fervently that his given name had been forgotten. But the Kid didn't hesitate.

"I ain't wanted nowhere," he said, "so you can call me by my name. I'm Harley Logan, and I growed up on the farm, so I reckon I ain't much of a cowboy."

"You'll do, Harley," said Stoney. "You just need to

spend more time with a rope and less time with a gun. How do you feel?"

"Sore, like my guts has been ripped out."

"You took a bad raking," Stoney said, "but that ain't as bad as having a horn shoved through you. We're pushing on to Dallas, and unless you're some better by then, we'll find you a doctor there."

Stoney rode back to meet the herd. Long John had seen him enter the wagon, and his eyes were full of questions.

"His name's Harley Logan," said Stoney, "and by the time we reach St. Louis, he'll be a cowboy."

"Wal, now," Long John said, a grin breaking up his craggy face, "that is a surprise. I been figurin' that before we got to St. Louis, you'd have to shoot him. Where's our water fer t'night?"

"From here," said Stoney, "another ten miles."

The herd reached the creek without a stampede. Once they had watered and bedded down for the night, Stoney and Long John went to the wagon to see how Harley Logan was doing.

"Talkin' out of his head," Sky Pilot told them. "Fever's risin'."

"No rain in sight," Long John said. "Stoney, let's git him outta this wagon an' lay him under that cottonwood by the creek."

Harley had been wrapped in blankets and then placed on a thick pallet of other blankets. With Long John grasping two corners of the pallet and Stoney the other two, it became a stretcher on which they carried the feverish Harley to the bank of the creek. The rest of the outfit gathered around.

"He won't make it to Dallas," said Deuce Gitano. "We need whiskey to sweat that poison out of him."

"Town ain't far," Sky Pilot said hopefully. "Somebody could ride in—"

"We don't have to ride nowhere," said Long John.

"Jist in case we run short on whiskey fer medicine, I stuck a extry quart in my saddlebag. I'll git it, and I'll personal see that this young jaybird swallers enough of it to start him sweatin'."

Long John returned with the whiskey and knelt beside young Harley Logan, working the cork out of the bottle with his teeth. Sky Pilot, his eyes on the bottle, licked his lips. Long John spoke to the feverish Harley.

"Kin ye hear me, boy? Ye got to swaller this whiskey so's ye can sweat out that fever an' fight infection. Now this is all the whiskey we got, an' we can't afford to waste none. Kin ye hear me?"

"Yeah," said Harley, his eyelids fluttering. "I . . . hear you."

On his other side, Stoney lifted Harley up enough so that none of the whiskey was spilled when Long John tilted the bottle. Harley took a long pull and lay back gasping. Slowly, each swallow more difficult than the last, he downed half the whiskey.

"I'll look in on ye again at midnight," Long John said, "an' if'n that fever ain't broke, ye git the rest o' this firewater. When I'm ready fer it"—he looked long and hard at Sky Pilot—"it'd damn well better still be there in my saddlebag."

When Long John came off the first watch, he found Harley Logan snoring. And sweating. Llano and Stoney were saddling up for the second watch when Long John approached.

"Fever's broke," Long John said, "an' he'll sleep off the whiskey by mornin'. That was a damn fine thing ye done, Stoney, haulin' the little peckerwood outta the river. He's been a mite troublesome."

"We can't afford to lose a rider," said Stoney. "Besides, like I told you, he's got the makings of a top hand."

Dent Briano and Quando Miller joined Llano and

Stoney for the second watch. But for the occasional yip of a coyote, the night was quiet.

When Darden brought up the stop near Dallas, Llano said, "I expected Long John to say somethin' about us stayin' overnight."

"Smart of him not to mention it," Stoney said. "So far as anybody knows, we'll be there just long enough to pick up another wagon wheel. If Darden suspected we're gonna be there overnight, he'd really throw a fit."

"He'll know it when we get there," said Llano. "That is, if Suzanne's been truthful with me."

"I believe she has been," Stoney said. "Why lie about something, knowin' you'd catch her in it?"

"You reckon Long John will turn us all loose for a trip to town?"

"I reckon he will," said Stoney, "half of us goin' at a time. He might have said somethin' tonight, if Darden hadn't shot off his mouth."

"If Long John rides into town, do you aim to stay with the herd?"

"Yes," said Stoney. "I'm trail boss, and with Long John away, I should be here. Why?"

"I promised Suzanne one of us would ride in with Long John. I reckon it ain't a good idea, havin' him learn the why of it."

Stoney laughed. "I reckon it ain't. My God, let Long John even suspect Suzanne's got us ridin' shotgun, and he'll blow like a keg of black powder."

June 12, 1858. A few miles south of Dallas.

At the end of the second watch, Stoney found Harley Logan awake and restless.

"How are you feelin', Harley?" Stoney asked.

"Like I been throwed and stomped about six times,

and my head's thumpin' like a war drum, with the whole tribe beatin' on it at once."

"You'll be ridin' the wagon as far as Dallas,' said Stoney.

"I ain't earnin' my keep. I'll likely be left in Dallas."

"That's what you think," Stoney said. "The worst of the Shawnee Trail's ahead of us, and we'll need every man that can fork a horse and swing a rope."

The horse remuda moved out, followed by the wagon and the longhorns. Stoney rode out seeking water. If Long John's calculations were even close, they were no more than three days out of Dallas, if that far. Substantial settlement that it was, Stoney didn't expect Indian trouble, but he dared not relax his vigilance. The Comanches might count on the very proximity of the town to catch the trail drive off its guard. Once Dallas was behind them, there was the crossing of the Red, near Doan's store. After that they might not see another friendly face. Stoney had ridden no more than ten miles when he found a runoff from what proved to be a spring. It was deep, the fast flowing runoff was substantial enough for the herd, and there was plentiful graze. That was enough. No frontiersman passed decent water and graze with the hope of something better, lest he end up in dry camp. Stoney rested and watered his horse, and then rode back to meet the herd.

"Water's mighty close," said Long John, when Stoney reported to him. "We won't make a good day's drive, but ye done right. Might of rode on without findin' good water an' graze fer ten more miles, an' maybe not even then. We won't be more'n two days from town anyhow, so we'll just have us an easy day. God knows, they'll be plenty o' long, hard ones 'fore we ever see St. Louis."

By the time they reached water, Harley Logan was much improved, and very tired of the wagon. After supper Stoney spoke to Long John.

"Tomorrow, after I've found water for tomorrow

night's camp, I aim to ride on to Dallas. At least near enough so that we know have far we still have to travel."

"I ain't wantin' to bed down right in the midst of the place," Long John said. "See kin ye find us some good water an' grass maybe ten mile out. I reckon that'll be plenty close enough. Then when we're ready to move on, we kin pass the town to the east, an foller the Trinity River north a ways."

After a quiet night, the herd was ready to take the trail at first light. Two days in the wagon hadn't cured Harley Logan, but he saddled his horse and mounted, as Long John watched approvingly.

"That horn slash looked bad," said Suzanne. "He shouldn't be riding again so soon."

"Glad he is," Long John said. "The boy's got sand. Stoney figgers he'll be a first-class cowboy."

"You were right, making Stoney Winters trail boss," said Suzanne. "I can see that now."

"So ye wasn't sure until now," Long John said. "What changed yer mind?"

"He's very mature for one so young, and I'll never forget how he rode into that crazy bunch of cows and rescued Harley Logan. The Kid has gone out of his way to be disagreeable, especially where Stoney's concerned. It takes a big man to risk his own life saving someone who's caused only trouble."

"It pleasures me that yer seein' it that way," said Long John. "Life on the frontier ain't easy. They's so many ways of dyin', a man just nacherly helps them that's in need, without tryin' to decide if'n they're deservin' er not. I reckon ye kin end up savin' some no account bastards that way, but if'n they ain't deservin', they'll git theirs. If not a strong dose of lead poisonin', they'll git their necks stretched at the end of somebody's rope."

Stoney rode out, seeking water and graze that wasn't too far from Dallas, but near enough for the drive to reach it before sundown. He had ridden not quite fifteen miles when he found the graze he'd been looking for, strung out along a clear, deep creek. When his horse had rested enough, he allowed the animal to drink, and then rode on. The wind was out of the northwest, and he'd ridden less than a mile when he heard dogs barking. He judged the town wasn't more than half a dozen miles distant. Wheeling his horse, he rode back to meet the herd, finding they had already covered a third of the distance to water.

"We been pushin' 'em hard," Long John said, "since we wasn't sure how many miles we'd have to make 'fore sundown."

"You can't lose, thinkin' like that," said Stoney. "We're maybe ten miles from water. From there I heard dogs barking. Once we reach the creek, we can't be more than five or six miles from town."

"Close enough," Long John said. "I kind of promised Suzanne we'd ride into town, so maybe we'll lay over a extry night. I reckon we kin allow the riders a night in town, so's they kin belly up an' wet their whistles. Sky Pilot kin take the wagon in tomorrer. Some of us kin ride in t'night, with the others goin' tomorrer er tomorrer night. That's up to you."

"Won't matter," said Stoney, "but I want you or me with the herd at all times. Why don't you ride in tonight, taking Suzanne, Llano, and Dent Briano with you? Tomorrow, or tomorrow night, I'll go, taking Miller, Darden, Gitano, and Harley Logan with me."

"I kin agree with that," Long John said, "but they's one thing I want ye to do. Git there 'fore dark an' be sure Sky Pilot's got that wagon wheel replaced. Then track down Sky Pilot and git the old coot in the wagon, if'n ye got to hog-tie him. I want him sober an' ready fer the trail, an' he won't be less'n he's had a night to sleep it off."

"I'll take care of that," said Stoney. "What about

Malo Coyote and Naked Horse? Should we offer them a chance to ride to town?"

"I reckon," Long John said. "Might as well be fair about it, but I'm hopin' they'll stay with the herd. They ain't Comanches, but they're Injuns, an' Texans can be damn sudden."

It was as good a time as any to put the question to the Indian riders, so Stoney caught up to the horse remuda, and the response was exactly what Long John had hoped for.

"No like town," said Naked Horse.

"Ninguno," Malo Coyote said. "Not go."

June 13, 1858. Dallas.

Thanks to their early start and Long John's pushing the herd, the drive reached the creek without difficulty. Once the herd was bedded down, Stoney told the riders in what order they would be allowed to ride into town.

"I aimed to ride to town tonight," said Bandy Darden. "Whose idea is it that I don't go till tomorrow?"

"Mine," Stoney said.

"That ain't surprisin'," Darden growled. "Suppose I don't choose to go tomorrow?"

"Then you don't go at all," said Stoney.

Darden choked back an angry response, for Dent Briano and Quando Miller were watching him. While they had said no more of Darden's end-of-trail proposal, they hadn't forgotten.

After supper, while Dent and Llano waited, Long John saddled a horse for himself and one for Suzanne. The four rode out, Long John taking the lead. Their first look at Dallas came at dusk, as lamps winked on like distant fireflies. They rode along broad dirt streets, and men paused on the boardwalks as they passed. There were no women in sight. Discordant pianos from the various saloons fought with one another, and the cacophony was punctuated with drunken shouts and female laughter. It was Sunday night, still early, so the town was just beginning to roar. All the shops were open, and Long John reined up before a vast unpainted building with a square false front. Tall black lettering applied with a heavy brush and untalented hand proclaimed it DALLAS MERCHANTILE.

"Suzanne an' me are goin' in here fer a while," Long John said. "You gents is free to go where ye like, but I reckon we'd ought to ride back to the herd around midnight. Suzanne an' me may not be here that long. If'n ye don't see us nowhere, just mosey on to camp."

"I'm goin' to that Lone Star Saloon across the street," said Dent. "You comin', Llano?"

"I reckon," Llano said. He turned away, avoiding the plea in Suzanne's eyes. He'd feel like a fool trailing Long John around town, especially if the Cajun got suspicious of Llano's motive. He followed Dent Briano into the saloon, and when they approached the bar, the bartender raised his eyebrows.

"Beer," said Dent.

"Same here," Llano said.

Most of the patrons, keeping a respectable distance, had gathered around a table where four men were playing poker.

"That hombre in the silk hat with the longhorn moustache is Ben Thompson," said Dent quietly. "I hear he's a reg'lar gentleman when he's sober, but get him likkered up, and he's the meanest, deadliest son of a bitch west of the Mississippi."*

"He's all that and worse," said one of the observers who had overheard Dent's conversation.

---

* In October 1858 Thompson shotgunned a man in Austin. In the back.

"Surprisin' he can find anybody to play poker with him," Llano said.

The stranger laughed. "Safest place in town, at the table with Thompson, long as you don't cheat. It's when he catches some damn fool bottom-dealin' that all hell busts loose."

The Dallas Merchantile had a narrow-roofed porch that ran all the way along the front of the building, serving as a boardwalk. When Long John and Suzanne entered the place, the mingled smell of oiled leather and smoked hams attested to the variety of merchandise. There were barrels from which brooms reared their brushy heads, tables piled high with bolts of cloth in various colors and patterns, kegs of nails, molasses, and in one corner, a barrel that smelled of coal oil. Near the door there was a table and four rickety chairs for those who had purchased edible merchandise and needed a place to partake of it. Three bearded men hunched over the table, using their Bowie knives to carve bite-sized hunks of cheese from their purchase, which lay unwrapped before them. Long John ignored the trio, and Suzanne was thankful, for one of the men looked at her with the light of recognition in his eyes.

"Long John," Suzanne said desperately, "I'm going to look at the dress materials."

"Take yer time," said Long John. "I'm lookin' fer the guns."

Her heart pounding, Suzanne looked back. The three men were laughing, kicking back their chairs. Suzanne turned quickly down an aisle where the bolted goods were piled higher than her head, and doubled back toward the door. She had to reach her horse! Returning to camp without Long John would set off his fury like the wrath of God, but the fearful alternative would be far worse. But the trio of strangers had anticipated her move, and met her at the door.

"Damn me eyes," said the man who'd first recognized

her, "I told ye it was ol' Suzy, from Madame Toussand's, in New Orleans."

"By Gawd," said a second man, "you're right. Ol' Suzie's all growed up and all decked out in britches. Suzy gal, we gonna have us a time!"

11

*F*or a terrible moment Suzanne was frozen in body and mind. Was it possible, after almost ten years, that her unsavory past had caught up with her? Grim reality assured her that the worst had indeed happened, when one of the men seized her arm and drew her to him. The whiskey on his breath almost floored her, and she swung her right fist as hard as she could, smashing it into his mouth. She carried a Colt beneath the waistband of her Levi's, and she had her hand on the butt of it when one of the burly men slammed his fist into the side of her head, below her left ear. Her vision blurred, and it seemed from a great distance she could hear them shouting and cursing. It was too late to spare Long John humiliation. Now she wanted him to hear, to save her from these brutal apparitions from a past she longed to forget. But when she tried to cry out to him, she found a leathery palm over her mouth. She kicked and fought to no avail, and as they dragged her across the boardwalk, she felt the cool night wind on her face. Her head pounded from the blow she'd taken, and seemingly from afar a drunken voice was talking to her.

"Suzy, we got money and we got us a room. It'll be like old times."

Then, also seeming far away, came the deadly voice of Long John Coons.

"Git away from her, damn ye."

"Like hell," said one. "We seen her first. Get your own woman."

"She is my woman," Long John said in a soft, deadly voice. "I'll fergive a man one mistake. Jist don't make the second one. Now git, the three of ye."

But Long John was in a poor position. He stood to one side of the store doorway, his back to the log wall. The three strangers who had Suzanne were at the hitch rail where they had left their horses, and the horses offered cover that Long John lacked.

"It's you that'll be leavin', friend," one of the strangers snarled. "We knowed this little gal in a New Orleans whorehouse, and we aim to renew our friendship." He fired from beneath the belly of a horse, and the lead ripped into the wall near Long John's head.

Long John fired twice, once at the muzzle flash and once directly to the left of it. There was an agonized groan.

"By God, he's shot Turk," one of the surviving trio bawled. "Kill the bastard!"

Long John dropped to one knee as their answering fire began slamming into the store's wall. They were firing from behind the horses, and Long John had no clearly defined target.

The gunfight in the street quickly became more interesting than Ben Thompson and the poker game. Llano and Dent were the first to slam through the bat-wing doors, and quick to guess the significance of the muzzle flashes from the street. Quickly they moved from the lighted door of the saloon to the shadows.

"Long John," Llano said guardedly, "we're here."

"Hold yer fire," said Long John. "I bored one o' the bastards, but they's two more, an' they got Suzanne."

Long John's response had the desired effect. The firing from the street resumed, one of the men firing at the sound of Long John's voice and the other at the position from which Llano had spoken. At that point Suzanne gave Long John, Dent, and Llano the edge they needed. She broke loose as the frightened horses began to rear, and scrambled into the darkness of the street.

"I'm free from them," Suzanne shouted.

As gunfire from the street tore into the front wall of the saloon, Llano and Dent had it all to themselves, as those who had run to the scene of the shooting just as quickly returned to the safety of the saloon. But from the moment Suzanne cried out that she was free from her captors, Llano Dupree and Dent Briano began returning the fire. With Long John across the street in front of the store, the pair in the street were in a deadly cross fire.

"This is the law," a voice shouted. "Hold your fire!"

It was an unnecessary order, for the firing from the street had ceased. Long John, Dent, and Llano had stopped shooting, for they no longer had anything at which to shoot. Suzanne, shirt torn, stood beside Long John. Once the shooting had ceased, a man emerged from the store with a lantern, and it was to him that the sheriff spoke.

"Hennessy, this is Sheriff Rankin. Bring that lantern out here so's we can see to these men by the hitch rail. Rest of you hombres that's burnt powder, get out there where I can see you. I got a scattergun loaded with bird-shot, and at close range it ain't gentle."

The horses, once the shooting was over, had settled down. Hennessy stepped out on the boardwalk with the lantern, and the revelation in the street wasn't pretty. The three antagonists were dead, and the first man Long John had shot had been mangled by the hooves of the frightened horses.

"Now," said the sheriff, "you gents that's still on your

feet, move out there in the street where there's light, and keep your hands where I can see 'em."

Hennessy had left the lantern on the boardwalk and retreated to the store. Long John and Suzanne stepped into the light and were joined by Dent and Llano. Suzanne had lost her hat, and her curly black hair tumbled down around her shoulders. Her torn shirt was obvious, and a purple bruise ran from her left ear to the corner of her mouth. Sheriff Rankin stepped into the light, a shotgun in the crook of his arm, and confronted the four. He was very blunt.

"Three dead men. They been here before, and I know them. I don't know none of you. You pilgrims had better have a reason. A damn good reason."

"I reckon we have," Long John said. "Suzanne's my woman. We was in the store when them three varmints grabbed her. They dragged her out here, an' when I demanded they turn her loose, they cut down on me. These riders of mine, Briano an' Dupree, come out of the saloon, and when Suzanne got loose, we salted them bastards down in a cross fire. You want proof of what they done, look at Suzanne."

"Ma'am," said Rankin, turning to Suzanne, "you ever seen them three gents before?"

"No," Suzanne said, hands behind her to hide their trembling. "I never saw them before in my life. They were crazy drunk."

"Sheriff," said Long John, "I'm Long John Coons, an' I got a place down on the Colorado. We're takin' a drive north, an' we're just layin' over a day er two. We ain't here lookin' fer trouble."

"Too bad," Rankin said. "Looks like you done bought a mess of it."

"Sheriff," Llano said, "Briano and me come out of the saloon in time to see those men firing at Long John. When Suzanne broke loose, Briano and me cut loose with our Colts, siding Long John, evening the odds.

We're claiming self-defense. What are you chargin' us with?"

"Nothin'," said Rankin. "When I said you got trouble, I wasn't referrin' to the law. Them three has been here before, and they been in trouble before, and I can see what they done to the lady. I ain't wastin' sympathy on them. But you just gunned down three of the Harkness bullwhackers. Harkness sends a dozen wagons from New Orleans every month. This bunch rolled in yesterday evening, so's they'd have the weekend to raise hell in town. The Harkness men are so hairy-legged, so poison-mean, Old Man Harkness brags they wear out their britches from the inside. You got problems, Coons, because I can't promise the rest of this Harkness outfit won't be gunnin' for you. There'll be an inquest in the mornin' at ten o'clock, and I'll still be needin' you here for that. But when that's done, I'd take that herd and slope on out of these parts before the rest of them Harkness whackers sober up enough to come lookin' for you. There's nine more of 'em, and I can't offer you protection from that many."

"I ain't expectin' you to," Long John said curtly. "I'll gut-shoot my own coyotes. Jist don't you go handin' me any surprises at that inquest."

"I don't aim to," said Rankin. "I think you was justified in cutting these hombres down, and I'm willin' to testify to that. That's all the more reason to be ready for these Harkness drivers. They ain't goin' to agree to my verdict, and when I turn you loose, there may be hell to pay."

"Then why can't you have the inquest without us?" Suzanne cried. "You're bringing Long John back to town so they can kill him."

"Can't do it no other way, ma'am," said Rankin. "We got no witnesses 'cept you and Coons. Unless these two riders seen somethin'." He turned to Llano and Dent.

"Dent and me was in the saloon," Llano said. "We

was in time to see Suzanne break loose, and we joined the fight after all them hombres opened up on Long John. But the shootin' had started before we knew there was a fight."

"I'll likely need testimony from all of you," said Rankin. "I'm lettin' you go now on your promise to be here tomorrow mornin' for the inquest. Do I have that promise?"

"You got it," Long John said.

"Ride, then," said Rankin. "Meet me at the courthouse at nine-thirty in the morning."

Long John rode out, followed by Suzanne, Dent, and Llano. They rode back to camp in silence, Llano mulling over what had happened. From what Suzanne had told him of her past in New Orleans, Llano thought he knew what had happened. Being from New Orleans, the three strangers had recognized Suzanne. Suppose the rest of the Harkness drivers showed up at the inquest, and some or all of them recognized the girl? If the town was convinced Suzanne was a decent woman molested by drunken teamsters, Long John wouldn't be faulted in the slightest. However, let Suzanne be branded a saloon woman, or worse, what westerners referred to as a "soiled dove," and the three dead men wouldn't be blamed for accosting her. It would put Long John in a bad light, and the affair might blossom into an unsavory mess that would force them to shoot their way out of town. It was still early, the fight having taken but a few minutes. Llano wondered how much Long John would tell Stoney. The rest of the riders would have to be told of the shooting, even if they weren't told the cause of it. Otherwise, they might be gunned down without warning by the vengeful Harkness outfit. When they reached camp, Llano pulled his roll and spread his blankets, but he wouldn't sleep. Long John had ridden on through camp, toward the slumbering herd. At least he was going to talk to Stoney, and sometime before the dawn, Llano would also be talking to his longtime friend. Despite Long John's determination to protect Suzanne, Stoney must know the truth, lest he and the rest of the outfit ride into a death trap tomorrow night. To Llano's dismay, Suzanne spread her blankets near him, and feigning sleep didn't fool her.

"You know what happened, don't you?" she said quietly.

Llano said nothing, and she continued.

"They recognized me, remembered me," she said bitterly.

"No matter," Llano said quietly. "That didn't entitle them to grab you and drag you into the street."

"When Long John came after me, they . . . taunted him. They called me a—a New Orleans whore."

"You told me you worked in a saloon."

"I did, at first," she said, "and then Madame Toussard sent me . . . upstairs."

"Great God," said Llano, sitting up. "Long John knew about the saloon, but not the . . . other?"

"He knows all of it," Suzanne said. "As I became more comfortable with him, I—I wanted him to know, to accept me in spite of . . . that. I didn't want to live a lie, and I was afraid he'd find out on his own, and end up hating me. It was a burden, fearing that he'd discover my past and drive me away. But tonight, I—I—"

"You're afraid of what it might have done to Long John, hearing it from those men who knew you in New Orleans."

"Oh, God, yes! In private, just him and me, he accepted it, but this . . . this may be the end for us. I could stand even that, but I don't want him to die because of what . . . I did. After what the sheriff said, about not being able to protect Long John, he'd ride into town tomorrow if there was a hundred men gunning for him. His pride—"

"Pride's got nothin' to do with Long John ridin' back

in the morning," said Llano. "You heard what the sheriff said. Gunnin' down some varmints that's needful of it on the prairie is one thing, but in town, where there's law, you have to follow the rules. Sheriff Rankin knows we'll be in some danger, and he warned us. Tomorrow, we'll ride in and take our chances. We may have to shoot our way through an ambush later, and if we do, I promise you I'll be right there beside Long John."

"Then so will I," she said, her voice hardening. "After that . . ."

"After that," Llano said, "you're on your own with Long John. All I can tell you is this: whatever happens tomorrow or on the trail, don't go all weak-kneed and teary-eyed. You got to have Long John's respect, and that purely won't get it."

The sound of a trotting horse ended the conversation, as Long John returned. He dismounted, unsaddled the horse, and spread his blankets. Llano lay there for an uncomfortable few minutes, knowing full well Long John wasn't asleep and probably had no intention of sleeping. Perhaps he felt the need to talk to Suzanne, but he would not with Llano present. Without a word Llano gathered his roll and set off on foot, toward the distant herd. Let Long John and Suzanne think what they liked. There was no moon, and Llano walked on until he could see the shadowy forms of horse and rider, as the nighthawks circled the herd.

"Dupree here," he said softly.

"Been expectin' you," Stoney said, reining up. There was the creak of saddle leather as he shifted position. "Where's your horse?"

"With the remuda," said Llano. "Couldn't sleep. Had Suzanne on one side of me and Long John on the other, both of 'em wide awake. I reckoned they might have some talkin' to do, and was right sure they wouldn't do it with me there. I reckon Long John told you about the fracas in town, and that we got to go back in the morning for an inquest."

"Yeah," Stoney said. "He told me three hombres grabbed Suzanne, and when the shootin' was over, the three of 'em were dead. He told me the four of you had to ride back tomorrow. He's not expectin' the sheriff to charge him with anything, but he thinks the rest of those Harkness teamsters may set up an ambush. But I have a gut feeling Long John's not tellin' it all. Why did those varmints grab Suzanne? This is the frontier, and while a man may be a thief, a killer, and just in general three notches below a yellow coyote, he won't show any disrespect toward a woman. In a saloon or whorehouse, maybe, but not on the street or in some public place."

"Pard," said Llano, "get a grip on your saddle horn. I reckon it's time you knew what Long John didn't tell you. Before Suzanne threw in with Long John, Suzanne spent some time in a New Orleans whorehouse. Them three gents in town remembered her, and aimed to pick up where they left off."

"My God," Stoney said, "and Long John didn't know?"

"He knew, Suzanne says, but havin' it throwed up to him in public might have played hell between him and Suzanne. She's scared out of her wits."

"I don't blame her," said Stoney. "Long John's a prideful man, but far as we're concerned, he's on his own with Suzanne. All we can do is try to keep him alive if the rest of that Harkness bunch comes gunnin' for him."

"Sky Pilot still has to take the wagon into town tomorrow and replace that busted wheel. What do you aim to do about the rest of the outfit ridin' into town? Even if we get in and out without a fight in the morning, them teamsters might discover the rest of our outfit's in town and jump them."

"I doubt Sky Pilot will have any trouble," Stoney said,

"but I'll warn him about hanging around the saloons. As for the others, I don't aim to tell 'em they can't go. Especially Darden. But I'll see that they know of these teamsters and possible trouble. Except for Sky Pilot, I'll see that the rest of them don't ride in until tomorrow night. The Harkness wagons will likely be unloaded tomorrow, and if they are, the drivers will soon have to return to New Orleans. Do you think I ought to send maybe two more riders to town for that inquest?"

"No," said Llano. "Sheriff Rankin carries a scattergun, and I reckon he'll keep order in town. I think if this Harkness bunch tries anything, it'll be after we're out of town. There's nine of them, and they may have friends we don't know about. If they ambush us, two more riders won't be that much help."

"But you'll have only four guns, when you count Suzanne," Stoney said, "and we don't know how she'll work out in a fight. That means if those Harkness men come after you, you're considerably outgunned."

"Outgunned or not," said Llano, "I've never had much enthusiasm for shooting my way out of an ambush. Now if that bunch jumps us in town, we're on our own. But if they aim to waylay us after we ride out, that means that while we're in town, they'll have to get ahead of us. Now we're talkin' about broad daylight, so the horse remuda and the herd won't be a problem. After the four of us ride in, send Malo Coyote and Naked Horse behind us. Have them close enough to town to see anybody ridin' south. Then if the Harkness men ride out to set up an ambush somewhere ahead of us, Malo Coyote and Naked Horse will know where it is. Right after the inquest, we'll start back. If the Harkness bunch is waitin' for us, the rest of you ride to meet us. Cut down on them before they hit us. That'll warn us, and we'll have them boxed in a cross fire."

"By God," said Stoney, "that'll work. If they try anything in town, it'll have to be in the open. Why don't you ease on back and tell Long John? Maybe it'll ease his mind some, and Suzanne's too."

Llano heard voices, and since he was afoot, he coughed to warn them of his approach. They waited in silence until Llano spoke.

"Long John, I've been talkin' to Stoney, and we've figured a way to keep them Harkness drivers from catchin' us in an ambush as we leave town."

"That's bothered me some," said Long John. "Tell me what ye got in mind."

Llano explained it as he had outlined it to Stoney, and Long John laughed.

"By the Eternal," the Cajun said, "that's sound thinkin'. They ain't so likely to start trouble in town, 'cause of the law. But we still got to git Sky Pilot in with the wagon, and the other riders won't like bein' cheated out of a night in town."

"They won't be," said Llano, and again he explained his and Stoney's thinking.

"Then we'll git out'n this yet," Long John said, rolling out of his blankets. "Git some sleep, Llano. I'm goin' to talk with Stoney."

When Long John had gone, Llano said nothing. He fully expected Suzanne to unload on him again, and he didn't have long to wait.

"It's good of you and Stoney to think of these things," she said.

"No more than we should do," Llano said. "We're an outfit. Has Long John said anything about . . ." His voice trailed off, embarrassment overcoming his curiosity.

"No," she said tiredly. "I wish he'd yell, swear, do something. It's like . . . I don't know. Something's gone out of him. He just doesn't seem to care, but I have no right to complain. Laying over in Dallas was my idea, and I've tried to take all the blame for this, but he acts like it just doesn't matter."

"Then maybe it don't," Llano said.

"Oh, hell yes, it does," she said heatedly. "It matters so much that he's refusing to think or talk about it. He's put it all completely out of his mind, and me along with it."

"I reckon it's been hard on him," said Llano. "Give him time."

"I'll give him until St. Louis. If he's as dead to me then as he is tonight, maybe I'll stay in St. Louis. I've heard there's houses along the river. Why, on a good night, I could make thirty dollars."

"Suzanne—"

"Or maybe," and her shrill laughter took on an insane note, "I could find me a cowboy that don't give a damn if the merchandise has been used by bullwhackers, gamblers, and anybody else with the money. What about you, Llano Dupree? Would you have a woman that was born old, been used since she was fourteen, rode hard and then hung out to dry? Who knows, cowboy? Maybe this old heifer's still good for a few rolls in the hay."

Llano grabbed his blankets and lit out for the horse remuda. He only hoped if this crazy female decided to ride the second watch, that Long John would be there to take the edge off her.

The following morning at breakfast Stoney told the riders who had been promised they could ride into town the second night what had happened the day before. He said nothing about Suzanne's past, only that she'd been taken by three men and that the abductors had died in a shootout with Long John, Dent, and Llano.

"So we're expecting trouble from the rest of those Harkness teamsters," said Stoney. "Long John, Llano, Suzanne, and Dent Briano have to be in town this morning for the inquest. We think we can get them out of there unhurt, but if we do, those friends of the dead men may go after those of you who plan to ride in tonight.

I've talked to Long John, and we ain't sayin' you can't go. What we are saying is that you go at your own risk. I'll be ridin' with you, and any man gettin' in gun trouble had damn well better be sure it's justified. To my satisfaction, not yours."

"I'm takin' my turn in town tonight," Bandy Darden said, "and when it comes to pullin' my iron, I ain't askin' nobody's permission."

"You heard me," said Stoney. "Break the law, and you'll do some time in the *calabozo*. Have your fun, but keep it legal."

Harley Logan, Quando Miller, and Deuce Gitano said nothing. If there was trouble, Stoney expected Bandy Darden to be at the bottom of it. Darden went out of his way to be disagreeable and antagonistic, and Stoney never ceased to wonder why the man stayed with the drive. Breakfast was a silent affair, and one who didn't know otherwise would have thought Long John and Suzanne were total strangers. She had dark circles around her eyes, and the big bruise on her left jaw was more hideous than ever. Long John didn't so much as look at her, and when it was time for them to ride to town, it was Llano who saddled her horse. Long John led out, followed by Llano, Suzanne, and Dent Briano. The courthouse, made of brick, seemed the most permanent structure in town. They dallied their reins about the hitch rail and waited for the sheriff. Men arrived in twos and threes, going inside, and Llano suspected some of them were the Harkness teamsters and their friends. Most of them wore Colts thonged to their thighs.

"Mornin'," said Sheriff Rankin as he looked them over. "I reckon the Harkness boys is all in there. One of 'em telegraphed Old Man Harkness in New Orleans, and he's hired a local lawyer. Last night in the dark, I wasn't sure who all them hombres was, but I found out this mornin', and it ain't good news for you. The youngest was Brandon Harkness, son of the owner."

"I reckon that complicates it some," Long John said.

"It does," said Rankin. "I hear this lawyer's been promised a thousand double eagles if he puts your neck in a noose. This may be more of a trial than an inquest. Let's go."

12

The courtroom was packed. Sheriff Rankin led the way to a long table to the right of the room facing the judge's bench. Rankin took a chair, and his four charges followed his lead. On the other side of the courtroom, at a similar table, sat a man in a town suit and boiled white shirt. The lawyer Harkness had hired.

"Everybody stand," the sheriff ordered as the judge entered. When he had seated himself, Rankin allowed the spectators to be seated. He then stepped forward to address the court.

"Judge Meeker, this has to do with them three killings last night, and this inquest is bein' done because the law requires it. I made no arrests because there wasn't any witnesses, and from the evidence and the testimony of Mr. Coons and his outfit, I'm callin' the shootings justified."

There was shouting, cursing, and stomping of feet, and when Judge Meeker finally restored order, he was furious.

"Just once more," he hissed, "and I'll have every last one of you removed from this room and kept out for the duration of this proceeding."

"Judge Meeker," said the man in the town suit as he

approached the bench, "I'm Isaac Ferguson, and I've been retained on behalf of the men who were killed."

"For what purpose, Mr. Ferguson?" Judge Meeker asked. "This is only an inquest, not a trial."

"Because the three men who died were employed by the Harkness Freight Lines in New Orleans," said Ferguson, "and Mr. Harkness is demanding a full-fledged hearing at which he intends to be present."

"Mr. Ferguson," said Judge Meeker, "this court does not take kindly to demands from anybody, including Harkness, your client. Where there is evidence of justifiable shooting, this court is inclined to take the recommendation of Sheriff Rankin."

"With all due respect to Sheriff Rankin," Ferguson said, "I'd like him to recount the evidence from which he's drawn his conclusion."

"Mr. Ferguson," said Judge Meeker, "you've heard my decision, and it stands as rendered. If Sheriff Rankin wishes to reveal any of his findings to you, that's up to him. Sheriff?"

"When Coons and his woman went into the Dallas Merchantile," Sheriff Rankin said, "the three Harkness men was already there, and from what Hennessy the storekeeper said, stinkin' drunk. 'Fore Mr. Coons knowed what was happenin', these three hombres grabbed the woman and dragged her outside. That's where Coons caught up to 'em, and when he demanded they free the woman, they cut down on him. I dug eleven slugs out of the wall where Coons was standin', and I'll be glad to have Mr. Ferguson look at that lead, if it'll make him feel better."

There was laughter in the courtroom, and Judge Meeker did nothing to restrain it. In fact, his honor ducked his head to conceal a trace of a grin. Ferguson flushed with anger, but he wasn't finished.

"This woman, Suzanne, is not legally married to Coons," the lawyer said. "Have you considered the possibility that she may have willingly left the store with the three men? Wouldn't that have angered Coons enough to kill them?"

"Mr. Ferguson," Judge Meeker cut in, "whether or not the abducted woman is married to Coons is totally irrelevant, and you know it. Her marital status, or lack of it, has nothing to do with the fact she was taken against her will. Go on, Sheriff Rankin."

"Mr. Ferguson," the sheriff said, "when Hennessy brought a lantern from the store, I could see this lady, here, had her shirt half ripped off, and somebody had smashed her upside the head. Now unless your eyesight is as rotten as your judgment, take a look at her face. If she was goin' with them varmints willingly, why would they have to beat her black and blue and rip her clothes? That's my evidence, and by God, for any reasonable man, it's enough."

"That concludes this proceeding," said Judge Meeker with a stroke of his gavel.

Long John and his companions waited for the spectators to clear the courtroom. Ferguson the lawyer made it a point to speak to Long John.

"This is not finished," Ferguson said angrily. "Mr. Harkness gets what he wants, one way or another."

"Threats don't scare me, Ferguson," said Long John, "an' if ye got ideas of sendin' a pack of killers after us, I kin save ye the trouble. Ever' man that comes gunnin' fer me, I'll send the varmint back belly down acrost his saddle. Then ye know what I aim to do? I aim to come lookin' fer ye, an' after ye been gut-shot, I aim to git mean an' cause ye some real hurt."

"You—You savage," sputtered Ferguson, "you can't threaten my life. I—I'll have you thrown in jail."

But other men, including Sheriff Rankin, had heard the exchange, and they grinned at the flustered lawyer. Ferguson hurried away, and Rankin turned to Long John.

"It'd be a good idea," said the sheriff, "if you folks rode back to your outfit, and was I you, I'd keep a close watch on the back trail for a ways."

"We aim to," Long John said. "Tomorrow. Tonight they'll be some of our riders in town, but they been told to shy away from gun trouble. They're Texans, though, and I reckon ye know they won't take no water."

The sheriff sighed. "I know the kind."

Long John led the way out of the courthouse, Llano, Dent, and Suzanne following. Silently they mounted and rode out of town. There was no jubilation, and when they met Sky Pilot on the way to town with the wagon, Long John only raised his hand in passing. They reached camp without hearing the ominous rattle of gunfire that would warn them of an impending ambush. If there was to be a fight with the Harkness bunch, it would come somewhere along the trail.

"Good news, I reckon," said Stoney as they dismounted.

"Some," Long John said. "I didn't git much shut-eye last night. I'm gonna pull my saddle an' use it fer a piller fer a while."

Suzanne followed Long John, who didn't seem to notice or care. Dent Briano rode on toward the grazing herd, leaving Llano and Stoney alone.

"Well," said Stoney, "do you aim to talk to me, or do I have to track down Suzanne?"

"Why don't you just track down Suzanne?" Llano grinned. "She give me a rakin' over last night. Says if Long John's still got his back up at the end of the trail, she aims to find work in a St. Louis whorehouse."

"Long John's a prideful man. If she throws that up to him, he's likely to tell her to go ahead, and I'm not sure I'd blame him. He's been through a hell of a lot, bein' forced into a gunfight because of her. I hope she's got the good sense to lay off until Long John sweats this out. Now, damn it, tell me what happened in town."

"Long John told it straight," said Llano. "Some good news, and some not so good. The sheriff and the judge called the shootings justified, but Old Man Harkness ain't satisfied. His lawyer showed up, wanted to turn the inquest into a trial, and then come after us with some threats. One of the three hombres we salted down was Brandon Harkness."

"Then it won't surprise me if Harkness arms the rest of those drivers and sends them after us."

"That's what the sheriff expects," Llano said. "Long John's pride is fierce enough anytime, but it's a powder keg with a short fuse after that mess last night. Once we move out, I reckon one of us had best keep a sharp eye on the back trail."

"Yeah, and there's still tonight. Did Long John happen to tell the sheriff there'll be some of us in town?"

"He did," said Llano with a grim laugh, "and all but dared anybody to try anything."

"They likely won't in town. It'd put them on the bad side of the law, but from here to the Red, I reckon they'll be as much or more a danger than the Comanches."

"You could stay here tonight," Llano said, "and I could ride into town with the rest of the outfit. With Suzanne on the outs with Long John, she's likely to come lookin' for me."

"So you want her on my trail. No thanks, you *asno.*"

The day dragged on, and to everybody's surprise, Sky Pilot returned a good two hours before sundown. More surprising, he was cold sober.

"Well, ye old coot," said Long John, his good humor momentarily returning, "they must of run ye out of town."

"Might as well of," Sky Pilot said, with a surly look at Long John. "That Harkness bunch is still there, oilin' their tonsils at ever' saloon in town. They kept lookin' at me like I was bein' measured for a pine box."

"Ye done the right thing, comin' back quick," said Long John. "Did ye git a new wagon wheel?"

"Why hell yes," Sky Pilot said hotly. "Wasn't that my reason for goin'?"

"Long John," said Stoney, "no reason the riders that's goin' town can't go on, unless you think otherwise."

"Go on," Long John said, "and let's be done with it. We're movin' out in the mornin' at first light."

Stoney rode out, followed by Quando Miller, Deuce Gitano, Bandy Darden, and Harley Logan. Darden dropped back, riding alongside Harley.

"Kid," said Darden, "when we hit town, I'm goin' down in the Mex quarter and git my ashes hauled. You wanta come along?"

Harley looked at him, uncomprehending.

"A whorehouse, kid. Hell's bells, are you so green you ain't never been to a bawdy house?"

"I been," Harley gulped. "Plenty times."

"When it's dark, then, we'll go."

There was little said during the ride to town, but when they reined up on the outskirts, Stoney spoke.

"We'd best be gettin' back to the outfit around midnight. Until then, you're on your own. Just don't forget we're moving out early, at first light. Me, I'm goin' after some town-cooked grub."

"I wouldn't mind gettin' on the outside of some of that myself," Quando Miller said. "I'll go with you."

"The Kid's goin' with me," said Bandy Darden, offering no details. Deuce Gitano said nothing, but when they rode into town, he reined up before the Alamo Saloon.

After supper, without a word to anybody, Long John saddled his horse and rode out to the herd. Close to town and with little danger from Comanches, he began singing a strange Cajun song.

"He sings right well," Dent Briano said, "but the words don't make sense."

"I reckon that don't matter to a cow," said Llano.

"Before it's dark," Suzanne said, "I'm going up to that patch of willows along the creek and take a bath."

"Why don't you go down the creek near where Long John is," said Llano, "and he can watch out for you."

"Because the cows and the horses are down there, and the water will be muddy. You can watch out for me from here."

She stomped away without another word, and Dent Briano looked at Llano, questions in his eyes. Llano said nothing. Only Llano and Stoney shared Suzanne's secret, so the rest of the outfit was unaware of the rift between Suzanne and Long John. It looked, Llano thought, as though he had some kind of surreptitious relationship with Suzanne. Briano finally broke the silence.

"Close as we are to town, I reckon she won't be in no trouble from the Comanches."

Llano had no answer to that, but he didn't need one. Suddenly Long John's Cajun song was lost in an unharmonious drunken wail from a different voice.

"Brangin' in the sheep, brangin' in the sheep. We gonna come rejoicin' . . ."

"He come back sober," said Briano, "but he brought the stuff with him. I hope we don't have to move out in the mornin' without breakfast."

"We won't," Llano said. "Long John—"

He was interrupted by a shriek from the willows where Suzanne had gone.

"That's Suzanne," Llano said. "Come on!"

But Dent Briano stayed where he was, and Llano found himself approaching the willows alone.

"Suzanne," Llano called cautiously, "where are you? Are you decent?"

Only silence greeted him, and there was nothing for it

but to go looking for her, and Llano pushed into the willows, ducking under low-hanging limbs. He came upon her suddenly and froze. She stood on the creek bank stark naked, and when she turned to face him, Llano caught his breath. Whatever she was now, whatever she had been, she was a strikingly beautiful woman.

"I saw a snake in the water," she said weakly.

Suzanne didn't move, but Llano did. He stomped back the way he'd come, furious even before he heard her jeering laughter. Suppose Long John had heard her startled cry and found him there? She had deliberately set him up in a compromising position that might well have provoked a fight with Long John. But Long John's Cajun song continued, clashing mightily with Sky Pilot's caterwauling.

"She saw a snake in the creek," Llano said, leaving it at that. Dent Briano said nothing, but he was no fool.

Stoney and Quando found a place called the Longhorn Cafe, and no sooner had they seated themselves at a table than a big man wearing a lawman's star approached them.

"You gents are part of Coons' outfit, I reckon."

"Yes," said Stoney. "I'm Winters, the trail boss, and this is Quando Miller."

"I'm Rankin," the sheriff said. "Them Harkness teamsters is still here, and most of 'em are drunk. I don't want no more gunplay, gents."

"You're talking to the wrong men, Sheriff," said Stoney. "Those drunken teamsters are the hombres you need to convince."

"I already talked to 'em," Rankin said.

"We'll start no trouble," said Stoney, "but we won't be pushed around. We'll defend ourselves, and that includes pullin' our guns."

A waiter arrived with mugs of hot coffee, and Rankin walked away without another word. Four men at a nearby table had heard the exchange, and one of them kicked back his chair. Stoney had just lifted his mug of coffee when a big bearded man slapped the upraised mug into Stoney's face, spilling the coffee down his shirtfront. The offender stepped back grinning, expecting anything except what he got. Stoney came out of the chair like a wounded cougar, driving his right knee into the big man's groin. The wind went out of him in an agonized grunt, and when his head came down, Stoney struck with the barrel of his Colt. The troublemaker weighed near three hundred pounds, and he hit the floor on his back with a jarring crash. It brought Sheriff Rankin on the run, although he had already left the cafe. He found Stoney Winters and Quando Miller with Colts in their hands, their backs against a wall.

"Sheriff," Stoney said, "the man on the floor wanted trouble, so I obliged him, but I was gentle this time. He only got a knee in his privates and a pistol barrel over his head, but next time I'm likely to lose my temper."

"The big bastard on the floor started it, Sheriff," somebody said.

The unconscious man's three companions still sat at their table. Sheriff Rankin turned to them.

"You Harkness men have been warned," Rankin said. "This big lobo on the floor is goin' in the *juzgado* for thirty days. The next one of you gents that starts a fracas, you're goin' in there with him. Starnes, you and Bascom tote him over to the jail."

Harley Logan followed Bandy Darden to a Mexican cantina, where they whiled away an hour. When Darden decided it was time, he led the way to an old house near the Mexican quarter. Heavy drapes covered the windows and the place seemed deserted, but Darden pounded on the door until it was opened by a buxom woman in a skintight red dress. It was low-cut, and Harley stared at her, for it seemed she was more out of the garment than in it. Darden laughed and Harley flushed with embarrassment.

"What's wrong with him?" the irritated madam demanded. "He never seen a woman before?"

"Likely not so much all at one time," said Darden. "We're needin' some company for a while. What you got?"

"It's early," she said, "but come on in, and I'll fetch a couple of the girls."

She led Harley and Darden into a fancy parlor. Deep-piled maroon carpet matched the floor-to-ceiling drapes. There were two plush sofas, a variety of upholstered chairs, and lamps with frosted globes. The madam quickly returned with two girls. One of them was large, having stuffed herself into a pale pink dress. Her hair was dark, and she might have been partly Mexican. The second girl was thin, her eyes were blue, and her fair hair was the color of new corn silk. She was dressed in white.

"The one in white is Pearl," said the madam, "and the one in pink is Juanita."

"I'll take Juanita," Darden said. "I like a woman with meat on her bones."

Juanita giggled as though it was the funniest thing she'd ever heard. She led Darden down the hall. Harley found himself alone with the madam and the slender girl in white. Quickly she took his arm and led him away, while the madam frowned after them. She opened a door, and Harley followed her into a room that contained a bed, a small dresser, and a single chair. On the wall above the dresser hung a mirror, and on the dresser was a porcelain pitcher and a washbasin. Harley sat down in the chair, nervous and uncertain. Pearl skinned the white dress over her head, and she wore nothing else. Harley Logan looked at her and his eyes dimmed as the years fell away. The girl before him became his sister Elvie. He was thirteen and Elvie just a year older, and after five years he could still hear Elvie's voice.

"I'm scared, Harley. I've done wrong, and I'm goin' to have a child. Pa will kill me when he finds out."

"Don't cry," Harley had said desperately. "We'll run off, come summer."

"Oh, God, Harley," she had cried, lifting her dress, "see how big I am. I don't think I can wait."

Time had run out, and when their pa, old John Henry Logan, had discovered the girl's condition, he had beaten her unmercifully. The child had come too soon and had been born dead. Elvie had lasted barely another day. Harley had stayed for the burying, leaving the same day with only the clothes on his back and one of John Henry Logan's mules. Harley was jolted back to the present by the pleading of the small naked girl who so reminded him of Elvie, his long lost little sister.

"Please, mister," she begged as she tugged at his boots, "I need the money awful bad."

Blindly Harley got to his feet. Taking her hand, he pressed into it a double eagle, all the money he had. His eyes burned and he could barely see the door. He stumbled out into the hall, and when he reached the parlor, he realized the madam was speaking to him.

". . . she didn't treat you right, I'll take a strap to the little fool."

"You lay a hand on her," Harley snarled, "and I'll burn this place down around your ears." He closed the door and stepped into the welcome night.

"I thought you was ready to git your ashes hauled," said Bandy Darden, when he found Harley waiting with the horses. "I reckon you ain't ready."

"No," said Harley to the grinning Darden, "I reckon I ain't."

Deuce Gitano lingered in the Alamo Saloon just long enough to have a look at the men gathered around the poker table. The man he sought—the man he'd sworn to kill—he hadn't seen in five years, but he'd know the bastard when he saw him again. Undaunted, Deuce wandered from saloon to saloon, for this was Kelland's town. Branch Kelland. That might not even be his name, or he might be dead, Deuce thought glumly. Without much hope, he took to searching the Mexican cantinas and the lesser saloons. One of them was a joint without even sawdust on the floor, called the Buffalo. Only three men sat at the poker table, but Deuce Gitano's heart leaped. The man facing the door was Branch Kelland! Older and heavier, but with the same pale albino features and the shock of snowy hair. Deuce ordered whiskey, and leaning against the bar, was but a few feet from the man who had mutilated him, the man he had hunted for five years. Deuce thrust his hand inside his coat, gripping the butt of his Colt. It was time.

"Kelland," he said. "Branch Kelland."

Kelland looked up without changing expression.

"Stand up, Kelland," said Deuce. "I want you looking at me when I kill you."

Slowly the albino got to his feet, his eyes on Deuce. He wore his Colt on his right hip, and he had no doubt his adversary already had his hand on the butt of his weapon. But fate and time had given the albino an edge that neither he nor Deuce Gitano was aware of. The muzzle of the Colt had worn a finger-size hole in Deuce Gitano's coat pocket just large enough to slow the gambler's draw.

"Now, you bastard," said Gitano, "draw."

Deuce ripped his Colt free, but he was slow. Even as his finger tightened on the trigger, he could see fire and smoke roaring from the muzzle of Kelland's Colt. The force of the lead slammed Deuce back against the bar, but there was no pain. His vision dimmed and he slid to the floor, only the bar supporting him. His head tilted forward as though he was studying the blood that had blossomed out on the front of his shirt. But the gambler's quest had ended and his eyes saw nothing, for Deuce Gitano was dead.

"Shootin' down yonder in that rundown saloon," said Bandy Darden. "Let's git down there and see what's happened."

So it was Bandy Darden and Harley Logan who first learned of Deuce Gitano's death, and it was Harley who insisted on tying the gambler's body across his saddle and taking him back to camp.

"Hell, he's dead," said Darden. "Why bother?"

"Because he was one of us," Harley said, "at least for a while. Every man, whatever he is, ought to have somebody that cares enough to see that he's buried fittin' and proper."

13

When darkness came, Dent Briano, Llano, and Suzanne joined Long John in circling the herd. Suzanne had always kept close to Long John at night, but that apparently had changed, for tonight Llano found her trailing him. Dent Briano seemed wary of her, and took Suzanne's place near Long John.

"Why the hell can't you just leave me alone?" Llano growled.

"Who's bothering you? We're both watching the same herd."

"Damn it, you know what I'm talkin' about. Is that how you get your thrills, shuckin' your clothes for different men?"

"Perhaps," she said brazenly. "Working in a whorehouse, I've done it often enough. There was some difference, though. The others appreciated it."

"Suzanne," said Llano, exasperated, "there's a time and place for everything, but there's no time and no place for you and me. Long as I've known you, you've been Long John's woman. Now I ain't about to let you play me against Long John. If you and him split the blanket, I don't aim to have a hand in it."

"That's your way of saying you don't want a woman that's been used."

"By God," he said wearily, "you just don't know when to quit, do you? It's my way of sayin' I don't want a flighty female that'd throw me down at the drop of a hat. A woman that'd risk gettin' me killed to satisfy a whim. Now is that plain enough?"

"No," she said sulkily. "How did I risk getting you killed? I've never had a man expire from looking at me yet."

"You damn little fool!" Llano exploded. "If Long John had showed up the same time I did, you reckon there wouldn't have been some powder burnt?"

To his dismay, she laughed. "Long John was too far away to hear me. You weren't."

"Neither was Dent Briano. Suppose he'd been with me?"

"What's one more," she said, "when you're dealing in used goods? Maybe he'd have been more interested in me than you are."

"You've lived with Long John eight years," Llano said in disgust. "How the hell can you shed all that and fall back to bein' a whore in just a day?"

"Why not," she said, "when I'm treated like one everywhere I go?"

"Long John hasn't treated you like one, has he?"

"Not until last night," she said bitterly. "It wasn't that hard, forgetting what I was ten years ago. But last night was different. It's like nothing has changed. Now, damn it, I have to start over, if I can, and I'm not sure I want to. When I was Suzy the whore, that was all I had to be. I've wasted ten years being the respectable Suzanne, only to have it all go to hell in one night. What's the use?"

"I don't know," said Llano. "All I know is, I don't want to end up in a fight with Long John because of you."

"You didn't mind seeing me then," she said, her boldness returning. "You just don't want Long John to know."

Exasperated, at a loss for words, he said nothing. Taking his silence for agreement, she laughed.

An hour before midnight Harley Logan and Bandy Darden rode in leading Deuce Gitano's horse. The gambler's blanket-wrapped body had been lashed across the saddle.

"God A'mighty," Long John shouted, "how'd it happen? Was it them damn Harkness men?"

"No," said Harley.

"He run across some hombre he knowed," Darden said, "and they had a shootout. Old Deuce come in second."

They were all in a somber mood when Stoney and Quando rode in less than an hour later.

"We heard there'd been a shooting," Stoney said, "and all we could learn was that the Harkness bunch wasn't involved. Quando and me had a fracas with one of 'em, and the sheriff threatened to jail any of them that caused any more trouble. I think Deuce has been on a manhunt, and it ended tonight. He was a good man. Too good to die at the end of a vengeance trail."

Despite Long John's intentions, the drive didn't get under way at first light. With shovels from the wagon, the riders took turns digging a proper grave for Deuce Gitano. They wrapped the gambler in his blankets and laid him to rest among the willows that lined the creek. From his saddlebag Stoney took a Bible, and from it read the Twenty-third Psalm. They filled the grave, piling the dirt high and packing it, to discourage wolves and coyotes. The sun was an hour high when the herd again took the trail.

"Move 'em out!" Stoney shouted. He found that Long John had again taken Llano's usual position at right flank, and that Llano was riding drag with Suzanne. Deuce Gitano having been killed, it had been a somber night, with little talk. Tonight, Stoney would talk to Llano. He was spending entirely too much time with Suzanne, and Stoney feared it might lead to big trouble with Long John. He rode back to talk to the Cajun before scouting ahead.

"We can't be far from the east fork of the Trinity," said Long John. "Wisht we could git there today. Sooner we git past this town an' headed north, the better I'll like it. I still think that Harkness bunch will foller us."

"Or get in front of us," Stoney said. "As I ride ahead, I'll keep them in mind."

Stoney doubted they were more than twenty miles west of the Trinity. With the herd well-rested, and after two days of good graze and water, they should reach the Trinity without difficulty. Slightly east of Dallas, Stoney remembered a long finger of water—a lake, or series of them—stretching for miles to the north. It would be a source of water for several days. Stoney reached the headwaters of the Trinity even sooner than he had expected, so it wasn't even twenty miles. Somewhere to the east of Dallas there had to be a wagon road to accommodate the freight wagons that traveled regularly from New Orleans to Dallas. Stoney rode north another ten miles until he reached the rutted, well-defined road. He found evidence of wagons bound for Dallas, but no sign that any had recently departed. The Harkness bunch had still been in town last night, so it was still too early in the day for them to have traveled this far. If they were coming by wagon, bound for New Orleans. Something bothered Stoney, and his mind wouldn't leave it alone. Old Man Harkness had lost a son, and had proven his vindictiveness by telegraphing Dallas and retaining a lawyer. The men Stoney and Quando had faced at the cafe in town had seemed a brutal lot. It wasn't hard to imagine them following orders from New Orleans, ambushing the trail drive once it was far from Dallas and the law. Stoney rode back to meet the herd. The attack, if there was one, wouldn't come tonight, and it was for tomorrow and tomorrow night that Stoney began making plans.

"Draw on yer own feelings," Long John said, when Stoney spoke of his suspicions. "I think ye'd do well, countin' on trouble from that Harkness bunch. They went to a hell of a lot of trouble to jist let us go."

The drive was going well. Harley Logan had dropped back and was riding drag with Llano and Suzanne. Stoney moved ahead to the point position. Tonight would be soon enough to talk to Llano. The riders kept the herd moving, and they reached the Trinity without mishap. In places the river was narrow and shallow, so there would be no hazardous crossing.

"Stoney," said Suzanne during supper, "I want to change to the second watch."

Since the start of the drive, it had been understood that Suzanne had the first watch, with Long John. Now all eyes were on Long John, but he said nothing, and Stoney took his silence for approval.

"Makes no difference to me," Stoney said, "but with Deuce gone, there's only eight of us. Somebody from the second watch will have to change to the first. Any volunteers?"

"I'll swap," said Harley. He had felt uncomfortable around Bandy Darden since their visit to the bawdy house. Changing to the first watch, he would have Long John, Llano, and Dent Briano for his companions.

"Thanks, pard," Llano said, when Stoney spoke to him after supper. "I been thinking of goin' to the second watch myself, just to get away from that woman."

"That bad, huh?"

"That bad," said Llano. "I could tell you some things about her, but I reckon you'll find out on your own. But I will tell you this. She ain't expectin' to get back with Long John, and she ain't above gettin' her claws into somebody else. Be on your guard."

When Stoney rolled out for the second watch, the sky was awash with stars, and with light from an ascending moon, he saddled his horse without difficulty. When Stoney went to awaken Suzanne, he found her already awake, and Bandy Darden was saddling her horse. If what the girl had told Llano meant anything, she hated Darden. Stoney decided to keep an eye on her for a while, and he did, but all seemed well. He had found Quando Miller an easygoing rider who liked to talk, and they paused for some conversation, discussing last night's trouble in town. Seeing them thus engaged, Suzanne dismounted, went behind some bushes and dropped her Levi's. No sooner had she done so than she heard a rustling.

"Who's there?" she hissed.

Darden laughed softly. "The gent that saddled your horse," he said.

"Damn you," she said, "leave me alone. I—I'll call Long John."

"I reckon you won't," he said. "Not after you just changed watches to git away from him. Besides, I seen you that night in the creek, but Coons is so damn sudden with a Colt, I couldn't hang around."

"What do you want of me?" she asked.

"Just a better look without riskin' bein' shot," he said. "Unbutton the shirt."

She hated the man, yet she unbuttoned the shirt and stood there facing him, her Levi's still around her ankles. She heard him catch his breath, and it was a long moment before he spoke again.

"I reckon that's enough. For now. Go ahead and do whatever you was about to do."

But Suzanne was suddenly afraid as she pondered the consequences of what she had done. With trembling fingers she buttoned the shirt, hauled up her Levi's and went to find her horse. When she reached it, Stoney Winters was standing beside it.

"When you dismount and leave your horse," he said, "you should tell one of the other riders."

"I'm not in the habit of telling others when I have to go to the bushes," she snapped.

"On a trail drive, when there's a possibility of Indian trouble, you'd better get in the habit, so there'll be somebody to go lookin' for you when you don't come back."

"I'll do better than that," she said sarcastically. "Next time I have to go, I'll find you and take you with me."

"You do that," he said just as sarcastically. "Better me than a certain other hombre that comes to mind."

With that he was gone, leaving her wondering how much he had seen or heard. Then her anxiety changed to fury, and she hated him for talking down to her as though he were her daddy. She decided she no longer cared if Bandy Darden came after her again. Damn them, she'd show them all, Long John Coons especially.

June 15, 1858. On the Trinity.

"Move 'em out!" Stoney shouted.

Once the herd was moving, he rode back to talk to Long John. "We'll soon be comin' to a string of lakes north of here," Stoney said. "They're long, stretchin' north, so water won't be a problem for a couple of days."

"No matter," said Long John. "We got these critters of a mind to stretch their legs, an' later on they might have to, so I ain't slowin' 'em down."

"Maybe ten miles north of here," Stoney said, "we'll cross that wagon road the freighters take to and from Dallas. I'm ridin' ahead to have a look at that road. If the Harkness bunch has pulled out, I want to know it. If there's departing wagon tracks, I aim to trail 'em until

I'm sure they haven't doubled back with an ambush on their minds."

"What if they ain't no new tracks? That don't mean we're free of 'em."

"No," said Stoney, "it could mean they've left the wagons in town and ridden north, planning to hit us after we've relaxed our vigilance. If I find no wagon tracks, I'll ride on and circle back to the northwest. Then if I cross a trail that looks suspicious, maybe we'll cut this day's drive short and some of us will follow that trail. If it's the hombres we're expectin', they won't be lookin' for us to show up after dark with our guns ready."

"Son," Long John said, "I purely like the way you think ahead. Ride on, an' we'll foller whatever plan ye decide on when ye git back."

Stoney rode out, appreciating Long John's confidence in him, but unsure of the Cajun's future insofar as the flighty Suzanne was concerned. Never had he been on a trail drive that had included a woman, and when this one was finally done, he'd think long and hard before embarking on another. But at the start they'd had Long John to keep Suzanne in line, and how could they have known that was going to change? Now Long John didn't seem to care a damn what she did, and Suzanne seemed to have taken that as a challenge to try everybody's patience to the limit. While Stoney was less than half Long John's age, the Cajun had allowed all the slack any trail boss could ask or expect. Soon Stoney would have to put Long John to the test. If the Cajun refused to keep Suzanne on a tight rein, Stoney intended to, with or without Long John's blessing.

Reaching the wagon road, Stoney felt better when he found the recent tracks of a dozen mule-drawn wagons. With three drivers dead and another in jail, Old Man Harkness had been forced to hire more men. Stoney rode east, following the road. This train would stop somewhere for the night, and as Stoney thought about it, he decided that if there was to be an ambush, the men would likely ride back after they'd stopped for the day. Naturally they'd take to the woods rather than following the road, so that if questions were ever raised, there would be only the tracks of the eastbound mules and wagons. Stoney rode back to meet the herd, a plan coming together in his mind. He wasted no time in outlining it to Long John.

"I think," said Stoney, "instead of us riding after them, hoping to take them by surprise, we'll choose a good defensive position and let them come after us. If they do, then we'll know what their intentions are, and we can retaliate as we see fit. Before sundown we'll choose our position. Then I'll send Malo Coyote and Naked Horse far enough north to warn us well in advance, if the Harkness men coming looking for us. I've found us a place along the lakeshore where a rock abutment rises up like a fortress for half a mile. To the south there's easy access to the water and plenty of graze, so that's where we'll bed down the herd and the horse remuda. If Malo Coyote and Naked Horse bring word we're about to have visitors, we'll hightail it to our position and be ready to welcome them."

"Short drive t'day, then," Long John said, "but it'll give us plenty of time to bed down the herd and the horses, and git supper outta the way 'fore dark. This'll be our chance to git that Harkness bunch offa our tails fer good."

"We don't know for sure they're comin'," said Stoney, "but if they do, I aim for us to be ready. If they don't show tonight, we may be rid of them, because each passing day will put more distance between us and them."

Stoney rode ahead, catching up to the horse remuda. He told Malo Coyote and Naked Horse only that he had chosen a campsite. As the time drew near to prepare for the expected ambush, he would tell the Indian duo what he wished of them. Stoney rode with the Cherokee wranglers until they reached the area where the horses and longhorns would be bedded down.

"We'll want supper well before dark," Stoney said, when Sky Pilot arrived with the wagon. "Soon as you can, douse the fire."

Sky Pilot eyed him pityingly and said nothing. When the herd arrived, the longhorns were watered and settled on the graze without difficulty. Now it was time to get the outfit together and tell them of the possible fight.

"Tonight," said Stoney, "I'm lookin' for the Harkness bunch to come after us. A mile or so north of here, there's a rock abutment strung out along the east shore of the lake. If riders come, it's natural for them to ride alongside the lake, and we'll take our stand behind the rock. I'm sending Malo Coyote and Naked Horse far enough north to warn us in plenty of time."

The afternoon dragged, and it was the first real opportunity for Llano and Stoney to talk since Stoney had ridden back from Dallas.

Llano grinned. "How do you like havin' Suzanne on your watch?"

"How do you reckon? She's started cozyin' up to Bandy Darden, now that she's on the outs with Long John and you won't have her."

"When we hired on with this outfit, there wasn't anything said about us ridin' herd on Long John's headstrong female."

"No," Stoney said, "and that fits in with a decision I made last night. Suzanne's on the prod, and she's hellbent on striking back at Long John. If he don't give a damn what she does, why should we?"

"You takin' her along if we have to fight them bullwhackers?"

"Damn right," said Stoney. "Why try to protect her like she's a lady, when she's determined to conduct herself like a New Orleans whore? I aim to leave only Malo

Coyote and Naked Horse with the horse remuda and the longhorns. Even with Suzanne, there'll be only eight of us, and Harkness has hired some more men. There was tracks of a dozen wagons."

The sun was down and a rosy glow on the western horizon was about to be swallowed by approaching darkness. Naked Horse and Malo Coyote rode in, and they didn't bother dismounting. Naked Horse made sign, spreading the fingers of both hands, then extending two fingers on his right hand.

"Them come," Naked Horse said. With that, he and Malo Coyote rode away toward the horse remuda.

"Let's ride," said Stoney.

Concealing their horses to the south of their position of defense, the outfit continued on foot. Stoney positioned Suzanne between himself and Llano, not for her protection, but to prevent her from doing something foolish.

"Hold your fire," Stoney cautioned. "Let me challenge them. There'll be plenty of light, and we'll be shooting from cover. If they ignore me, then that'll be your call to return their fire and shoot to kill. Remember, we don't fire until they fire on us, or until we're sure they don't aim to back off. Follow my lead."

From the attackers' standpoint, it was a poor time and place. Stoney could hear them coming long before they were close enough to be challenged. When they were finally visible, they came two abreast, riding mules.

"That's far enough," Stoney shouted. "We know who you are and why you're here. You're covered. Drop your weapons and ride back the way you came."

"And if we don't?"

"Then you'll die here," Stoney said. "The choice is yours."

"You got the drop," somebody snarled, "but damn you, this ain't over."

"I think it is," Stoney said. "Next time, if there is one,

you'll get no warning. We'll drop you on sight. Now shuck your guns and ride."

"We ain't leavin' our guns!".

"After the count of three," said Stoney, "you'll be shot dead. One . . ."

"Hold your fire, dammit. We're droppin' 'em."

Slowly, reluctantly, they parted with their weapons. Then, without a word, they rode back the way they had come.

"By God," Bandy Darden said angrily, "we could of kilt 'em ever' damn one. Winters, what ails you?"

"I don't believe in cold-blooded murder," said Stoney, "when there's no call for it. Those men are being paid by old Harkness in New Orleans. Now if they make the mistake of coming after us again, they die. But not tonight. Now let's gather up those guns and get back to the herd."

When the second watch began, Stoney virtually ignored Suzanne, and she didn't know whether to be elated or angry. He seemed to have washed his hands of her, and she decided she didn't like that. She trotted her horse around the herd and caught up to him.

"Last night," she taunted, "it bothered you that the Comanches might find me with my britches down and carry me off. Tonight you don't seem to care."

"Why should I?" Stoney said. "I'd have fought for you to the death as long as you at least *acted* like a lady, but I've never felt that strong about New Orleans whores."

"God, that's a relief," she said, with all the sarcasm she could muster. "I've been scared to death you were going to spank me."

"I wouldn't dirty my hands on you," Stoney said. "Llano and me decided that for the rest of this drive, we're goin' to do what we was hired to do, which is punch cows. Now if you hanker to nuzzle up to Bandy Darden, you just go right ahead. It'll serve the little varmint right."

"Maybe I will," she snarled. "At least he's interested in me."

"That's not surprising," said Stoney. "When he hit town, the first place he went was a whorehouse. Birds of a feather flock together, and as long as you don't care a damn what you roost with, why should I?"

Suzanne reined up her horse and dismounted, but Stoney rode on, ignoring her. Bandy Darden had been behind them, and seeing her dismount, he trotted his horse and caught up.

"Well," he said, "the boy segundo ain't interested, but I am."

"Leave me alone," she said. "Do you think I'm some . . . town whore, to be had for the asking?"

"I didn't at first, but you been makin' all the moves, 'specially since the big Cajun shucked you out of his blankets. I seen the goods twice, so I reckon some kinda offer's been made."

Suzanne tried to mount her horse, but Darden reached down and caught her by the collar of her shirt. Suzanne fought, and Darden, off balance, came out of the saddle. He grunted when Suzanne kneed him in the groin, and free of him, she grabbed the Colt from the waistband of her Levi's. Sight of the pistol overcame Darden's misery and he seized Suzanne's arm as she tried to bring the Colt to bear. The weapon roared once, twice, blasting into the midnight sky. Frightened, Darden's horse lit out, followed by Suzanne's, the pair of them headed for the drowsing herd. The nickering of the horses and the thud of hoofbeats brought the longhorns to their feet, and within seconds the herd was off and running. While the gunshots had awakened the camp, only Stoney and Quando were in a position to try and head the thundering, bawling longhorns. They ran south, headlong into the horse remuda, and despite the efforts of Naked Horse and Malo Coyote, the horse remuda was sucked into the stampede. Long John stomped into his boots and stalked through the night. The first one of the outfit he encountered was Bandy Darden, and he got the full force of Long John's fury.

"Ye was out here to watch the herd," Long John roared. "Them brutes is scattered all over hell an' half of Texas, an' here ye are stumblin' around without yer horse. Who'n hell fired them shots? I'll kill the son of—"

"I dunno," Darden cut in desperately. "I was comin' to see, when my hoss bucked me off."

Long John went on, his fury unabated, and Llano caught up to him. The thunder of the stampede had died away, and at first there was only silence. Then there was the shuffle of footsteps and low moans, punctuated with sobs. Suzanne stumbled toward them like a lost soul, still clutching the Colt. It was all the answer Long John needed as to who had fired the fateful shots. He snatched the pistol from Suzanne and then he hit her. Struck under the left ear, the blow lifted her off her feet and then dropped her in a small crumpled heap, but Long John wasn't finished with her. He lifted her by the collar of her shirt and was about to hit her again when he suddenly froze. Llano had drawn and cocked his Colt, and when he spoke, it was with a coldness Long John had never heard from the young rider.

"Leave her be, Long John. Whatever fool thing she's done, she's still a woman."

Long John let go of the shirt and stood there breathing hard. Suzanne lay unmoving, and the arrival of Stoney and Quando seemed to restore some sanity to Long John. He actually seemed surprised to find Llano holding a Colt on him, but no more so than Stoney and Quando.

"We couldn't head 'em," Stoney said. "Did you find out who was firing, and why?"

"Yeah," said Long John mildly. "We know who, but not why." With that, he walked away.

With Long John out of the picture, Llano holstered his Colt, nodding to the crumpled, unmoving Suzanne.

"Good God," Stoney cried, swinging out of the saddle, "did she get throwed and stomped?"

"Worse'n that," Llano said. "Long John found her with a Colt in her hand and walloped hell out of her. He just went stomp-down crazy, and if I hadn't pulled a gun on him, he'd have killed her."

"Foolish move on his part," said Stoney. "It won't undo the stampede. Tomorrow we'll round 'em up again. For now, I reckon we'd better see what can be done for Suzanne."

Stoney mounted his horse and Llano lifted the unconscious girl up to him. Back in camp they bathed her face in cold water until she opened her eyes. She looked around as though seeking Long John, and when she didn't see him, she spoke to the rest of them.

"I fired the shots," she said. "I'm sorry. I—I thought I heard something. . . ."

In the darkness Bandy Darden sighed with relief, licking his thin lips.

14

"Roll in your blankets and get what sleep you can," Stoney said. "We'll start the gather at first light."

Nobody knew where Long John was, and it seemed a poor time to be asking questions, so nobody did. Suzanne sought her blankets and seemed to be avoiding everybody. Llano and Stoney spread their rolls far enough away from the others so they could talk without being overheard.

"I couldn't help feelin' a mite sorry for Suzanne," Llano said. "She's got to be hurtin', Long John turning against her so sudden. Makes me wonder if she ain't throwin' herself at everybody else in the hope that she'll make Long John jealous enough to turn him around."

"Was I you," said Stoney, "I'd not lay awake trying to figure her out. Long John ain't the kind to fall for any female tricks. You did the right thing tonight, stepping in and stopping him before he killed her, but I'd let it go at that."

Breakfast was a hurried affair. Since Bandy Darden and Suzanne had lost their horses in the stampede, they were left behind until their mounts—still saddled—could be found. Suzanne tried to avoid Darden, but found it impossible.

"You saved my bacon last night," he said. "I'm owin' you."

"Then leave me alone," said Suzanne shortly, "and we'll call it even."

"Can't do that," Darden said, grinning. "Besides, it ain't what you want. After old daddy Long John slugged you last night, you're ready for somebody to jump his claim, and I'm ready."

Suzanne said nothing, disturbed that he'd come so close to the truth. She'd lain awake most of the night, her head aching, vowing to hurt Long John Coons in as many ways as she could devise. Now, with the devious Bandy Darden a willing accomplice, the whole idea seemed repulsive. The many months with Long John on the Rio Colorado were strong on her mind. Was it now too late to recapture what she'd lost, to finish this drive, to return with Long John to the only home she'd ever known? Savagely she turned on Darden, and her response wiped the grin off his face.

"I can't fault Long John if he's done with me forever, but that don't mean I'm ready to slither down to your level. You've had your look, but what you've seen don't mean that's what you're going to get."

With that, she walked away, retreating to the wagon, leaving Sky Pilot wondering what was going on. Harley Logan brought her horse and she rode away to join the gather. The first rider she encountered was Long John, and it took all her courage to approach him. His surprise was evident, but he said nothing.

"Long John," Suzanne said, "I'm sorry about last night. The stampede was my fault, and I promise you it won't happen again. Now may I have my pistol? I may be needing it."

Long John still had the Colt under his belt. He removed it, and without a word handed it to her butt first.

"Thank you," she said. She slipped the Colt's muzzle beneath her waistband and rode away. Suzanne wanted to look back, but she dared not. Long John's pale blue eyes softened just a little, and almost imperceptibly the hard lines around his mouth relaxed. It was a start.

The nearest source of water was the series of lakes that stretched to the north, and with the dawn, much of the herd had bunched near the water.

"Not all that bad," Llano said as they went about gathering the herd.

"No," Stoney agreed. "It's not like having them stampede because they're thirsty, or running before a bad storm, with thunder and lightning. Today will be a short drive, but it won't be a day lost. Long as we're traveling north along this lakeshore, water won't be a problem. When we've rounded 'em up and are ready to move out, I'll ride ahead ten miles. I want to be sure those Harkness men rode on back to their wagons."

"They left their guns with us," said Llano. "Not much else they could do."

"They might have had other guns in their wagons," Stoney said, "or they could have sent a couple of men back to Dallas and rearmed themselves. I reckon I'll track down Long John and find out what kind of mood he's in."

"I'll go with you," said Llano. "After pullin' a Colt on him last night, I'd better find out how he's feelin' toward me."

Suzanne was working with Harley Logan, and once they were past, Llano turned to Stoney and laughed. "You saw the gun," Llano said.

"I saw it," said Stoney, "and that's the first promisin' sign since all hell busted loose in Dallas. Suzanne's got her Colt back, and that means she or Long John's decided to bend a little."

"Stampede wasn't all that bad," Long John said, flashing them his lopsided grin. "We'll have these critters on the move 'fore the sun's noon high."

"Once they're movin'," said Stoney, "I aim to ride ten

miles north. I want to be sure those Harkness drivers don't get their hands on some more guns and decide to do somethin' foolish."

"Damn good idee," Long John said. "I reckon we'll have to fight 'fore we git to Missouri, but let's stave it off as long as we kin."

Stoney rode north following the trail of the Harkness men, and when he reached the rutted wagon road, he was elated to find that the dozen riders had turned eastward. He followed the road a ways to be sure. Their keeping to the road was evidence enough they wouldn't be returning, for they were no longer concerned with concealing their tracks. Thus reassured, Stoney rode back to meet the trail drive. Getting a late start, they had covered less than ten miles when Stoney called a halt. Tomorrow he would ride at least twenty miles ahead, scouting.

"Mighty quiet," Llano said when he awakened Stoney for the second watch. "Ain't heard a coyote all night. But you got Suzanne; you won't have a chance to listen to the coyotes."

"Don't remind me," said Stoney.

But to Stoney's surprise, Suzanne was subdued and quiet. She rode behind him, saying nothing. After an hour of silence Stoney reined up and waited until she was alongside him.

"I see you have your Colt again," he said, "so I reckon you and Long John have talked."

"I talked," she said, "and he listened. I asked for the pistol and he gave it to me."

"Do us all a big favor," said Stoney. "Next time you decide to shoot Bandy Darden, get him away from the herd."

"How do you know—"

"Because I heard the horses—two horses—galloping away after you fired the shots. Darden told Long John and Llano his horse bucked him off. The truth is, your horse *and* Darden's ran because they were spooked by the shots, and neither of you were in the saddle."

"I . . . it's not what you think," she said.

"I reckon it don't much matter what I think," Stoney said, "but I'm fair to middlin' sure you had a damn good reason for pullin' that Colt, and even though you caused a stampede, I want you to know I'm not faultin' you for pullin' the iron."

"You—You're not?"

"No," said Stoney. "You carry a gun to protect yourself, and I reckon that's what you had in mind. It was just a bad time and place, far as the trail drive is concerned."

"Oh, God," she cried, "I made a fool of myself. Darden didn't do . . . anything, but he—he thought he could. But what you said about him going to the whorehouse . . . I . . . it got to me. I had dismounted, and he rode up. When I tried to mount my horse, to get away from him, he grabbed my shirt. Then I pulled the pistol, he came out of the saddle, and we fought over it. The shots scared his horse and mine, and that's why they ran away. And that's the truth."

"I believe you," Stoney said, "but you didn't have to tell me."

"I know, but I feel better for it. Last night I couldn't sleep, thinking of the end of this drive, wondering what would become of me."

"Llano said you were talkin' about finding yourself a place in one of the houses in St. Louis."

"I was a fool," said Suzanne. "I'd rather be dead than go back to that."

"I know," Stoney said. "That affair in Dallas hit Long John pretty hard, and he backed away from you. So you took to feelin' sorry for yourself, and you started thinkin' of ways to get back at Long John."

"I was selfish. Long John had more reason to be hurt than I did. The closer Bandy Darden got to me, the more I saw myself for what I—I used to be, and I knew I could never go back to that. Lord God, I'd go back to that ranch on the Colorado if all I could ever be to Long John is a cook and somebody to wash his clothes. He kept me even after he knew what I'd been. It's the only home I've ever had. If he knew the things I've said, what I've done . . ."

"He won't," said Stoney, "unless he hears it from you. Like I told you, Llano and me hired on to punch cows. We don't see or hear a thing that ain't associated with a cow or cayuse."

He said no more, waiting until her sniffles had subsided. When she spoke, it was with a plea that touched him, for it was honest.

"Do you think he—Long John—will ever want me again? What more can I do?"

"Leave him be," Stoney said. "He's had to wrassle with them three men grabbin' you in public. Don't go makin' it any harder on him. Try to be like you've always been, and the time will come when he'll be doing what you're doin' now. He'll think of the days there on the Rio Colorado, and forget the rest."

"I'm sure Llano hates me," said Suzanne. "Will you tell him I'm—I'm sorry for the terrible things I said and . . . for what I did?"

"No," said Stoney. "Tell him yourself."

June 17, 1858. On the trail north.

"One more day," Stoney said, "and we'll be leavin' this handy chain of lakes behind. From there, I'd say we're less than fifty miles south of the Red, and Indian Territory."

"I'm glad ye been this way b'fore," said Long John. "I been west all the way to Californy, an' south into Old Mexico, but never north of the Red."

"You been east of New Orleans, I reckon," Quando Miller said.

"Naw," Long John said. "What'n hell fer? They ain't nothin' east of New Orleans. Stoney, how we fixed fer water betwixt here an' the Red?"

"We cross the Sulphur River twice," said Stoney. "It forks maybe eighty miles east of Dallas. We'll cross the south fork maybe forty miles south of the Red, and the north fork not quite twenty miles beyond."

"More of them damn twenty-mile drives," Bandy Darden said. "For a pair of hombres that's supposed to know this country, Winters, you and Dupree don't show me nothin'."

"There'll be creeks and springs we don't know about," said Llano. "We're countin' on the Sulphur because we *know* it's there, and because it won't be dry. It's always a good idea, Darden, to count only on water you know is there. Then if you find some in between you didn't know about, count your blessings."

"We got water fer three days, then," Long John said, "and that'll git us to Indian Territory."

"Yes," said Stoney, "but I'll be scouting ahead. There's renegades who hole up in the territory, making it their business to ride across the Red to plunder and kill. They'd murder us all for the horse remuda. The longhorns will make it twice as tempting."

June 19, 1858. At the south fork of the Sulphur.

It was an easy drive along the lake's eastern shore, but the following day was everything Bandy Darden had predicted. They pushed the herd until dark, the longhorns thirsty and cantankerous, and the last three or four miles was a cowboy's idea of hell. Stoney had half the outfit at drag, for the longhorns remembered the good graze and water behind them, along the lakeshore. Most of them were hell-bent on returning to it.

"I dunno which is worse," Long John said. "Havin' 'em hittin' the back trail fer the water they had last night, er gittin' a whiff of what's ahead an' stampedin' to it."

"It's always worse when they light out down that back trail, headin' for yesterday's camp," said Dent Briano. "When they smell water ahead and go for it, at least they're headed in the right direction."

Sky Pilot doused the fire as soon as he could, for they had no idea what dangers lay ahead.

"Stoney," Suzanne said, "I think I'd like to change back to first watch."

"It's all right with me," said Stoney, "but it might not suit Harley."

"I'll swap," Harley said, and was rewarded with a grateful look from Suzanne.

The following morning, Stoney rode out at first light. This day's drive, if they made it, would take them to the north fork of the Sulphur. While there might be water in between, they couldn't count on that. Another twenty-mile drive would take them within a day of the Red. Stoney rode all the way to the north fork of the Sulphur without finding suitable water. Llano again rode his position at right flank, and Long John was at drag with Suzanne. While the two of them still hadn't fully returned to their former comfortable relationship, there were signs of progress. Llano breathed a sigh of relief, but it was short-lived. Suddenly a Texas jack bounded across in front of the herd, spooking the lead steers. They ran to the east, Llano trying to head them, when a horn raked the flank of his horse. The animal screamed and began to buck. The only other rider near enough to have headed the herd was Bandy Darden, and his efforts left something to be desired. At least Llano thought so. When Stoney returned to the trail drive, there was no herd. Just the wagon and the horse remuda, which had been far enough ahead of the longhorns that the horses hadn't been involved in the stampede.

"Cow gone," said Malo Coyote needlessly.

Stoney rode eastward, the stampede's passing still evident by a pall of dust that hung in the air. He met Suzanne afoot, leading her limping horse.

"Something scared the leaders," she said, "and Llano couldn't get ahead of them. Nobody else was near enough except Darden, and I don't think he tried very hard."

Stoney rode on, unsure as to what he must do about Bandy Darden. Anything he said or did might result in Darden provoking a fight with Long John by telling him lies involving Suzanne. Stoney didn't believe anything had taken place between Suzanne and Darden, but it might set off a new brushfire of doubt in Long John's mind. After he'd ridden several miles, Stoney began seeing grazing longhorns. Ahead of him there was a dust cloud, and more of the longhorns began emerging from it. Behind them rode Llano, Long John, and Bandy Darden.

"No water between here and the north fork of the Sulphur," Stoney said. "From the looks of it, I think we'll be stuck in dry camp tonight."

"We'll do the best we kin," said Long John. "If'n we don't make it to the north fork, then dry camp it is. When them brutes take a notion to run an' ye can't head 'em, then all ye kin do is beat the bushes an' round 'em up again."

It was the logical way of looking at the situation, although Long John was thoroughly disgusted. Stoney rode on, eventually joining Dent Briano, Quando Miller, and Harley Logan. The trick was to follow the path of the stampede until the longhorns began to thin out. Then, while driving the bunch that was farthest away, the riders added to it as they returned to the main herd.

"Damn it," Long John said when they'd rounded up every cow in sight, "a hunnert of 'em is still missin'. They ain't no river brakes fer 'em to hide in. Wher' kin they be?"

"That many," said Stoney, "they'd almost have to have followed some old bull. For sure they didn't follow the stampede until it petered out. Llano, Quando, and Dent, come with me. We'll find 'em."

The running herd cut a wide swath, and it had been easy to miss the bunch that had veered away. Eventually they found where the missing longhorns had quit the bunch and had headed south.

"They won't have run far on their own," Llano said.

"I don't think they're on their own," said Stoney. "I reckon we've been so busy lookin' at cow tracks, we've overlooked the obvious."

"It's kind of brushy through here," Quando Miller said, "but when there's a hundred cows been through, you just kind of know it. You don't have to see every track, or even any tracks."

"That's true," Stoney said, "but wait'll we get clear of these last years' leaves. There's a sandy slough up ahead."

"Them brutes was pickin' 'em up and layin' 'em down," said Dent Briano when they reached the sandy arroyo. "Look at the length of them strides."

"That's what I mean," Stoney said. "They wouldn't be runnin' this hard on their own. Now you can see the horse tracks. Three riders. Let's ride 'em down."

The trail continued south for two miles and then turned sharply eastward.

"Damn fool thing to do," said Llano. "They know we won't lose a hundred head and not go lookin' for 'em. This is just plain old-fashioned rustling."

"We're near enough to Indian Territory," Stoney said,

"for this to be the work of a gang. These three may have been stalking us, taking our measure. When the herd decided to run, these varmints saw a chance to cut out a hundred head. They may have a camp to the east of here. If they get close enough to that camp before we catch up to them, some of the gang could ride out, flank us and set up an ambush."

"Then we got to overtake 'em before they get too near their camp," said Quando. "The dust ain't settled, so they're not far ahead of us."

"There they are," Llano shouted as he broke through the trees at the top of a rise.

The three riders and their rustled herd had passed through a narrow arroyo and were climbing the farthest slope. Stoney drew his Colt and fired a single shot. One of the distant riders looked back.

"They know we're after 'em now," said Dent Briano.

"I want them to know," Stoney said. "If they don't leave the longhorns and ride for their lives, we'll know these three are part of a gang, and that they likely outnumber us. If they don't cut and run pretty soon, we'll have to back off."

But the distant trio gave up the herd. Flanking the longhorns, the riders galloped their horses on up the slope and disappeared over the crest.

"Well," said Quando, "either they ain't part of a bigger gang or the others are too far away to be of any help against us."

"I believe there's more of 'em," Stoney said, "and they've tipped their hand, so this stampede's been helpful to us. We can still be on our guard, and if they decide to come after us in a bunch, we'll be ready. Now let's go recover our cows and get them back to the main herd."

By the time the herd was again ready to take the trail, it was late afternoon, not more than four hours shy of sundown.

"By God, I don't believe I ever seen it this hot,"

Quando Miller said, wiping his sweaty face on the sleeve of his shirt. "Not a breath of air stirrin'."

"Reckon we buildin' up to a storm," Long John said. "Ye see how dirty the sky looks over yonder to the west? 'Fore dark they'll be clouds. Look fer the sun to set early."

"I hope you're right about the storm," said Stoney, "if it means rain. We're still more than fifteen miles from the north fork of the Sulphur. By mornin' these brutes will be crazy for water."

"They'll be crazy for it before then," Llano said, "if the wind brings 'em the smell of rain. Hell of it is, the rain might be a hundred miles away."

"No help fer that," said Long John. "All we kin do is keep the drive movin', hopin' if they is rain, that it'll hit us afore these longhorn varmints goes lookin' fer it."

The sun set red against the gray of the western horizon, and still there was no wind. The twilight seemed thick, oppressive, forbidding. Far to the west, lightning danced above the clouds, but there was no thunder. The longhorns bawled uneasily, and some among the horse remuda began nickering.

"I don't like the looks and the feel of this," Stoney said. "We might as well bed down the herd here. I want everybody in the saddle until this storm passes."

"This is some hell of a place to make camp," Bandy Darden complained. "There's a stand of cottonwoods over yonder that would of been some protection."

He was ignored as the riders set about trying to calm the restless herd. Suddenly every rider paused, listening. It started with the faraway sound of rushing wind, but as it drew closer, it became an ominous roar.

"Great God A'mighty," Long John shouted, "ever'body git on th' ground an' lay flat. Git yer hosses down aside ye. She's a killer wind!"

A towering black funnel cloud came out of the south-west, dipping earthward, leveling the stand of cottonwoods Bandy Darden had found tempting. Insofar as the longhorns and the horse remuda were concerned, it couldn't have been worse. While the monster lifted off the ground and missed the cows, horses, and riders, it showered the herd with limbs, leaves, and brush. The riders had left their saddles and held on to their reins, and that was all that spared them being left afoot. Broken branches and tree trunks raining from the sky was just too much. Bawling in terror, the longhorns fogged out to the south, followed by the spooked horse remuda. Ironically, at the tag end of the storm the rain came, borne by a cooling wind.

"I've heard of them big devil clouds," Dent Briano said, "but this'n is the first I ever seen."

"I seen one," said Long John, "but it wasn't this close. God, that thing could of picked up all of us, ever' cow an' ever' hoss, an' dropped us in the Gulf."

"That's about how far we'll have to ride 'fore we find them damn spooked cows and horses," said Bandy Darden sourly.

"Too bad you wasn't in that stand of cottonwoods," Llano said cheerfully, "and you wouldn't have to do no ridin'. You'd already be there with 'em."

There was laughter, despite the twist of fate that had hit them with two stampedes in one day, but Bandy Darden was silent.

"Wal," said Long John, "tomorrer we hunt cows an' horses, but t'night, thanks to the rain, we got water fer coffee. When Sky Pilot gits the grub ready, we'll eat an' turn in. Tomorrer we lose another day, but that can't be helped."

June 20, 1858. Two days south of the Red.

The outfit arose before dawn, prepared to spend a second day gathering stampeded stock. To everybody's surprise, they found themselves short a rider. Harley Logan was gone.

"He rode south," Llano said, "headin' for Dallas. Can't be more'n forty miles. He'll be there tonight."

"Wal, by God," Long John growled, "jist two days ago the little varmint hit me fer a thirty-dollar advance. I figgered he wanted it fer Doan's store, when we git to the Red. If I'd knowed he aimed to vamoose whilst we had a scattered herd to gather, I wouldn't of let him have it."

"Maybe he'll come back," said Suzanne. "If he can ride there today, he can ride back tomorrow."

"If he does," Stoney said, "he'd better have more than a passable good reason for runnin' out on us. He knows we're shorthanded, and this is the second damn stampede we've had in a matter of hours."

"It ain't all bad news," Llano said. "After last night's rain, there'll be enough scattered water to see us to the north fork of the Sulphur."

Harley Logan neared Dallas with his confidence at an all-time low. He'd known better than to ask permission to ride back to town. Not only would he have been denied, he'd have been laughed out of camp when he'd told them what he aimed to do. Now he feared that not only would the ride be for nothing, but that he had lost his position with the trail drive. It was dark when he rode into Dallas, but that suited his purpose. He found the address that he wanted, and pounded on the door until it was opened.

"I want to see Pearl," he told the startled madam.

15

"*I*'ve dragged these same damn cows out of the brush so many times, I believe I could do it in the dark," Llano said.

Stoney laughed. "Yeah. By the time we get 'em to St. Louis, they'll be such good friends, we likely won't be able to part with 'em." Then Stoney shifted focus: "I purely can't figure what's got into Harley Logan."

"You was in town the same time he was," said Llano. "Where did he go and what did he do?"

"Went off somewhere with Bandy Darden," Stoney said. "I'm just guessin', but I'd say Darden lit a shuck to the nearest whorehouse."

"And took Harley with him."

"Likely," said Stoney, "but I don't think Harley was ready for it. When Suzanne wanted to change to the second watch, Harley was mighty quick to take her up on it."

"He wasn't comfortable with Darden."

"That's how I figure it," Stoney said.

"Harley had a bad experience, so he's hit Long John for thirty dollars and gone back for more. That just don't add up."

"I reckon we'll have to wait until he comes back," said

Stoney, "if he does. Whatever he has in the way of an explanation oughta be damn interesting."

The sun was noon high before the gather was finished.

"Took us jist long enough fer the sun to suck up the water last night's rain left us," Long John observed.

"Maybe not," said Stoney. "Bound to be some shade and some wet weather springs along the way. We know the north fork of the Sulphur's there, so we can shoot for that. But I aim to ride ahead, and there's a chance we'll find some water holes the sun has spared."

But Stoney's optimism wasn't justified. The temporary water holes had been just that, and by the next afternoon following the rain, all evidence of it was gone.

"Sorry," Stoney said when he rode back to the herd. "The sun's left us where we started. A good fifteen miles from the north fork of the Sulphur, and no water in between."

"They's a moon t'night," said Long John. "What's the use of tryin' to bed these critters down in a dry camp, when all they gonna do is tramp around bawlin' their fool heads off? By God, let's drive 'em till they're ready to drop, an' we'll be that much closer to water."

"We might as well," Stoney said. "It'll be cooler at night, and by the time we bed down the herd, there'll be dewfall. That'll wet the grass and help some."

Sundown came and went, and despite the confused bawling of the herd, they were pushed on, the moon and stars lighting the way. Stoney watched the Big Dipper, and when he judged it was midnight, he stopped the drive.

"I reckon I figgered that right," Long John said. "Ye know they're thirsty, but they's so damn tired they ain't got the strength to raise hell."

"They ain't by theirselves," said Dent Briano. "I feel like I been pitched off, stomped, and then dragged maybe ten mile."

"Don't get too comfortable when you roll in your

blankets," Stoney said. "It's two hours sleep and two hours watch, and then we do this whole thing all over again."

"If I'm any judge," said Llano, "we killed better than half that fifteen miles to the north fork of the Sulphur. We oughta make it by tomorrow evening."

"Wal," said Long John, "no matter how early we git there, we'll bed 'em down fer the night. No sleep t'night, but tomorrer we make up fer it. Once we git there, it's no more'n a day's drive to the Red. Right, Stoney?"

"That's how I figure it," Stoney said.

Long John's theory had proven itself. The herd, exhausted, hadn't even begun to graze until near dawn, and the dewfall helped slake their thirst. But the brutes had no desire to take the trail at first light, and had to be driven.

"So ye ain't had enough rest," Long John said to the stubborn longhorns. "Wal, that's jist too damn bad. Neither has we. Ye kin rest when ye git to the north fork of the Sulphur. Now rattle yer hocks, ye varmints."

It was important that the drive get under way as early as possible, to put as many miles behind them as they could before the sun's heat became so terrible. Thanks to the dewfall and the early grazing, they were on the trail awhile before the longhorns' thirst again got to them. The brutes took to pausing at dry streambeds and at wet-weather water holes where the mud was already cracked and dry. They continually bawled their misery.

"Keep 'em bunched, keep 'em moving," Stoney shouted.

It was another of those miserable days of which Texas seemed to have more than its share. There wasn't a hint of a breeze. The flanks of the longhorns and the shirts of the riders were dark with sweat. Just beneath the brims of their hats they had tied bandannas around their heads, trying to keep the sweat out of their eyes. Stoney rode ahead and caught up to the horse remuda.

"Take the horses on to water," he told Malo Coyote and Naked Horse, "and then move them across the river to graze."

"One thing we got goin' for us," Stoney told Long John. "There's no wind, so we likely won't have a stampede when we're near the river. I've sent the horse remuda on ahead, so they'll be out of the way."

"Tomorrer," said Long John, "we git to the Red. I'm ready to cross it an' git on with this drive."

They reached the north fork of the Sulphur with a good four hours of daylight to spare. The longhorns were practically at the river before they were aware of it. Once the herd was watered and grazing, Long John made a welcome announcement.

"I'll be up an' around, keepin' watch. Rest of ye stretch out somewhere an' sleep till suppertime. I'll give ye a holler if they's any need."

It was a rare opportunity in a cowboy's life, and they all hastened to take advantage of it. All except Suzanne. She followed Long John along the river until they were well away from the camp. He became aware of her and waited.

"Long John," she said, "while the others are asleep, I . . . I just want to talk."

"I reckon it's time," he said. "Come along."

Sky Pilot had supper ready an hour before sundown. Thanks to the unaccustomed rest and the immediate prospect of food, the outfit was jovial. But that came quickly to an end when Harley Logan rode in. Riding behind him was a slender girl with fair hair and blue eyes. She wore Levi's pants and seemed ill at ease. Harley dismounted and helped her down. He too was nervous, and after swallowing hard a couple of times, he spoke.

"This here's Pearl."

Clearly on the defensive, Harley stood beside the girl, the two of them seeming like a pair of lost sheep. Bandy Darden was the first to react. He stalked over to Pearl and stood there grinning. When he spoke, he ignored the girl and spoke to Harley.

"Well, by God, kid, you not only got your ashes hauled, you brought the whore back with you. First drive I ever been on where that was allowed. I reckon I'll ride back to town and git my own piece of baggage."

It was the most offensive thing he could possibly have said, and Harley Logan attacked him with his fists, but all the young rider had in his favor was his fury. Darden had the edge, outweighing Harley forty pounds, and the fight was one-sided from the start. Darden ducked under the first swing and stunned Harley with a blow to the chin. Harley went down on his back and had only gotten to his knees when Darden again flattened him with a second blow. Darden then dropped astride Harley, grabbed his hair and began slamming his head against the ground. Furious, Pearl overcame uncertainty and pounded Darden's broad back with her small fists. Darden paused in his punishing Harley long enough to slap Pearl away like a bothersome mosquito. Long John, Llano, and Stoney moved at the same time, but Llano got there first. He grabbed Darden by his shirt collar and flung him away from Harley.

"He started it," Darden snarled, his hard eyes on Long John.

"Wrong," Long John said. "Ye done it. Wasn't no call fer ye sayin' what ye did. Now ye apologize to the young lady, else I'll stomp hell out'n ye m'self."

"I ain't apologizin' for the truth," Darden said. "The gal come from a whorehouse. I seen her there myself."

There was a terrible silence. While they hated what Darden had said and hated him for saying it, there was a ring of truth that could not be denied. Pearl proved it when she turned to Harley's still-saddled horse, hiding her face against the animal's flank. Nobody seemed to know what to do except Suzanne. She led Pearl away from the men and down along the river.

"Wal," said Long John, "this needs some talkin', I reckon."

Harley had gotten to his knees, his eyes on Bandy Darden, his hand near the butt of his Colt.

"Go ahead, kid," Darden said through a nasty grin. "Draw, and I'll kill you. That, or tell 'em I didn't lie. Tell 'em the truth."

"It—He . . . told it straight," said Harley miserably. "I just hated him sayin' it to Pearl. She didn't want to come here, but I . . . had nowhere else to take her."

"Wal," Long John said, "whar ye found her ain't none of Darden's business an' none of mine, but what are ye aimin' to do with her?"

"I don't aim for her to be a burden," said Harley. "I reckon we'll be goin' on to St. Louis. We just stopped so's you'd know why I left."

"Pearl's a mite young," Long John said. "The law—"

"The law ain't after us," said Harley. "Pearl ain't but seventeen, but the preacher didn't say nothin' when we went before him this mornin'."

That threw everything into a new light. Long John suspected Suzanne was hearing all this from Pearl, and what effect it might have, Long John dared not contemplate. One thing he knew for sure: Suzanne would readily see herself all over again, as she heard Pearl's story. Stoney Winters came to Long John's rescue.

"Long John," Stoney said, "why don't you talk to Sky Pilot and have him make room in the wagon for Pearl? With Deuce gone, we're already short one rider, and we need Harley. He's aimin' to go to St. Louis anyhow."

"I like the idee," said Long John. "All 'cept me tryin' to talk sense to that stubborn old coot, Sky Pilot."

Stoney looked at Bandy Darden, silently daring him to say anything in rebuttal, but Darden did not. Stoney then went looking for Suzanne and Pearl, and when he found them, Suzanne wasted no time in taking responsibility for the younger girl.

"Stoney," said Suzanne, "please talk to Long John and see if he won't make room in the wagon for Pearl. She's going with us."

"Long John's already taking care of that," Stoney said, "and it was his idea. Now why don't you see to gettin' Pearl some supper before it gets dark and the grub gets cold?"

"By God," said the disgruntled Sky Pilot when Long John was finished with him, "time we get to St. Louis, we'll be stoppin' every Sunday evenin' for a tea social."

At first Pearl kept to herself, except for Harley and Suzanne, but as the others accepted her, so would she accept them. The drive took the trail north at first light, and before sundown the longhorns were grazing on the banks of the Red River. Indian Territory lay ahead.

June 22, 1858. Red River.

"Doan's store," Long John said. "Likely the last place fer grub, plug, er anything else 'fore we git to St. Louis. Ye that's needin' anything, ye better git it here, er plan on makin' do."

"Pearl needs another change of clothes," said Suzanne. "She has only what she's wearing."

"Take Llano with ye," Long John said, "an when ye go to the store, don't stay no longer'n ye need to."

Fresh in Long John's mind was what had taken place in Dallas. Suzanne's past had sparked that fight, and now here was Pearl with a similar and far more recent background.

"We'll cross the Red in the morning at first light," Stoney told the rest of the outfit. "Anybody needin' to go to Doan's, go ahead. Malo Coyote and Naked Horse will be watchin' the horses. Long John and me will stay with the herd, and we're almost within sight of the store."

Llano saddled horses for Suzanne and Pearl, and then one for himself. Dent Briano and Quando Miller were about to saddle their own mounts. When Llano, Suzanne, and Pearl reached the store, there were seven horses tied to the hitch rail. Llano recognized none of the brands, but there was nothing to arouse his suspicion, except the fact that Doan's was an isolated trading post and there was no other trail drive in sight. Who were these seven riders and what business did they have at Doan's? Llano, Suzanne, and Pearl reined up, Llano dismounting first. He helped Suzanne and Pearl dismount, then dallied the reins of their horses around the hitch rail. Mounting the steps to the narrow porch, Llano opened the door for Suzanne and Pearl. Doan's was almost a copy of the Dallas Merchantile, with goods piled high along the walls and some even suspended from the ceiling. But Llano was more concerned with the store's patrons than with its variety of goods.

"Suzanne," said Llano, "you and Pearl get what you need as quick as you can, and let's get out of here."

Llano followed Suzanne and Pearl as they searched the aisles for what they needed. Doing as Llano had asked, they completed their purchases and were ready to leave. Suddenly a big man with two tied-down Colts stepped from behind a counter piled high with bolted goods. He grabbed a fistful of Llano's shirt front.

"Cowboy," he snarled, "Me and my boys is ridin' north, and we decided to ride with your outfit. Any objections?"

"Pilgrim," said Llano through gritted teeth, "you just made one mistake. Don't make another. Get the hell out of my way."

"You ain't answered my question," said the big man.

Llano said nothing, fisting his right hand and bringing

it up from his knees. The offending stranger took the blow on the point of his chin and was slammed to the floor on his back. Spitting blood, he sat up, then made his third and last mistake. The muzzle of his Colt had barely cleared leather when Llano's slug flattened him again, and this time he didn't move.

"Suzanne," Llano said, "you and Pearl head for the horses. I'll be right behind you."

Llano waited for the dead man's companions to arrive, and they did, before the sound of the shot had faded. First they eyed the dead man, and then the Colt that was steady in Llano's hand.

"He tried to shoot me," said Llano. "Anybody else of the same mind?"

"Not fer now," said one of the strangers, "but don't you go makin' no plans, 'cause you ain't gonna be around. You just kilt one of Buck Tundree's boys. Last gent done that, he died hard an' slow."

"Come on, Llano," said Quando Miller from the doorway. "Me and Dent's coverin' 'em."

Llano backed out the door, still gripping his Colt. He pulled the door shut just in time to avoid a fusillade of gunfire from inside the store. He found Suzanne and Pearl on the narrow porch, their backs against the wall. Dent and Quando had their own horses ready, along with those of Llano, Pearl, and Suzanne.

"Let's ride," Llano said. "This place is bound to have a back door, and that bunch won't waste any time findin' it."

They urged their horses into a fast gallop, and before they reached the herd, they met Long John, riding hard. Seeing they were all safe, the Cajun said nothing, wheeling his horse and riding with them. He would hear their story when they were safely with the herd. Stoney was waiting for them, and Llano told him and Long John what had happened.

"Seven of them," said Llano, "and they're part of

Buck Tundree's gang. I'd bet my last peso them three that tried to grab part of the herd after the stampede was part of this bunch. They'd know we'd be crossing the Red here, and this would be the time and place to size us up. One thing purely don't make sense, though. Why'd they start gun trouble here at Doan's, when they're likely plannin' to hit us after we get into Indian Territory? Now we'll be lookin' for 'em, especially since they promised to gun me down."

"That hombre you shot, the one that drawed on you," Long John said, "he likely was actin' on his own. After ye shot the bastard, they're aimin' to git even, so what does it matter that we're expectin' 'em? It'll come as a mighty big surprise to me if'n they ain't outnumberin' us considerable. Once we cross the Red, I reckon they figger they got us by the short hairs, an' they flat don't care if'n we know they's on our trail."

"That's sizin' it up damn close," said Stoney. "I'd say they've been plannin' to hit us anyway. This fight today just tells us we're in for it later on. We'll have to be ready, because we don't know when they'll strike."

"When the rest of them varmints rides out," Long John said, "I'll mosey back to the store an' talk to Doan. Sooner er later they'll be some Rangers through here, an' I'll want 'em knowin' the truth. 'Nother thing, if'n Doan ain't scared to talk, mebbe I kin git some idee as to how many hombres they is in this Tundree gang."

"Startin' tonight," Stoney said, addressing the others, "we'll have to be ready for them. I want nobody wanderin' away from camp after dark. Those of us on watch will likely be nervous enough, so if you're sleepin' and you got to get up—for any reason—make yourself known to the nighthawks."

Before sundown Long John rode back to Doan's, but learned little.

"He didn't see the fight," Long John told Llano, "but he knowed them seven hombres was part of the Tundree gang. Bein' up here on the Red, Doan can't depend on the law, so he's got to stay neutral if'n he can. Says he ain't sure how many Tundree riders they is, 'cause they don't talk around him, an' they never come in more'n five to seven at a time."

With Suzanne again on the first watch, Llano found himself in her company, but thanks to her improved relationship with Long John, her attitude had changed entirely. Llano listened to her talk and was silently thankful for Pearl's addition to the drive. Suzanne had identified with the younger girl and had set about allaying her fears and making her feel welcome.

"The poor girl's fresh out of a whorehouse," said Suzanne, "and she needs to know she has a chance at something better. I've been away from that awful life for ten years, and you saw what almost happened to me."

"I'm wishin' her the best," Llano said, "but I got some doubts about her and Harley's chances in St. Louis. For certain there'll be war, and Texans are gonna be almighty uncomfortable in Missouri."

"I've been talking to Pearl about her and Harley going back to Texas and settling along the Colorado," Suzanne said.

"It'd be for their own good, I reckon," said Llano. "Besides, you'd have neighbors to that godforsaken Colorado River ranch."

She laughed, and Llano sighed with relief. Whatever lay ahead, anything would be better than having a hot-tempered female on the prod.

June 23, 1858. Indian Territory.

'All my life," said Harley Logan, "I been hearin' about how bad it'd be, crossin' the Red. It wasn't near as bad as the Brazos."

"It depends on rain to the west," Stoney said. "A

week from now it may be over the banks, making the Brazos look like a spring branch. Don't get your hopes too high. Halfway across Indian Territory, we'll be crossing the Canadian, the North Canadian, and the Arkansas."

Stoney's first day's scouting after crossing into the territory gained them some valuable knowledge. Despite the dangers they might otherwise have to face, there seemed to be no shortage of water.

"I rode more than twenty miles," Stoney told Long John, "and if the rest of eastern Indian Territory is watered as well as what I've seen, there'll be no fifteen-mile days. Today we'll only make a little more than ten miles, but it'll be better than pushing the herd until midnight."

Their first two days and two nights in Indian Territory were peaceful, but that all changed on the afternoon of the third day, when Stoney rode back to the herd after scouting ahead.

"Indian sign," said Stoney. "I found tracks of seventeen horses. They spent last night where we'll be bedding down for tonight."

"Where'd they go when they rode out?" Llano asked.

"North," said Stoney. "I followed them another ten miles, to the next water. They rested their horses, watered them, and rode on."

"Don't mean nothin'," Long John said. "They know we're here, and they'll know we're travelin' north. They kin cover fifty er sixty mile a day, to our ten. All er some of 'em can turn east er west, an' double back. Seventeen of 'em, and we're outnumbered two to one. Hell's fire, they could hit us in daylight. We'd best have the drag riders keepin' a sharp watch on our back trail."

"Maybe I'd better have Malo Coyote and Naked Horse slow the remuda some," Stoney said. "Like it is, they could grab every horse we have before we could close the gap."

But Stoney's decision came too late. Ahead there was the rattle of gunfire, followed by an ominous silence. Stoney waved his hat to the flank riders, a signal to mill the herd. He then rode ahead at a fast gallop, Long John right behind him. When they were within sight of the horse remuda, there was no activity, except for the milling horses. Stoney and Long John rode through the dust and found their Indian wranglers afoot, the left sleeve of Malo Coyote's shirt soaked with blood. On the ground lay two very dead Indians. Stoney and Long John dismounted, and with a question in his eyes, Stoney looked at Naked Horse.

"Them come, them shoot, them die," said Naked Horse.

Stoney pointed to the dead men and raised one hand, his fingers spread. How many men? Just the two dead Indians, or had there been more? Naked Horse raised his right hand, extending three fingers. One had escaped.

"Him run like coyote." Naked Horse laughed.

16

Suddenly to the south there was the roar of guns.

"Let's ride," Stoney said. "These three must have been a diversion. The rest of 'em are attacking the drag riders."

Stoney kicked his horse into a fast gallop, Long John right behind him. They rode west and then south, taking themselves out of the path of the herd, for the stampede was coming hell-for-leather. They could hear the frenzied bawling of the longhorns and the thunder of hooves. Ahead, through rising clouds of dust, Stoney could see two horsemen. The flank riders, Dent Briano and Quando Miller, were galloping to the aid of their comrades at drag. The shooting seemed closer, and Stoney realized Dent and Quando had taken a hand in the fight. Stoney drew his Colt, but he was out of range, and the rising pall of dust robbed him of any possible target. Finally, in the wake of the stampede came three riders. Llano and Harley rode looking backward, their Colts in their hands. Suzanne slumped in the saddle, the ugly shaft of an arrow protruding from her left thigh. Blood had already soaked the leg of her Levi's. Long John rode alongside Suzanne, steadying her in the saddle. Llano and Harley whirled their horses, prepared to face the attack, but it appeared to be over. Quando Miller and Dent Briano were riding back.

"They saw us comin'," Dent said, "and lit out. Kiowa, I'd say."

"They're a bold lot," said Quando Miller, "hittin' us in daylight. What was that shootin' about up front, before they attacked the drag?"

"Three of 'em jumped Malo Coyote and Naked Horse," Stoney said, "and two of 'em are dead. What happened back here, Llano?"

"They come at us from two sides," said Llano, "stampedin' the herd, knowin' we was outnumbered. We tried to outride 'em, but with 'em on both sides of us, it was follow the herd or turn and ride south. When they nailed Suzanne, we kept her ahead of us, shot at them as best we could, and tried to stay close enough to the stampede so's the dust would cover us. We hit two or three of 'em, but not so hard they couldn't ride."

"I don't understand their thinking," Stoney said. "Three of 'em go after Malo Coyote and Naked Horse, while the rest attack the drag. Stampeding the herd won't gain them a thing, and with the herd running north, it won't hurt us all that much."

"I don't think stampedin' the herd was what they had in mind," said Llano. "They didn't ride in whoopin' and yellin', and we had no warning. They shot Suzanne first thing, and if it hadn't been for the dust stirred up by the herd, they'd have cut down Harley and me. I think the bloodthirsty bastards just aimed to kill us. Our shootin' stampeded the herd, I reckon."

"You could be right," Stoney said. "That kind of tallies with the three of 'em going after Malo Coyote and Naked Horse. Let's ride on and find out how hard Suzanne's been hit."

Stoney led out, Llano, Harley, Dent, and Quando following. When they caught up to Sky Pilot's wagon, Pearl was mounted on Suzanne's horse and the wagon was moving north. Long John rode beside it, and Stoney trotted his horse next to Long John's. He said nothing, waiting for Long John to talk.

"Nasty wound," said the Cajun. "She's in the wagon. That arrer's got to be drove out, an' we'll need lots of hot water. First decent water we come to, we'll stop there."

Stoney rode on ahead, wondering if the stampeding herd had taken the horse remuda with it. As he recalled, they weren't that far from a creek he had in mind for the night's camp. He rode on, mystified as to what had become of the horses, thinking they'd been caught up in the stampede. Soon he was seeing grazing longhorns, then bunches of five or more, and finally what appeared to be most of the herd. They were scattered along the creek, some of them beyond it, grazing near the horses.

"We no wait for cow *estampeda*," Naked Horse said. "Horse gallop."

"*Bueno,*" said Stoney. While the pair of Cherokees had their faults, they were resourceful when it counted. Malo Coyote's wound hadn't been serious, and he already wore a bandage on his arm.

When the wagon reached the creek, Long John wasted no time in starting a fire and getting a pot of water on to boil. Suzanne lay on a pallet of blankets. Long John took one end of the pallet and Llano the other, and they lifted Suzanne out of the wagon, placing her in the shade beside the creek. Llano left Long John with her. He had seen Indian arrows driven through the flesh before, and he didn't envy Long John the task. Only Pearl had remained with Long John, and he looked questioningly at her.

"I want to help you with her," Pearl said.

"I don't need no help drivin' an arrer through," said Long John gruffly.

"I can't help you with that," said Pearl, "but I can do other things. Please let me stay."

There was a pleading note in her voice and a look in her eyes that Long John might not have understood, but there was no doubting her desire to help. Suzanne had stood by Pearl, daring anybody to treat her unkindly, and Pearl was remembering.

"Ye kin stay," said Long John. "Here. Take m'knife an' cut away the leg of them Levi's, whilst I git the quart of whiskey I bought at Doan's."

When Long John returned with the whiskey, Pearl had Suzanne bare from the waist down. It didn't seem to bother Pearl, but Long John was obviously nervous.

"See kin ye raise her up," Long John said. "I got to git enough of this poison down her to kill the pain whilst I'm drivin' the arrer out."

Pearl lifted Suzanne, and Long John pulled the cork from the bottle with his teeth. He tilted the bottle, but Suzanne resisted it. When he tried to force the open bottle past her lips, he found she had clenched her teeth.

"Damn it, Suzanne," he said in exasperation, "open up. Open yer mouth an' take this whiskey. How'n hell am I s'posed to git it down ye with yer mouth shut?"

But if Suzanne heard, she didn't respond. Pearl eased Suzanne down on the blankets and looked at Long John.

"I'll go to the wagon for a tin cup," she said. "Perhaps I can get her to take some of it."

"Git one, then," said Long John. He waited impatiently until Pearl returned, and then raised Suzanne enough so that none of the whiskey spilled.

"Suzanne," said Pearl softly, "you must drink this whiskey." She took the bottle and poured the cup a third full. With a steady hand she touched the cool rim of the cup to Suzanne's lips.

"Suzanne," Pearl said, "drink. Please drink."

For just a moment Suzanne opened her eyes, and then drank a little of the whiskey. Pearl quickly took away the cup until Suzanne's coughing and wheezing subsided. The cup was swiftly returned, and Suzanne drank again. The ordeal was repeated until Suzanne had swallowed almost three cups of the vile liquid.

"That'll be enough," said Long John, easing Suzanne down. "Now we jist wait fer the stuff to knock her out."

Long John and Pearl waited, neither speaking. Finally Long John lifted Suzanne and she was totally limp, the only sign of life her shallow breathing.

"Best I git it done," Long John said. "Ye don't have to watch."

But Pearl appeared not to hear him. Long John broke his Colt, unloading the cylinder. He then took his Bowie and cut the feathered shaft of the arrow, leaving just enough of its length to drive it on through. Taking the Colt by its muzzle and using the butt for a hammer, he began the trying ordeal. With every blow to the broken shaft of the arrow, Suzanne groaned. It was an agonizingly slow process, and although it was now the cool of the evening, patches of sweat darkened Long John's shirt. Repeatedly he stopped to wipe his hands on the legs of his Levi's, and to sleeve the sweat off his lean face. During one of his pauses, Long John spoke to Pearl.

"Go to the wagon an' tell Sky Pilot I'm needin' that bolt of muslin. Git as many blankets as he kin find, an' bring the pot of water from the fire."

Long John intensified his efforts, trying to complete this nerve-wracking procedure before Pearl returned. He worked with clenched teeth, and it was taking a lot out of him. Pearl was stronger than he'd thought, and he was reluctant to have her witness what this was doing to him, to see the trembling of his hands. Suzanne had her faults, but they were the furthest thing from his mind. Suzanne's pain-wracked face and agonized groans had driven away everything except Long John's desire to see her through this ordeal. He had finished the gruesome task by the time Pearl returned.

"You're give out," Pearl said. "Let me finish."

Long John said nothing, signifying his agreement by getting unsteadily to his feet and moving out of her way. The exit wound was bleeding, and Pearl used most of the hot water cleansing it and the angry purple gash where the arrow had entered. That done, she poured some of the whiskey into the wound and placed a whiskey-soaked pad over both wounds before wrapping Suzanne's thigh with a long strip of the muslin. From the bundle of blankets Pearl had brought, she took a clean pair of Levi's pants. Without a word, Long John knelt and raised Suzanne enough for Pearl to get the Levi's on and buttoned. The legs of them were well over Suzanne's feet.

"Them britches is way too big," Long John observed.

"They're yours," Pearl said, a twinkle in her eyes. "Sky Pilot said they oughtn't be so tight, so the wound can breathe."

"Why, that mossy horned old varmint. What's he know about wounds?"

With Long John's help, Pearl wrapped Suzanne in blankets and they left her in the shade of the cottonwoods beside the creek. Long John was ill at ease, knowing he should say something to Pearl, but not sure what. Pearl understood.

"If you'll leave the rest of the whiskey with me," she said, "I'll see that she takes some more during the night, if she's feverish."

"I'd be obliged," Long John said, handing her the bottle.

While the rest of the outfit hadn't witnessed Pearl ministering to Suzanne's wounds, they had seen her go to the wagon for bandages and blankets, and take the pot of water from the fire.

Llano laughed. "I reckon old Long John's been gettin' some help, whether he wanted it or not."

"He should of been thankful for it," said Quando Miller. "Them arrow wounds is hell to deal with."

When Long John and Pearl returned to the wagon, the Cajun was still uneasy, but Pearl's timidity had been replaced with a new air of confidence. Harley Logan said nothing, but when Pearl's eyes met his, he knew her biggest challenge had been met and conquered.

June 25, 1858. Indian Territory.

Long John had left Suzanne in Pearl's care during the night, and before breakfast, Pearl had good news.

"She had fever during the night," the girl said, "and I gave her the rest of the whiskey. Move her back into the wagon and I'll ride her horse."

When the drive again took the trail, Pearl rode at drag, with Llano and Harley. Once, when Pearl was riding a little ahead, Llano trotted his horse alongside Harley's.

"She'll do, kid," said Llano.

"Long John," Stoney said, "I'm ridin' out. After that Indian attack yesterday, and the threat from the Tundree gang, I think we can pretty well count on one thing: hell could bust loose from any direction."

Stoney rode out, but instead of riding due north, he rode northwest. Once he had traveled a dozen miles, he would swing eastward, crossing the path the drive would take, and eventually riding south. When he returned to the drive, he would have ridden a giant horseshoe trail across the path of any potential enemy, red or white.

By the time Stoney had ridden what he judged was ten miles, he found himself on the banks of a deep running creek. It would be just about the right distance for tonight's camp, and if there were enemies, he might find some evidence of them along this creek. Since he had to ride eastward a ways before he headed south, he decided to follow the creek. He had ridden only a mile or two when he reached a stretch of water where the banks were low and there was easy access. The tracks, when he found them, were not what he'd been expecting. The horses had been shod, and it wasn't a trail left by passing riders who had spent the night or paused to water their horses. This was myriad tracks where many horses had been watered for days at a time. That meant some well-defined trail down which the horses had been driven, and since they were driven to water, that meant a corral or holding pen. When Stoney found the trail he was looking for, he tied his horse well out of sight in a scrub oak thicket and continued on foot. There might be many horses, and he dared not risk having one of them nicker and his own horse answer.

The cabin, when he came within sight of it, seemed deserted, for the large corral, six poles high, was empty. With its shake roof and mud-and-stick chimney, the cabin had a look of permanence. There was no porch and no steps, and the entrance—which faced south—consisted of a cowhide hung from the top of the doorway. There were no windows, at least not at the front. Stoney approached the building from the west. His back to the log wall and his Colt in his hand, he pulled the cowhide away just enough to see inside. There was little enough to see. On a crude split-log mantel there were a few tins that might have contained staples such as coffee, beans, or flour. The floor was dirt, and there was no table or chairs. Stoney returned quickly to his horse. The crude cabin was barely sufficient to shelter men from the elements. He left the creek, circling the cabin until he found a trail leading north. It was days old, and the many tracks accounted for the empty corral. But there had been rain since the horses were driven away, so he couldn't tell how many of the horses had carried riders. Could this be the Tundree gang? Indian Territory was immense enough, wild enough, and lawless enough to harbor many such renegade bands. His mind awhirl with questions needing answers, Stoney rode south.

"Mebbe that's good news fer us," Long John said when Stoney reported to him. "If'n them hombres rode north with a herd of horses, they'll likely be gone fer a while. Ain't likely they'd find a market any closer'n Kansas City er Abilene."

"I figured the tracks at maybe a week old," said Stoney, "and that means it couldn't have been the Tundree gang. Not unless there's a hell of a bunch of 'em, because there was seven at Doan's less than a week ago."

"Wal, damn it all," Long John said, "that's right. I was jist figgerin' to rid us of some of them bastards. Now I reckon we'll end up killin' the lot of 'em. Wisht we had us 'nother rider er two, handy with their irons."

"Pearl's ridin' drag, and she's unarmed," said Stoney. "Why don't you ask her if she can shoot? She can use one of the Colts we took from those Harkness bullwhackers."

"That little gal's got more'n her share of sand," Long John said, "and I reckon she'd take a Colt, but I ain't sure it'd be fair to her. Not after what happened to Suzanne. Mebbe ye better ask Harley what he thinks."

"I'll talk to him," said Stoney, trying to suppress a grin. Long John had taken Pearl in as a helpless little waif, and she had surprised him, proving herself resourceful and strong. It said much for Suzanne's judgment in standing up for Pearl, and Stoney suspected Long John was impressed.

Stoney rode back to the drag. The herd was trailing well, and Harley rode a few yards behind Llano and Pearl. Harley Logan hadn't forgotten that Suzanne had been the first—and only—rider hit during the Indian attack. Stoney rode back and turned his horse, trotting it alongside Harley's. In as few words as possible he told the young rider what Long John had suggested, but mentioned Long John's fears as well.

"I'll leave that to Pearl," Harley said. "She's got no kin, nobody 'cept me. She knowed we was shorthanded, even 'fore Suzanne was hurt, and ridin' back here is what she wants to do. If she's gonna take the risk, I'd favor her carryin' the Colt."

"I can shoot," said Pearl when Stoney put the question to her. "I'm a Texan, and my daddy taught me to use a gun."

"You can have your pick of a dozen," Stoney said, "but I'd recommend a Colt."

The drive reached the creek without difficulty. Long John immediately went to the wagon to look in on Suzanne, and found Pearl right behind him.

"This gal's been givin' me hell since noon," Sky Pilot complained. "For God's sake, put her on a hoss so's I can have some peace."

"I'd rather be tied belly down over my saddle," said Suzanne, "than spend another hour being bounced around in this damn wagon."

"Yep," Long John said cheerfully, "she's agonna make it, if'n she don't cash in from the hangover."

"I don't suppose there's any of the whiskey left," said Suzanne.

"I dunno," Long John said, leaning over the wagon's tailgate. "I give the whiskey to Pearl, an' she give it to ye as it was needed."

"You drank it all last night, Suzanne," Pearl said, and it was the first time they'd heard her laugh.

Stoney spoke first with Long John, and after supper had something to say to the outfit.

"Tonight and every night until the end of this drive, we're goin' to be more careful how and where we spread our blankets. Indians or renegade whites could slip in close and kill half of us as we're sleepin'. From now on nobody sleeps anywhere even close to the wagon, but I want it to appear that we are. We'll take extra blankets, and with leaves and brush build us some humps that in the dark will look like sleepin' riders. When you do sleep, spread your blankets in the shadow of trees, so you'll be hard to see, and don't shuck anything but your hats. When your watch is done and before you sleep, saddle fresh horses and picket them close by."

"I don't sleep worth a damn in my boots," Bandy Darden grumbled.

"One other thing," said Stoney. "Nobody wanders around in the dark. I've told you this before, but I'm tellin' you again. Once the horses are settled down for the night, Malo Coyote and Naked Horse will take turns prowling through the area. If you're not supposed to be up and about, then don't be. I don't want any of you gettin' your throats cut or a Bowie in your gut. We're shorthanded enough already."

"It's mighty quiet," Llano said when he awakened Stoney for the second watch. "I feel a mite better with Malo Coyote and Naked Horse driftin' around out there."

"So do I," said Stoney, "and with them and their Bowies on the prowl, the horses are in no danger."

Stoney was two hours into the second watch when it happened. There was a scream of mortal agony, ending as suddenly as it had begun.

"Great God!" Long John shouted, rolling out of his blankets. "What'n hell was *that?*"

"I reckon somebody just made the acquaintance of Malo Coyote and Naked Horse," said Llano. "Everybody stay put until Stoney gets here."

It was a while before Stoney arrived, and he slowed his horse, speaking quietly. "Hold your fire. It's Stoney."

"That sounded like a white gent havin' his throat slit," Llano said.

"He got a bad case of it, compliments of Naked Horse," said Stoney. "Quando swears he's one of the Tundree gang you faced at Doan's store. Why don't you have a look? He's down the creek a ways, beyond the horse remuda."

"Damn lucky that screech didn't stampede the horses," Llano said. "I've always heard that an Indian with a Bowie can kill quietly."

"They can," said Stoney, "but there's times—like tonight—when the cry of a dying man can be a powerful weapon. If this dead hombre had anybody with him or waitin' for him, they'll still be runnin' this time tomorrow night."

Llano and Stoney reined up and dismounted. Quando Miller spoke from the darkness.

"I believe this varmint was one of them Tundree riders at Doan's store, Llano."

"Light a match, Quando," Stoney said, "but shield it with your hat."

Quando did, and Llano knelt to have a look at the dead man.

"Looks like one of 'em," said Llano. "In fact, I think this hombre was the one that done all the talkin' and made all the threats."

"I hope the rest of 'em was close enough to hear this coyote squall," Quando said. "God, that screech would of raised the hair on a dead Comanche's head."

"Quando, you and Darden get back to the herd," said Stoney. "Llano and me will roll this skunk in a blanket so's he'll keep till morning. Where's Harley?"

"He went to tell Pearl what happened," Quando said. "She's in the wagon with Suzanne."

When Llano returned to his blankets, he found Long John and Dent Briano awake. Quickly he told them of the dead man and of his being a member of the Tundree gang.

"Somewher' along the trail," said Long John, "we

gonna have one hell of a fight with this Tundree bunch. Time we meet, they'll have a considerable mad on. We'd best have ourselves in a position to pull our irons first."

A dozen miles to the north, renegade Buck Tundree and his fourteen followers sat around a small concealed fire. One of the men had just finished relating the death of his comrade in the hands of Naked Horse. Tundree was a big man weighing well over two hundred pounds. He had black hair like an Indian, and wore a bristly black beard to hide his scarred face. He got angrily to his feet, towering over the man who had just spoken.

"Vidner," Tundree said, "I sent you and Shando to have a look at that trail drive, to take their measure, to size them up. Now you ride in with your tail between your legs like a whipped coyote, handin' me some fool yarn about Shando bein' gutted by some devil Injun, and you still didn't learn one damn thing."

"Wrong," Vidner growled. "I learnt plenty. This ain't a bunch of short horns with no savvy. They're mean-as-hell Texans with the bark on, and by God, I warned Shando. That camp was just too quiet, and with mighty good reason. Gettin' around the nighthawks wasn't no trouble. You know why? 'Cause them damn *cuchillo** Injuns was out there in the dark, just waitin' for us. You think Shando was a *malo* hombre, you should of heard him squall whilst they was cuttin' his guts out."

Vidner's words had the ring of truth, laced with awe, fear, and a hint of the supernatural. Shando had killed many men, and not a man in the gang would have dared accused him of cowardice. Yet he had died in the darkness at the hand of an unseen foe, screaming like a woman.

"By God, if'n they got ol' Shando, that's enough fer me," one of the gang said. There were growls of assent, and Tundree sensed a rebellion. His response was

* Knife

conciliatory. "Let me think on it some," he said. "Maybe we'll set up an ambush and hit 'em in daylight."

June 26, 1858. Indian Territory.

Pearl changed the dressing on Suzanne's wound, and despite all her complaints to the contrary, Suzanne was forced to spend another day in the wagon.

"No wonder Sky Pilot's such an old grouch," Suzanne said, within his hearing. "This miserable wagon's punishment enough to ruin a person for decent company."

Stoney waited until the herd was trailing well before he rode out, and before he departed, he spoke to Long John.

"I'll scout ahead at least twenty miles. So far, we've cashed in two of Tundree's gang, and I don't look for him to let that pass. We'd best be on our guard, even in daylight. I reckon they'll be comin' after us."

After changing Suzanne's dressing, Pearl rode alongside Sky Pilot's wagon. For a while the old cook said nothing, and when he finally spoke, it shocked Pearl.

"Ye got sand, girl. Ye handle yerself like a western woman."

"Thank you," said Pearl, and encouraged by his kind words, surprised old Sky Pilot.

"Sky Pilot, could you . . . would you teach me to cook? The way you do, to make dutch oven biscuits and dried apple pies?"

"Reckon I could," said the old cook, pleased, "but it purely ain't no easy job, feedin' this bunch of ongrateful coyotes. Why would ye be wantin' to learn?"

"I want to do my share, to fill in where I'm needed," Pearl said. "I'd take over for you if you were . . . well . . . sick."

Sky Pilot grinned. He suspected the girl was referring to the times he got his hands on a bottle of rotgut and suffered the effects of what seemed a terminal hangover.

"Tell ye what," said Sky Pilot. "Talk to your Harley and to that cantankerous old walrus, Long John. If they ain't got no objections, then I'd be proud to make ye a first-class trail drive cook."

Pearl wasted no time in approaching Harley and Long John.

"I'd like that," Harley said. It would lessen Pearl's danger if there was a stampede or if the herd was attacked.

"I'll still help with the herd when I'm not cooking," Pearl assured Long John, when she approached him with the proposal.

"Girl, if ye want to cook," said Long John, "and that mule-headed old varmint is willin' to teach ye, then ye got my blessin'. Jist don't take no foolishment off'n him. If'n he gits uppity with you, box his ears."

Pearl only smiled and rode away.

Stoney rode warily, virtually certain the Tundree gang wouldn't allow last night's killing to go without some attempt at retribution. If that wasn't enough, they were subject at any time to a return visit by the Kiowa. Reaching a creek, Stoney estimated that he'd ridden a little more than ten miles. There was an abundance of last year's fallen leaves, and no evidence of anyone's passing. It would be an ideal campsite at the end of this day's drive. Stoney was tempted to accept the tranquility without further scouting and ride on, but he dared not. Instead he rode eastward until the trees thinned out and the leaf accumulation gave way to open stretches of bare ground. There he found tracks of more than twenty unshod ponies. Tracks only hours old!

"Damn," he muttered, "nothin' to do but find out how close they are."

Stoney led his horse well away from the creek, concealed it as best he could, and continued on foot. It was

possible this band of Indians had no mischief in mind
and would continue riding eastward. However, if they
had made camp anywhere near the northward path the
trail drive must take, they were trouble. Stoney had already passed several convenient places they might have
stopped if all they wanted was a decent campsite. On the
heels of these sobering thoughts came the not-too-dis-
tant nicker of a horse. His venturing closer would only
risk discovery, and he'd already learned what he needed
to know. While the creek would be ideal for watering
the horses and longhorns at the end of the day, such a
thing was impossible with the Kiowa camp less than two
miles distant. Stoney rode on, determined to see what
lay beyond this creek. Might they get past this Indian
camp without a fight? It didn't seem likely.

Four or five miles north of the creek, Stoney paused
at what appeared to be the runoff from a spring. Although the water was being swallowed up at this distant
point, leaving only mud, the spring still might provide
decent water, the runoff becoming more substantial as
he neared the source. Stoney rode cautiously on, pausing occasionally to listen. Finally he dismounted and
continued afoot. If there was a mounted enemy near,
the horse would quickly have given him away. But the
enemy wasn't mounted, and a cold voice froze Stoney in
his tracks.

"Stand where you are, mister."

Stoney said nothing. The voice had come from behind
him, to his right. Stoney could drop, roll, and come up
shooting, but his adversary could well be firing from
cover. He must play for time and somebody at which to
shoot.

"I lost my way," Stoney said.

"Sure you did," scoffed the unseen gunman. "A gent
that's lost his way don't leave his hoss an' go cat-footin'
ahead. Now you and me will slope on down to the spring

and let Buck Tundree decide what to do with you. Usin'
your finger an' thumb, lift that iron clear and drop it."

There was the sound of footsteps as the unseen man
drew closer. He was away from whatever cover had concealed him, and it was Stoney's last chance to avoid
falling into the hands of the Tundree gang. He buckled
his knees, falling backward, twisting so that he came
down on his left side. Before he hit the ground his Colt
was spitting lead. His opponent overshot, two shots driving into the ground ahead of Stoney, but Stoney Winters
didn't miss. Both his shots were true, the lead slapping
puffs of dust from the front of the renegade's shirt.
Stoney was up and running toward his horse, but before
he reached it there was a clatter of hoofs and the shouts
of his pursuers. They were coming, and he was more
than fifteen miles from his comrades!

"Sky Pilot," Suzanne said, "you stop this damn wagon
right here. I want my horse and saddle."

Sky Pilot was more than happy to do her bidding.
Yesterday she'd had an excuse, having consumed most
of a quart of whiskey and having awakened with a killing
hangover. Today, however, he had discovered she could
raise as much or more hell when she was sober. Long
John was at right flank, and he rode ahead to find out
why the wagon was no longer moving. He listened as
Suzanne expressed her opinion of wagons in general and
Sky Pilot's in particular, ending with an impassioned
plea for her horse and saddle.

"Sky Pilot," said Long John, "git the wagon off to the
side, so's the longhorns don't git spooked. Suzanne, I'll
send Pearl up here to bind that wound as tight as ye kin
stand it. Pearl's been ridin' yer horse an' usin' yer saddle."

"Deuce Gitano's saddle is here in the wagon," Sky
Pilot said, fearful of being stuck with Suzanne for the
rest of the drive. "Bring me a hoss and I'll saddle it."

* * *

Stoney loaded his Colt as he rode, but withheld his fire. Even if he was in range, shooting from a galloping horse at his pursuers would be a waste of ammunition. Likewise, the hard-riding renegades held their fire, content to let him exhaust his horse and then kill him at their leisure. Three of their number had been cut down by Stoney and his outfit, so they wanted him bad. That was something he might use to his advantage, so he began devising a desperate plan. When he judged they'd ridden far enough, Stoney deliberately slowed his horse. Let them believe the animal was tiring. It had the desired effect, and when he looked back, he counted twelve riders and they were gaining. As he neared the creek, Stoney turned his horse slightly to the southeast. The Indian camp was typically well-concealed, and Stoney was on top of it before he saw it. But he had slowed his horse to the extent that the pursuing renegades were practically on his heels, so close they had begun shooting, and they roared into the Indian camp with guns blazing. A dozen hard-riding, gun wielding white men meant only one thing to the Indians, and they responded exactly as Stoney had expected. Four of the Tundree gang were shot out of their saddles, and the others—including Tundree himself—were routed in confusion. Not a Kiowa was hit, and as quickly as they could catch and mount their horses, they lit out in pursuit of Tundree and his retreating riders.

"Well, old hoss," Stoney laughed, "Tundree and his bunch wanted a fight, and I reckon, by God, they got one."

Stoney found the herd trailing well, Suzanne back in the saddle, and Sky Pilot almost jovial.

"Wal," said Long John when Stoney had told him of the introduction of the Tundree gang to the Kiowa, "that was somethin' I'd of paid money to see. But what about t'night? When we git to that creek, that bunch of

Injuns may still be there, jist waitin' to peg our hides out to dry. They had to know about us an' the drive."

"I reckon they did," Stoney said, "but when the Tundree gang hit the Indian camp, suppose they thought it was us?"

"That'd be damn strong medicine fer us," said Long John. "I don't reckon Tundree's bunch is gonna git a chance to explain it was all a misunderstandin'."

"I'll be ridin' back to the creek ahead of the herd," Stoney said. "I don't look to find the Kiowa at that same camp, but I'll have to be sure. I'll want to see where they went when they gave up chasin' Tundree's gang."

"Mebbe they kilt 'em all," said Long John.

"No such luck," Stoney said. "I don't think we've seen the last of that bunch. Not after we've salted down three of 'em and I've led the others headlong into a band of Kiowa."

Stoney grinned to himself when he reached what had been the Kiowa camp. Nothing remained but the ashes of an old fire and four scalped, mutilated bodies. The Kiowa had returned for the grisly finale only because they had left in too much of a hurry to complete the ritual. Stoney had no trouble following the trail north. There was a dead horse, still saddled, but no more bodies. Stoney rode almost ten miles north of the creek before the tracks of the Indians' horses veered off to the east. They had given up pursuit so that they could scalp their victims before dark. Stoney rode south until he got to the creek, and then southwest to meet the trail drive.

"Wal," Long John said, "I feel some better, knowin' them Injuns ain't camped along the creek. But I'd give odds that Tundree bunch ain't give up on gettin' even. They got even more reason now."

"Long as we're in Indian Territory," said Stoney, "I think we'll do just as we did last night. Malo Coyote and Naked Horse will be circling the camp, the herd, and the horse remuda. If they ain't already, Tundree's bunch is gonna git damned reluctant to sneak around in the dark."

Buck Tundree and his remaining riders were exhausted, and so were their horses. They had ridden west, finally managed to evade their Kiowa pursuers, and had worked their way south to the dirt-floor cabin Stoney had discovered.

"By God," said one of the renegades, "I wisht we'd never heard of them damn Texans an' their trail drive. Ain't nothin' went right for us since they showed up."

"Buck," said a young rider, "I'm sick of these damn woods, greasy grub, and dirty blankets. Why can't we go back to St. Louis?"

She was only seventeen, a hellcat in Levi's and a too-big shirt. Buck Tundree had decided she was his kind of woman after he'd murdered her parents in St. Joe and she'd left with him willingly. He eyed her tolerantly now, and then he spoke.

"Mauvie, there ain't a damn lawman in Missouri that wouldn't give five years of his life to get my neck in a noose. Get a fire goin' and boil us some coffee."

"No coffee," she said. "I can boil you beans or flour. Which do you want?"

One of the gang laughed, but it died to a nervous titter when Tundree glared at him. It was a critical time, and they all knew it. They had lost seven of the gang in a week, and nobody but Tundree had any enthusiasm for further attempts at vengeance. Their comrades were dead, and giving the Texas outfit hell wasn't going to change that. Besides, this Texas bunch didn't take kindly to anybody giving them hell. They repaid in kind, with interest.

"Tomorrow," said Tundree, "we'll ride north and set up an ambush. I owe those bastards, and I pay my debts."

Nobody said anything, but with the exception of the girl, their minds were on those who had died attempting to execute Buck Tundree's idea of vengeance. None of them dared look Tundree in the eye, lest he suspect what they were thinking. But when Tundree slept, who was going to stop them from riding away into the night?

The trail drive reached the creek so recently occupied by the Kiowa, and Stoney again instructed Malo Coyote and Naked Horse to prowl the area.

"I never knowed a pair of Injuns could cover so much territory in the dark, an' do such an almighty good job of it," Long John said. "When this drive's done, I jist hope Malo Coyote an' Naked Horse will go back to Texas with us."

"I don't know where else they'd go," said Llano. While he and Stoney hadn't mentioned it to Long John, they suspected the Indian duo might be wanted for horse stealing in some of the more civilized parts of the country. Remaining on the Rio Colorado for a while might keep their necks out of a noose.

"I'm going back on the second watch tonight," Suzanne said.

"Come on," said Long John. "Jist don't git shot again. I ain't sure Sky Pilot could stand it."

"I'm going to ride with Harley on his watch," Pearl said.

Despite Pearl's newly gained confidence, she still feared Bandy Darden. She had said nothing, not even to Harley, but she didn't like the look in Darden's eyes. While he had done nothing, and since that first day had said nothing, Pearl felt like he was just waiting. He hadn't forgotten her checkered past, nor did he intend to.

"Long John," said Suzanne during the first watch, "I want Harley and Pearl to go back to Texas with us."

"I reckon that'll be up to them," Long John said. "Ye know life on that Colorado River ranch is hard. Don't ye go givin' the little gal no false hope."

"I haven't," said Suzanne, "except . . ."

"Except what?"

"Except I said we'd help them get a start."

"By God," Long John said, "we're broke as they be, gal. Ye gonna talk us right into the pore house."

"We won't be broke after we sell the herd. I owe a lot to Pearl. I felt sorry for her, tried to help her, and then she ended up helping me. I want her for a neighbor. What will you do, without another woman for a hundred miles, when I'm about to have a child?"

"Wal, I . . . *what?* Ye ain't . . . ?"

"No, I ain't," she laughed. "Not yet. But I got your attention, didn't I?"

"Ye sure as hell did." Long John sighed. "I like Pearl. The little gal's strong an' true, an' I got nothin' agin' havin' her an' Harley close by. Jist go slow, an' don't be spendin' the gold from this drive 'fore we git our hands on it."

Unless the weather was bad, Tundree's men spread their blankets outside, in deference to Tundree's woman. So it came as no surprise when the remaining six men left the cabin with their bedrolls. The surprise came at dawn, when Tundree discovered that he and Mauvie were alone. The men had taken their bedrolls and their horses and departed. The tracks led north.

"Them cowardly sonsabitches," growled Tundree. "I oughta track 'em down and gut-shoot the lot."

"I'm glad they're gone," said Mauvie. "Now we can leave here. Let's go today."

But Tundree was in a foul mood. He grabbed the front of Mauvie's shirt and lifted her off the floor. "We'll go when I say," he snarled.

"Damn you," she shrieked, "put me down."

He flung her against the log wall and she slid to the dirt floor. From her boot she drew a stiletto and came at him, springing off the floor like a cat, the blade ripping his shirt at the waist. He caught her arm, twisted it until she dropped the knife, then slammed his fist against the side of her head. She sagged against him, and with his free hand he unbuttoned her Levi's. They slid to the dirt floor, and recovering, she began unbuttoning her shirt. . . .

June 27, 1858. Indian Territory.

When the herd was again on the trail, Stoney rode out. Yesterday he had freed them of the Kiowa and the Tundree gang, playing one against the other. But today would be different. They might meet both factions somewhere along the trail. But Stoney found no tracks along the creek he had chosen for the night's camp, and when he rode back to the herd, he found the longhorns trailing well.

"I figger we ain't more'n three days south of the Canadian River," Long John said. "We'll pass next to Fort Gibson betwixt the Canadian an' the North Canadian."

"I didn't think you knew the territory," said Stoney.

"Don't," Long John said. "When I was with the Austins on that drive to Californy, they had some maps the Rangers had got from the guv'mint. They showed the rivers an' the forts in Indian Territory, but nothin' else."*

"One thing I like about the territory," said Stoney, "and that's the water. We haven't been stuck in dry camp yet."

It became one of their better days, and nothing disturbed the quiet except the occasional cry of a coyote, followed by a distant answer. Despite the tranquility, Stoney continued having Malo Coyote and Naked Horse scout the area, and shortly after midnight the camp awakened to a squall that a cougar might have

* Trail Drive Series #5, *The California Trail*

envied. But it was human. Everybody, including the nighthawks, was at the wagon when Long John arrived. Naked Horse held the screeching, kicking captive by the waistband of her Levi's. Her shirt had been ripped or cut away, leaving no doubt of her gender, for there was light from the moon and stars.

"Squaw," Naked Horse said contemptuously. *"Malo bruja."*

"What'n hell's a young gal doin' here in the territory in the middle of the night?" Long John demanded.

"Catch Squaw *perra,"* said Naked Horse. *"Bandido hombre* run. *Cansado. Malo* Coyote *caza, matar."*

"Set the little gal on her feet," Long John said, "so's I kin talk to her."

But it was easier said than done. The moment she was upright, Mauvie spat in Naked Horse's face. It was something no squaw dared do if she valued her life. Naked Horse slammed her in the face with the flat of his big hand. It lifted her off the ground, and she fell on her back. She did not move.

"Suzanne," said Long John, "git a shirt an' git it on her whilst she's out. It purely ain't decent, her layin' there thataway."

The girl didn't move while the shirt was being buttoned, and not even while Suzanne bathed her bleeding nose and mouth with cold water. She was still for so long, Long John knelt down and took her hand, seeking a pulse. But Mauvie had been playing possum, and tore into Long John like a catamount. By the time she was subdued, she was again without a shirt. Long John finally slammed her down on her back, knocking the wind out of her.

"Now, damn it," Long John panted, "who are ye, an' what was ye doin' here?"

"I am Buck Tundree's woman," she hissed, speaking for the first time. "Buck will kill you."

"Gal," said Long John, "ye ain't old enough to be

gallivantin' around with a varmint like Tundree. I reckon we'll have to take ye on to St. Louis an' let the law look out fer ye. Suzanne, git me some of that muslin. I reckon we'll have to tie her hand an' foot an' haul her in the wagon."

"Hell's fire and damnation," Sky Pilot groaned, "ain't they no end of tribulation?"

Suzanne brought the muslin. It was a situation not to Long John's liking, and Suzanne quickly came up with a solution.

"Long John," she said, "all of you leave her alone. Let Pearl and me see to her."

Nobody argued with that. Naked Horse, with a final contemptuous look at the girl, left to join Malo Coyote, as they again began scouting the area. Stoney, Darden, Quando, and Harley returned to nighthawking, while the rest of the riders went back to their blankets and their interrupted sleep. An uneasy silence prevailed the rest of the night. During breakfast, just as it became light enough to see, a distant rifle spoke. The slug slammed into a cottonwood tree just a few feet from the wagon. Colts in their hands, the riders sought cover. But there were no more shots. The captive girl understood the significance, and there was wild laughter from the wagon. Buck Tundree was out there, and he was making them aware of his presence.

"Sharps buffalo gun," Long John said. "The bastard aims to stalk us, an' he's lettin' us know what to expect."

"Turn the gal loose," said Bandy Darden. "You aim to git us all gunned down fer a woman that ain't wantin' to be rescued?"

"It's more'n that," Long John said, "an' ye know it. This Tundree varmint blames us fer saltin' down seven of his gang. He was out there last night with some devilment in mind, and that was 'fore we caught the gal. Ye give in jist a little to some bastard that's crowdin' ye, an' he'll shoot yer ears off."

"Long John's right," Stoney said. "Nothing will rid us of this Tundree short of killin' him, and we'll have to do it before he kills some of us. He won't just give up and go away."

"We could trail him and gun him down," said Llano. "He's showed us he's got a Sharps and that he can shoot. Next time it won't be a cottonwood that takes the lead. He won't have to come slippin' around in the dark. He can pick us off in the daylight."

"He'll be lookin' fer us to trail him," Long John said, "and I reckon there's nothin' he'd like better. He can hole up with that Buffalo gun and cut us down 'fore we're even close to bein' in range."

Naked Horse and Malo Coyote had already had their breakfast when Tundree had fired on the camp. The Indian duo had remained silent while the outfit discussed the dilemma. Now Naked Horse spoke.

"Naked Horse follow. No get close big gun. Come night, *cuchillo* kill."

"Long John," said Stoney, "that may be the answer. Tundree's out there somewhere with a long-range Sharps, and if we wait for him to make the next move, some of us will die. Naked Horse on his trail will put him on the defensive. As long as Tundree's a threat, Naked Horse or Malo Coyote can scout ahead. I'll stay with the drive so we're not shorthanded."

"You got problems lots bigger'n Buck Tundree," Sky Pilot said. "I ain't ridin' from here to St. Louis with that female catamount at my back."

"Jist one damn thing at a time," growled Long John. "Ye kin stand it fer a day er two, till we git this Tundree varmint off'n our backs. Suzanne, 'fore we hit the trail, will ye git that gal in the wagon some grub? She's gaunt as a lobo."

"I'll help," Pearl said. "We'll have to untie her hands, and Suzanne's wound is still healing."

The wagon's canvas pucker was closed. Pearl had

loosened the canvas and was about to climb over the gate when, from the dim interior of the wagon, the captive girl sprang. Pearl drew back barely in time, the knife slashing her shirt from shoulder to shoulder. Mauvie made another pass with the knife, but Pearl caught the renegade girl's wrist, dragging her from the wagon. The two of them fought for the knife, Mauvie with her back to the wagon's gate. Sky Pilot crept through the wagon's interior, and as he was about to get his arm around Mauvie's throat, she sank her teeth into his hand. He bawled like a fresh-cut bull, and Mauvie threw all her weight against Pearl. They went down, Mauvie on top, trying to drive the thin-bladed knife into Pearl's throat. Long John seized Mauvie's shirt and only succeeded in ripping off what was left of it. Before anybody else could get a grip on the girl, they had swapped places. Pearl was on top, and the two of them fought for possession of the knife, which was still between them. Pearl cried out as the knife point ripped into her shoulder, but she still had the strength to force the knife-wielding hand away from her.

The struggling women rolled under the rear of the wagon, still fighting for possession of the knife. Pearl was still atop the outlaw girl, and Mauvie suddenly heaved upward, slamming Pearl's head against the heavy wagon axle. Mauvie broke Pearl's grip and drew back the knife for a final thrust, but Pearl wasn't finished. She caught Mauvie's wrist and drove the hand and the knife between the spokes of the wagon's rear wheel. With her other hand, Pearl seized the hand holding the knife, forcing it hard against the wagon spoke. Slowly but surely she broke Mauvie's grip on the knife, and it dropped to the ground.

Mauvie then got both hands on Pearl's throat and began slamming her head against the underside of the wagon. Her head pounding, unable to see for blood and dirt, Pearl seized one of the wagon spokes and from there began searching for the fallen knife. Dizzy and weak for lack of air, she fought to bring the knife into position. Mauvie released her grip on Pearl's throat and began fighting for possession of the knife, and suddenly Pearl drove her head down as hard as she could, directly into the other girl's face. The shock of it freed Mauvie's grip on Pearl's wrist, and she drove the knife into the renegade girl's throat. There was a gasp, a cry, and the struggle ceased.

Harley Logan was first under the wagon, and there was a glad cry when he found Pearl was alive. Slowly, carefully, he eased her out. She got to her knees but could go no farther. She sobbed, tears streaking the blood and dirt on her face. Only the collar and sleeves of her shirt remained. There was a bloody knife slash from shoulder to shoulder, just under her collarbone. Her nose and mouth were a bloody mess, and blood ran out of her hair from a lacerated scalp. Suzanne was first to recover from the shock. In an instant she was at Pearl's side, helping her unsteadily to her feet. Without a word to anybody, she led the bloodied, weeping Pearl down along the creek until they were shielded by a growth of brush along the bank. Harley Logan stood looking after them as though undecided as to what he should do. He, along with the rest of the outfit, was shocked speechless.

"Lord God," said Dent Briano, "I ain't never seen nothin' like that, and I don't never want to again."

Without a word Llano and Quando Miller lifted the dead girl from beneath the wagon. Blood still welled from the terrible wound in her throat, and she looked pitifully young. The men were Texans, and had seen death in most of its forms, but never had they witnessed anything like this. They swallowed hard, for it touched them in a manner that left them strangely uncomfortable, as though each of them had suffered a personal loss.

"I reckon we'll be gittin' a late start," Long John said.

"Couple of ye git the shovels from the wagon. We'll find her a place along the creek."

They wrapped her in a blanket, for they had nothing else, and buried her deep so the wolves and coyotes couldn't get at her. Stoney took his Bible from his saddlebag, and his throat was so tight, reading was difficult. He read the Twenty-third Psalm, and while it all seemed so inadequate, there was nothing more to be said or done. Pearl, her wounds tended and in a clean shirt, had been unable to witness the burying. She had sat on the wagon tongue, and Suzanne had stayed with her. The trail drive moved out two hours late, and whatever she was or had been, they mourned for her. There was only the steady, plodding hooves of the longhorns, the creak of saddle leather, and the sigh of the wind in the cottonwoods. Her lonely grave was unmarked, for they hadn't known her name, no more than they knew the name of the creek where she lay. . . .

Buck Tundree rode in from the south, reining up at the creek. Dismounting, he walked to the new-made grave. From there he walked along the creek until he found the tattered bloody shirt Mauvie had worn. Returning to the grave, he stood there cursing bitterly, clutching the Sharps until his knuckles were white. Finally, his cruel lips set in a grim line, he mounted and rode north

17

While Naked Horse would be seeking water as he scouted ahead, strong on his mind was the renegade killer and his long-range Sharps. It was well to scout the trail ahead, lest they ride into an ambush, but what of the back trail? Already the Kiowa had attacked from the south, and Long John's woman had been wounded. Naked Horse had his suspicions, having looked at the cottonwood that had taken Tundree's slug. The shot had come from a southerly direction, and before Naked Horse rode north, he intended to find the position from which Tundree had fired. If the killer had ridden north from there, it would be a simple matter to circle wide and trail him. If he had gone south, then Stoney Winters should be told. The danger would not lie ahead, but behind. Naked Horse found Tundree had left little sign, but had no difficulty in finding where the renegade had left his horse. And that was all the Indian needed. He wasn't in the least surprised when the trail led south, doubling back to their last night's camp, or when he found Tundree's tracks near the grave of the *diablo* squaw. Naked Horse followed Tundree's trail north until it turned sharply northwest. The killer would circle wide and get ahead of the trail drive, or perhaps ride parallel to it, awaiting his chance to fire from the south. Naked Horse was no coward, but had a healthy respect for the long-range killing power of the Sharps. If Tundree intended to stalk the Texans from the south, he wouldn't be ahead of them, but somewhere to east or west. He could easily fall back to the south as he saw fit, and that would effectively destroy Naked Horse's defense. He must either scout the trail to the north, or drop back and attempt to pursue the killer. He couldn't do both, and he rode due north, catching up to the trail drive. He found Long John, Pearl, Suzanne, and Harley riding drag. Long John looked questioningly at Naked Horse.

"Sendero jefe," said Naked Horse.

"Suzanne," said Long John, "ride an' git Stoney *muy pronto.* I reckon we got us some talkin' to do."

Finding Naked Horse at drag, Stoney turned to Harley Logan. "Harley, keep the herd moving. I'll want to talk to you, Suzanne, and Pearl after I've talked to Naked Horse."

Stoney rode back to Long John and Naked Horse, and he didn't have to question the Indian. Long John had already questioned Naked Horse, and he quickly related to Stoney what he had learned.

"The bastard's driftin' along with us," Long John said. "He's been to our last night's camp, foun' the grave, an' knows about the girl. When the cover's right, he kin drop back an' shoot hell out'n our drag, an' they ain't a damn thing we kin do about it."

"Night come," said Naked Horse.

"I reckon it will," Long John said irritably, "but we can't wait fer it. It's the daylight an' that damn Sharps that'll kill us."

"You're right," said Stoney. "It'd be just like the cold-blooded sidewinder to gun down Pearl and Suzanne for the girl we buried beside the creek. We'll have to box this hombre in and force his hand. Naked Horse, you and your *cuchillo* are *muy bueno,* but we cannot wait for the night."

Stoney pointed to himself and to Long John, and then drew his Colt, pointing it west and southwest. Finally he pointed to Naked Horse and then to the north. The Indian nodded his understanding, mounted his horse and rode after the herd. His *cuchillo* was no match for the long gun of the renegade Tundree. He would scout the trail ahead and seek water for the night's camp.

"If'n I'm readin' ye right," Long John said, "ye aim fer us to flush this Tundree hombre out so's we kin git at him with our Colts."

"It's that or risk havin' him gun some of us down from long range," said Stoney. "Catch up to the drag and talk to Harley. Tell him the drag riders are to stay right on the heels of the herd. The dust will keep them from bein' easy targets. Then you and me are goin' to box Tundree, you from the north and me from the south. Keep to cover so he's got nothin' to shoot at. I want him to know we're after him, keepin' him so busy watchin' us that he's got no time to use that Sharps on our riders."

"By God," Long John said, "I like yer thinkin'. Sooner er later, we git this polecat to shoot at us, an' fore he kin reload, we'll rush the bastard."

"That's the only chance we have," said Stoney. "Once we get him boxed, with the Sharps empty, it's his Colt against ours. Long as he's a mile away with a loaded buffalo gun, all the chips are on his side of the table. Just don't give him anything to shoot at, keep to cover, and let's not give him a minute's rest. I want to force his hand before dark. If we don't, he could get close enough to gun our nighthawks out of the saddle, but not close enough for Malo Coyote or Naked Horse to reach him."

Long John rode ahead to speak to Harley Logan, while Stoney rode westward. While the trail drive kept to the high plains and open spaces, Stoney turned north, keeping to cottonwood and scrub oak thickets. The riding was more difficult, but it was excellent cover. He offered a poor target, even at close range, with a Colt. From a great distance he couldn't even be seen.

"I feel this is all my fault," Pearl said when Long John told the drag riders what he and Stoney had planned.

"Ye done what ye had to," said Long John. "We had Tundree after us 'fore ye had the fight with Tundree's woman. I'm sorry fer the gal, but she was a hellion that wouldn't of had it no other way. It's a bother, havin' to track down this Tundree, but it's somethin' that's got to be done."

Long John rode on past the herd, and when he was well ahead of it, he rode west. There was a chance Stoney had misread Tundree's intentions, that the renegade might ride on ahead of the herd and cut down the lead riders. With Naked Horse scouting far ahead, Malo Coyote was a lone target with the horse remuda.

To the south, from a stand of stunted oaks, Buck Tundree had witnessed the conversation between Stoney and Long John. Naked Horse eventually rode after the herd and was soon followed by Long John. That meant nothing to Tundree, but his lips skinned back over his teeth in a wolf grin when Stoney Winters rode west. So they knew he was somewhere to the south of them, thanks to the Indian, but his plans could change. He too could ride west, and when he was far beyond the herd, he could then ride north. From there he could ease in from the flank, keeping to cover, and cut down on the flank riders.

But Tundree didn't know that far ahead of the trail drive, Long John Coons was riding west. With Long John ahead of him to the north, and with Stoney advancing from the south, the renegade was about to be forced into a showdown where the Sharps buffalo gun would be of little use to him. It would be his Colt against that of Stoney Winters and Long John Coons.

Naked Horse rode north, and while his duty had been

clearly defined, he felt cheated. True, the *diablo* gun could kill him long before he could creep close enough to use his *cuchillo*, but he believed his failure had been a keen disappointment to Long John Coons and his Texas outfit. But Naked Horse soon had to free his mind of all except what lay ahead, for he was approaching not just a creek, but a river of some importance.*

The water was swift and the banks much too steep for crossing, especially for the old cook's *carreta*. Looking for a suitable crossing, Naked Horse rode downstream a mile, without the banks diminishing. Turning his horse, he rode back the way he'd come. Reaching the point where he started, he rode a mile in the opposite direction, until the river's banks began to flatten out. Finally Naked Horse reached a long stretch where not only were the banks low enough for the wagon to cross, the water was shallow enough that the *carreta* wouldn't have to be floated. Heavy rain could change all that, but Naked Horse saw little possibility of it. Cautiously he rode his horse into the river, testing for quicksand, but found none.

He was about to ride out and return to the trail drive when a bit of white on the opposite bank caught his eye. When he rode across and retrieved the object, he found it was the butt of a white man's cigarillo. It was enough to ignite the Indian's curiosity, and he circled until he found the tracks of a shod horse followed by the lesser prints of a mule. Could it be two riders, one of them mounted on a mule? Naked Horse didn't think so. While the mule's tracks were deep enough for the animal to have been ridden, it had more likely been used to carry packs. One white man leading a pack mule didn't seem threatening. Naked Horse followed the trail west for several miles and found nothing to arouse his suspicion. But his curiosity had him wondering what business

* The Canadian

did one man and a mule have here in a wilderness that seemed to harbor only *bandidos* and killers? Naked Horse didn't know. He would report what he had seen.

Stoney rode on, keeping to whatever cover there was, knowing that if Tundree had ridden north in pursuit of the trail drive, there had to be some sign. But the renegade was no fool, and while the Sharps buffalo gun gave him an edge, he wasn't taking anything for granted. He had kept to grassy plain and to wooded land where fallen leaves made tracking difficult. Finally there was a stretch of upthrust rocks that had blackened and mossed over, and one of these had been nicked by the shod hoof of a horse. Stoney dismounted, and while there was no other prominent sign, a few yards farther north he found a partially rotted log with a bit of bark dislodged. Had this sign been left by Tundree as he'd ridden north earlier in the day, or was it his trail as he'd recently ridden south? Stoney needed to know. If Tundree was still to the south, then Long John was wasting his time farther north, leaving Stoney to face the renegade's buffalo gun alone.

Stoney got his answer, and it almost cost him his life. His horse nickered and he went belly down as the Sharps roared. The heavy slug slammed into an oak near where he lay, and he rolled into what might have been the shallow bed of a dry stream. It was poor cover at best, but he lay still, counting on Tundree being too distant to see him in this prone position. However, Tundree might be able to see his horse, and could fire at any movement near the animal. That, Stoney knew, could pin him down until dark. But he now knew that Tundree was to the north of him, which meant Long John was north of Tundree. While the Cajun was armed with only a Colt, he had one advantage: Tundree wouldn't know he was there, while Long John had heard the boom of the Sharps. It would give him some idea as to where the elusive Tundree was.

To the north, Long John reined up as the crash of the Sharps died away. Stoney had drawn fire, and if Long John was any judge, the young trail boss would take cover and prolong the standoff. They couldn't get close to Tundree as long as he had the deadly Sharps loaded and ready, but now they had a chance to take the buffalo gun out of the fight. Long John rode cautiously south. If his thinking was right, Stoney would somehow provoke Tundree until the renegade fired again. It would bring Long John that much closer to the showdown.

Stoney, as quietly as he could, rolled over on his back. Feeling around among the leaves, he found a slender dead branch a yard long. It was strong enough to support his hat, and he raised it up just high enough that the renegade with the Sharps might see it, if he was close enough. And he was. The buffalo gun roared and the heavy ball snapped the branch supporting the hat. Stoney sighed. The best he could do was continue to draw Tundree's fire. Long John would then have a chance to rush the renegade before he could reload the buffalo gun.

Long John grinned to himself as the .50 caliber long rifle roared again. He had no idea what Stoney Winters was doing to keep Tundree shooting, but it took courage to taunt a man with a Sharps who could hit what he was shooting at. Long John rode as far as he dared. He then dismounted and tied his horse, since he had no idea how near to Tundree he was. Somehow he must locate the man's position, and when Tundree again cut loose with the Sharps, be close enough to rush Tundree before he could reload. Tundree might suspect that very tactic and refuse to give away his position by continued firing. But Stoney Winters was more resourceful than that, and Tundree was too deadly with the Sharps.

Stoney tried another tactic that was more helpful to

Long John in locating Tundree. "Tundree," he shouted, "this is gettin' you nowhere. Why don't you mount up and ride out while you can? Come dark, I have some Indian friends who'll be looking for you, and the buffalo gun won't be of any help."

"Won't make no difference to you, Texas," Tundree shouted, "because you ain't gonna be alive till dark. I can move, and you can't. I can't see you from here, but that gully you're bellied down in ain't worth a damn at the open ends. You got just a few more minutes, bucko."

"Wrong, Tundree," said Long John. "I'm behind ye, an' I got the drop. Now git up, leavin' the long gun on the ground. Do it slow, with yer hands where I kin see 'em. I'm givin' ye more of a chance than ye'd of give us."

Slowly Tundree got to his feet, leaving the Sharps where it lay.

"Now," said Long John, "with yer finger an' thumb, ease that Colt out'n the holster an' drop it. Then ye kin turn around."

Slowly Tundree did as he was told, lifting the Colt and dropping it at his feet.

"Turn around an' face me," Long John said.

Stoney was out of range, and while he couldn't fire, he could see what was coming. "Long John!" he shouted.

Tundree carried a second Colt under his belt, and when he whirled to face Long John, the weapon was roaring and spitting lead. The first slug ripped off Long John's hat, while the second burned a fiery path along his neck beneath his left ear. But Long John didn't flinch, and he fired just once. Dust puffed from Tundree's shirt, his knees buckled and he fell. Lying on his back, his life pumping out the hole in his chest, he turned hate-brimming eyes on Long John.

"You bastards . . . killed my . . . woman," he gritted.

"We didn't aim to," Long John said. "It was her choice, an' we give her a decent buryin'."

But Tundree's hate-filled face had relaxed in death and his wide open eyes were unseeing.

"God," said Stoney, "this has been the kinda day you don't want to ever think about again."

"That's gospel," Long John said. "He was a killer, but I reckon he cared fer the gal. Git his horse. We'll rope him acrost the saddle, an' I'll pack him back to the creek wher' we buried his woman. Ye kin ride back, ketch up to the wagon, an' git the shovels. We'll plant him alongside the gal."

Without a word, Stoney went and found Tundree's horse. The two of them roped the renegade across the saddle, and Long John rode away, Tundree's skittish horse on a lead rope. Stoney took the Sharps, mounted his own horse, and rode to catch up to the trail drive.

"It's got to be the Canadian River," Long John said, after Naked Horse had returned from his scouting, "an' as fer them tracks, I'd gamble it's jist one hombre with a pack mule. Dunno what'n hell he'd be a doin' here, but I can't see it as a danger to us. Kin ye, Stoney?"

"No," said Stoney. "Llano and me spent some time in Omaha, and we heard that Jesse Chisholm's got a tradin' post somewhere on the Canadian, a hundred and forty miles or so west of Fort Smith. Chisholm's always ridin' off somewhere tryin' to make peace between the Indians and the whites."*

"He must be some hombre," Llano said. "They say he speaks the language of fourteen tribes, and the government relies on him pretty strong."

"Them tracks was some hombre headin' fer Chisholm's post, then," said Long John. "We ain't lookin' fer trouble, but when we git to the Canadian, I reckon we'd best do some scoutin', 'specially to the north. If'n I be any judge of distance, when we cross the

* Trail Drive Series #3, *The Chisholm Trail*

Canadian an' the North Canadian, we'll be mebbe a day's drive from the Arkansas. From there, we ain't more'n five days from the Missouri line."

June 27, 1858. The Canadian River.

While Stoney and Long John had forced a showdown with Buck Tundree, the rest of the outfit had kept the herd moving, and so the drive reached the Canadian with some daylight to spare. Long John and Stoney rode to the potential crossing Naked Horse had spoken of, and found it better than they'd expected. Stoney rode west, following the week-old tracks for ten miles, and found nothing to alarm him.

"I been givin' it some thought," Long John said around the supper fire, "an' I'd like to talk to this Jesse Chisholm, if'n it ain't more'n a day's ride to an' from his place. We got mebbe a week 'fore we git into Missouri, an' I'd like some talk with a gent that likely knows what the feelin' is. I reckon we kin lay over a day here, usin' the time to wash clothes an' blankets."

"You aim to ride alone?" Stoney asked.

"I reckon," said Long John. "We ain't got that many riders that two kin be gone fer a day. 'Sides, if'n I don't see some sign of Chisholm's post by midday, I'll have to fergit it an' ride on back. I ain't layin' over here more'n one day."

June 28, 1858. The Canadian River.

Long John rode out at first light, following the Canadian west. He had begun to think his ride was in vain when the sun started its daily journey toward the western horizon and Chisholm's post was nowhere in sight. Long John reined up, preparing to ride back the way he'd come, when his horse nickered. Deep in Indian Territory, it was an unwelcome sound. It meant other riders, and the odds were against them being friendly. Buck Tundree's bunch had been proof enough of that. Long John dismounted, the reins in his left hand, his Colt in his right. There were three riders, a white man in the lead, the two Indians that followed leading pack mules. They fanned out on each side of their *patrono,* for they were armed and he was not.

"We come in peace," said the stranger. "I am Jesse Chisholm, and these are my Cherokee riders."

The Indian riders had made no move toward their belted Colts, so Long John eased down the hammer and holstered his own.

"I'm Long John Coons," he said. "From Texas."

Long John appraised Chisholm and found Chisholm conducting an appraisal of his own. While there was some Indian in him, Chisholm had eyes as blue as Long John's, and those eyes held steady, never leaving Long John's own. He had the most compelling stare of any man the Cajun had ever met. He wore homespun shirt and trousers, and a flop-brimmed hat that had seen more than its share of rain. He inspired a confidence that Long John rarely felt for any man.

"I got a herd o' Texas longhorns back down the river a ways," said Long John. "We're bound fer St. Louis, an' I'm hopin' ye kin tell me how things is up ahead."

"Not good," Chisholm said. "I have business at Fort Smith. Mount up, and we'll talk as we ride."

Long John rode alongside Chisholm, and the Indians followed with the pack mules. It was an opportunity for Long John to size up the other man without seeming to stare. Chisholm wore moccasins instead of boots, and his gray hair was long and shaggy. His neck and face were burned as brown as an old saddle, making his ragged moustache appear more white than it actually was.

"You'll have trouble getting your herd into Missouri," Chisholm said, "because of the tick fever problem. Besides that, you have the pro-slavers and abolitionists, with night riders from both factions killing and plundering. Then there's the renegades, like Quantrill, playing one side against the other while he steals and kills."

"I thought Quantrill was mostly causin' trouble in Kansas."

"He started there," said Chisholm, "but now he's spending as much or more time in Missouri. It's estimated that his gang numbers between sixty and a hundred men."

Long John found Jesse Chisholm to be the most knowledgeable, literate man he'd ever spoken to, and the ride back to the herd seemed short.

"It's near sundown," Long John said. "Yer welcome to stay the night."

"Much obliged," said Chisholm. "There's a cured ham on one of the pack mules. We'll share with you."

They had supper before dark, and even Bandy Darden listened with interest as Chisholm told them of his efforts to negotiate peace with the plains tribes.

"Someday the territory will become a state," Chisholm said, "and the government hopes to relocate many of the tribes here."*

"If'n all the tribes was to come here," said Long John, "mebbe they'd be peace. That is, if'n the guv'mint would leave 'em be. If'n the Injuns give up their land an' come here, this ought to be their land fer all time."

"I'm told it will be," Chisholm said. "That's why I'm trying to get the tribes to give up their traditional lands and resettle here. The government is telling them this will be their land forever."**

* * *

* Indian Territory became the state of Oklahoma in 1907.
** Such was not the case. By the turn of the century, most of the territory had been opened to white settlers.

At first light Chisholm and his Indian companions rode east, toward Fort Smith. The longhorns were well watered and grazed, and once they were again moving north, Stoney rode ahead to scout the trail. He found they were just a day's drive from the North Canadian, and reaching it, he scouted at least ten miles east and west. Finding nothing to arouse his suspicion, he rode back to the herd.

"If'n I'm rememberin' it right," Long John said, "it can't be more'n a day's drive from the North Canadian to the Arkansas. If'n we're lucky, it ought to be easy trailin' from here to the Missouri line."

But their luck didn't hold. Three hours before sundown, big gray thunderheads began gathering far to the west, swallowing the sun in an explosion of flaming red.

"By God," said Long John, "we're in fer somethin' 'fore the night's done."

"One thing worked out in our favor," Stoney said. "Today was a good drive, and we'll have supper before dark. After that, I want everybody in the saddle until that storm has done whatever it aims to do."

After supper Stoney spoke to Malo Coyote and Naked Horse. They were to move the horse remuda well away from the longhorns. More than once, when the herd had stampeded, Malo Coyote and Naked Horse had been able to control the horse remuda. Stoney hoped they could do it again.

"I've never been through a stampede before," Pearl said nervously.

"If'n they run," Long John said, "don't ye try an' git ahead of 'em. If'n they's any way to head 'em, we got enough riders. If'n they's lots of thunder an' lightnin', they likely won't be nobody that kin hold 'em. They'll run like scairt wolves, an' they won't stop till they're plumb tuckered out."

"Haw, haw," Bandy Darden laughed, "why don't we

all roll in our blankets, let 'em run, and then gather 'em up in the morning?"

The insult was directed at Pearl, and it wasn't allowed to pass. Llano turned angrily on Darden.

"I reckon it's her turn to skip this stampede, Darden. You set out the last one. My horse got hooked and damn near pitched me off, and what was you doin' toward headin' the herd?"

"Ever'body pull in yer damn horns," Long John shouted. "We purely ain't got the time to fight amongst ourselves, even if'n we had somethin' to fight about. Nobody but a damn fool gits himself kilt by runnin' in front of a stampede that ain't about to be headed. I'd ruther spend tomorrer roundin' up the herd than in buryin' some of ye. Now mount up an' let's do what we kin."

The coming storm had much the same effect on the riders as it had on the longhorns and the horses. It was a nervous time when the elements seemed to gather their fury to make war against man, and man had nothing with which to retaliate. Storms that struck in the night left riders all but helpless when it came to trying to head the thundering herd. Long John was a practical man and a fair one when it came to the safety of his riders.

"I reckon this'll be one hell of a storm," said Dent Briano. "It's been a while since we had one, and she's just been too hot for the last few days."

It was a prophecy that wasted no time being fulfilled. Blue, green, and gold lightning rippled from one horizon to the other. Riders lashed down their hats with piggin string as the first rain blew in on the wings of a screaming west wind. Thunder became a continuous drumroll, and the earth trembled. A cow bawled, and as though on cue, others joined in until there was a chorus that could be heard above the roar of the storm. Riders circled the herd, themselves ill at ease, as lightning seemed at any moment about to strike the earth. When it did, three hundred yards west of the skittish long-horns, a resinous old pine literally exploded in blue fire. In the pitch-black of the night, it seemed the very world was on fire, and the herd—of a single mind—decided it wanted to be somewhere else. Anywhere else. The troublesome Corrientes bulls taking the lead, they thundered away to the east, along the banks of the North Canadian.

"By God," said Quando Miller, "it'd take a prairie fire comin' at 'em head on to change their minds."

"Well," Llano said resignedly, "we know what we'll be doin' tomorrow. The horse remuda's gone too."

"Tomorrer," said Long John, "we'll start the gather. T'night we kin sleep. Jist two riders fer the watch. Suzanne an' me will take the first. Anybody volunteerin' fer the second?"

"Pearl and me," Harley Logan said.

18

*L*ong John awakened Harley at midnight.

"Ye best not move around too much," Long John said. "They's a skunk wanderin' about, likely after the scraps from supper."

Harley took Long John's advice. While their horses cropped grass, Harley and Pearl sat with their backs to an oak and talked.

"We didn't even try to stop the herd from running," said Pearl. "Why did Stoney have all of us mounted?"

"So we wouldn't be left afoot," Harley said. "It ain't easy for your horse to pile into a stampede when you're in the saddle."

"If we go back to Texas with Long John and Suzanne," said Pearl, "I hope Bandy Darden won't go."

"I expect Long John will have somethin' to say about that," Harley said. "Right now we're shorthanded and need every rider. Even Darden."

"He won't ever let me forget what I've done . . . what I was," said Pearl.

"Nobody else is holdin' that against you. There's nothin' Darden can do."

Pearl didn't agree, but she said nothing. From the very first time Darden had insulted her, Harley had fought for her, and he would again. But Harley Logan was no killer, and certainly not a gunman the equal of Darden, and Darden was much heavier. While Pearl dared not tell Harley, she feared Darden would kill him, and she yearned for some way to strike back at the arrogant gunman.

"That skunk's still around here," Harley said. "He's stronger'n ever."

"What do they eat?"

"I dunno," said Harley. "Meat, I reckon."

"I was nervous about the storm and didn't eat much supper. I have some beef wrapped in my bandanna."

"You'd best eat it or get rid of it," said Harley. "We don't want that varmint lookin' for us."

Pearl laughed. "No, but suppose he went looking for Bandy Darden?"

"If you're thinkin' what I *think* you're thinkin'," Harley said, "don't you dare. You go sneakin' around Darden in the dark, and he could shoot you dead."

"Aw, come on, Harley," Pearl begged. "He always takes off his boots. I can drop it in one of them. I'll be ever so quiet, and he'll never know."

Harley thought as little of Darden as Pearl did, and the idea appealed to him mightily. Finally he agreed. Silent as a shadow, Pearl dropped the morsel, and she and Harley settled down to wait.

"It'll likely be for nothin'," Harley said. "The stink of Darden's boot might kill the smell of the meat."

But that wasn't the case. Something awakened Bandy Darden, and unsure as to what it had been, he lay there in the dark trying to get a handle on it. The moon was already down, and little or no starlight filtered through the leaves of the cottonwood beneath which he'd spread his blankets. Suddenly there was the soft ching of a spur rowel. Somebody was after his boots! Slowly Darden drew his Colt and sat up. His movement, slight as it was, was enough. The intruder became frightened and reacted in the manner of all its ancestors since the beginning of time. Bandy Darden took the blast full in the face. He coughed and wheezed, cursed, and emptied his Colt in the general direction from which the attack had come.

"What'n hell . . . ?" Long John bawled.

He and the rest of the riders were out of their blankets in seconds, Colts in their hands.

"Skunk!" Harley laughed from a safe distance.

Darden continued to choke and gag, and for obvious reasons, nobody came close to him. His acid tongue, foul mouth, and antagonistic manner had cost him whatever sympathy might have been his.

"You been actin' like a skunk for so long, Darden," Llano said, "you're startin' to smell like one."

Dent Briano and Quando Miller said nothing, but they were grinning in the darkness. Stoney at first thought Suzanne had been overcome by the skunk smell, but then realized her choking was the result of suppressed laughter. Only Long John managed to remain serious.

"Darden," said the Cajun, "git rid o' them blankets, the duds that yer wearin', an' go dunk yerself in the river. If'n ye aim to go on with this outfit, ye'd best be rid o' the worst o' that stink by mornin'."

Darden did not, or could not, respond. He continued coughing and wheezing, and the rest of the riders left him to his misery.

"By God," Long John wondered when he and Suzanne were back in their blankets, "many of us as they is, why'd that stinkin' little varmint go after Darden?"

"Like attracts like," Suzanne said cheerfully.

"God," said Harley, when he and Pearl were again alone, "that was a dirty, sneakin', low-down thing to do, even to the likes of Bandy Darden."

"Yes," Pearl agreed, "and I just wish he knew it was me that done it."

"He'd shoot you dead, even if they hung him for it."

"I know," Pearl sighed. "You ain't sorry I done it, are you?"

"I just said it was a dirty, sneakin', low-down thing to do," Harley said. "I never said I was sorry."

In daylight Bandy Darden was a ghastly figure. His eyes were swollen and his breath came in painful gasps. His face, neck, hands, and arms were as red as turkey wattles, for he had scrubbed himself with the terrible lye soap that was only used to wash clothes. There was a pair of bullet holes in each of his boots, but no sign of the skunk's remains. The offending animal had escaped. Despite his having spent most of the night in the river, scrubbing himself raw with lye soap, Darden still stunk to the extent that nobody could stand being near him. Nothing was said about Darden's condition. He helped himself to breakfast and ate far from the rest of the outfit.

"Now," said Long John when breakfast was done, "we'll start our gather. I don't look fer 'em to be too scattered. Since they was runnin' alongside the river, it ain't likely they crossed it."

Unfortunately, as they rode eastward, the river deepened and the banks became higher. In the darkness two of the Corrientes bulls had gone over the edge, breaking their necks on an upthrust of rocks that lay just beneath the water.

"Wal," Long John said, "that ain't a good sign. A sharp bend in the river could wipe me out."

"They was slowin' when they got here," said Dent Briano. "But for them high-steppin' Corrientes bulls, the strides is shorter."

The horses had quit the stampede first, and the remuda was almost intact, grazing along the river.

"Once the storm eased up, the stampede slowed," Stoney said. "Unless we find some more dead ones, this won't be all that bad. With the river cuttin' 'em off to the south, they can't have scattered too far."

The river remained at a depth that made crossing difficult, and with a longhorn's limited intelligence and ambition, the herd had been content to graze along the north bank. By early afternoon Long John and Stoney were ready to run a rough tally.

"I count 2005," said Stoney.

"I got 2012," Long John said. "We'll take the low count."

"Now," said Stoney, "do we spend another night here, or push on to the Arkansas?"

"We got near six hours o' daylight," Long John said. "These varmints is well-rested, grazed, an' watered. Let's head 'em north, swat their behinds, an' git on to the Arkansas."

"Damn right," said Llano. "One side of the river for us, the other side for Bandy Darden."

"We're losin' half a day," Stoney said. "I'll ride on to the Arkansas and look for Indian sign. Push the herd, because it may be farther than we think. There'll be a moon tonight, and unless there's rough country ahead, with dropoffs, we'll go on after dark."

When Stoney reached the Arkansas, he realized they'd bitten off more than they could chew, for he had ridden more than twenty miles. It would be next to impossible to push the herd that far, even if they kept to the trail until midnight. He rode upstream and then downstream far enough to be sure there was no Indian sign, reminding himself that last night's storm would have erased any trail made as recently as the day before. But there would always be some risk. On the frontier, a man rode with a loaded Colt, a quick eye, and a quicker hand. Stoney rode back to the herd, and starting with the Indian horse wranglers, told every rider of the difficult drive to the Arkansas. For the first time, at the mention of such an ordeal, Bandy Darden said nothing. He contented himself with a surly stare and rode on.

"Wal," said Long John, "we're into it, an' they ain't nothin' to do but go on. We'll drive 'em till moonset if'n we kin keep 'em movin'. If'n they git too damn cantankerous, they's nothin' we kin do but stop the drive an' go again at first light."

Because of their late start, the longhorns trailed well until sundown, but there their cooperation ended. It was time for them to stand belly deep in cool water, drinking their fill. A time to graze and rest. But they had no graze, no water, no rest, and their continuous lowing became a mournful dirge. The drag riders got the worst of it, as the longhorns near the tag end of the herd began to break ranks, galloping madly down the back trail.

"That's the trouble with cows," Quando Miller said wearily. "They don't remember a damn thing but the last water hole they drunk from."

"Not a breath of wind," said Llano. "If there was just a little breeze from the north, these cantankerous brutes wouldn't stop runnin' till they was standin' in the Arkansas."

"With our luck," Stoney said, "if there was any wind, it'd be from the south, and in the mornin' we'd find this bunch standin' in the North Canadian."

They continued pushing the rebellious longhorns, losing time as they had to head numerous bunch quitters. Finally, two hours shy of midnight, Long John called it quits.

"By God," the Cajun growled, "we're killin' ourselves fer nothin'. They ain't no way in hell we gonna git to that river t'night. Mill the bastards, an' we'll start early, whilst they's some dew on the grass."

"Watches as usual," said Stoney, "and we'll change at two o'clock."

"My God," Suzanne said, "who can sleep with all that bawling?"

"You'd better try," said Stoney. "Tomorrow will be worse than today."

Despite Stoney's admonition, nobody slept enough to make any difference. The longhorns spent the night lowing and moving restlessly about, so that the nighthawks had trouble keeping them bunched. There was a nickering from the horse remuda, as the horses picked up the skittish mood of the longhorns. Llano didn't have to wake Stoney for the second watch. After less than two hours of fitful dozing, Stoney was riding beside Llano, circling the nervous herd.

"Give it about two hours in the mornin'," Llano said, "and it'll be hot as the hinges on the gates of hell. By noon this bunch of stubborn brutes is gonna know what *real* thirst is."

"And we're gonna know what *real* trail drivin' is," said Stoney. "I'd say we're still a good ten miles south of the Arkansas, and by the time we chase bunch quitters all day, we'll be lucky to reach water before dark."

"I'm lank as a starved lobo," Llano said. "We had no supper, and if you got ideas of us movin' out without breakfast, you're gonna be in big trouble. Startin' with me."

"We'll eat before we move out," said Stoney. "The longhorns—and maybe even the horses—will be at their worst, so we'll have to be at our best."

Far to the west there was a flicker of lightning, but it wasn't repeated. The sky was awash with stars, and there was no cloud cover.

"Heat lightning," Stoney said. "No rain."

With approaching dawn, the riders ate a few at a time. There was some dewfall, and the longhorns had begun to graze. They had no desire to take the trail again, and defied every effort to bunch them. Even before the sun rose, the riders were dusty, sweat-soaked, and hating longhorn cows in general and this herd in particular. Malo Coyote and Naked Horse had better luck with the horse remuda, for while the animals were thirsty, they lacked the deep-rooted, cantankerous disposition of the longhorns. Stoney waved his hat, pointing to the trail ahead, and the Indian wranglers caught on quickly. The horse remuda was brought into line, and some of the less unruly of the longhorns began to follow.

"Thank God," Long John sighed, "some of 'em ain't forgot they was part of a herd. Swing them lariats, gents, an' let's refresh the memories o' the rest of the varmints."

It took the moving horse remuda ahead and a lot of hard riding behind before the longhorns were again trailing north, leaving Sky Pilot following the herd with the wagon. Long John dropped back, speaking to Sky Pilot.

"Them longhorn bastards needs somethin' to foller fer a while, an' they's more inclined to foller the horse remuda than a wagon. Fer t'day, until we git to the Arkansas, keep behind the drag riders. A mite dusty, but it won't kill ye."

"Injun arrers might," said Sky Pilot shortly.

"Injuns show up," Long John said, "preach to the bastards. That'll git rid of 'em quicker'n a comp'ny of U.S. Cavalry."

It was by far the worst day they'd had on the trail since leaving Texas, and Stoney had privately begun to doubt they'd reach the Arkansas before dark on this second day's attempt.

"Wal, hell's fire," said Long John, "I'm some tempted to get behind this bunch an' cut loose with my Colt, an' jist stampede the hell out'n 'em."

"I'd agree and join you," Stoney said, "if we was within two or three miles of the Arkansas, but we're still too far away. Force this ornery bunch to run, and they'd just scatter from hell to breakfast. We'd be stuck with another gather and another night in dry camp, and we don't want that. We'll just have to force them ahead as best we can. Come sundown, if we're still fighting them, maybe we'll be close enough to force them to run the rest of the way."

Unable to handle a rope, Pearl was of little use at drag, but Long John left her there with Harley, because she'd have been even less useful anywhere else. Llano, Dent Briano, Quando Miller, and Bandy Darden were the flankers, while the rest of the riders rode drag. With Naked Horse, Malo Coyote, and the horse remuda leading the drive, Stoney dropped back and joined the hard-riding drag riders. In the distance he could see Llano and Darden scrambling to head deserters along the right flank, while Dent Briano and Quando Miller were fighting a similar battle at the left.

"My God," Suzanne gasped as she and Stoney drove a trio of rebellious longhorns back to the slow moving herd, "how much farther to the Arkansas?"

"Less than five miles," said Stoney. "Maybe not that far, but don't be surprised if we're until after dark getting there."

"Wind or not," Suzanne said hopefully, "when we get a little closer, maybe we can stampede the herd and run them the rest of the way."

"Maybe," said Stoney, and that reminded him of something. In between battles with the backtrailing longhorns, Stoney had a chance to speak to Long John.

"Just in case the herd should get a whiff of the river and decide to run," Stoney said, "we really should have Malo Coyote and Naked Horse take the horse remuda on ahead, as they've been doing. Otherwise, we could end up with a stampede that'll include the horses. Thirsty as these longhorn brutes are, once they smell water, they'll gore anything gettin' in their way. Trouble is, with the horse remuda gone on ahead, the herd won't have anything to follow."

"They ain't trailin' worth a damn," said Long John, *"with* somethin' to foller. Ye reckon they could actual do any worse?"

"I doubt it," Stoney said, his grin cracking the trail dust that had dried on his sweaty face. "I'll ride ahead and have Malo Coyote and Naked Horse take the remuda on to the Arkansas. First chance you get, drop back and have Sky Pilot pull ahead of the longhorns and follow the horses on to the river."

Having sent Malo Coyote and Naked Horse on to the Arkansas with the horse remuda, Stoney returned to the drag. They didn't have enough riders for him to remain at the point position. Sky Pilot had swung wide of the herd and was rapidly overtaking it. Not too difficult, as slowly as the longhorns were moving.

"By God," said Long John, sleeving the sweat from his face, "I'd take thunder, lightnin' bolts, an' whatever else they is up there, long as they was some rain comin' with it."

"So would I," Stoney said, "but there's not a cloud in sight. Wind or not, once the sun's down, the herd can sense water once we're within a mile or two of it. They'll tear out of here like hell wouldn't have it, and that'll end our trouble for today. There'll be another gather in the morning, but I don't look for 'em to get too far from the water."

"I'd do a new gather every day, from here to St. Louis," said Harley Logan, "if it meant there'd be no more days like this."

The herd plodded on, bawling their discontent, but having grown weary enough that they had ceased breaking ranks. Slowly the sun made its way to the western horizon, and every hard-won mile seemed like two. The blue of the sky was swept away, evening shadows spreading a purple backdrop for the first stars. If nothing else, there was blessed relief from the relentless sun. There was still no wind, but a coolness suggestive of the river somewhere ahead. It was enough for the lead steers. With a frenzy of bawling and a thunder of hooves, they were off and running.

"Yippeeee," Llano shouted.

"Thank God," Suzanne sighed. "Whatever it takes to round them up again in the morning, it'll be worth it."

The outfit came together, trotting their horses through the coolness of the evening, bound for the Arkansas. Bandy Darden, having sweated out most of the stink, now rode closer. His first utterance since tangling with the skunk was fully in character.

"We never should of left the North Canadian in the middle of the day," he growled. "Just whose damn fool idee was that, leavin' us in dry camp, and puttin' us through all the hell we had today?"

"My idee," said Long John, dangerously calm. He said no more, nor did Bandy Darden.

Reaching the Arkansas, Stoney could see the horses grazing on the other side of the river. Longhorns were still drinking, many of them belly deep in the water. Sky Pilot's small fire had burned down to coals, suggesting that supper was ready, or nearly so.

"Ever'body unsaddle an' see to yer horses," Long John said. "Then we'll eat. With them cows scattered up an' down the river fer a mile er two, they ain't much need fer nighthawkin'. We'll keep watch over the camp, two of us at a time. After that god-awful bawlin' last night, I reckon ever' one o' us is needin' sleep."

"Amen to that," said Dent Briano. "I feel like I got half the trail dust in Indian Territory down my gullet, and the rest under my eyelids."

Sky Pilot had outdone himself, and there was dried apple pie for supper. Malo Coyote and Naked Horse were allowed to take their supper first, because the horse remuda had not scattered and would need watching during the night. The Indian wranglers were especially fond of the dried apple pies, and they each took two, much to Bandy Darden's disgust.

"Damn Injuns," Darden said, loud enough for Stoney to hear. "What kind of outfit is it that lets them hea· thens eat ahead of a white man?"

"Darden," said Stoney, "this outfit ain't in the least concerned with a man's hide. When a man does what he's hired on to do, conductin' himself like a man, then he gets treated like one. Nothin' else matters to me, and I purely don't give a damn how you feel about it."

Darden said no more. Dent Briano and Quando Miller were watching him, and so was Long John. The three of them were thinking similar thoughts. While the trail drive was shorthanded, and they needed Darden, there was going to be a reckoning. While Briano and Miller had some idea as to when and how the showdown would come, Long John knew only that it would come at the end of the trail, after they had reached St. Louis.

July 1, 1858. At the Arkansas.

Despite the terrible two days it had taken to reach the Arkansas, some sleep and good food made all the difference. The herd took the trail at first light, Stoney riding ahead to seek water and scout for Indian sign. If Long John was correct in his distances, they were less than ninety miles from the Missouri line. From there, according to what Jesse Chisholm had told him, they were about 250 miles from St. Louis. If nothing happened to slow their progress, the drive should reach the end of the trail early in August.

Stoney rode almost twelve miles before finding water for the night's camp. It was a fast-running creek that looked as though it might empty into the Arkansas somewhere to the east. While they were almost out of Indian Territory, Stoney took no chances, scouting the creek in both directions for Indian sign. While hostiles were always a concern, he couldn't discount the possibility that their potential enemies would be riding shod horses. Strong on his mind was the warning they had received from Jesse Chisholm regarding the renegades who plundered and killed in Kansas and Missouri. From whence such an attack might come, they had no way of knowing. They must be ready. Finding nothing to arouse his suspicion, Stoney rode back to meet the herd.

"How will we know when we enter Missouri?" Suzanne asked.

"From what Chisholm told us," said Long John, "the second day after we've crossed the Arkansas, we'll hit the Neosho River. It crosses the Kansas line jist a little ways west o' the Missouri line, runnin' southeast to join the Arkansas. We'll foller the Neosho to jist shy o' the Kansas line. From ther' we keep to the northeast, an' we're in Missouri."

The herd was trailing well, allowing Harley and Pearl to ride alongside Long John and Suzanne.

"Plenty of water," said Harley, "while we're followin' the Neosho."

"Fer about seventy-five mile," Long John said. "Chisholm said this part of the Neosho twists an' winds somethin' fierce, an' there'll be lots of backwater an' little lakes. Kind of like that stretch north o' Dallas, but here we'll be follerin' the Neosho lots farther. I reckon, fer the five days 'fore we cross into Missouri, water won't be a problem fer us."

Stoney rode in before noon, finding the herd trailing well. He rode back to drag, reporting to Long John.

"We got water fer t'night, then," said Long John, "an' tomorrer sometime we'll pick up the Neosho where she turns to the southeast. Follerin' the river, however crooked she is, we'll make up some time. It'll be a rest fer us all, not havin' to wrassle the herd to the next water."

"I reckon we'd better enjoy it while we can," Stoney said. "I have the feeling it's the calm before the storm."

Without difficulty they reached the creek Stoney had chosen, and before sundown the longhorns had been watered and bedded down for the night. While everything seemed serene, Malo Coyote and Naked Horse had taken the horse remuda well away from the longhorns. It was a tactic that had served them well.

"Tomorrer," said Long John, "we ought to reach the Neosho where she turns southeast, an' we'll foller her north till she cuts away west to the Kansas line. From there I reckon we kin consider ourselves in Missouri. We got mebbe a week o' good trailin' an' good water. All we got to look out fer is renegades an' mebbe Injuns."

"Then comes Missouri," Llano said, "and God knows what we'll find waitin' for us there."

19

A day and a half north of the Arkansas, as Chisholm had promised, the trail drive reached the bend in the Neosho where it turned southeast. The Neosho was clear-running and deep, and the sight of it brought a deep sigh of satisfaction to the riders. It meant plentiful water for the next five or six days, with the promise of rest wherever darkness found them.

"Wal," Long John said cynically, "it's damn near perfect. I reckon we'd best keep our eyes open fer hostiles an' renegades. On the frontier, nothin' ever goes right all at the same time."

Nobody laughed, for it was all too true. While water wasn't a problem, Stoney continued riding ahead, scouting the river to the north. The second day after they reached the Neosho, he found the tracks of a dozen shod horses. The tracks had come from the west, reaching the Neosho three or four miles north of where Long John's outfit had bedded down the herd the previous night. The tracks had turned north, following the Neosho, as though the riders might have known nothing of the trail drive to the south. But Stoney didn't believe that. He rode cautiously north, studying the trail, and decided the tracks weren't more than a few hours old. With the river near, the trail drive had the freedom of bedding down the herd at any time, but Stoney rode on. While these riders might mean trouble along the trail, Stoney didn't intend to sacrifice all or part of a day's drive because of them. He rode an estimated ten miles without any deviation in the trail he followed. He turned and rode back to meet the herd, and found Long John skeptical as to the destination of the riders Stoney had been trailing.

"By God, I'd bet the herd it's a bunch o' them renegades Chisholm warned us about," Long John said. "Why else would a dozen hombres be gallivantin' around in this godforsaken country?"

"No reason I can think of," said Stoney, "and while they can't have known we were here, I can't imagine them ridin' so close without findin' out."

"Me neither," Long John said, "an' them ridin' north don't mean doodly. Right now, the bastards could be somewher' to the east er west of us, ridin' south to our flank."

"That's my thinking," said Stoney, "and while they might not be after us, we can't afford to give 'em the benefit of the doubt. I reckon we'd better let this be a ten-mile day, bed down the herd, and find out just where these hombres are. Slick as they may be, I don't think they can outslick a pair of trailwise Indians. I think we'll let Malo Coyote and Naked Horse follow that trail."

"Good idee," Long John said, "an' don't wait fer us to bed down the herd. They're trailin' good, so I reckon Harley, Pearl, an' Suzanne can handle the drag fer a while. Let's the two o' us take the horse remuda, so's Naked Horse an' Malo Coyote kin git on that trail pronto."

"You're right," said Stoney. "If they're up to no good, the sooner we know it, the better chance we'll have."

They found the Indian duo eager to take the trail, and especially Naked Horse, for he felt he had failed in the pursuit of Buck Tundree. Long John and Stoney watched the pair ride out. They each rode one of the solid black Mendoza horses bred from the stock Gil and Van Austin had brought back from Mexico in 1845.*

"Look at 'em ride," Long John said admiringly. "Was them two in a quarter mile race on them blacks, I'd bet ever'thing I own an' all I could borry."

"It'd be a temptation," said Stoney, "but I'd think on it some."

Once Naked Horse and Malo Coyote knew what was expected of them, they had their own unique method. They rode north until they found the trail Stoney had followed, and when they reached the point where he had turned back, they reined up. Clearly, Stoney Winters and Long John Coons suspected that the *docena* riders would eventually double back. They would ride north far enough to allay suspicion, ride east or west four or five miles, and ride south. While their tracks indicated that they'd ridden north, they would actually be but a short distance east or west of the unsuspecting trail drive. There was little point in following the actual trail. Malo Coyote spoke.

"Este?"

"Este," Naked Horse said. "Me *oeste.*"

Malo Coyote rode east while Naked Horse rode west. If the twelve riders had doubled back south, Malo Coyote or Naked Horse would cross their trail without tracking them farther north. If neither of the Indian riders found where the riders had doubled back, then they would have to follow the trail north. It wouldn't mean there was no danger of an ambush. It might mean the renegades had found good cover somewhere to the north and would simply wait until the unsuspecting Texans rode into the trap. Malo Coyote rode ten miles to the east, while Naked Horse rode an equal distance to

* Trail Drive Series #4, *The Bandera Trail*

the west. The pair met near the point from which they had started.

"*Nada*," said Malo Coyote.

"*Igualmente*," Naked Horse said.

Long John Coons and Stoney Winters had guessed wrong. Naked Horse and Malo Coyote picketed their horses in an oak thicket and there they waited. The sun was but an hour high, and the darkness that followed was their *bueno companero*. . . .

"Them Injuns has been gone a hell of a long time," Long John said.

"Yeah," said Stoney, "and that tells us we were wrong about one thing. That bunch of riders may try and ambush us farther north, but they won't be comin' after us tonight. Doublin' back, they could have come at us from east or west. If that's what they had in mind, we'd know it by now. Malo Coyote and Naked Horse found no evidence of that, and they're havin' to follow the original trail north. They don't know what they're ridin' into, and they're settin' it out somewhere, waitin' for dark."

"Ye ain't got a lot o' years behin' ye," Long John said admiringly, "but ye know a powerful lot about the way them Indians think."

"A white man can learn from them," said Stoney. "Have you ever seen an Indian ride into an ambush?"

"I reckon I ain't," Long John said with his lopsided grin. "One thing I got to say, I never seen a more valuable pair o' hombres than Malo Coyote an' Naked Horse. I'm countin' it a lucky day they showed up, along with ye an' Llano."

"I reckon I might as well tell you what I hadn't aimed to tell you for a while," Stoney said. "Llano and me found Malo Coyote and Naked Horse in the clutches of some Comanches, about to be burned at the stake. After we risked our scalps to save their hides, we found they'd been caught tryin' to steal Comanche horses. They're notorious horse thieves, and God knows what kind of price may be on their heads."

Long John slapped his thigh with his hat and laughed until there were tears in his eyes.

"Llano and me had just crossed the Red," said Stoney, "and after we freed them thievin' varmints, the four of us rode damn near a hundred miles before we lost them Comanches."

It threw Long John into a new fit of laughter, and it was a while before he could speak.

"Why didn't ye find some good cover an' ambush the bastards?"

"It ain't been more'n two minutes," Stoney said, "since you admitted you'd never seen an Indian ride into an ambush. How long since you went up against twenty Comanches, all of them mad as hell, clamorin' for your scalp?"

"By God," said Long John as he sleeved new tears of laughter from his eyes, "ye mean them two Injun wranglers snuck into a Comanche camp an' tried to make off with every damn hoss?"

"Exactly what they tried to do," Stoney said, "and before we finally lost them Comanches, Llano and me was wishin' we'd left Malo Coyote and Naked Horse to roast over a slow fire."

"I'm glad ye didn't," said Long John, serious now. "When ye measure a man's courage, the right er wrong o' what he's doin' don't figger into it. I've knowed some hombres that should of been strung up, but what they was deservin' bein' strung up fer took guts. Remember that gun-throwin' Clay Allison out in Colorado?"

"I've heard of him," Stoney said. "Got in a fight over a boundary with one of his neighbors. Allison dug a grave, and the two of 'em got down in that hole and fought with knives."

"He done that," said Long John, his eyes afire with admiration, "an' he's alive t'day. A damn fool mebbe, but that don't take nothin' from his havin' sand in his craw."*

Once the sun was down, darkness came swiftly. Malo Coyote and Naked Horse loosed their horses, mounted, and rode north. They noted with approval there was a light breeze from the northwest. White men liked to linger before a fire, and however small and well-concealed it might be, there was always smoke. After the Indian duo had ridden for an hour, they slowed their horses. Their quarry was ahead, and not too far.

"*Humo,*" said Naked Horse, sniffing the wind.

"*Fuego,*" Malo Coyote agreed.

They dismounted, securing their horses. They were downwind, but they dared not ride any closer, for in this camp there would be many *bandidos*. While at some later time they might take part in battle, tonight they could only observe and report what they had seen. They proceeded on foot, Naked Horse a few paces behind. There was a deep arroyo that angled in from the northwest, ending at the Neosho. Once it had been the bed of a creek or perhaps a lesser river. Now there was what amounted to a small lake, backwater from the Neosho. It was an obstruction the trail drive would be unable to cross without moving considerably west of the river. It was near the mouth of this arroyo where water backed up from the Neosho that the renegades had their camp. There was no moon and the small fire was down to coals, and even in starlight this would not be the time to ambush these *bandidos*. Perhaps the renegades had chosen this particular arroyo as the site for an ambush, but as Malo Coyote and Naked Horse studied the situation, that didn't make sense. In daylight the arroyo would become a death trap for those within it, so for tonight it was no more than a concealed camp. The trail drive

* Trail Drive Series #1, *The Goodnight Trail*

would reach this arroyo late the following day. Malo
Coyote and Naked Horse believed it would play some
part in whatever plan the *bandidos* had devised. The duo
crept westward along the rim, determined to follow this
gash in the earth to a point where the trail drive might
cross. As they left the river, the vegetation and trees
thinned out, giving way to stunted growth. Even in the
limited starlight they were better able to see into the
arroyo, and they quickly found it was bending northward
as the depth diminished. Eventually they reached a
place where the trail drive would be traveling parallel to
the arroyo, where its banks were no more than shoulder
high to a man. Malo Coyote and Naked Horse had seen
enough. They returned to their horses and rode south to
report to Stoney and Long John.

"I reckon that tells us 'bout what we needed to
know," Long John said, after Naked Horse and Malo
Coyote had related what they'd seen. "With us comin'
along the west bank o' the Neosho, it'd be the sensible
thing to do, swingin' to the west to avoid this arroyo. All
them pelicans got to do is wait where them arroyo walls
drops down, an' they got natural cover."

"Won't do 'em no good if they're dead," said Bandy
Darden. "All we got to do is be on them canyon rims at
first light, and we can gun down the whole damn lot."

"No," said Stoney. "Those men have done us no
wrong. We're guessing, and we can't massacre a dozen
men based on our suspicions."

"Winters," said Darden, his eyes on Long John,
"you're some poor damn excuse fer a trail boss. You aim
to let them bastards gun down a few of us so's you can
be sure of their intentions? By God, I'm fer goin' after
'em at first light, and if you got some better idea, talk."

There was an uncomfortable silence among the riders, and Long John said nothing. Darden, despite their
dislike for him, had presented a powerful but brutal solution. While it hadn't been mentioned yet, there was

the Indian camp into which they'd crept, gunning down the Comanches while they slept. Had that been any different than the circumstance that faced them tonight?

"Darden," Stoney said, "you jumped up and shot off your mouth without me havin' a chance to say anything. I aim for us to be there at first light, on those canyon rims, but not with guns blazing. I aim to call these men out, learn why they're there, and there'll be no shooting unless they start it. You pull a gun without cause, and I'll kill you where you stand. *Comprender?*"

Darden said nothing, turning away and vanishing into the darkness. It was Long John who finally spoke.

"I reckon that's the only fair way to handle it. We'll have the drop, an' I ain't lookin' fer gunplay. But ye got one thing to consider. When that bunch rides out, we ain't necessarily rid of 'em."

"I know that," Stoney said, "but unless you're of a mind to do as Darden suggests, and gun down the lot of 'em on suspicion, what choice do we have?"

"None," Long John sighed.

"We'll ride in the morning at four o'clock," said Stoney. "Suzanne, Sky Pilot, and Pearl will remain with the herd. We'll have nine guns as opposed to their twelve, but we'll have the drop."

"If I'm part of this outfit," Suzanne said, "why do I always have to stay with the herd?"

"Two reasons," said Stoney. "You're a woman, and somebody has to stay with the herd. Besides, we'll be in a position where we'll have enough guns, and I won't risk havin' you shot when there's no need for it. And the same goes for Pearl. Any more questions?"

There were none. Stoney rode out to the horse remuda and explained the predawn ride to Malo Coyote and Naked Horse. Their response was typically stoic; they said nothing. Stoney suspected their private feelings were akin to those of Bandy Darden, that they likely couldn't understand Stoney's reluctance to gun down the suspected renegades without warning. He couldn't help questioning his own decision. It *was* a temptation to follow Bandy Darden's brutal suggestion, slaughtering these potential troublemakers without warning. But he could not, even if it meant facing them somewhere along the trail.

They rode out, nine strong, with Malo Coyote and Naked Horse in the lead. Even with the stars, the predawn darkness seemed more intense than ever. It would be necessary that they dismount and walk the last mile or two, because of the distance even the smallest sound carried in the night. Even the creak of saddle leather could be heard for a great distance. Malo Coyote and Naked Horse reined up and dismounted, sign enough for the rest of the riders to follow. Naked Horse was in the lead, and after a mile he signaled a halt. Quietly he touched Llano's arm, then Quando Miller's, and finally Harley Logan's. They were to follow him as he led them to the farthest high bank of the arroyo. Malo Coyote would position himself, Long John, Dent Briano, Bandy Darden, and Stoney on the arroyo's near bank. Come the dawn, the suspected renegades in the arroyo would be in a poor position to do anything except mount up and ride on. The stars had begun to recede, withdrawing into whatever invisible haven was theirs between dawn and dusk. Stoney concentrated on the depths of the arroyo beneath them, but could see nothing. The first sign of life they saw was the firefly glow of a cigarette, and a moment later they smelled tobacco smoke. Stoney would challenge them at first light, while sleep still slowed their reflexes. Stoney realized there was a chance —a small chance—that these men were unaware of the approaching trail drive, and if that was the case, he was about to make them aware of the drive's existence. However, it didn't seem possible or even probable that these men were ignorant of the herd of longhorns and horses but a few miles to the south. Why would a dozen law-abiding men be riding through the wilds of Indian Territory with no apparent destination in mind? The gray of the eastern horizon had suddenly become a faint rose, growing deeper, heralding the arrival of the sun. Slowly there appeared the shapes of sleeping men in the depths of the arroyo. Several sat up in their blankets, having their first smoke of the day. It was time, and Stoney approached the edge, his Colt in his hand.

"You men in the arroyo," Stoney shouted, "you're covered. Don't do anything foolish."

One of the men discarded his cigarette and carefully got to his feet, keeping his hands clear of his belted gun. He directed his angry response toward the rim where Stoney stood.

"What'n hell you throwin' down on us fer? We ain't done nothin' to you."

"Not yet you haven't," said Stoney, "and we aim to see that you don't. There's a herd of Texas longhorns down the trail a ways, and we reckoned it was a mite too much coincidence, havin' twelve of you hombres hunkered down in this arroyo, just ahead of us. Under the circumstances, we got a right to know who you are and what you're doin' here."

"You got no such right. Besides, it ain't none o' yer damn business."

"Wrong," Stoney said. "You're covered from both rims. That gives us the right and makes it our business."

For a moment there was no response, as the man below spoke to one of his companions. He then turned back to Stoney.

"We're a deputized sheriff's posse from Fort Smith."

"I don't see a badge or lawman's star on any of you," Stoney said. "What identification do you have?"

"None, and we ain't needin' none."

"Then you can't prove you're who you're claimin' to be," said Stoney.

"And you can't prove we ain't," said the voice with a smirk to it. "What are you aimin' to do, gun us down?"

"This time," Stoney said, "I'm givin' you the benefit of the doubt, but I won't do it again. You got ten minutes to mount up and ride. If we catch the lot of you laid up on the trail ahead of us again, we'll come shootin'. The talk's been done."

"We'll ride," said the surly voice.

Stoney watched as they saddled their horses. Without a word the twelve of them mounted and rode toward the end of the arroyo that led northwest. As they disappeared around the bend, Malo Coyote turned to Stoney.

"Seguir?"

"Seguir," Stoney said. "You and Naked Horse." He pointed to the rising sun, then to the position it would attain by midday. By then Malo Coyote and Naked Horse would know if the riders who called themselves lawmen intended to double back.

When the outfit again came together where they had tied the horses, Malo Coyote and Naked Horse rode north. Stoney and the rest of the riders mounted and rode south, back to the herd.

"By God," said Long John angrily, "that bunch ain't no more lawmen than we be."

"I don't believe they are either," Stoney said, "but we did all we could do, short of gunning them down in cold blood."

"That's what they'd of done to us," said Bandy Darden venomously.

"That don't keep what we done from bein' right," Long John said. "They been warned. If'n they show up again, ye kin shoot all ye like."

Suzanne and Pearl waited anxiously, and Sky Pilot had breakfast waiting. "Come and git it, you ongrateful varmints," he shouted, "or I'll chuck it in the river."

The outfit took the trail an hour later than usual, Long John and Stoney riding behind the horse remuda.

"Ye reckon that bunch is goin' to ride on an' leave us be?" Long John asked.

"For a while," said Stoney. "They can ride sixty miles in the time it'll take us to make ten. All we'll know when Malo Coyote and Naked Horse return is that the twelve of 'em *did* ride on. But they'll know we can't trail 'em forever, and there's nothin' to stop them from doubling back during the night."

"An' facin' us at dawn, like we done them," Long John said.

"They may try to," said Stoney, "but I aim to use the same defense against them that we used against Buck Tundree. We'll have Malo Coyote and Naked Horse out there in the dark, waitin' for 'em."

"That's twelve o' the bastards against Malo Coyote an' Naked Horse."

"No," Stoney said. "It'll be twelve of them against all of us. I don't aim for Malo Coyote and Naked Horse to attack them. I want them to warn us that these hombres are comin', and we'll all face them as an outfit."

The drive moved on, making camp just north of the arroyo where the suspected renegades had been holed up. Stoney had told Malo Coyote and Naked Horse to roam the camp, specifically with their attention to the north. Should the riders approach the camp, Malo Coyote and Naked Horse were to alert Stoney or Long John.

"Mebbe ye ought to of told Malo Coyote an' Naked Horse to grab a pair o' the varmints an' slit their throats. That'd scare hell out'n the rest of 'em, an' they'd likely leave us be," Long John said.

"Maybe," said Stoney, "but we can't count on that. I'd rather just face the whole bunch and be done with 'em. They've been warned, so they get no mercy. We've planted some mighty real-lookin' empty blankets near the wagon."

An hour before dawn Quando Miller and Stoney were

watching the drowsing herd, holding the reins while their horses cropped grass. Suddenly the two animals lifted their heads, breaking the pattern. Stoney and Quando had Colts in their hands when Naked Horse spoke softly.

"*Banditos* come."

"Wait here," Stoney said, "while Quando and me wakes the other riders."

Stoney and Quando quietly roused the rest of the outfit, and Stoney led them to a thicket near the wagon. In the diminishing starlight the blanket rolls near the wagon looked for the world like sleeping men. The renegades had left their horses and were afoot. Stoney had arranged nine blanketed "riders" with the intention of drawing most if not all the renegade fire. The trap had been set as near the river as possible, utilizing the shadow of the overhanging trees. The deep shadow would inspire a false sense of security in the approaching men, but once they began firing, their muzzle flashes would provide perfect targets for the defenders.

"Fire," a voice suddenly shouted from the darkness. A dozen Colts cut loose, lead slamming into the bundles of blankets Stoney had arranged. The firing of the attackers was the prearranged signal for the defenders to open up, and they had targets aplenty. Stoney fired once at a muzzle flash and again to the right of it, and all around him the rest of the riders were laying down a hail of lead. Suddenly it was over, and the silence seemed all the more profound. It was now light enough to see the bodies of some of the attackers. Naked Horse and Malo Coyote had moved cautiously from cover, lest some of the gunned-down attackers still be alive.

"By God," Long John grunted, "we got 'em all."

"Not quite," said Stoney as Naked Horse drew his Bowie.

"My God," Suzanne cried, "this is awful." The empty

Colt in her hand was still warm, and she looked at the weapon as though wondering how it had gotten there.

"I got one of them," said Pearl.

Assured that the attackers were dead, Malo Coyote and Naked Horse drifted silently into the brush.

"Where are they going?" Suzanne asked.

"Likely to get the horses," Stoney said. "Come on, Long John, and let's have a look at what's left of them hombres. I just hope we don't find lawmen's badges on none of 'em.

"I ain't worryin' about it, if'n we do," said Long John. "They cut down on us, an' we give 'em what you promised 'em."

20

When Malo Coyote and Naked Horse had brought the renegades' horses, Long John and Stoney searched the bedrolls and saddlebags. Their findings verified what they had suspected and cleared Stoney's conscience.

"God A'mighty," Long John said, "them thievin' bastards took ever'thing. I never seen so many gold an' silver doodads. One of em' had a silver plate with some writin' on it."

"If there's any way, all this should be returned to the rightful owners," said Stoney.

"I reckon," Long John agreed, "but wher'n hell did all this stuff come from? That bunch o' thieves might of been stealin' all over Kansas an' Missouri."

"Even if we knew how and where, we don't have the time to right all their wrongs," said Stoney. "Let's just consolidate all this in three or four of their saddlebags, pile them in the wagon, and turn them over to the first sheriff we meet."

"Onliest choice we got," Long John said. "I jist hope the sheriff ain't standin' at the line with a gun, tellin' us we can't cross into Missouri."

Again they took the trail north, leaving the dead men where they had fallen.

"It's inhuman, leaving them there for the buzzards and coyotes," Suzanne said, looking back.

"Mebbe," Long John said, "but we jist ain't got the time to plant ever' skunk betwixt here an' St. Louis. Anyhow, we ain't done no worse by them than they'd of done by us."

Despite the late start, the drive covered what Stoney estimated was ten miles.

"I figger we ain't more'n two er three days' drive from the Missouri line," Long John said. "Tomorrer, let's git as early a start as we kin, an' try fer more miles."

"Tomorrow," Stoney said, "I aim to ride out early and try to reach the Missouri line. Or at least to the place where we'll leave the Neosho. If this one band of renegades knew we were comin', there may be others."

"There's somethin' I been wonderin' about," said Dent Briano. "We keep hearin' about farmers and cattlemen bandin' together to keep Texas longhorns out of Missouri. With all the war talk goin' on, there ain't been hardly any trail drives north. How is all them folks gonna know we're goin' to Missouri?"

"I don't know," Stoney said, "unless it's because Missouri's a mite more populated than we're used to. Once we pass a farm or ranch, the word will spread, and I reckon they'll gang up on us."

"I thought that's why you're always scoutin' ahead," said Bandy Darden, "to keep us from ridin' headlong into trouble."

"I aim to do what I can," Stoney said shortly, "but like I said, this is more settled country. I can't just pick up a ranch and put it in my pocket until the longhorns have passed through."

But the authorities in Missouri already knew of the approaching trail drive. Once the Harkness bullwhackers had returned to New Orleans, reporting their failed retribution, the fury of Old Man Harkness had known no bounds. One way or another, he had vowed to have his vengeance on the Texans who had murdered his son. From his desk he had taken a quill, stationery, and an envelope. Finishing the letter, he had sealed it in the envelope and had addressed it to the Attorney General of the State of Missouri. . . .

July 8, 1858. Missouri.

Stoney had ridden ahead as far as the trail drive would follow the Neosho. The morning they parted company with the Neosho, Stoney rode ahead a dozen miles until he reached a swift-running creek that came in from the northwest and turned eastward. It turned in the general direction they would be traveling, and their first night in Missouri, they made camp in the bend of the creek.*

"The creek will have to turn more to the south somewhere ahead of us," Stoney said, "but we'll use it as a source of water while we can. Tomorrow I'll ride ahead far enough to see where we'll be leavin' it."

Stoney rode out the following morning at dawn, just after the longhorns took the trail, and he had ridden only three or four miles when he came upon the tracks of a horse. A shod horse. The trail led in from the northwest and continued along the creek in the direction the drive would take. Stoney rode twelve miles, to a bend in the creek that took it south. The tracks of the single horseman continued to the northeast, the direction the trail drive must go. The implication was clear. The trail drive had been discovered, and somebody was spreading the word. . . .

"I can't be sure, Long John," Stoney said, "but we're talkin' about a single rider, and nothin' else makes sense. He's ridin' ahead of us, making no attempt at

* Shoal Creek, fifteen miles south of present day town of Joplin, Missouri

hidin' his tracks, and I think sometime tomorrow we'll be meetin' these hombres that don't like Texas long-horns."

"Wal," said Long John, "it looks like the trouble we been tryin' to avoid ain't wantin' to avoid us. If'n these gents shows up an' gits ugly, I reckon we'll have to turn back a ways. Er make them think we're goin' to. Fer sure, we can't shoot our way in. We'd git some o' them, but they'd git some o' us, an' that's a trade I ain't willin' to make. I reckon these folks is got a reason fer keepin' us out, an' we got a reason fer goin' on. I ain't wantin' to kill nobody over a herd of Texas cows, but I ain't aimin' fer nobody to kill us over 'em, either. It's one o' them porkypine problems. Ye jist don't know wher' to grab the damn thing. I reckon we'll wait fer tomorrer an' do what's got to be done."

"We can follow this creek for another twelve miles before it turns south," Stoney said. "Tomorrow, water won't be a problem, but I'll scout ahead, looking for riders. If they come after us, I'll try to get back with as much warning as I can. If nothing else, we can halt the drive and all of us come together in time to confront them."

July 9, 1858. On the trail to St. Louis.

Once the herd was on the trail, Stoney rode northeast, following the creek. He would ride to the bend where the creek turned south, and if the way still seemed clear, a few miles beyond. Reaching the bend in the creek, he rode on another half a dozen miles without finding water. Each time he rode across bare ground, he looked for the tracks of the single horseman, and they were always there. The tracks were a day old, and if his suspicions were correct, there had been time enough for the lone rider to have spread the word. He was tempted to ride farther, virtually certain that men would be coming, knowing he should warn the outfit. But suppose these men, when they came, did not return along the trail this lone rider had taken? They could always ride in from the north, taking the outfit by surprise. With this possibility in mind, Stoney rode back the way he had come. Far to the west there was a gray smudge against the sky that seemed to rise up from the horizon. There was a storm building, and hot as it had been, chances were better than even there would be thunder and lightning. Stoney hoped the drive could reach the bend in the creek ahead of the storm. Once the longhorns and the horses had been watered and bedded down for the night, there was a chance the riders could hold them, even if there was thunder and lightning. Reaching the herd, Stoney found they had trailed well. Long John was making good his boast of a better day and more miles.

"I rode six or seven miles beyond the bend in the creek," Stoney told Long John, "and saw nobody. But there's another possibility we'll have to consider. The riders we're expecting may not come at us head on, but from the north."

"I reckon it won't much matter which way they come," said Long John, "if'n they don't ride in shootin'. From what I hear, they'll try an' force us to turn around an' hit the back trail. I reckon the trouble will start from there, dependin' on whether we do er we don't."

"Storm's comin', and we need to reach that bend in the creek before it hits us. I'd like to have the longhorns and horses watered and bedded down by then."

"We will," Long John said. "Storm won't git to us 'fore sometime late t'night er early in the mornin'. Hot as she's been, we gonna git a reg'lar frog strangler, with plenty o' rain. Ye won't be lookin' fer water tomorrer."

"It's just as well," said Stoney. "I look for us to have problems enough. I just have a gut feeling we're in for a showdown with these Missouri folks over this tick fever problem. You know they passed a law three years ago, makin' it illegal for Texas cattle to enter Missouri. If this bunch we're lookin' to meet includes a lawman, we're in for it."

"I reckon," Long John said. "Like I said, it's one o' them things nobody kin figger ahead on. We'll jist play whatever cards we git dealt."

As Long John had predicted, the storm held off, and the trail drive had no difficulty reaching the bend in the creek. The sun lingered for an hour behind gray thunderheads, tinting them with varying shades of red and rose. A light wind sprang out of the northwest, moist with the promise of rain, and occasional lightning leaped above the gathering cloud mass.

"Be early mornin' 'fore it gits to us," said Long John. "Might rain on us all day tomorrer."

"I'd welcome that," Quando Miller said. "If we're gonna be wet, let it be with rain. God knows, there's been enough sweat."

Long John had been right. While there was a cooling wind, the night passed without thunder, lightning, or rain. The dawn broke chill and gray, low-hanging black thunderheads hiding the sun.

"Long John," Stoney said, "I'm of a mind to ride out this storm where we are. There's goin' to be a bunch of thunder and lightning, and I think we'll be better off just keepin' 'em bunched an' holdin' 'em where they are."

"I think yer right," Long John said. "Be a hell of a lot easier fer 'em to run if'n they's already movin'. We'll all jist stay in the saddle an' circle the varmints till the storm passes."

"Stoney," Llano shouted, "riders comin' from the north."

There were fifteen men, the lead rider a big fellow with a long beard, astride a solid black horse. But the most striking thing about him was the badge pinned to his vest, not to mention the brace of Colts he wore and the shotgun in the crook of his arm. He reined up, and the rest of the riders fanned out on either side of him. He wasted no time.

"Who's the owner of them tick-infested varmints?" he demanded.

"Yer lookin' at him," Long John said. "I'm Long John Coons, of Texas. Who be ye?"

"Nolan Venters." said the lawman. "I reckon you know why we're here."

"I reckon we do," Long John said calmly, "but what proof ye got that they's anything wrong with my cows?"

"I don't need no proof," said Venters. "The law says them cows ain't welcome here. Bein' a kind and considerate man, I'm offerin' you and your riders the chance to turn them varmints around and get the hell out of here."

"An' supposin' we don't?" Long John asked. "I'm needin' to git this herd to market."

"Then I reckon you'd best weigh your need for that against bein' shot dead," said Venters. "The law says we got the right to shoot every damn Texas cow settin' foot in Missouri, and if need be, the riders that brung 'em. Now do you ride, or do we shoot?"

"We'll ride," Long John said, "but dammit, not till the storm's done."

"I'm a reasonable man," said Venters, "and I'll allow you that much time. Just so's you don't change your mind, we'll be waitin' up the trail a ways. When the storm's done, just don't make the mistake of travelin' any way except the way you come."

With that they rode out northeast, the direction the trail drive would have gone.

"Damn," Long John said, slapping his thigh with his hat.

"But we can't take them back to Texas," Suzanne

cried. "Not after bringing them this far, and all we've been through."

"When the storm hits," said Stoney, "we can stampede the herd on through that bunch of hombres."

"No," Long John said, "temptin' as it sounds. That'd put us on the outs with the law. I reckon we'll have to drive to the east, an' hope we kin circle around this bunch an' their lawman."

But everything changed in a heartbeat. The first gust of rain blew out of the northwest, and on the trail ahead there was the thunder of guns. It was a vicious fight, transcending the roar of the storm. But Long John and his riders were in their saddles, galloping to calm the herd. Whatever had taken place on the trail ahead would have to wait until the storm abated. Lightning swept toward the earth and the boom of thunder started the longhorns to lowing uneasily. Rain came tearing out of the northwest in gray sheets, lashing the riders and their horses, the wind squalling like a wild thing. But the thunder and lightning diminished and there was only the rain. Long John trotted his horse alongside Stoney's.

"They was some hell of a fight up the trail," said the Cajun. "The herd's settlin' down. Git Llano, an' we'll ride up there an' see what's happened."

The trio had ridden only a short distance when they found themselves facing five riders. The men were heavily armed. Three of them, including the lead rider, wore two guns. Long John, Stoney, and Llano reined up, waiting.

"I'm Quantrill," the lead rider said. He was a young man and he spoke pleasantly, but his thumbs were hooked in his pistol belt, near the butts of his Colts. "Are you men part of the bunch that jumped us up the trail a ways?"

"No," Long John said. "I'm Long John Coons, and we're takin' a herd of Texas longhorns to St. Louis."

"Then you have good horses," said Quantrill, his manner still pleasant. "Many of my men are needing fresh mounts, and we'll be makin' a deal for some of yours."

The four men behind him had fanned out to either side, leaving little doubt as to the kind of deal they had in mind.

"We're needin' the horses we got," Long John said, his eyes on Quantrill.

Quantrill and his men were fast, but the Texans were faster. Long John's slug tore into Quantrill's shoulder and the renegade dropped his Colt. Three of his companions were down, victims of the accuracy of Llano and Stoney. Quantrill wheeled his horse and galloped madly back the way he'd come, as Long John cut down Quantrill's fourth companion.

"We oughta ride the varmint down," said Llano.

"We oughta git the hell outta here," Long John said. "This is the bastard Jesse Chisholm warned us about, an' he's got sixty to a hunnert riders. God only knows how many of 'em is up the trail, an' they'll be comin' after us, hell-bent fer election."

Long John's warning was punctuated with shots, shouts, and the thunder of hoofs. The Quantrill gang was coming, and there was a bunch of them.

"Ride," Stoney shouted. "Our only chance is to stampede the herd and run 'em down!"

The rest of the riders were still mounted, and having been alerted by the gunfire, were waiting. They could see Long John, Llano, and Stoney riding hard, and they could see the many riders in pursuit.

"My God," Suzanne cried, "there must be a hundred men after them!"

"Come on," shouted Quando Miller, "they'll have guns enough to kill all of us ten times. If we can stampede the herd, we got a chance."

Dent Briano, Bandy Darden, Harley Logan, Suzanne and Pearl rode after Quando, and once they were behind the herd of longhorns, they all cut loose with their Colts. Amid the cowboy yells and the thunder of Colts, the herd lurched to its feet and ran wildly toward the coming riders.

"Yippeee," Llano shouted, "what a beautiful sight!"

Long John swung his horse hard to the right, followed by Llano and Stoney. They circled wide of the herd, joining their companions in the wake of the stampede. Quantrill and his superior force quickly discovered their quarry had been replaced with a four-legged avalanche of Texas longhorns. Most of the front runners were the ill-tempered Corrientes bulls, prepared to gore anything or anybody in their path, for any reason or for no reason at all. The herd had fanned out, cutting a wide enough swath until there seemed no way to escape except to turn and flee ahead of them. Quantrill's band did exactly that.

"Let's keep 'em runnin' a ways," Long John shouted. "Be to our advantage if'n we kin run some o' the bastards down!"

When the longhorns began to tire, the Texans backed off and allowed the stampede to slow.

"By God," said Long John when the riders again came together, "startin' them longhorns to runnin' saved us. That was Quantrill, the hombre Jesse Chisholm warned us to look out fer. He's got enough men fer a small army."

"It was Quando's idea to stampede the herd," Suzanne said. "The rest of us just followed him and did our best."

"I'm thankin' ye, Quando," said Long John. "A fast gun ain't the only thing that keeps a man alive on the frontier. Takes a quick mind jist as it takes a quick gun."

Embarrassed with the praise, Quando Miller turned

away. Dent Briano grinned at him, while Bandy Darden kept a surly silence.

"Well," Stoney said, "I reckon we've had one problem replaced with likely a bigger one. Likely, that Missouri lawman and his posse have been wiped out by the Quantrill gang, and we may have them on our trail, since we gunned down four of them. They were after horses."

"They was fifteen men in that posse," said Long John. "When Quantrill an' them four riders come lookin' fer us, I'm bettin' the rest of the buzzards was strippin' that posse an' takin' their horses."

"Maybe," Stoney said, "but they could still come after us and our horses."

"If they do," said Llano, "we'll never see St. Louis. There's enough of 'em to surround us and cut us to ribbons."

"What are we going to do?" Suzanne asked.

"Go on with the drive," said Long John. "Nothin' else we kin do, unless we take that lawman's advice an' hightail it back to Texas."

"We'll go on, then," Suzanne said, "and take our chances with Quantrill."

"Damn right," said Llano. "For all we know, they're on the way back to Kansas. You don't gun down that many lawmen and not have somebody come lookin' for 'em, and who'd be more suspect than Quantrill's bunch?"

"Us, maybe," Stoney said. "We're in violation of Missouri law, taking a herd to St. Louis. Venters and his posse were sent to stop us, and now they're dead. But for that, we'd either have to turn back, or try to sneak in another way."

"Damn it," said Suzanne angrily, "we didn't kill that sheriff and his men, and nobody can prove that we did."

"We can't prove that we didn't," Stoney said, "and who besides us have anything to gain by them bein' dead?"

"Wal, hell," said Long John, "we can't do nothin' but go ahead, takin' our chances. I reckon we're 230 mile out o' St. Louis. Figurin' ten mile a day, that's mebbe three weeks. They's a chance we could git there 'fore anybody finds out about them dead lawmen. Folks is welcome to their suspicions, but they ain't a damn thing to tie us back to them gents. Bein' the buzzards they are, Quantrill an' his bunch stripped 'em of their belongings an' took their horses. We don't know nothin' about that posse, an' we kin always truthfully tell that we was attacked by Quantrill an' his bunch. If'n folks is lookin' fer somebody to lay the blame on, we kin tell 'em that Quantrill an' his gang was here."

"That's a good argument," Stoney said, "unless we get tangled up with a bunch of radicals that believe strong in circumstantial evidence. I reckon our best hope is that we can reach St. Louis before somebody discovers that posse is dead. As long as they're supposed to be out here taking care of us, there's a chance we won't run into another bunch with the same idea. I'd say we'd best gather up the herd and get as far away from this bloody ground as we can, as fast as we can. It looks like there may be rain the rest of the day, and that's in our favor. It won't hide the bodies, but it'll wipe out all trails, includin' that of the posse ridin' in from the north."

Quickly they went about gathering the scattered herd, and with the help of the continuous rain, it wasn't that difficult. During a storm, even rain, the longhorns had a tendency to bunch together, if not all in a single herd, then in a series of smaller ones. By midday the longhorns were again moving northeast. The rain continued, offering a welcome respite from the merciless sun. Water was no problem, being hock deep in places, and the day's drive ended when darkness caught up to them. By the time the first watch had begun circling the herd, the rain had ended. A chill wind swept away what remained of the clouds, and millions of stars blossomed in a field of panoramic purple splendor.

"How grand they are," Suzanne said, admiring the heavens. "I like to think there's another world up there, and that someday we'll ride among them."

Long John said nothing. He was remembering his friend Bo, who had so often spoken of riding a range beyond the stars. Nine years ago Bo had died at the hands of Mexican bandits, and today slept on the bank of the Rio Colorado, near faraway Fort Yuma.*

"There are times," said Suzanne irritably, "when I don't think you hear anything I say."

"I heard what ye said," Long John responded calmly, "an' I was thinkin' of a gent I once knowed that talked of that range up yonder."

"Is . . . was he your friend?"

"Onliest friend I ever had."

"What happened . . . where is he now?"

"Up yonder," said Long John, "on that range beyon' the stars. . . ."

Suzanne had never heard Long John speak with such reverence. She longed to continue the conversation, to learn more about this man of whom she actually knew little. But Long John wasn't ready for that. He said no more.

July 10, 1858. On the trail to St. Louis.

The sun rose, and having been absent for a day, seemed determined to become hotter than ever.

"By tonight," Stoney said, "we won't be able to depend on last night's rain for water. I aim to ride at least twelve miles, lookin' for water and trail sign."

Nobody needed to ask what trail he was seeking.

* Trail Drive Series #5, *The California Trail*

Vivid in every rider's memory was the fifteen-man posse slaughtered by Quantrill and his band, and the realization that so many men sanctioned by the law didn't just disappear without others seeking to learn what had become of them. While the killings had been done by renegades, Quantrill and his men were long gone, probably in Kansas. A second group of lawmen, intent on avenging the first, might simply attack in unreasoning fury. The Texans might become convenient scapegoats, for they were defying Missouri law, and who had a better motive for disposing of a troublesome posse?

Water not having been a problem the day before, Stoney had no idea what distance he might have to ride to find decent water. To his surprise, he had ridden not quite twelve miles when he came to a swift-flowing stream that cut across their trail from the northwest. It was more substantial than a creek, so it had to be a minor river.*

Stoney had no trouble finding a place the wagon could cross. He rode on for several miles before turning back. He had found no tracks, nor had he expected to, for yesterday's rain had left the earth seeming fresh and clean. By the time he met the herd, the July sun had every rider longing for the overcast sky and chill wind of yesterday. But the longhorns were trailing well, having had plenty of rest, water, and graze.

"Wal," Long John said, after Stoney had reported to him, "ever' day we git through without seein' nobody, the better I feel. I ain't wishin' trouble on nobody, but I jist hope that Quantrill an' his bunch raised enough hell b'fore leavin' Missouri to git the notice o' the law. Then even if us an' them longhorns git run out o' the state, at least we won't git hung fer killin' Venters an' his posse."

* Spring River, about thirty miles west of present-day Springfield, Missouri

* * *

July 15, 1858. Cole County sheriff's office, Jefferson City, Missouri.

"Sheriff Brundidge," said a deputy, "two gents just come in from Butler, over in Bates County. They been ridin' all night and they're give out. That bastard Quantrill and his bunch hit the town, and three of 'em was shot out of the saddle."

"None of 'em was Quantrill, I reckon," said Sheriff Brundidge hopefully.

"No," the deputy said, "but these gents that just rid in—"

"I'll talk to them," said Brundidge. "Where are they?"

"Over to the hotel, sleepin'," said the deputy. "They ain't all that important, but what they brung with 'em is. You'd better come out and see."

Three horses were tied to the hitch rail, their heads drooping wearily. One of them was a big black, and Sheriff Brundidge caught his breath.

"That's the three horses them Quantrill men was ridin'," said the deputy.

"I'll have to do some checkin' on the other two," said Brundidge, "but by God, that's Nolan Venters's black. He raised it from a colt, and he'd die before havin' another man take that horse."

"I reckon he did," the deputy said. "Him and all his men."

"We'll have to raise another posse, then," Brundidge said, "if only to find their remains and give 'em a decent burying."

21

July 16, 1858. On the trail, 130 miles southwest of St. Louis.

"*I*t's downright scary," Llano said. "A week with plenty of water, no outlaws, no lawmen, and no stampedes. When trouble finally catches up to us, it's gonna be hell with the lid off."

There was some laughter, but not much. There were so many hazards on the frontier in general and on the trail in particular, few of the riders disagreed with so pessimistic an outlook. They were saddling their horses, preparing to take the trail north.

"Push 'em hard," Stoney told Long John. "If our figurin' is anywhere close, we're within two weeks of St. Louis. If we can drive twelve miles or more a day, we can shave a couple of days off that."

"We'll stay on their behinds an' keep the varmints rattlin' their hocks," Long John promised.

Stoney rode out, and despite all his efforts, Llano's pessimistic prophecy lay heavy on his mind. Life *did* seem that way. You rolled all sevens or all snake eyes, but never a mix of the two. When there was drought, you were on a mountain, and in the valley when the flood came. He grinned to himself. The comparisons went on and on. He had ridden a little more than twelve miles when he reached a creek that zigzagged off to the south. From force of habit he rode upstream, downstream, and then several miles beyond the stream without finding any sign. At least since coming into Missouri they hadn't been plagued with hostile Indians, he thought gratefully. That reminded him of something Long John had said.

"Hell's fire, I'd ruther fight Comanches than faunch around with troublesome lawmen an' renegades the likes o' Quantrill. With Injuns it's simple. Ye kill them, er ye end up with an arrer in yer gut an' yer hair gone."

Satisfied with the water and a lack of unfavorable sign, Stoney rode back to meet the herd.

"Ye ain't run into no towns, I reckon," Long John said. "The littlest town's gonna have law of some kind, if'n it ain't nothin' but a justice o' the peace."

"That's why I'm ridin' ahead," said Stoney. "We'll drive around any of the villages we come to, like we did Springfield. I don't look for a town that'll be large enough to worry us until we reach St. Louis. Once you've sold the herd, we're in the clear."

"I reckon yer right," Long John conceded. "The folks that are raisin' hell about the longhorns is ranchers an' farmers. Once these longhorn critters is in the stock pens, we kin hightail it to Texas."

July 21, 1858. Eighty miles southwest of St. Louis.

"I can't believe we come this far without the law catchin' up to us," said Quando Miller. "We can't be more'n a week out of St. Louis. I reckon there's gonna be some celebratin' when we git shut of these longhorns."

"Celebratin' like nobody's ever seen," Bandy Darden said. The look in his eyes told Quando Miller what Darden was referring to.

Once the herd was again on the trail, Stoney rode out

seeking water, and to be certain they avoided any villages where there might be potential trouble. But the villages directly in their path weren't the only problem. Just before sundown, when the longhorns and the horse remuda grazed along a creek, four men rode in from the north. Only one wore a belt gun, but all were armed with shotguns. Llano, Stoney, Long John, and Quando Miller rode out to meet them. The four strangers reined up, their faces grim. They had ridden in abreast, fanned out in a pattern, and at a range that would make the scatter guns deadly.

"You ain't welcome here," the lead rider snarled.

"We kinder gettin' that impression," said Long John. "We're just passin' through, on our way to St. Louis."

"We got spreads to the north," said the spokesman, "and any one of them longhorn bastards settin' foot on our land is dead. The same goes fer any rider that's with 'em. Don't come no farther north. We'll be waitin', with our guns."

With that, they turned their horses and rode back the way they'd come.

"Wal, by God," Long John said, "that's better'n havin' 'em ride in shootin' at us. I reckon it won't hurt us none, bearin' a little south. I ain't one to go kickin' no sleepin' dogs."

"Neither am I," said Stoney. "This kind of thing we can handle. It's the lawmen we have to worry about. Just another week is all we need."

But time and luck had run out. Before they could take the trail the next morning, a twelve-man posse rode in on their back trail. . . .

July 22, 1858. Seventy miles southwest of St. Louis.

Breakfast was finished and the riders were mounting up to take the trail when they became aware of the mounted men approaching from the southwest. On the vest of the lead rider, reflecting silver in the morning sun, was a badge. All the men were heavily armed, some of them carrying two belted Colts. They reined up forty yards away, spreading out in a skirmish line. Long John and his riders stood their ground, and when the Cajun moved to the forefront, Llano and Stoney were to his right and left.

"I'm Deputy Marshal McCullough, from Jefferson City," said the lead rider.

"Long John Coons, from Texas," Long John replied.

"We'll be escortin' you the rest of the way to St. Louis," said McCullough, "and I'm askin' you to shuck your guns. With finger and thumb, slow."

"We want no trouble with the law," Long John said. "Ye got my word on it."

"You have mine as well," said Stoney. "I'm Stoney Winters, trail boss. Are we being arrested?"

"No, sir," said McCullough. "We got orders from the attorney general to take you to St. Louis for questioning. Under the circumstances, I'll accept your word, and you may keep your weapons. But I could change my mind. That's depending on your conduct."

"Ye'll have no trouble from us," Long John said. "What about the herd?"

"You'll drive them on to the stockyards in St. Louis," said McCullough. "They'll be held until the question of ownership is settled. You may be subject to prosecution for theft."

"Theft!" Long John bawled. "Jist who'n hell—"

"That's enough," McCullough snapped. "I'm not at liberty to divulge any information. There'll be a hearing in St. Louis. Now mount up and get that herd moving."

McCullough and his men rode well behind the drag, avoiding the dust. Long John's outfit rode in silent fury, their future and that of the herd uncertain. Llano, ever pessimistic, tried to find a bright side.

"At least," he said, "we're gettin' the herd to St. Louis, and that's what we set out to do."

"My God," Suzanne cried, "they can't just take our herd, can they?"

"I reckon they can," Long John sighed. "They have."

"The important thing is," Stoney said, "we're gettin' the herd to St. Louis, and once there, somebody's got some provin' to do. Even if bringin' the herd into the state is a violation of Missouri law, I can't believe the state can legally take the herd. A fine, maybe, but we won't stand ground-hitched while they confiscate the herd."

The hard lines around Long John's mouth relaxed a little, and there was a flood of gratitude in Suzanne's eyes. In the confusion following the arrival of McCullough and his men, they had forgotten the need for water. Once the herd was on the trail, Stoney rode back to speak to McCullough, explaining the need for scouting ahead.

"I'm a reasonable man," McCullough said. "Ride on, find your water."

Stoney rode out, his mind awhirl with these circumstances that seemed so overwhelming. Who could be claiming ownership of the herd? Who could possibly prove the herd belonged to anybody except Long John Coons? Every cow had been dragged out of the brakes along the Colorado, and it wasn't just Long John's word, but that of the entire outfit. To steal a man's herd with such patently false an accusation, justice had not only to be blind, but stupid. Having ridden a dozen miles, Stoney reached a creek that wound its way down from the north. Being escorted by the law, there was no longer any need to seek out and avoid the small villages where offended farmers and ranchers might be waiting with their shotguns. Stoney rode back and met the trail drive, and since nobody had yet explained these new circumstances to Malo Coyote and Naked Horse, he took the time to do so. The Indians listened gravely, and Malo Coyote responded with the same anger the rest of the riders felt.

"Dark come," said Malo Coyote. "Take *cuchillo*, we fix."

"No," Stoney said, *"cuchillo* is *bueno*, but not this time. We'll have to take our chances with the white man's law."

July 29, 1858. St. Louis.

After several days it became obvious to the lawmen that Long John and his outfit intended to keep their word, and while McCullough and his men were always there, they did nothing to hinder the trail drive. Stoney continued to ride out seeking water, and there was only the uncertainty of what lay ahead to diminish their joy when they eventually reached the outskirts of St. Louis.

"It's too late in the day to talk to the court," McCullough said. "We'll ride in tomorrow."

"Why can't we jist leave the herd out here?" Long John asked. "It'll be here when the court decides what it wants to do. Run these longhorns into the stock pens, an' somebody's got to feed 'em. They've never et nothin' but grass, an' they ain't gonna know how to eat nothin' else. Anyhow, the state's gonna end up with one hell of a feed bill. Out here, the graze is free."

"I can understand that," McCullough said. "Unless the court rules otherwise, leave them here, with your riders watching them."

"Good move," Stoney told Long John. "Possession is still nine-tenths of the law. Get them in the pens at the stockyards, and even if we settle all the rest of it, you'd end up paying for their feed, and maybe for use of the pens. I don't know what they've got up their sleeves, but come mornin' we'll find out. I aim to take Llano with us, and I want Suzanne there too."

July 30, 1858. An unexpected friend.

With McCullough's permission, Long John and his outfit were allowed to ride into town. Long John, Llano, Stoney, and Suzanne went first, not that they had any money to spend.

"If'n they figger some way to bamboozle us outta the herd," Long John said morosely, "I won't have the money to pay nobody, an' nothin' to buy grub fer the ride back to Texas."

"Nobody's faultin' you for that," said Stoney. "Besides, they don't have the herd yet."

For those bound for the frontier, St. Louis was the jumping off place.

Mountain men carried their packs and long rifles, the buffalo hunter had his Sharps .50 caliber, and although it wasn't even sundown, the town had begun to roar. Indians roamed the wide streets, seeming to see nothing, yet seeing everything. From the railroad yard came the bellow of a locomotive, and as though in answer, the hoot of a steamboat at the landing. Almost daily there were steamboats to and from Louisville, New Orleans, and Fort Smith.

"Let's ride down to the landing and see the steamboats," Suzanne said. "I haven't seen one since . . ." She paused, uncomfortable with her past.

"Since New Orleans," Long John finished. "Come on, then. T'won't cost us nothin', an' that's about what we kin afford."

St. Louis being a river town, there was a veritable jungle of saloons and cafes strung out, fronting the river, a boardwalk running before them. As they rode along the river toward the landing, Long John spotted a familiar figure approaching them on the boardwalk.

"Wal, by God," said Long John, "that's Jesse Chisholm. He said he was goin' to Fort Smith."

"He'd have to go there to take a steamboat here," Stoney said.

They rode to the other side of the street, trotting their horses alongside the boardwalk until they met him. Chisholm looked up, a grin of recognition on his weathered face. There was no pretense about the man. He wore the same old flop-brimmed hat and homespun clothes he'd worn on the trail.

"I'm bound for my favorite eating place," said Chisholm. "Come along."

They followed, painfully aware that among them they didn't have the price of a cup of coffee. Chisholm paused before a cafe that seemed the cleanest of the lot.

"We won't go in," Long John said. "We already et."

"I imagine all of you can find room for a piece of pie and some coffee," said Chisholm, a twinkle in his eyes. "It's on me. Come on."

They followed him inside, and when they were seated at a table, Chisholm ordered for them all. He spoke to them as though he'd known them all his life, and he insisted on hearing of their drive. He listened gravely as Long John explained their painful situation, ending with their appearance in court the following morning.

"In another two or three years," Chisholm said, "there's going to be war. I have a son that I'm planning to send to the St. Louis Academy, and I have to meet with them, but not until tomorrow afternoon. I'll meet you at the courthouse in the morning. I'm known here, and not without influence. I have been to the capitol at Jefferson City, and the state's attorney general knows who I am. I think there's been a serious misunderstanding here. Perhaps I can be of some help to you."

Long John was astonished. "Why would you put yer

name on the line fer me? Ye never seen me till the day we met along the river."

"That day when we met beside the river," Chisholm said, "your eyes never left mine, nor have they while you were speaking to me just now. I believe you have a powerful enemy who has taken unfair advantage of you. We must have men on the frontier who can endure the hardships and survive, and that means if you're a cattleman, you must have a market for your herd."

"They're going to say we've broken the law," said Suzanne, "because of the tick fever."

"That's a bad law," Chisholm said, "and it'll be struck down as the rails move west. It'll fall to the law of supply and demand, because the East wants beef, and Texas has it in plenty. Your herd's already here, and if the state is determined to enforce that law, then I can't see them being legally able to do more than fine you. I think, if we handle this properly, they'll not be allowed to do even that. I'll meet you in the morning at the courthouse."

They stood beside their horses and watched him stride along the boardwalk the way he had come.

"My God," Suzanne said in awe, "no wonder the government has so much confidence in him as a negotiator with the plains tribes. He believes he can solve anything."

"Hell of it is," said Long John, "he's got me believin' it too. We jist might git out'n this with our hides in one piece."

But as their friendship with Jesse Chisholm brightened their chances in court, a new crisis was in the making. There was a horse race planned for Saturday, and it called to a pair of weaknesses in Malo Coyote and Naked Horse that would jeopardize the entire horse remuda. The Indian duo enjoyed stealing horses, but even more so did they like racing them, gambling on the outcome. And when they gambled, it was all or nothing. . . .

* * *

July 31, 1858. In court.

From habit, Long John and the outfit were up at first light, more than three hours before their appointed time in court. To their surprise, there were riders from town, some of them Indian. They bypassed the camp and the longhorns, riding directly to the horse remuda. In an instant Long John was in the saddle, unsure as to what might happen when these Indians confronted Malo Coyote and Naked Horse. But he needn't have worried. When he reached the remuda, there was nothing more serious going on than the new arrivals admiring the Mendoza blacks. Malo Coyote and Naked Horse showed no emotion, unless it was pride. But not all the admirers were Indian. A white man in town clothes spoke to Long John.

"Fine hosses. Any of 'em runnin' in the race tomorrow?"

"No," Long John said shortly. While he didn't like all this attention, there seemed little he could do. God knew they had enough enemies in this town already. He turned his horse and rode back to camp. The other riders, seeing him riding to investigate, had waited.

"Folks from town," said Long John. "They's a horse race tomorrer, an' some gent was wantin' to know if our blacks was gonna be runnin'. I told 'em no. If'n we kin settle this court thing t'day, an' sell the herd, I aim to be one hell of a long ways from here by tomorrer night."

Long John, Suzanne, Llano, and Stoney rode out at eight o'clock, a full hour before they were to be at the courthouse. They chose not to go inside, waiting for Chisholm, observing those who entered the building.

"Hey," said Llano, "one of them hombres comin' up the steps is that jack-leg lawyer Ferguson, from Dallas."

"By God, yer right," Long John said, "an' I'd bet the

whole damn herd that old buzzard with him is Harkness."

"Now I reckon we know who's layin' claim to the herd and chargin' us with thievery," said Stoney.

"My God," Suzanne cried, "he has no claim on the herd. All he has against us is what happened in Dallas. How can he drag that into Missouri?"

"He can't bring any charges against us over the shootings in Dallas," said Stoney. "The only way he can hurt us here is by taking the herd, and I reckon that's what he aims to do. The charges will be false, but we can't afford to fight him in the courts. Crooked lawyers and bought courts have stolen more than every owlhoot and bank robber in the history of the world."

"The bastard's got power," Long John said angrily, "else he couldn't pull strings from New Orleans an' have the law here dancin' to his tune. I reckon if'n Mr. Chisholm has any influence, we're gonna need ever' bit of it."

"Then if he's going to speak on our behalf," said Suzanne angrily, "he's going to know the truth. I'm going to tell him what happened in Dallas, why Harkness is after us."

"Now, Suzanne—" Long John began.

"He's going to be told," said Suzanne, "and I'm going to tell him. The law—the court—must see what's behind this . . . this low-down scheme to take our herd. That means they must be told what happened in Dallas, that Harkness is out to avenge his son by destroying us."

"Long John," Stoney said, "she's dead right. I don't think we'll have to go beyond the fact the three men were stinking drunk when they took Suzanne, and that they forced the fight by pulling their guns, but let's leave it there."

Jesse Chisholm arrived moments later, and was told of the fight in Dallas and that Harkness and his lawyer had gone into the courthouse.

"I think you're right," said Chisholm after he'd been told the facts of what had happened in Dallas. "We'll allow Mr. Harkness to call the first tune. Give a man enough rope and sooner or later he'll hang himself. I have friends in New Orleans, as most of my trade goods are shipped there, so Mr. Harkness is not unknown to me. He has enemies there, and if word of this miserable scheme gets back to the newspapers, his hide won't hold shucks. Let's go in and see what he has to say."

While the courtroom was large, there were few spectators. On the left, facing the bench, was a table for the prosecution. At that table sat Ferguson and the older man presumed to be Harkness. There was an identical table on the right, facing the bench, for the defendants. Chisholm, Long John, Llano, Stoney, and Suzanne took their seats. The deputy who had escorted the drive to St. Louis sat behind the railing that separated the prosecution and defense areas from the rest of the courtroom. Half a dozen men sat behind the railing near the prosecution's table.

"Some of those hombres over there behind Ferguson are the bullwhackers who were in Dallas," Stoney said. "Harkness aims to lie, and he's brought some gents to swear to it."

"Everybody stand," said the bailiff. The judge came in and took his seat.

"Court's in session, Judge Pendleton presiding."

For a minute the judge read or pretended to read the papers before him. When he finally spoke, he was abrupt and to the point.

"Mr. Coons," he said, glaring at Long John, "Jeremiah Harkness of New Orleans claims that in Dallas, Texas, you took a herd of longhorn cattle belonging to him and drove them here. He is asking this court to confiscate them, restore them to him, and to prosecute you for theft. What have you to say for yourself?"

"He's a lyin' son of a bitch!" Long John shouted angrily.

"We have witnesses!" Ferguson bawled from the other side of the room.

"They's lyin' sonsabitches too!" Long John shouted, more angry than ever.

"Order," Judge Pendleton roared. "Order in the court!"

When silence again prevailed, Judge Pendleton glared at Long John, but his anger was directed at Ferguson.

"As attorney for the prosecution, you were out of order," said Pendleton. "Another such outburst and you will be fined and held in contempt of court. Now," he said, turning to Long John, "we are not concerned with your opinion of Mr. Harkness, his attorney, or any witnesses that may testify before this court on his behalf. We are concerned only with what you have to say in your own defense."

"Judge," said Jesse Chisholm, rising, "I'd like to address the court on behalf of Mr. Coons. I am Jesse Chisholm, from Indian Territory."

"Are you a practicing attorney?"

"I'm not an attorney, period," Chisholm said. "I am a personal friend of Mr. Coons and his outfit, and I'm here to see justice done. I often serve as a negotiator for the government with the plains tribes, and I am recognized by the governor and by the attorney general of the State of Missouri."

There was a stunned silence in the court room. Finally, although it seemed to pain him considerably, Judge Pendleton actually smiled.

"I am familiar with you," said Pendleton. "What have you to say in defense of Mr. Coons?"

"Nothing," said Chisholm. "Even in the wilds of Indian Territory it's customary to show some proof before hanging a man. I have many friends and business associates in New Orleans, and I've heard considerable about

your Mr. Harkness. I'd like to see some of his proof, if
he has any."

"Objection!" Ferguson shouted. "I object to the snide
references this man has made regarding my client!"

"Objection overruled," snapped Judge Pendleton.
"Defense has requested that you present any evidence
that you have to substantiate the charges being brought
before this court. Are you so prepared?"

"I—We . . . have witnesses," Ferguson stammered,
"but my client's word—"

"Without some conclusive evidence," Judge Pendleton said, "your client's word means nothing to this court,
nor that of your witnesses. It's no more than their word
against that of Mr. Coons, and if that's all you have, I
am going to dismiss this case."

"Before you do, Judge," said Chisholm, "I think we
should clear Mr. Coons of these charges, and I believe
we can do that to the satisfaction of the court. This man,
Harkness, has no claim on this herd, nor has he ever
had. The truth is, Brandon Harkness, his son, was killed
in Dallas. The sheriff and the court declared it fully
justified, but Mr. Harkness was unwilling to accept that,
and he's gone to great lengths to wreak vengeance. Mr.
Coons was forced into a gunfight with three Harkness
employees, one of whom was Brandon Harkness. I want
Mr. Coons to tell you, in his own words, what this was all
about."

"I object!" Ferguson shouted. "This is most irregular."

"I dare say it is," said Judge Pendleton, "and I'd like
to hear the truth behind it. Objection overruled."

Long John stood up at the defense table and told of
the night in Dallas when the three men had dragged
Suzanne into the street, of his demand that she be released, and of the gunfight that had followed. Then he
sat down.

"I want you to hear it from the lady herself, Judge," said Chisholm, "and then we'll say no more."

Suzanne stood up and began to speak, and when her voice trembled, it was with anger. She looked not at the judge, but across the room at Ferguson and Harkness.

"The three of them were drunk," she said. "They knocked me senseless, tore my clothes, and dragged me outside. The three of them started shooting at Long John, and that's when I got loose from them. I'm sorry your son was killed, Mr. Harkness, but what he did was wrong. Just as wrong as what you tried to do to us." She said no more and sat down.

"This is a one-sided approach to justice," Ferguson shouted. "I object."

"Your objection is overruled," said Judge Pendleton, "and I am dismissing this case."

"Judge," said Deputy McCullough, getting to his feet, "what about them cows? Them bein' here is a violation of Missouri law."

"That law was hastily and poorly written," Judge Pendleton said, "and I am not going to enforce it. It says only that Texas longhorns are not to be allowed to enter Missouri, and that violation can result in the animals and riders being shot. This herd is already here, the state has wrongly prosecuted the owner, and I believe the only sensible thing to do is to drop the entire matter."

With that, Judge Pendleton left the bench and Deputy McCullough got up and approached Long John.

"Congratulations, Mr. Coons," he said, grinning. "I was sent to do a nasty job, an' I'm glad it's over. I wanted him to say somethin' specific about them cows. Now if anybody don't like 'em bein' here, I can always say you got Judge Pendleton's permission."

"Thank ye," Long John grinned, "an' much obliged fer bein' decent to us fer that week on the trail."

McCullough shook Chisholm's hand and the two were

talking when a third man approached. Long John, Suzanne, Llano, and Stoney went on outside, waiting for Chisholm, unwilling to leave without properly thanking him. When at last he emerged, McCullough and the stranger were with him. Chisholm caught up to them and introduced them to the man they didn't know.

"This is Andy Bonner," said Chisholm. "He's a stringer for a newspaper in New Orleans. He's going to write a story about the sandy Mr. Harkness and his lawyer tried to run on you folks. Mr. Harkness, as I believe Shakespeare put it, is being hoisted by his own petard."

After Chisholm left them, they spent almost an hour in a cafe with the young reporter, who insisted on riding with them to see the Texas longhorns. Reaching the herd, they found the rest of the riders anxiously awaiting the verdict.

"By God," Long John shouted, "the judge says the herd's ours!"

"You'd best unload it today, then," Dent Briano said, "because after tomorrow, you may not have a horse remuda."

"It's them damn heathen Injuns that's such good hoss wranglers." Bandy Darden laughed. "They're ridin' in a hoss race tomorrow, and they've bet the whole blasted hoss remuda they're gonna win!"

"The horse remuda ain't theirs to bet," said Long John. "They kin jist pull out."

"I reckon they can't," Quando Miller said. "They're in too deep. All the gamblers is backin' some fancy horses from back East."

"Then by the Eternal," said Long John, "them sneakin' varmints had better win, else I'll skin 'em like coyotes an' make piggin string outta their hides!"

22

Long John found Malo Coyote and Naked Horse grooming the pair of blacks they normally rode, and the duo seemed not in the least perturbed by Long John's fury.

"Ye lowdown, sneakin' varmints," Long John bawled, "lose my horses an' I'll kill ye dead."

"No lose," said Naked Horse calmly.

"If there's a way to cheat," Llano said under his breath, "they'll find it."

Once his temper cooled, Long John was one who took things in order of their importance. He would seek out a cattle buyer for the herd.

"Stoney," he said, "ye been right alongside me from the first, an' I'd like ye there fer the close." Then, turning to the rest of the outfit, he said, "I'll have some gold fer ye some time t'day. Jist stay with the herd, so's Malo Coyote an' Naked Horse don't gamble it away 'fore I git it sold."

Livestock being dependent upon the railroad, the cattle buyers and the cattle pens were strung out along the Missouri Pacific. The first buyer they spoke to was a little man named Hackett, who also owned the livery.

"I hear you got hosses that're runnin' tomorrow," he said. "Got a pair m'self. Good luck."

"We got two thousant longhorns to sell," said Long John. "How much?"

"Thirty-five," Hackett said, without removing his cigar.

"We'll think about it," Long John said, and he and Stoney went on to the next buyer.

Quinn Medano's Medano Cattle Company was the least prestigious of them all, but the old-timer knew Jesse Chisholm, and when he offered forty-one dollars, Long John took it.

"I ain't got that kind of money," said Medano. "I'll have to get it from the bank, borryin' against the herd. You'll want gold, I reckon."

"Nothin' else," Long John said. "Show us the pens ye aim t' use. We'll drive 'em in, an' ye can run a tally."

"Come on, then," said Medano. "Then we'll mosey down to the bank, show 'em a bill of sale, and you can get your money."

It was a day none of them would ever forget, when at last they drove the longhorns down alongside the tracks and into the cattle pens.

"I've gotten used to them," Pearl said, "and I almost hate to see them go."

"Lord, I don't," said Suzanne. "I'm glad we didn't lose them to that Old Man Harkness, but I'm glad to be rid of them."

"I tally two thousand and nine," said Medano.

"I count two thousand and five," Stoney said. "We always take low count."

"Rest o' ye stay here by the pens, so's I kin find ye," said Long John. "Stoney an' me are goin' to the bank an' git our money. Then ye kin all hit the town."

Long John took only several thousand dollars in gold, choosing to leave the rest in the bank until he was ready to leave St. Louis.

"I promised ever' rider a hunnert dollar bonus when we sold the herd," Long John said. "But we been through hell, an' shorthanded ever since we left Dallas, so I'm raisin' that bonus to a hunnert an' fifty dollars."

"That's mighty generous, Long John," said Stoney. "Nobody will expect that. On top of their wages, that'll be more money than most of 'em have seen at one time in their lives."

When Long John returned with the money, the riders reacted in different ways. Malo Coyote and Naked Horse received their wages, and their eyes lighted at the added bonus. Most of the white man's ways they neither cared for or understood, but money was the exception.

"Much gamble," said Naked Horse.

"I'm gonna wet my whistle, eat town grub, and sleep in an honest-to-God bed," said Dent Briano.

"I'll go with you," Quando Miller said.

"I'm lookin' for some fun," said Bandy Darden, his eyes on Harley. "You wanta come along, kid?"

"No thanks," Harley said, as calmly as he could. "I want just one thing from town. I reckon we'll go buy a ring for Pearl."

They all rode away, leaving Long John, Suzanne, Llano, and Stoney.

"Ye got somewher' to go," said Long John, "feel free. Malo Coyote an' Naked Horse kin watch the remuda. Nothin' else fer anybody to bother 'cept Sky Pilot, an' nobody'd have that old buzzard if'n he was gold plated."

"I reckon we'll ride in and nose around some," Stoney said. "We might track down Jesse Chisholm and buy his supper. What about you and Suzanne?"

"Ever' time we have a fight," said Long John, seeming dead serious, "she gits to hollerin' about runnin' off to New Orleans. I about had enough o' that, an' while we're here, I aim to do somethin' about it. I'm burnin' my brand on this gal. Suzy, you an' me is goin' to town an' buyin' you a ring."

Suzanne slapped him hard, sending his hat flying. "That," she said, "was for calling me Suzy," and before he recovered from that, she threw her arms around him, kissing him violently. "That," she said, withdrawing, "is for getting me the ring."

Of one mind, Llano and Stoney mounted and headed for town. They'd had a blessed plenty of the violent relationship between Long John and Suzanne.

"It's kinda nice settin' down to eat without dust blowin' in your face," Llano said as he and Stoney left the cafe. "Malo Coyote and Naked Horse were mighty helpful on the trail drive, but I feel kind of bad about bringin' them to roost on Long John's shoulders. Especially after this fool thing they did with the horse remuda. I've been expecting them to do something, but I didn't think it would be this bad, unless they just stole the remuda and headed for Indian Territory."

"I'm afraid the result is going to be the same," said Stoney, "unless there's a miracle. I know these Mendoza horses are fine animals, but they haven't been raced. I know they can move like chain lightning over a short distance, but we don't know anything about the other horses that will be running."

"No," Llano said, "but we do know it'll be a quarter mile run. Let's ride back to camp and see if we can find out what them sneakin' Injuns has got on their minds."

Other horses had been brought to town, and the locals had seemingly lost interest in Long John's horse remuda. Malo Coyote and Naked Horse were busy with a pair of blacks, but not the Mendoza blacks. These were two of the horses stolen from the Comanches, back in Texas.

"My God," Llano said, "don't tell me they aim to run Injun ponies in that race tomorrow!"

"I hope not," said Stoney. "They're not bad-looking horses, but they're no match for the Mendozas."

Malo Coyote and Naked Horse had listened in silence to the exchange between Llano and Stoney. It wasn't easy, reading their impassive faces, but there might have been a trace of pity.

"Town come," Naked Horse said, nodding to the Comanche horses. "We ride."

Stoney winked at Llano. Maybe this pair had something going for them, after all. Obviously they hadn't made any claims, and while the town watched, they had been working out with the blacks taken from the Comanches. Without a word, Naked Horse went to the picketed remuda and led back the blacks that he and Malo Coyote had ridden from Texas. During the trail drive they had been forced to use Texas saddles, but now the drive was over. Without saddle, bridle, or even a blanket, the Indians sprang to the backs of the magnificent Mendozas. The horses were off and running, and when their Indian riders bid them turn, they wheeled without the loss of a second. They thundered back to the point from which they had started, and they weren't even breathing hard. The Indian duo slid to the ground and their mounts nuzzled them fondly.

"No lose," said Malo Coyote, pointing to Stoney and then to Llano. *"Apuesta mucho dinero."*

Llano and Stoney mounted and rode back to the wagon, wondering why Sky Pilot hadn't taken the opportunity and driven to town. They found him sitting on the wagon tongue, where he had likely observed the impromptu race.

"I still ain't fond of Injuns," Sky Pilot said, "and feedin' that pair is like droppin' grub down a bog hole, but don't sell 'em short. If somebody don't git in their way, they'll take that race, by God."

"I think you're right," Stoney said, "and if they win it honestly, then I aim to see that nobody steals it from them."

"That's how I feel," said Llano, "and so will the others, with maybe the exception of Bandy Darden. I reckon we need to talk to Long John and give Malo

Coyote and Naked Horse a chance to win. If they lose, that's one thing, but to have it taken from them because they're Indian, that's another."

Harley and Pearl were the first to return from town, and everything they had purchased was for Pearl. Everything she wore was new, including her hat and boots, but most important of all, the gold band on her ring finger. The girl had gained some weight, had become tanned by the sun, and nobody—even Bandy Darden—questioned Harley Logan's judgment. When Long John and Suzanne returned, there was no evidence they'd bought anything except the ring Suzanne wore. But the several dresses she had longed for were packed carefully in her saddlebags.

"Llano and me have been talkin' to Malo Coyote and Naked Horse," Stoney said.

"I ain't wantin' to hear nothin' about them low-down varmints," Long John growled, "an' they needn't be makin' no plans to go back to Texas with me. I got enough trouble, by God, without packin' it along with me."

"Don't be too hasty, Long John," said Llano. "That pair of Injuns is got plenty of savvy, and they're gonna win that race tomorrow."

"I'll have to see it to believe it," Long John said. "You really think they kin win?"

"In an honest race they have a damn good chance," said Stoney.

"Ye don't think this is gonna be honest, then," Long John said.

"I've got my doubts," said Stoney, "because there's too much at stake. We learned that Hackett, the livery owner, has two horses entered, and that he's got a thousand dollars on each of them. His entries are heavy favorites, and if they lose, Hackett will be cleaned out."

"If they's any hope that Malo Coyote an' Naked

Horse kin win," Long John said, "we'll git behind 'em with our guns an' see that they ain't cheated."

"Llano and me are goin' down along the river and ride that track," Stoney said. "I think we'll find the sheriff and have a talk with him too."

"Jist don't do er say nothin' to git us involved with the law," said Long John. "I done had enough o' that."

Dent Briano and Quando Miller found a cafe that had fresh fish, and to that they added potatoes, onions, sliced tomatoes, pie, corn bread, and a gallon of cold lemonade. From there they went to a saloon and were watching a poker game in progress when Quando noticed a big bearded man at the bar staring at him.

"That's one of the Harkness hombres that was in the cafe in Dallas," Quando said. "Four of 'em was at the next table. One of 'em got up and throwed coffee in Stoney's face. Stoney laid him out on the floor, and we was ready to take on the others when the sheriff showed up."

"What'n hell are they doin' in St. Louis?" Dent wondered.

"Harkness may of fired the whole damn bunch," said Quando. "Remember, they come to ambush us, and we sent 'em back to their wagons without their guns and with their tails between their legs."

"That big ugly varmint at the bar knows you," Dent said. "Maybe for the sake of avoidin' trouble, we better vamoose. There's other bars."

"Yeah," said Quando, "but it rubs my fur the wrong way, havin' some overgrowed bullwhacker thinkin' I'm scared of him."

"Come on," Dent said. "We ain't runnin' away. We'll go to another place, and if they show up there, we'll know they're houndin' us. Let's go to one of them cutthroat joints down along the river."

They mounted their horses and rode away, apparently

without being followed. At that time, the river was a more important means of commerce than the railroad, and between the many warehouses that prevailed along the river, there were countless riverfront dives and greasy spoon eateries.

"That one looks interesting," Dent said. "Let's go in there." They dismounted, dallied their reins about the hitch rail, and from a once-elaborate sign mounted on the roof, a faded green dragon leered at them. Fancy scroll letters above the door said the name of the place was the Emerald Dragon.*

"We'll have a beer or two," said Quando, "and give that hombre time to find us, if that's what he's got in mind. If he's got any eye for horses, he won't have no trouble."

When Quando and Dent were ready to leave, they stood on the boardwalk for a moment. Farther along the winding street, in both directions, other horses were tethered before the various saloons and cafes. The single shot came just as Quando had one foot in the stirrup, and he clung to the saddle horn to keep from falling. Blood stained the back of his shirt above the left shoulder blade. Colt in his hand, Dent Briano ran along the boardwalk in the direction from which the shot had come. It was still too early for the waterfront's usual hell-raising to have begun, and the shot drew men from various saloons and eateries.

Llano and Stoney had no trouble finding the sheriff's office, and found the sheriff, Ode Lomax, interested in what they had to say.

"We have this race ever' summer," said Lomax, "and I ain't gonna say we don't have trouble. Ever' damn Indian within a hundred miles will be here, and so will all the gamblers that usually roost in the saloons aboard

* Trail Drive Series #3, *The Chisholm Trail*

the steamboats. Ever' last hombre will have a gun, a knife, or both, and them that ain't directly involved in the race will likely be roarin' drunk. I aim to keep order as best I can, but I can't be ever'where."

Suddenly there was a flurry of hooves outside, the thump of boots on the boardwalk, and a man burst through the door.

"Sheriff, they's been a shootin' down to the Emerald Dragon. One of them cowboys from the trail drive took one in the back."

Before he could say more, Llano and Stoney were past him, running for their horses. They had ridden past the Emerald Dragon the day they'd met Jesse Chisholm on the waterfront, and they rode there now, as fast as their horses would take them. By the time they arrived, somebody had fetched a saddle blanket, and Quando Miller lay facedown on the boardwalk. Onlookers had gathered around as a little man in a dark suit knelt beside Quando. Dent Briano was there as Llano and Stoney dismounted.

"That's Doc McConnell with him," said Dent Briano. "He was up yonder in the Baltimore, and he's half crocked, but he was handy."

"Any idea who shot him?" Stoney asked.

"Crazy as it sounds," said Dent, "I believe it was one of them Harkness bullwhackers. Some big hombre with a beard kept starin' at us, and Quando said it was one of that bunch from the cafe in Dallas. We left the place and come here to the Emerald Dragon, figurin' to see if the big gent was following us. We didn't see nobody, and just as we went to leave, Quando got it in the back. I went up and down the boardwalk, but couldn't see nobody. With all them saloons and cafes, he could of ducked back inside one of them."

Sheriff Lomax rode up and dismounted. Stoney wasted no time in getting to him, introducing Dent Briano, and having Dent repeat what had happened.

"So you figger it's some hombre you had trouble with back in Texas," the sheriff said, "and he's follered you here."

"We know there's at least six of them here," Stoney said. "The man they work for is likely still here. He tried to take our herd from us, bringing these men here as witnesses. Judge Pendleton ruled against them this morning, and we reclaimed our herd. Deputy Marshal McCullough can verify what I'm telling you, including the reason the Harkness outfit has it in for us. You won't know the man we think shot Quando, but I may recognize him, and I'm sure Dent will. Now we aim to find that back-shootin' varmint, along with any of the others that are involved, if we have to level every damn saloon in this town. Are you goin' with us?"

"I'm going with you," said Lomax.

"First," Stoney said, "we'll see how Quando is, and be sure he's being taken care of."

Doc McConnell had Quando's shirt off, had already disinfected the wound, and was applying a bandage. He looked up as Dent, Llano, and Stoney drew near.

"No lead in him," said the doctor, "but there'll be some pain. I can look in on him later tonight, and again tomorrow. Keep infection away from him, and he'll live. He needs a bed and plenty of rest."

"Sheriff," Stoney asked, "where can we take him, until he's on his feet?"

"The St. Louis Hotel," said Lomax. "McConnell, can you see that he's taken there and assigned a room?"

"Why, hell yes," said the peppery little doctor. "You know I don't get petrified until midnight. Conner, Peavey, Rockport, Burris, don't just stand there lookin' foolish. Each of you grab a corner of the blanket and tote this man over to the St. Louis Hotel. Get going. I'll be right behind you."

"Now, Sheriff," Stoney said, satisfied Quando was being cared for, "let's track down this Harkness varmint and see what he's got to say for himself."

They worked in the direction from which the shot had come, taking one saloon at a time. The sheriff entered first, followed by Dent, Stoney, and Llano. When they reached the third saloon beyond the Emerald Dragon, the barkeep had some information for them.

"The big bearded gent was here. Left just a few minutes 'fore we heard the shot, and there was a tall hombre with him. Had two Colts tied down, and a mean scar on his right jaw."

"He's one of 'em," said Llano. "I remember seein' him in the courtroom this morning."

"If these two are gunning for us," Stoney said, "I reckon we can figure on the rest of 'em bein' of the same mind. I won't be surprised if Harkness has put a price on our heads."

"God Almighty," Lomax groaned. "Just what I need. A bunch of killers roamin' the town, and that damn race comin' up tomorrow."

"You'll only have the race to hassle with tomorrow, Sheriff," said Stoney. "I aim to end this Harkness vendetta today, one way or another. We've been hounded by this bunch all the way from Texas. We thought it ended in Judge Pendleton's court this morning, but Harkness is never satisfied. We've bent over backward to avoid trouble, but by God, that just come to an end. We ain't bendin' no farther. Let's go on to the next saloon."

Their search was fruitless until they reached the ninth saloon. Sheriff Lomax had barely stepped inside when two men ran for the back door.

"Halt," Lomax shouted.

The tall man wearing two Colts drew one and fired. The slug ripped off the sheriff's hat and he returned the fire. But the fugitives made good their escape, the back door slamming behind them. Lomax followed, pausing at the back door only long enough to be certain the two weren't waiting to ambush him. Then he stepped out into a narrow alley, his Colt in his hand. Stoney, Llano, and Dent were right behind him.

"Every damn saloon and cafe along this row has a back door," said Lomax.

"Then we'll split up," Stoney said. "I reckon by now you're convinced this bunch is everything we've said they are."

"I reckon I am," said the sheriff. "When a man cuts down on me with a Colt, I take that as an admission of guilt. If they don't halt in the name of the law, you got my permission to shoot."

But that wasn't necessary. The tall man stepped out from between two buildings, a Colt in each hand, his bearded companion behind him. One slug burned a path along Llano's left thigh, while a second ripped through the flesh of Dent Briano's left arm, just above the elbow. Stoney and Sheriff Lomax fired in the same instant, and the tall gunman was flung violently to the ground. A second later Llano fired, and the bearded man dropped his Colt, Llano's shot having crippled his gun arm. He raised his left hand.

"Don't shoot no more!" he cried.

"Oh, I don't aim to shoot you," Lomax said grimly. "First, I'm takin' you to jail, and where you go from there depends on you. Then you're going to do some talking. Say the right things, and you just might keep your neck out of a noose. Now move!"

"I'm hurt!" the bearded man cried.

"That ain't near as painful or as permanent as bein' hung," said Lomax. "You get a doc when I get you to the jail."

"Sheriff," Stoney said, "before you question this man, I'd like to find Deputy Marshal McCullough and have him present. This Harkness bunch got McCullough involved by comin' after us through the attorney general's office in Jefferson City. Now I'd like for Mr. McCullough to learn firsthand what we've been through because of Jeremiah Harkness."

"I believe that request is fully justified," said Lomax. "Go and bring McCullough."

On his way to the courthouse Stoney saw Doc McConnell leaving the St. Louis Hotel. Stoney reined up, waiting for the little doctor.

"Sheriff Lomax has another customer for you down at the jail," Stoney said.

McConnell said nothing, and Stoney rode on. When he and McCullough reached the jail, they found Sheriff Lomax, Llano, and Dent Briano in the outer office. A door stood open, revealing an aisle that ran between two rows of cells. In the first cell the wounded man lay on a bunk, a doctor working on his wounded shoulder. The doctor was not the half-drunk McConnell.

"Howdy, Ben," the sheriff greeted McCullough. "I went ahead and had the doc patch up this hombre. I want him able to talk, because I suspect he's goin' to have some interesting things to say. By the way, you don't know where we can get our hands on this Jeremiah Harkness, do you?"

"He's likely at the St. Louis Hotel," said McCullough.

When the doctor had finished with his patient, Sheriff Lomax went into the cell and stood looking down at the man who lay on the bunk.

"We'll start with your name," said Lomax. "Who are you?"

"Gib Dismukes."

"Why are you in St. Louis, where are you from, and why did you shoot that cowboy outside the Emerald Dragon?"

"Why I'm here an' where I'm from ain't none o' your business," Dismukes snarled, "an' you can't prove I shot nobody."

"No," said Lomax, "but I can prove you shot at me and three other men. That'll be enough to convict you for attempted murder, and if I have anything to say about it, you'll hang."

"You'd better talk, Dismukes," said McCullough. "There's a steamboat leaving for New Orleans in less than two hours, and your boss, Harkness, will be aboard. He don't care a damn about you, so why are you protectin' him?"

"I ain't protectin' nobody!" Dismukes shouted.

"Have it your way," said Sheriff Lomax. "I'll charge you with attempted murder and see that you're held without bail." The barred door clanged shut with a finality that shook Dismukes.

"Wait!" he cried. "Wait!"

Sheriff Lomax didn't unlock the barred door.

"What—What happens to me if . . . if I talk?"

"It depends on what you say," Lomax replied. "Tell us what you're doing in St. Louis, why you shot a man in the back, and I'll see that the judge takes that into consideration. What you say can make the difference between you living and dying."

"I'll talk," said Dismukes. "Old Man Harkness brought six of us here from New Orleans. We was to testify that them Texans stole that herd of cows in Dallas, cows that belonged to Harkness."

"Did the herd, or any part of it, belong to Harkness?"

"No," Dismukes said. "Them three Harkness men dragged a woman out of a store in Dallas and then started a gunfight. The three was killed, one of 'em Brandon Harkness, the old man's only son. He just went crazy, swearin' to get even. He sent a dozen of us to ambush Coons and his outfit, but they was waitin' for us. They took our guns and run us off. Then Harkness set up this thing in court and brung six of us here to testify. When the court throwed it all out this mornin', the six of us that come to testify was told we'd git five hundred dollars for ever' one of Coons' riders we killed. He put a bounty of five thousand on Coons himself."

"This foolishness started in Jefferson City, at the capitol," McCullough said. "I reckon we'll have to backtrail and see just who it is over there that's cozied up to Jeremiah Harkness."

"There's more important things than that," said Sheriff Lomax. "You've just heard Harkness accused of sending half a dozen hired killers after Coons and his entire outfit. Are you goin' to swear out a warrant for Harkness, or am I?"

"I'll do it," McCullough said. "This is a conspiracy, and by God, it's of a magnitude that it deserves a federal warrant. We'll let the state prosecute Harkness, and in so doing, follow this all the way back to Jefferson City. I'll go get the warrant, and then I'll get Harkness before he has a chance to slither away."

"I reckon we'd better get back to camp and take word to Long John," said Stoney. "We'll be back to see how Quando's doing."

"I'll need to talk to Coons," Sheriff Lomax said. "There's going to be a hell of a stink before McCullough's done, and likely a full-blown trial, so you folks had best plan on bein' here a few days."

"Point me toward that doc," said Dent Briano, "so's I can get a bandage on this nicked arm."

23

"Wal," Long John said, "it's been some hell of a day, ain't it? I like the part about McCullough goin' after Harkness with a federal warrant, but not the part 'bout us bein' stuck here whilst it's bein' took care of."

"We couldn't leave anyway," said Stoney. "Not while Quando's laid up."

"Yer right," Long John said. "He's a *bueno* hombre, an' 'fore I bother with talkin' to the law, I aim to look in on Quando. I ain't wantin' him to think we'd leave without him. Ye got nicked in the arm, Dent. Ain't bad, I hope."

"It'll be sore," said Dent, "but I've hurt myself worse shavin'. Least I had a chance to shoot back. Quando took the bad one."

"We still have time before dark," Suzanne said. "Let's ride in and see how he's feeling."

"He'll likely be sleeping for a while," said Stoney, "but we'll need to make arrangements with the hotel. You're not exactly broke anymore," he said to Long John, "so why don't you and Suzanne take a room there until we're ready to pull out of here? There's enough of us to look after the horse remuda, and Sky Pilot can stay with the wagon."

"I reckon we'll jist do that," Long John said. "C'mon, Suzanne." As she turned away, there was a look of gratitude in Suzanne's eyes, and Stoney winked at her.

"Wal," said Llano as Long John and Suzanne rode away, "you're in solid with her. After the hell she put us through back yonder on the trail, I never thought they'd be sharin' a hotel room. Or for that matter, even a blanket on the ground."

"She's basically a good woman," Stoney said, "and it says a lot for them that they've been able to resolve their differences. Long John Coons has always been a big man, but he's grown a mite taller since Dallas."

"Now that we got Long John and Suzanne took care of," said Llano, "why don't we put up Harley and Pearl in that same hotel until we're ready to start back to Texas? I'll kick in a double eagle, if you'll match it. I know they ain't flush and wouldn't spend the money, but forty dollars would pay for a room and keep 'em in grub."

"I'll match you," Stoney said. "It may be the first and last time they'll ever live this high. With the possibility of war, it may be a lot of years before they'll see anything but the wild country along the Rio Colorado."

Long John and Suzanne reached the St. Louis Hotel in time to meet Jesse Chisholm preparing to leave.

"I'm taking a steamboat to Natchez, and from there to Fort Smith," said Chisholm. "I was just talking to young Bonner, the stringer for the paper in New Orleans, and he's going to be looking for you. He's rushed together a story that he's sending back to New Orleans on the same boat I'll be taking. I think you finally gave Mr. Harkness enough rope, and he's tied his own noose."

"Ye give him the rope, tied the noose, an' pulled it tight," Long John said, "an' ye got friends in Texas. Ye ever need a fightin', gun-throwin' bunch o' Texans, jist holler, an' we'll come a'runnin'."

"I hate to see him go," said Suzanne. "With war coming, I have a feeling we'll never see him or St. Louis again."

"He's a man that believes in the West an' in the frontier," Long John said. "If'n this war comes, it'll be hell on ever'body, 'specially Texans. That's why we had to git this drive through to the railroad whilst we could. God knows when—er if—we'll ever git the chance fer another'n."

As expected, Long John and Suzanne found Quando Miller asleep. Suzanne felt his forehead, and he had no fever.

"C'mon," said Long John. "We'll go down to the desk an' git us a room here on the secont floor, wher' Quando is."

Harley and Pearl were just entering the lobby when Long John and Suzanne came down the stairs. Pearl's eyes were bright with excitement, and Harley seemed nervous.

"We couldn't of afforded this," Harley said. "Llano and Stoney each put up twenty dollars, and we couldn't get out of it."

"Wal, hell's fire," said Long John, "here's 'nother twenty. If'n it's gift-givin' time, ye ain't leavin' me an' Suzanne out."

Harley became all the more flustered, and Long John pushed him and Pearl toward the desk to register.

"Give 'em a room on the secont floor," Long John told the clerk. "That's wher' we want to go too."

"Long John," said Suzanne, "let's find a newspaper. I'd like to know what's going on in the world."

"There won't be a current one till tomorrow," said the man behind the registration desk, "but you're welcome to some back issues."

"Thank you," Suzanne said, and when she and Long John reached their room, she spread them out on the bed. They were all copies of the *St. Louis Globe-Democrat,* some of them a year old.

"Here," said Suzanne, "take some of them."

"You read 'em," said Long John, "an' if they's anything interestin', tell me about it."

"Last September," Suzanne said, "the government signed a contract with the Butterfield Overland Mail Company to provide service from Memphis and St. Louis to Fort Smith, to El Paso, to Fort Yuma, to Los Angeles and San Francisco. They'll go twice a week, the run taking twenty-five days."

"Wal, they's jist follerin' the route we took back in 'forty-nine, when I rode with Gil an' Van Austin to the Californy gold fields. 'Course we didn't go through Memphis, St. Louis, er Fort Smith, but from San Antone to San Francisco, we was ten year ahead of 'em."*

"Here's a paper from June of this year," Suzanne said. "Abraham Lincoln is going to run as a Republican against Stephen A. Douglas, the Democratic senator from Illinois. There's already talk of running Lincoln for president."

"Don't read me nothin' about politics," said Long John. "I'd bet the ranch that ever' damn one of 'em's a lawyer, an' I don't trust lawyers. If'n this country goes to hell, it'll be lawyers greasin' the skids. Ever' one of 'em oughta be strung up, startin' with Ferguson, the varmint Harkness turned loose on us in Dallas."

"There's rumors of a gold strike in northwestern Kansas Territory," Suzanne said. "They say it's near Cherry Creek, along the South Platte River."**

"That don't matter to us," said Long John. "Ain't they nothin' about the war?"

"Nothing for sure. It's mostly congressmen and sena-

---

* Trail Drive Series #5, *The California Trail*
** Little gold was found. The area became part of Colorado Territory in 1861.

tors fighting among themselves about slavery versus non-slavery, I think."

"Them damn Yankee politicians tryin' to figger some way they kin git at us," Long John said. "The hell with it. Let's git Harley an' Pearl an' go look fer some grub."

"It's getting late," said Suzanne. "Hadn't we first better go talk to Sheriff Lomax and Deputy Marshal McCullough?"

"I reckon," Long John said. "I'd fergot about them."

Long John, Suzanne, Harley, and Pearl were leaving the hotel when they saw Ben McCullough approaching. They waited.

"We got Harkness," said McCullough, with a grin, "and Ferguson raised so much hell, we locked him up too. We may not be able to hold him, but he'll spend the night in jail anyhow."

"We was jist on our way to find ye," Long John said. "Stoney said I'd need to talk to Sheriff Lomax too."

"Not necessarily," McCullough said. "Since Harkness started all this in Jefferson City, through the attorney general's office, I've jailed him under a federal warrant. I'm charging him with crossing state lines with the intention of committing murder. I think we'll backtrail Harkness and find out why he had enough influence at the capitol to set all this up, him bein' from New Orleans."

"We run into Jesse Chisholm as he was leavin'," said Long John, "an' it looks like Bonner, this newspaper gent, is sendin' news of all this back to the paper in New Orleans."

"God, yes," said McCullough. "He thinks the paper there will dig into some questionable things in which Harkness has been involved. It seems he's a ruthless old buzzard, not just in your case, but all down the line."

"Wal," Long John said, "we're obliged. God knows, we come here needin' some friends, an' ye done us right. I ain't fergittin'."

"When Jesse Chisholm stood up for you in the courtroom, I knew there was something wrong with the Harkness charges. Judge Pendleton is a hard man to convince, but he thought so too."

"We took rooms at the St. Louis Hotel," said Long John. "We'll be here a few days, if'n ye need us."

Long John selected one of the better cafes near the hotel, and that's where he, Suzanne, Harley, and Pearl were when Llano and Stoney found them.

"Drag up a chair," Long John said, "an' git the biggest steak they got. We got some celebratin' to do, an' it's on me."

Long John told them of the meeting with Ben McCullough and of the twist of fate that had thrown both Harkness and Ferguson, his lawyer, behind bars.

"I'm glad to hear that," said Stoney, "but what about those other four Harkness men, the teamsters that came here to testify? With two of them going after Dent and Quando, how do we know the rest of them aren't out there waiting for a chance to back-shoot as many of us as they can?"

"By God, yer right," Long John said. "After we eat, I reckon we better find McCullough er Lomax, an' see what's bein' done about them hombres. If'n they come here with Harkness, they got to know he's in trouble with the law. They got to know one of them varmints ye helped the sheriff catch is spilled his guts, makin' the rest of 'em guilty as hell."

They had just begun to eat when Long John saw Quinn Medano entering the cafe. Long John stood up and, when Medano saw him, beckoned to the amiable cattle buyer.

"C'mon, Quinn," said Long John, "an' join us."

"Reckon I will," Medano said. "Walked down to the landing with Chisholm. He don't get to St. Louis more'n once or twice a year. He says there's goin' to be war. Jess has a son that's maybe ten years old, and 'fore the war busts loose, he aims to enroll the boy in the St. Louis Academy."*

"I got slickered into the horse race tomorrer," said Long John. "What d' ye know about the horses that'll be runnin'?"

"Must be fifty Injuns aimin' to ride," Medano said. "Most of the big money's behind a pair of thorough-breds Doak Hackett's brought in from the East. Nobody around here's seen 'em run, but I hear they're beauties, long-legged and sleek as greyhounds."

"What'd Hackett run last time?" Stoney asked.

"Officially, nothin'," Medano said. "Prince Guthrie, the house dealer in one of Hackett's saloons, claimed to own the horse, but it wasn't no secret that Hackett laid all his money on it. Won him a bundle too, but didn't win him no friends. Let's just say he won under questionable circumstances."

"I'd take it as a favor if ye'd tell it straight," said Long John.

"All I could tell you is what's rumored," Medano said, "and I'd not want that repeated. Hackett's a power in this town."

"I had me a bellyful of hombres like him," said Long John. "Tell us what ye kin, rumor er not, an' mebbe we kin keep him honest."

"There's Injuns in this town that's never lackin' for whiskey," Medano said, "and last year, ever' blessed one of 'em had a horse in the race. Now there's nothin' wrong with that, 'cept two of them Injun horses was run into the only pair of horses that was givin' Hackett's horse a run for the money."

"There's a chance, then," said Llano, "that some of the Indian riders are spoilers, there to slow any horse that might beat Hackett's."

"I didn't say that," Medano said. "You did."

* Trail Drive Series #3, The Chisholm Trail

"Ye said enough," said Long John. "We're runnin' a pair o' blacks, an' in a honest race, we think they kin beat anything Hackett's got, includin' them hot bloods from back East."

Long John sat facing the cafe's plate glass window, and when he looked up from his steak, he found a longhorned apparition staring at him through the glass.

"Great God A'mighty," Long John shouted, "I been lookin' at longhorns fer so long, I'm seein' the critters ever'wher'!"

There was still enough light outside for the longhorn bull to see his reflection in the window, and when he hooked at his own image, the plate-glass disappeared with a tinkling crash. Furious, his adversary having eluded him, the bull vented his wrath with a thunderous bellow, sending the cafe's patrons scrambling for the back door.

"Damn it," Medano cried, "the cattle are loose!"

"Git down there to the pens quick as ye kin," Long John said. "Mebbe they ain't all got out. We'll see kin we run the varmints out of town so's they don't wreck the place."

Long John dropped two double eagles on the table and ran for the door, Suzanne, Llano, Stoney, Harley, and Pearl right behind him. The scene that greeted them in the twilight was unreal. Half a hundred longhorns trotted along the street, some of them on the boardwalk, poking their noses into lighted doorways. One of them had invaded a dressmaker's shop, sending a pair of ladies shrieking through an open window, one of them so poorly clad she would be the subject of gossip for months. Yet another bull found his way into the barbershop and into the adjoining bathhouse, forcing two men to flee into the street wearing only their hats.

"Grab yer lariats," Long John shouted, "an' let's run 'em back toward the river."

That was sound advice only insofar as the longhorns

on the boardwalks and in the streets were concerned. Llano finally got a horn loop on the bull in the bathhouse, only to have the beast charge him. Llano's horse back-stepped out the door, and the bull smashed headlong into the door frame. It buckled, bringing part of the ceiling down with it. Llano managed to drag the bull through the wreckage, only to have it charge him with the single-minded intention of goring him, his horse, or both. Harley threw a loop over the bull's hind legs, and when the brute hit the ground in a cloud of dust, Harley went after the hind legs with piggin string while Llano secured the front legs in like manner. They left the bull there, bellowing his indignation, and went after another.

Long John and Stoney chased a bull through the batwing doors of a saloon, and the dozen men bellied up to the bar crawled over it. But the bull, trying to elude Long John and Stoney, ran behind the bar, his massive horns sweeping off bottles and racks of glasses as he went. Tables and chairs flew as the bull raced through the back door, Long John and Stoney riding in pursuit. Some of the longhorns were cows. Pearl and Suzanne began swatting them with lariats, trying to bunch them. Order was slowly restored as the bulls were chased or dragged from the various shops they had invaded. Finally the entire lot of them were driven toward the railroad yard and back into the stock pen from which they had escaped. The last portion of the journey was accomplished by starlight. Quinn Medano was waiting to hoist the rails in place.

"Thank God only one pen was opened," said the cattle buyer.

"Somebody let the varmints out, I reckon," Long John said.

"The rails was on the ground," Medano said.

"Lucky they didn't drop the rails on all the pens," said Stoney.

"God, yes," Medano sighed. "This was bad enough, and I'm liable for all the damage."

"This ain't near all of 'em that was in that pen," said Long John. "The rest of 'em's still out there, likely down along the river. They'll look fer graze an' water. Come first light, we'll gather 'em up fer ye and drive 'em back in the pen."

"I'm obliged," Medano said. "I reckon I'd as well go find Sheriff Lomax and take my beatin' for all this."

He didn't have far to go. Lomax rode up before any of them could mount their horses. Nobody said anything, waiting for the sheriff to speak.

"What happened, Quinn? I never heard such a hell of a ruckus, and right in the middle of supper."

"Be glad you wasn't over to the bathhouse, taking a bath," said Llano.

Nobody laughed. Quinn Medano sighed.

"Some no account bastard let them cows out," Long John said. "By God, we drove them brutes into the pens, an' when we left here, they was secure. Them rails was took down after we left, an' it warn't the cows that done it."

"We can't do much in the dark," said Lomax. "I'll come down here in the morning and see if there's any tracks. You're almighty lucky that whoever let down the rails on this pen didn't do the same for all the others. That's what makes me wonder."

"Sheriff," Stoney said, "there was six of those Harkness men who had it in for us, and we've only accounted for two of them. Could the others have done this?"

"I doubt it," said Lomax. "They had disappeared by the time we got to Harkness, and he swears he has no idea what became of them. They're bound to know that Harkness is in trouble and that Quinn's bought the herd. I can't figure a motive for this, except pure cussedness."

"Come daylight," Stoney said, "we aim to round up

the rest of the longhorns for Quinn. There shouldn't be any more trouble tonight."

"I hope not," said Lomax, "but I wouldn't count on it. Quinn, was I you, I'd pay a gent to mosey around down here with a scattergun at night, for as long as you have these brutes on your hands. Now, Mr. Coons, I got somebody else in jail that might be of interest to you."

Long John and his companions followed Lomax, and long before they got to the jail, they could hear an all too familiar refrain.

"Brangin' in the sheep, brangin' in the sheep. We gonna come rejoicin', brangin' in th' sheep. . . ."

By habit, Long John and Suzanne were up well before first light. Long John had elected to leave Sky Pilot in jail until he sobered up, so Dent, Llano, and Stoney had ridden into town to join the rest of the outfit for breakfast. Afterward, when it was light enough to see, they would begin the search for Quinn Medano's missing longhorns.

"That was a low-down, skunk-mean thing to do," Long John said as they gathered around the table for breakfast. "Quinn was fair with us, and I'm hatin' t'see him takin' a loss on what them damn longhorns tore up last night."

"I feel the same way," said Stoney, "but I doubt we're going to find anything around the cattle pens that'll shed any light on who took down those rails. I can't help believing Quinn Medano's being persecuted for dealing with us."

"I think them four Harkness hombres that disappeared had somethin' to do with turnin' the cows loose," Llano said. "Harkness had time to arrange for that before Quando was shot, before we went after that pair of gunhawks, and before that confession landed Harkness in the *juzgado.*"

"Wal," Long John said with a sigh, "all we kin do to

help Quinn is round up the rest of his cows, an' we'd as well git started."

"I have a lot of confidence in Sheriff Lomax," said Stoney, "but I still want to look for sign around that cattle pen."

"Go on an' do that," Long John said. "The rest of us kin start lookin' fer them longhorns. I expect 'em to be grazin' down along the river, an' I reckon we'll look there first."

When Stoney reached the cattle pens he found Sheriff Lomax was already there. He didn't seem surprised to see Stoney.

"Plenty boot prints," said Lomax, "but knowin' western men, I doubt they walked from town. I'm figurin' they was mounted, before or after Harkness was picked up. I reckon if we take the time, we'll find where they left the horses, likely over yonder beyond the railroad tracks."

Lomax and Stoney were unable to find any tracks beyond the railroad, and it was Stoney who finally found a bit of mud on one of the railroad ties.

"They walked the ties until they were well away from the cattle pens," Lomax said. "That means they had horses. If they'd been headed for town, they wouldn't have cared about leavin' boot prints."

"I aim to find where they left the horses," said Stoney.

"Then we'll follow the track a ways away from the cattle pens," Lomax said, "until we find where they left the railroad."

The trail wasn't easy to find. A deep bed of ballast had been laid for the ties, and the egg-sized rock extended well beyond the ends of the ties on either side of the rails. It was Stoney who found what they were seeking.

"Here," he said. "Somebody missed the tie end and dug a boot heel into the ballast. The slag ain't quite dry on the underside."

Beyond the railroad right-of-way there was thick grass and weeds, but Stoney wasted no time looking for tracks. He headed for a nearby pine thicket, the obvious place to have concealed the horses. The horse droppings were still moist, and on the first piece of bare ground beyond the thicket there were hoofprints. Four horses traveling southwest.

"I reckon that settles it," Lomax said. "If they rode out right after they loosed the cows and kept riding, they're sixty or seventy miles away by now. I reckon we've seen the last of them."

But Stoney wasn't so sure. These men would expect Long John and his outfit to return to Texas, probably with fewer riders, and it wouldn't have been too difficult for them to discover that Long John would be carrying eighty thousand dollars in gold.

Within three hours Long John and his riders had gathered the scattered longhorns and returned them to the pen from which they'd been released.

"Now," said Long John, "I reckon we'd best git over to the hotel an' see how Quando's comin' along. Soon as he kin talk, they's somethin' I'm needin' to ask him, an' whilst it's on my mind, I got the same question fer ye, Dent. I'd like fer ye to ride back to Texas an' be part o' my outfit. Will ye go?"

"I reckon I'd like that," said Dent. "I'll go."

"Bueno," Long John said, "an' welcome. Now let's go see ol' Quando, an' I'll put the same question to him."

"I can't answer for him," Dent said, "but I'm bettin' he'll go."

Nothing was said about Bandy Darden, and Dent Briano wondered how that would affect the little gunman's plans.

"Rest o' ye wait in the hall," said Long John when they reached the second floor of the hotel. "Give me a minute er two. They won't be room fer us all at the same time. Come on, Suzanne."

They found Quando apparently asleep. Suzanne tested his forehead.

"No fever. Perhaps we should let him sleep and come back later."

"No," Quando said. "I'm awake. Tell me what's happened."

"I aim to," said Long John. "How ye feelin'?"

"I'll live," Quando said, "but I can't afford a room like this. It's fancy diggin's."

"Ye ain't payin' fer it," said Long John. "I am. Now lemme tell ye what ye gittin' shot has did fer us."

Long John recounted the killing of the Harkness gunman, the arrest of the second man, and his confession. He closed with the jailing of Harkness and his pending trial.

"That makes me feel some better," Quando said.

"Wal," said Long John, "mebbe I kin make ye feel better yit. I'd like fer ye to ride back to Texas an' be part of my outfit. Will ye do it?"

"I'll do it," Quando said, "and I'm thankin' you for the offer."

"*Bueno,*" said Long John. "Dent Briano's goin' too. He's outside, with Llano, Stoney, Harley, and Pearl. We'll go, so's they kin come in, but we'll be back."

After their visit with Quando, Llano and Stoney made the rounds of the saloons and many of the cafes, saying little, listening to the talk of the coming horse race. When they reached the saloon where Price Guthrie dealt for the house, they each bought a beer, listening to the talk, to the taking of bets. The odds seemed overwhelmingly in favor of Hackett's thoroughbreds.

"Folks got an almighty lot of confidence in a fancy pair of nags nobody's ever seen run," said Llano.

"Maybe their confidence ain't so much in Hackett's horses as in his hard-fisted methods. For all we know, that's Hackett's money all these gents are layin' down. He's just not choosin' to be too obvious about it."

"We found where the race will be run, while we was roundin' up all them scattered longhorns," Llano said. "It's down along the river. I reckon it's time we rode down there and had a closer look at it."

24

Three hours before the race there was activity all along the course. Everything from canvas squares to entire tents had been erected to ward off the July sun. Pits had been dug and beef and pork were roasting over open fire. Someone had brought a wagonload of watermelons, and virtually every saloon in town had set up a tent from which drinks would be sold. Beer was being delivered by the keg, and some of the Indians hanging around the tents were already glassy-eyed.

"It must be the saloons that keeps these races goin'," Llano said. "I'll bet they sell more rotgut today than they'd normally unload in a week. Anybody that don't get owl-eyed durin' the race, they'll get him in the saloons after the race is over."

"The course is pretty clean," said Stoney after they'd ridden the length of it. "Not much cover along the river for anybody with mischief on his mind. That means if Hackett aims to steal the race, he's countin' on his spoilers to blunder into any horses that might challenge the thoroughbreds."

"It's worked before for him, so why shouldn't he try it again? What can we do to keep his Indian riders from slowing or crippling our horses?"

"I'm thinkin' Malo Coyote and Naked Horse may

have some defense against that," Stoney said, "but I think we need to talk to them again, to make them aware of what we suspect. From what I've seen, I believe they have two big advantages. First, they'll be riding without any weight except the rider, and second, those Mendoza blacks can move like forked lightning from a standing start. I believe if there's any interference, it'll have to come right at the start. None of Hackett's spoilers can hinder our horses if they can't catch 'em. Give those Mendoza blacks a second and they'll be gone."

Before again riding out to talk to Malo Coyote and Naked Horse, Llano and Stoney stopped at a cafe to eat. They found Quinn Medano and Sheriff Lomax at one of the tables, writing tablets and pencils before them.

"Come on," said Medano, pushing things aside. "We're just goin' over what it's going to cost me to repair all that damage from last night."

"Well," Stoney said, "I hope it won't hit you too hard."

"He ain't comin' out all that bad," said Sheriff Lomax. "I've talked to everybody involved. They know who let the longhorns out, and they know why, so they ain't makin' it all that hard on Quinn."

"We've been down along the course the race will be run," Stoney said as he and Llano took their seats. "As many horses as will be runnin', it's gonna be mighty crowded."

"Not any more it ain't," said Quinn Medano. "The judges have decided there'll be two races, the first at two o'clock and the second at three. Everybody likes the idea 'cept for Doak Hackett. He's raisin' hell, but it won't do no good. The saloons that's puttin' up the purses has put up the same money for the second race. Rule is, no rider can ride in both races. It's one or the other. The way it was, horses would of been fallin' over one another."

"I can see why Hackett don't want two races," Llano

said when they had left the cafe. "That means it'll be pretty damn obvious on a track that ain't crowded if some rider intentionally runs his horse into another."

"It'll take away most of Hackett's edge," said Stoney. "Now I'm wondering how this is going to affect us. Will Malo Coyote and Naked Horse both ride in the same race, or will they split up?"

"I can answer that for you. With a chance at twice the money, that pair of gamblin' fools will split, Malo Coyote ridin' in one race and Naked Horse in the other. Why compete against one another when they'll each have a chance to win?"

"We'd better get out there and talk to them," Stoney said. "Way things were, they had all our horse remuda bet on that first race. Now we have to be sure they don't win that first race and then bet everything—including the horse remuda—on the second."

"By God, you're right," said Llano, "and it'd be just like them to do that very thing. But with odds so heavy in favor of Hackett's thoroughbreds, if Malo Coyote and Naked Horse can take the first race, they'll have a fortune of their own to bet on the second. That'll be enough."

"No it won't," Stoney said. "When it comes to gambling, have you ever seen an Indian that knew when to quit?"

"You're right," said Llano. "They'll bet everything, right down to the buckskin britches they're wearin'. Long John's remuda is in double trouble. We'd better lay some heavy threats on that pair before they find out there's a second race."

But they were too late. Sky Pilot had been released from jail and had learned of the second race. All his animosity toward Indians in general and Long John's horse wranglers in particular had vanished. Llano and Stoney found the garrulous old cook with Malo Coyote and Naked Horse.

"By God," Sky Pilot crowed, "I'm gunna be rich. I'm layin' half my cash on Malo Coyote in the first race and the rest on Naked Horse in the second."

Stoney took the time to explain to Malo Coyote and Naked Horse that some of the Indian riders might be spoilers, but neither of the wranglers showed any emotion.

"Why, hell's fire," said Sky Pilot, "these here Mendoza blacks has got wings on their feet. None of them other nags will get close enough to do more'n eat dust."

"For your sake," Stoney said, "I hope you're right. We aimed to have 'em keep the horse remuda out of that second race, but thanks to you, Long John has two chances of losing."

"No lose," said Naked Horse, glaring at Stoney.

Recognizing the futility of further conversation, Llano and Stoney rode away. It was little more than an hour until time for the first race to begin, so they rode back to town.

"We've put it off as long as we can," Llano said. "Do we lay some money on this pair of sin valor Indios, or do the sensible thing?"

"I read somethin' once," said Stoney, "about this great warrior who went across the water to fight. Once he got there, to be sure he'd win, he burned all his ships. He had to win, and that's the same kind of deep hole Naked Horse and Malo Coyote have dug for themselves. They have to win, and that bein' the case, I'm layin' a pair of double eagles on each of them."

"Well, I reckon I got no better sense than to do the same thing," Llano said. "At twenty-to-one odds, you sure forty dollars is enough?"

"Fifty, then," said Stoney. "Why be satisfied with losin' your shirt when you can lose your britches too?"

Llano and Stoney were headed for the St. Louis Hotel when Long John, Suzanne, Dent, Harley, and Pearl came out. They were ready to leave for the races.

"Wal," Long John said sheepishly, "we all laid some money on them sneakin', low-down, slick-dealin' Injuns."

"Both races?" Llano asked.

"Hunnert dollars on each race," said Long John, "an' I can't lose. If'n Naked Horse an' Malo Coyote wins, I'll git a pile. If'n they lose, then I still win, 'cause I'll git two hunnert dollars' worth o' satisfaction from killin' the two of 'em."

Both of Hackett's thoroughbreds were bays, one with a white sock on its right front foot and the other with a white star on its forehead. They were lean, sleek, and everything the Mendoza blacks were not. There were thirty horses in the first race, two-thirds of them with Indian riders.

"Purty critters, them thoroughbreds," Long John said, "but they ain't no match fer our Mendoza blacks."

"There's another black and a dun out there that's more competition for us than the thoroughbreds," said Stoney. "If Malo Coyote can stay ahead of them, he'll win it."

When Malo Coyote and Naked Horse arrived, Sky Pilot was right behind them in the wagon.

"What'n hell are ye doin' here?" Long John demanded.

"I'm here to collect my winnings," said Sky Pilot haughtily.

When the horses were taken to their starting positions, Malo Coyote had a pair of Indian riders on either side of him.

"I wonder who decided who gets what position," Llano said.

"Hackett, maybe," said Stoney. "His bay with the star is on the very end, while the other black and the dun are both among the Indian riders, just like Malo Coyote is."

Just as the starting gun was fired, one of the Indian riders shouldered his horse into the dun. But before the riders to the left and right of Malo Coyote could make such a move, the Mendoza black was three lengths ahead.

"Run, you Mendoza black!" Suzanne shouted.

The Indian riders began kicking their mounts and screeching as the Mendoza black left them behind. Hackett's bay got off to a slow start and the rider took a quirt to the horse. Startled, the bay broke stride and sidestepped into one of the other horses. The Mendoza black flashed across the finish line with the other black a dozen lengths behind and the dun a distant third.

"That damn Indian on the black jumped the gun," Hackett shouted.

"Well, I fired the starting gun," Sheriff Lomax said, "and nobody jumped the gun."

"Wouldn't of made no difference to you, Hackett," a heckler shouted, "if the black was disqualified. Your hoss still would of come in third."

There was much laughter, proof enough that most of the money bet on the Hackett thoroughbred had been Hackett's own.

"Yippeeee," Dent Briano yelled, "I put fifty down for me and fifty for Quando. I'm raisin' that to a hundred on the second race."

"By God," said Long John exultantly, "that Malo Coyote and Naked Horse is the savviest pair o' Injuns I ever seen."

"That's some turnaround," said Sky Pilot. "You been threatenin' to gut-shoot 'em both ever' since we left Dallas."

"Wal, ye backtrailed a mite yerself," Long John growled. "All I been hearin' since we left the Rio Colorado is how much grub it was takin' to feed them horse wranglers. Now, ye mossy-horned ol' varmint, shut up."

"I won't be surprised," said Llano, "if Malo Coyote and Naked Horse have dried apple pie every day, all the way back to Texas."

"I just hope the old coot ain't stashed too much pan-ther juice in that wagon," Stoney said. "If he has, there'll be days when none of us will have anything, includin' dried apple pie."

There were twenty-eight horses entered in the second race. Naked Horse was near the middle of the course, surrounded by other Indian riders. Except for a lone gray and Hackett's bay, there was little competition. It became difficult to believe the Mendoza blacks had never raced before, for the black Naked Horse rode seemed to understand the significance of the starting gun. The horse was off like greased lightning, and Hack-ett's spoilers managed only to slow the gray, allowing Hackett's thoroughbred to finish a poor second. Hackett was waiting at the finish line, a doubled lariat in his hand, and he lashed the unfortunate bay across the hind quarters. He had drawn back for a second blow when Naked Horse caught his upraised arm from behind. Na-ked Horse twisted Hackett around, fisted his right hand and smashed the fat man's nose and mouth. Hackett reared up on his elbows and reached for his Colt, only to discover Sheriff Lomax already had him covered.

"That—That heathen bastard *hit* me," Hackett bawled.

"If he hadn't, I would have," snapped Lomax. "Now get up. If there's a race next year, I think we'll think of some way to keep you out of it."

"Long race, him win," said Naked Horse, who had made friends with the frightened bay.

Those who had bet on the Mendoza blacks were jubi-lant. Malo Coyote and Naked Horse found themselves heroes, and accepted the praise and their winnings with no obvious change in their emotions. Nobody knew for sure how much the Indian duo had bet on their horses, so their winnings couldn't be calculated, but by Indian standards they had become wealthy.

"Damn," Long John said, "I hope Malo Coyote an'

Naked Horse ain't got so rich they won't be goin' back to Texas with us."

"You'll have time to win them over," said Suzanne. "We'll be here for a while, waiting for Harkness to be tried."

But there would be no trial. Sometime during the night, Jeremiah Harkness took a sheet from his bunk and hanged himself in his cell.

"I want to leave St. Louis," Suzanne said, "but in a way, I don't want to. We have friends here, and I feel like we'll never see them again."

"But we got to go," said Long John, "an' Quando's healin' fast. In the mornin' it'll be five days since he was shot. He's ready to ride, an' goin' back, that's all he'll have to do. We'll give it one more day. Tomorrer Sky Pilot kin drive the wagon in, an' we'll load up with grub."

They had been in town for a week, and none of them had so much as seen Bandy Darden until the day before they were to leave St. Louis. Dent Briano met Darden on the boardwalk outside a saloon.

"We're leavin' tomorrow," Dent said. "You ain't been mentioned, so I reckon you ain't invited."

"No matter," said Darden. "I'll give you a day's start, and then I'll be along. You and Quando gonna be ready fer me?"

"We'll be ready for you," said Dent.

July 6, 1858. The trail to Texas.

Long John took Stoney with him to the bank, and they left it with four canvas bags, each containing a thousand gold double eagles.

"One more good reason fer bringin' the wagon," Long John said.

"I wish we had some means of concealing it," said Stoney. "Just having the herd and a big horse remuda was temptation enough. This is more than enough to get us all shot dead."

"I reckon ye're right," Long John said, "but they ain't no help fer it. War's comin', sure as hell, an' a Texan with his money in a bank in St. Louis might's well be broke. Them Yankees ain't gon' miss a trick. Ye think they won't nose around an' find any money from the South that's stashed in other banks? We got to have this gold to see us through whatever hell that'll be comin' our way when the shootin' war starts."

They rode out at first light, following the wagon. Again Stoney scouted ahead, for they were in more danger than ever from renegades. Water would be no problem, for Stoney had recorded every spring, every creek, and every river as they trailed toward St. Louis. There would be no dry camps, for even when it was thirty miles from one stream or creek to the next, they could just go on until they made it. But they were careful, dousing their supper fire well before dark, withdrawing from the wagon to spread their blankets. But there were no tracks ahead, and when trouble arrived, it came down the back trail. They had just made camp at the end of their second day out of St. Louis, and Sky Pilot had supper under way, when Bandy Darden stepped out of a thicket. He had waited for Malo Coyote and Naked Horse to ride in for supper, so all the outfit would be together. The little gunman had a smirk on his face and a Colt in his hand.

"Don't nobody move," Darden said. "I'm here fer the gold. Dent, you and Quando know where it is. Get it."

Dent Briano and Quando Miller had been hunkered by the fire. They got to their feet and turned to face Darden.

"I figgered you hombres in this," Darden growled. "Now get the gold, and we'll finish this. *El muerto hacer no hablar.*"

Long John had his back to Darden, while Stoney faced him, but Long John, Suzanne, and Llano were in the line of fire. Stoney caught Long John's eye, and almost imperceptibly the Cajun shook his head. He was putting his faith in two men he had once caught stealing one of his cows. Dent Briano and Quando Miller had turned to face Bandy Darden, and it was Quando who spoke.

"It's already finished, Bandy. The gold ain't yours, and it's stayin' where it is. You'll have to start by gunnin' down Dent and me, if you're man enough."

"So that's how it is," Darden snarled. "The years we was saddle pals don't mean nothin'."

"For the sake of those years," said Dent Briano, "we're willin' to see you ride away, long as you keep ridin'."

"You damn fools," he bawled, "I got the drop—"

In a single motion Dent Briano and Quando Miller drew, their lead tearing into Darden as he got off just one wild shot. He flopped on his back in a puff of dust, and the wind caught his hat, sending it skittering toward the creek. Dent and Quando holstered their Colts, and it was Quando who spoke to Long John.

"We ride for the brand," Quando said, "and when there's a need, we fight for it too."

Stoney rode out the next morning, scouting ahead. There had been no rain since they'd come this way with the herd, bound for St. Louis. So there was a beaten path, but from what Stoney could tell, no recent horse tracks. He reached a creek which was less than twenty miles south. They could easily reach that, so he rode upstream three or four miles without finding any recent sign. He then rode downstream an equal distance, and was about to ride back when something on the other side of the creek caught his eye. It was an oblong piece of rice paper that some men used to roll a quirly. From the look of it, the paper had been there a few days, for the dew had wrinkled it. Uncertain what it meant, Stoney rode along that bank of the creek until the overhanging trees thinned out and there was bare ground. Carefully he studied the tracks of the four horses, seeking something by which he might recognize one or more of them farther on. But the shoes were new enough that there were no distinguishing marks. The tracks were almost a week old. Thoughtfully, Stoney rode back to meet his companions, and when he told Long John of the tracks, the Cajun's suspicions matched his own.

"We can't be sure," Long John said, "but I'm figgerin' it to be them damn Harkness men that jist disappeared when the law went lookin' fer 'em."

"We can't be sure it's them," said Stoney, "but we're goin' to have to be prepared, because we can't be sure it's *not* them."

"But they wouldn't go this far to avenge Harkness," said Suzanne. "Would they?"

"Them comin' after us ain't got nothin' to do with Harkness," Long John said. "If'n these bastards was willin' to kill fer bounty, what wouldn't they do fer the kind o' gold we're carryin'?"

It was something to think about, and in addition to having Malo Coyote and Naked Horse with the horse remuda, Long John began designating four riders for each night's watch, two of them on duty until midnight, the other two from midnight until dawn. But nobody disturbed them, and although Stoney continued scouting for sign, he found nothing. He had begun to think all their worries were for naught when he again found sign left by four riders.

Again the tracks were well off the beaten path, along a creek, and Stoney estimated they were maybe three days old.

"They're never on the trail behind us or ahead of us," Stoney said. "I feel like they're riding parallel to us, leaving no sign that makes any sense, just waiting for the right time."

"What *is* the right time?" Long John asked, exasperated. "Hell, we got to be a hunnert an' fifty mile from St. Louis. Since we left there, we ain't seen one human bein', less'n ye count Bandy Darden."

"We'll just have to keep our guns handy," said Stoney. "We outnumber them considerably, so whatever they have in mind, I look for it to come at night."

"Then why don't we turn Malo Coyote and Naked Horse loose every day at dark?" Llano said. "It worked when Buck Tundree's gang was prowlin' around in the dark. A couple of us can watch the horses, but they're in no danger, long as Malo Coyote and Naked Horse are out there with their long knives."

"Let's do it," said Long John. "Hell, ain't none o' us gonna sleep anyhow, knowin' them varmints is stalkin' us."

"I'll talk to Naked Horse and Malo Coyote, then," Stoney said. "We might not have to get all four of them. Just one, with Malo Coyote or Naked Horse givin' him the Indian treatment, might make believers out of the other three."

They all slept better knowing Malo Coyote and Naked Horse were silently making their way through and around the camp, and the night passed with no sign of the expected invaders. By early afternoon of the following day the western horizon darkened, but instead of rain, there was hail. Some of the stones were as large as eggs, and they took shelter beneath the trees. There was nickering as many of the horses were struck, for the hailstones stripped many of the trees bare. When the barrage had ended, the outfit rode on, making camp near one of the lesser rivers, somewhere south of Springfield. There they spent a second night with Malo Coyote and Naked Horse prowling in and around the camp, with no sign of the suspected invaders.

"By God," Long John said, "this is worse'n ridin' through Comanche country, always lookin' over yer shoulder fer the bastards to come swoopin' in. Even the Injuns would of struck by now. If'n we knowed wher' the varmints was, I'd be in favor o' huntin' 'em down, jist to put a end to this damn standoff."

"I'm of the same mind," said Stoney, "but all I've found is occasional tracks along the creeks. Maybe that's what they're waitin' for, thinkin' we'll get anxious enough to split up and come lookin' for 'em."

The stalkers struck the following morning at first light, just as all the riders had come together for breakfast. They came galloping down the back trail, their Colts roaring, forcing Long John and his companions belly down. Three slugs chunked into the water barrel on the side of the wagon, while others thudded into the ground among the fallen riders. When the four mounted attackers were gone, Long John got to his feet and began calling names. None of their wounds were fatal, but some were painful, and at least one was embarrassing.

"Damn it," Dent Briano said, "they nicked me in the *other* arm."

"They burnt one across my back," said Llano, "right above my shoulder blades."

"Pearl's going to have to stand in the stirrups for a while," Suzanne said. "She's been butt-shot."

Everybody laughed, even Harley, and Pearl was careful not to turn her back on them. A slug had plowed across her backside from left to right, slashing her Levi's almost in half.

"Suzanne," said Long John, "ye stay an' do whatever's got to be done fer Pearl. Quando, ye an' Harley stick close to camp an' keep yer guns handy. Dent, Llano, an' Stoney, I want ye ridin' with me. We're goin' to ride that flock o' *busardos* into the ground an' end this foolishness once an' fer all."

The four of them rode out at a gallop, the trail fresh

and easy to follow. They rode southwest for half a dozen miles, reining up when they reached a creek. The four riders they pursued had ridden downstream.

"They're expectin' us to foller," Long John said, "an' I reckon they got a rat hole they're headin' fer. Llano, ye an' Stoney circle wide an' go down the river two er three mile. Dent an' me will leave our horses here an' go ahead on foot. Whatever they got planned, we ain't gonna stumble into it in a bunch. Jist be careful. We can't count on a cross fire 'cause we don't know wher' they're holed up er what kinda cover they got."

Llano and Stoney rode wide of the creek so the men they pursued wouldn't hear them coming. When they had ridden an estimated three miles, they left their horses and began working their way upstream. As they progressed, the creek deepened until it flowed through an arroyo where the water had undercut the steep banks. The bed had eroded down to solid rock with a substantial overhang under each bank.

"We need to be on that farthest bank," Stoney whispered. "When Long John and Dent are in position, we'll have them boxed."

"I ain't too sure of that," Llano whispered back. "If there's room for them and their horses, must be a cave down there."

Llano and Stoney made their way back to a low-running stretch of the creek where they could cross. From there they proceeded back to the undercut banks beneath which they suspected the men they sought were hiding. From the opposite bank Long John waved his hat, and Stoney responded.

"We know ye skunks are down there," Long John shouted. "It's yer move. Ye ain't gittin' another chance to come out."

"Why don't you come in and git us?" a voice bawled from below.

Long John and Dent cut loose with their Colts, directing their fire beneath the opposite bank's overhang. Llano and Stoney followed with a barrage beneath the overhang on which Long John and Dent stood. They were depending on a ricochet when they had no idea how deep was the concave concealment into which they were shooting. Stoney took a tally book from his shirt pocket and a piece of piggin string from his belt. With a stub of pencil he wrote on a page from the tally book: *Keep firing. Got a plan downstream.* With piggin string Stoney tied the written message to an oblong rock, then waved his hat to get Long John's attention. He then heaved the message across the chasm to the opposite bank. Long John retrieved the rock, read the message, and waved his hat.

"Come on," Stoney said. "We're about to drown some rats."

Stoney led the way, Llano following, until the banks began to level out. They also became more sandy, harboring large stones, some of them weighing hundreds of pounds. Stoney began stomping along the sandy bank, and it caved in readily.

"What we need is a strong limb," said Stoney. "Cedar if we can find it. We're going to drop some of these stones down there, cave in these sandy banks, and raise the water level a mite. We can't go into their overhung hideout and we can't see to shoot, but there'll be no stoppin' this water."

"That's why I've followed you all over hell and half of Texas," Llano said, "you're so damn good at figurin' ways to keep us from bein' ventilated with lead. Let's find that limb."

What they finally found was a young oak that had been dead long enough for them to break off the limbs and the spindly top. The topmost part of it was slender enough to be driven under the backside of some of the boulders. Their first attempts snapped off portions of the oak until it became too thick and too tough to break.

From then on it was the boulders that gave instead of the oak, and by the time they rolled five of them into the deep channel below, the water level began to rise.

"A few more," said Stoney, "and then we'll drop some leaves, brush, and rotted logs. I hope there's nobody down yonder dependin' on this creek for water."

When the creek's flow had been reduced to a trickle, Llano and Stoney returned to their former position on the arroyo rim. Long John waved his hat, pointing below. The water level had risen dramatically, and there was frantic cursing from the depths.

"Drop yer guns an' come out, er stay there an' drown," Long John shouted.

They came out shooting, and since they'd been under the overhang on Long John's side, Llano and Stoney had first choice. All had come out mounted, and the second pair ceased firing and tried to escape downstream. That took them within sight of Dent and Long John. They were shot from the saddle and their horses went on without them.

"Come on," Long John shouted, "and let's go home. Let's put as much of this territory behind us 'fore dark as we can. They may be more varmints on our backtrail, but this time we ain't got the herd to slow us down."

But the trouble wasn't over. When Long John and his riders returned to the rest of the outfit they found Sky Pilot, Naked Horse, and Malo Coyote hunkered around a blanket spread on the ground. Each man held a hand of cards while the rest of the deck lay facedown on the blanket. But Naked Horse held something more than his cards. In his right hand he gripped a cocked Colt, its muzzle under Sky Pilot's nose.

"What'n hell's goin' on here?" Long John bawled.

"Him take gold, hoss, saddle," said Naked Horse grimly. "Him cheat. Him die."

"Naked Horse," said Long John, "put away the pistol. Nobody's goin' to die over a lousy card game. Anything he's took from you, I'm givin' it back. Now lay down them cards, all of you. Llano, do me a favor and round up the whole damn deck and give 'em to me."

Reluctantly Naked Horse eased the Colt off cock and returned it to his waistband, while Llano gathered up the cards and handed them to Long John.

"Now mount up," said Long John.

When they forded the creek where the outlaws had met their fate, Long John flung the deck of cards into the swift current and they were carried quickly away.

"Sky Pilot must have had some hell of a hand," Stoney said, "with old Naked Horse threatenin' to shoot him."

Llano laughed. "Oh, he did. Four aces. Trouble was, Naked Horse had two more, and Malo Coyote had one."

They rode south, taking the long trail back to Texas, to the lonely ranch on the banks of the Rio Colorado. . . .

EPILOGUE

William Clarke Quantrill was also known as Charles W. Quantrill, and there is some doubt as to where he was born. Some accounts say in Canal Dover, Ohio, on July 31, 1837, while others say Hagerstown, Maryland, on July 20, 1836. He had an irregular alliance with the Confederate army. After he captured Independence, Missouri, in 1862, Union officials declared him a menace and an outlaw. He raided in Kansas, Missouri, and Kentucky. In 1863 and again in 1864 he and his band escaped to Grayson County, Texas, camping near Sherman. Quantrill was shot during a raid on Taylorsville, Kentucky, and died in a Louisville military hospital on June 6, 1865.

Jesse Chisholm was born in Tennessee. His father was Scottish, his mother Cherokee, and they moved to Indian Territory while Jesse was a child. Jesse Chisholm was never a cattleman. He owned a trading post on the Canadian River, 140 miles west of Fort Smith. He has been referred to as "Ambassador to the Plains" because of his ability to negotiate with the plains Indians. He is said to have spoken fourteen Indian languages.

Although Jesse Chisholm is remembered for the famous "Chisholm Trail," it was originally a wagon road. Chisholm blazed it in 1865 at the request of the government, and then moved a band of Wichita Indians south to their new land in Indian Territory. The railroad reached Abilene in the spring of 1867, and it was a year later before Chisholm's wagon road came into general use as a cattle trail. While history credits Chisholm for the famous "Chisholm Trail," Jesse never witnessed the glory days of his namesake. He died in Indian Territory on April 4, 1868.

DON'T MISS *THE VIRGINIA CITY TRAIL*—
THE NEXT GREAT EPISODE IN THE
TRAIL DRIVE SERIES:

After a hasty breakfast, the outfit set out along the Arkansas, seeking the herd that had stampeded during the night. The rain had let up, but the sky was still overcast, and the wind from the northwest promised more rain, and soon.

"Ain't but one thing in our favor," said Dutch Mayfield. "They had to run east or south. It ain't likely they went chargin' across that overgrowed river."

"They nearly always run with their tails to th' storm," Shanghai said. "I figger we'll find 'em scattered along th' river."

Back at the wagon, Sandy Bill filled a tin cup from the still simmering coffee pot. Careful that nobody was observing him, he dipped corn mush onto a tin plate, to which he added three sourdough biscuits and a slab of fried ham. He placed the food and coffee on the wagon's lowered tailgate and spoke through the canvas pucker.

"Kid, you must be hungry, 'cause you ain't et for three days. I brung you some breakfast, some coffee, an' eatin' tools."

There was only silence from the dark interior of the wagon.

"I know you ain't sleepin'," the old cook persisted, " 'cause I heard you givin' them gals hell. They been here two er three times a day, doin' ever' thing they could to keep you alive."

There still was no response from within the wagon.

"There's more rain comin'," said Sandy Bill, "so I got to close this tailgate. I'll set your grub an' coffee inside, an' you can take it or leave it. I got nothin' else to say, kid, 'cept this. You'd likely git treated like you was growed up, if you took to actin' like it."

With that, he placed the food and the coffee behind the canvas and raised the wagon's tailgate.

"There they are," said Shanghai, with satisfaction, as they sighted the first bunch of grazing longhorns. "I look to find ever' blessed one of 'em strung out along th' river."

"We'll ride on and get the farthest ones first," Story said, "and pick these up on the way back."

"Look yonder," said Tom Allen. "More calves."

"They been dropped long 'nuff t' be on they feet," Oscar Fentress said. "All our luck don't be bad."

Most of the longhorns had become trailwise to the extent that they did not resist efforts to gather them into a herd. The rain started again at mid-morning, hampering their efforts, and it was past noon when they had what appeared to be most of the herd. There were five new calves. Shanghai and Cal ran a quick tally.

"We got 'em all," said Shanghai, "an' three extry. Three of 'em is branded D H Connected."

"Part of Dillard McLean's stampeded herd," Story said. "We'll take them with us. I invited him to ride back, in case we found any of his cows."

Sandy Bill saw the herd coming and prepared to hitch up the mules. But first he went to the rear of the wagon and fumbled around inside until he found the tin cup, the plate, and the eating tools. He grinned to himself, for the cup and the plate were empty. At least the cantankerous little varmint had been hungry, and that was a good sign.

"If we don't accomplish anything else today," Story said, "at least we can cross the Arkansas."

"If what I think means anything," said Cal, "I think we ought to take the herd across all at once."

"We already soaked to de hide," Oscar said, "an' ah

think we oughts t' keep our britches an' boots on. I be goin' to."

"We'll cross the herd all at the same time, then," said Story, "and come back for the wagon."

It seemed they were going to cross the herd without difficulty, but as the drag reached midstream, disaster struck. Tom Allen, Oscar Fentress, Hitch Gould, Jasmine, and Lorna were riding drag. The last dozen longhorns were some of the wildest, and for some reason—or no reason—they spooked. Bawling in confusion, they turned, determined to hit the backtrail. Horses screamed as they were raked by horns, and riders scrambled to get out of the way. They almost made it. A steer flung its massive head, and a horn slammed into Jasmine's face, just above her eyes. The girl was flung from the saddle into the maelstrom of horns and hooves.

"Jasmine!" Lorna cried.

But Tom Allen was already fighting to reach the point where Jasmine had gone under. He beat the plunging longhorns with his doubled lariat and slugged them with his fists. Jasmine's horse had escaped the turmoil and was headed for the farthest bank. Tom had no idea how deep the water was at that point. He clung to the horn with his left hand, leaning from the off-side, searching the water with his free hand. He was ready to cry out in despair when his hand touched the crown of Jasmine's hat. It had been thonged down against the storm. Allen released the horn, leaned far from the saddle, grasping Jasmine under the arms. She was unconscious, a dead weight, and it wasn't easy getting her onto his horse. The animal was winded from fighting the river and the rampaging longhorns, and they still had to reach the farthest bank. Oscar, Hitch, and Lorna had managed to head the troublesome longhorns, and the brutes were headed for the farthest bank, where they should have gone to begin with. Oscar, Hitch, and Lorna reached Tom, siding him, lest his horse should falter. Story and the rest of the riders waited on the north bank, having witnessed the disaster, but being unable to help. When Tom Allen rode out of the water, he swiftly dismounted, and lifting Jasmine off the horse, stretched her on the grass, face-down. He then drove the water from her lungs, and she began to cough. Tom turned her over, and there was a livid bruise above her eyes. The first thing she saw was the concerned face of Tom Allen.

"Thank you, Tom," she said. She spoke so softly that nobody heard her except Tom, and something in her eyes told him that was her intention . . .

By the time the riders got the wagon across the Arkansas, the rain had become more intense, and the sky had become so dark, it seemed that night was approaching.

"We'll stay where we are," Story said. "It's going to be a bad night. . . ."

***THE VIRGINIA CITY TRAIL*—BOOK 7 IN RALPH COMPTON'S EXCITING TRAIL DRIVE SERIES—AVAILABLE FROM ST. MARTIN'S PAPERBACKS!**

THE TRAIL DRIVE SERIES

by Ralph Compton
From St. Martin's Paperbacks

The only riches Texas had left after the Civil War were five million maverick longhorns and the brains, brawn and boldness to drive them north to where the money was. Now, Ralph Compton brings this violent and magnificent time to life in an extraordinary epic series based on the history-blazing trail drives.

THE GOODNIGHT TRAIL (BOOK 1)

THE WESTERN TRAIL (BOOK 2)

THE CHISOLM TRAIL (BOOK 3)

THE BANDERA TRAIL (BOOK 4)

THE CALIFORNIA TRAIL (BOOK 5)

THE SHAWNEE TRAIL (BOOK 6)

THE VIRGINIA CITY TRAIL (BOOK 7)

THE DODGE CITY TRAIL (BOOK 8)

THE OREGON TRAIL (BOOK 9)

THE SANTA FE TRAIL (BOOK 10)

THE OLD SPANISH TRAIL (BOOK 11)

THE GREEN RIVER TRAIL (BOOK 12)

THE DEADWOOD TRAIL (BOOK 13)

AVAILABLE WHEREVER BOOKS ARE SOLD
FROM ST. MARTIN'S PAPERBACKS

TD 1/00

In his thrilling saga of the Nez Perce War,
Terry C. Johnston combines unmatched authenticity,
fascinating details, and a broad tapestry of vivid
characters—to make frontier history come alive
as never before.

LAY THE
MOUNTAINS LOW

A PLAINSMEN NOVEL

TERRY C. JOHNSTON

TO THE U.S. ARMY the Non-Treaty Nez Perce tribes
were an inconvenience—soon to be eliminated from
Idaho's Salmon River territory. But the soldiers discovered that their enemy was a skilled and ferocious
opponent, and that the war had only begun . . .

"Johnston is a skilled storyteller whose words ring
with the desperation, confusion and utter horror
of a fight to the death between mortal enemies."
—*Publishers Weekly*

"Johnston's books are action packed . . . lively,
lusty, fascinating."
—*Colorado Springs Gazette Telegraph*

AVAILABLE WHEREVER BOOKS ARE SOLD FROM
ST. MARTIN'S PAPERBACKS

LML 12/00